A KISS BETWEEN FRIENDS

Without thinking, Davis yanked up the emergency brake and jumped out of his car. He didn't even take the time to kill the lights or pull the keys out. He caught up to Celia as she was turning the key in her front door, and when he skidded to a stop behind her, she turned and shrieked.

"Davis! You scared the crap out of me!" She tilted her head. "Did you want something?"

"I . . ." He swallowed. "I wanted to make sure you knew."

She squinted at him. "Knew what?"

Words came out in a rush. "That I think you're just about the most wonderful person I've ever known. I mean it. I—"

It was a little difficult to go on now. Celia's face had sagged in shock, as if it were imprinted on Silly Putty and someone had pulled it like taffy. His verbal momentum ground down, and he finished, less than spectacularly, "I . . . think the world of you, Celia."

They stood there for an eternity, she with her Silly Putty face and he with egg all over his. What should he do now? She already looked as though she needed smelling salts, but he couldn't just disappear. Some gesture seemed called for.

He didn't know where the impulse came from. He would always wonder. As if he'd practiced it a million times, he reached out, grabbed her shoulders, and hauled her against him as if he were s⎯⎯⎯⎯⎯eing entirely.

But when his li⎯⎯⎯⎯⎯⎯⎯⎯⎯⎯⎯⎯⎯who he was. What mat⎯⎯⎯⎯⎯⎯⎯⎯⎯⎯⎯ing he possibly could ⎯⎯⎯⎯⎯⎯⎯⎯⎯ all the months of wan⎯⎯⎯⎯⎯⎯⎯⎯⎯ed to do this before. . .

Books by Liz Ireland

HUSBAND MATERIAL

WHEN I THINK OF YOU

Published by Zebra Books

WHEN
I THINK
OF YOU

Liz Ireland

ZEBRA BOOKS
Kensington Publishing Corp.
http://www.kensingtonbooks.com

One

Chan-Milstein

You would never guess the couple met on the number seventy-five bus. Neither the willowy Chinese-American bride in her beaded Vera Wang gown nor her polished lawyer groom looks the type to spend much time on public transportation. And perhaps they never would have met, Lucy Chan admits with a rueful laugh, had Michael Milstein's ferret, Pepe, not dislocated his shoulder the very morning Michael dropped off his Jaguar to have the tires rotated. . . .

"Celia!" The voice of Sara Morton, receptionist, trumpeted across the honeycomb of gray cubicles. Short of temper and strong of lung, Sara often resorted to communicating the old-fashioned way. Especially when dealing with coworkers who were screening their calls. "Pick up your line! Some guy's been calling you all morning. Sounds important!"

Celia dove for the phone. And not just because "sounds important" sounded, well, important. After wrestling with the matchmaking ferret story all morning for her Sunday "Unions" column, she was open to any distraction. Not to mention "some guy" sounded intriguing.

She snatched up the phone and answered in the reporter voice she'd been practicing since she was a twelve-year-old dreamer in Bend, Oregon, and fell in love with Cary Grant in *His Girl Friday*. After over a year spent editing wedding and obituary announcements for the *Portland Times*, she was beginning to sound less like wisecracking Rosalind Russell and more like Droopy the dog, but she gave it her best shot. "Celia Snowden."

There was a second of noisy hesitation at the other end of the line. Glasses clinked, and somewhere in the distance she could hear the muted noise of ESPN. Then came a wheezy breath. Suddenly, she had Art Carney on the line. "Uh, yeah, this is Celia Snowden?"

Celia's breath, which she realized now she had been holding baited in journalistic anticipation, gushed out of her in one irritable gust. She knew that voice—a dead ringer for Ed Norton on *The Honeymooners*. It had been deviling her for months. She drummed her fingers impatiently and gritted her teeth. "Yes?"

"The local electrician's fifty-nine's going to have a union meetin' at the Lion's Club hall in Sellwood next Wednesday. Think you could put us in your column, babe?"

Art Carney had barely finished his question before he broke into uproarious laughter. In the background, she could hear a chorus of whoops and guffaws as his cronies joined in.

"Buzz off!" She slammed down the phone.

It was just a ridiculous prank call, a joke, but she was fuming. She automatically turned to her friend Davis's cubicle, right across the aisle from hers. She and Davis had landed their respective positions about the same time and had been working side by side now for nearly a year. She counted him as one of her best friends. He was the best listener, the best adviser, the best shoulder to cry on she'd ever run into. Plus, he shared her weakness for cheap diner food.

Unfortunately, he was now AWOL.

Damn! Was it lunch already?

She glanced at her watch and let out a panicked bleat. It was almost twelve-twenty, and she'd promised to meet her friend Natalie for lunch at half past twelve. A person would be better off tickling a rattlesnake than keeping Natalie Glass waiting.

But Celia's urge to vent got the better of her. Since Davis wasn't available, she stood and poked her head over the gray partition of her cubicle. Sometime in the past decade the higher-ups at the *Portland Times* decided it would be more democratic to get rid of offices and follow the high-tech company model of having everyone from receptionist to managing editor slaving away in cubicles. The same higher-ups were still in their offices on the eighth floor. On the fifth floor, home of the *Portland Today!* section, Marie Warden, aka the Warden, a suit-wearing feminist of the old school, presided over her hive from a massive steel desk at one end of the room. Marie had done the *Times* policy one better and eschewed portable walls around her own desk altogether. The hierarchy couldn't have been clearer, and less democratic, if she were a teacher in front of a roomful of second graders.

"Marie, we've *got* to change the name of this column." For a full year she had been telling her boss that calling the special Sunday wedding column "Unions" was just begging for harassment.

"For God's sake, Snowden, cool your jets. What's the problem?"

"I've got some geezer pestering me every time he gets a couple of drinks in him, that's the problem."

Marie shrugged until her stiff Joan Crawford shoulder pads almost reached her ears. "A few calls? Lighten up."

"But—"

The Warden fired off an infuriating so-you-can't-take-the-heat? stare. Any moment now she'd start spouting off about how hard it had been for female reporters back in the seventies.

Celia took a deep breath and gave herself a reality check. Weren't a few crank calls a small price to pay for such a cushy position? She got to write about good things—happy couples, weddings, lavish receptions. The "Unions" column, which came with a byline, highlighted a wedding every Sunday. Okay, so she spent *most* of her week editing obits and marriage announcements . . . but that wasn't so bad, was it?

The trouble was, deep in her heart Celia felt a weekly feature about good old holy matrimony wasn't as important as chasing a juicy political corruption story. Or following a murder trial. Sometimes she despaired that she was going to be buried in the *Portland Today!* ghetto forever. She didn't even have much of a prayer of advancement, either, because her boss thought she was a coddled Gen-X ninny.

Being sneered at, even by old drunks in a bar, just rubbed salt in the wounds of her thwarted newswoman's ego. For this she had spent four years in journalism school? In Columbia, Missouri?

"Couldn't we just consider changing the name to something more, well, weddinglike?" she asked, trying to strike a diplomatic tone.

"Oh, sure, let me put my thinking cap on," Marie said, oozing sarcasm. "How about the 'I Do' column? 'Bouquets and Butter Icing'? We might as well call it 'For Prissy Females Only.' "

Marie was a great morale booster.

"The trouble with you is, you need to toughen up," Marie lectured.

A tough wedding reporter. Right. In another year she would be as insane as Marie, who kept adding fluff pieces to her section, all the while braying about the backpedaling of hard journalistic standards. Celia and Davis had begun to doubt Marie even had a life outside of *Portland Today!* She was *always* at the office. In fact, they had spent quite a few coffee breaks speculating whether Marie actually had a home, or if that massive desk of hers was secretly a multi-use, Ron Popeil-type contraption. Celia could just imagine the TV ad. *It* looks *like an ordinary office desk—but wait! In just minutes it folds into a bed!*

"You think a few crank phone calls are harassment?" Marie asked. "You should have been around back, oh, twenty-five years ago. Then you'd know harassment when you saw it."

Fearing Marie was about to launch them back in time to the Ford administration, Celia backed down. "Okay, okay. Never mind. I'm going to lunch." She added, "To meet a *real* journalist."

Marie's brows, sternly plucked into two dark arches, launched with interest. "Who?"

Celia squared her own unpadded shoulders. Having a semifamous friend was a source of pride at least. Self-esteem by proxy. "Natalie Glass."

"Who?"

"You know," Celia reminded her, a little peeved. "She does the morning news on Channel Seven."

Marie snorted. "Television!"

At least Natalie doesn't do stories about matchmaking ferrets, Celia grumbled to herself as she marched to the elevator and jabbed the down button.

Well, actually, Natalie did do those . . . but she also covered real news, too. Natalie, who had been a class-

mate of Celia's at Mizzou, had always dreamed of becoming the next Barbara Walters. And if she hadn't
exactly succeeded yet, she was at least on her way.
Sure, she was a little disgruntled at being stuck doing
the early bird telecast and the dregs of the on-the-
scene reporting assignments, but she was bound to
move up someday.

And what had Celia Snowden accomplished in the
five years since she'd graduated? Well, since setting off
on her career as a *serious print journalist*, she was a
barely paid assistant at a wildly unpopular liberal
weekly that had gone belly up soon after she got there.
Then she was a flunky for an egotistical travel magazine editor. Then she landed at the *Portland Times*,
where for two years she did everything from doctoring
horoscopes to proofreading the school lunch menus.
Then the previous weddings and obits editor became
the restaurant reviewer, and Marie offered the job to
Celia. The prospect of seeing her name in those small
bold letters under the Sunday "Unions" column was
so seductive that she didn't question, at the time,
whether writing about a couple getting married on
Mount Hood in snowsuits could in any way, shape, or
form be interpreted as *serious print journalism*.

Since then, she'd covered marriages of minor TV
stars, old hippies, local kooks, and garden variety social types. She'd been to weddings at the seashore, on
sailboats, and practically every church from Seattle to
San Francisco. She'd witnessed Catholic ceremonies,
Hindu ceremonies, and atheist anticeremonies.
Through her column she'd reported on people who
had met through marriage brokers, at dog parks, and
in elevators.

The journalist in her wanted something meatier.
Something that would utilize her rusty investigative
skills. Something to kick-start her stalled career.

By the time Celia sprinted through the door of the *tapas* restaurant, Natalie was already waiting at a table. Though she seemed keyed up about something, she didn't appear to be simmering with outrage. She even smiled as Celia scuttled into her chair. More astonishing still, she'd already tucked into some bread. Natalie was usually very sparing with the carbohydrates. According to her, to look trim on camera, you had to be ten pounds thinner than what the rest of the non-telegenic world would consider normal. So Natalie was fifteen pounds thinner.

"Sorry," Celia said.

"No problem!"

Natalie's tone sounded so genuine that Celia wondered if this wasn't some kind of trick. "You look great," she said, trying to make amends for her tardiness. "Nice outfit."

Natalie, who was five feet ten and would have been a knockout in a potato sack, always looked like a million bucks—as if she were trying to prepare for that day when flocks of people would recognize her and pester her for autographs. Today's outfit was an incredible blue dress that clung perfectly on her carefully guarded size-six frame. Her ash blond hair was moussed to appear spiky and stylish but still somehow suburban and nonthreatening.

Nearby, a table of women were staring at her, puzzled, as if trying to figure out why she looked so familiar. This happened a lot with Natalie. Probably because the people who did watch her broadcasts were too bleary eyed to remember much of what they had seen. It was difficult to become a media icon at six A.M.

"Chanel," was Natalie's brusque response to Celia's compliment. "I went ahead and ordered some of your favorites, Celia. I only have a half hour, tops."

"Great." For Natalie, a half hour was practically a leisurely meal.

"The vice president's in town today," she said in a rush. "And they're sending *me* to the press conference. This could be really, really big. Maybe my ticket out of morning news purgatory."

"Wow, that's terrific, Nat."

"It makes me wonder if management is going to punt Jane Russo soon." Jane Russo was Natalie's nemesis—Channel Seven's six P.M. news anchor was also a tall, toothpicky bottle blonde. Jane's face was on buses, however. Natalie's wasn't. Yet. "About time, I would say. The woman's been around a decade, at least."

"A relic," Celia said.

The sarcasm sailed right past her friend. Natalie might bemoan the short shelf life of the anchorwoman, but she was champing at the bit to boot Jane Russo out of her chair at the first sign of crow's feet. "I've *got* to make a good impression tonight at the press conference," Natalie said. "I've already prepared a question about gas prices."

"Anything else to report?" Celia asked. "Besides the vice president and his gas?"

Natalie smiled excitedly. "Actually, yes."

Celia started packing away the bread, scooping it into an olive oil and pepper puddle on the little plate in front of her. Print journalism might be tedious and not particularly remunerative, but at least it didn't come with calorie restrictions. "Uh-oh. Has your weatherman gone off the wagon again?"

Natalie shook her head. "Actually, this gossip's more interesting. More personal."

Celia had to restrain herself from leaping across the table. "What is it?"

"I've got a wedding for you."

Wedding! The word filled her with gloom. "Whose?"

"Mine."

Celia was flabbergasted. This sudden announcement was tantamount to a betrayal. Natalie was one of her oldest friends. "I didn't know you were even seeing anyone!"

Naturally, given Natalie's looks, men swarmed around her like flies on an overripe banana—but she had never been able to keep a relationship afloat for very long. Natalie said it was because men were intimidated by assertive, beautiful women. Her ex-boyfriends had a different, less flattering take on the matter.

So who had she found who had managed to stick?

Excited though she was for Nat, Celia was also struck with friendly envy. She hadn't been in a serious relationship since her last boyfriend, Ian, had dumped her six months ago. She hadn't had a nonserious relationship, either. Or even a sleazy little fling. She'd had nothing. Zilch. If it hadn't been for Davis squiring her around town, she was afraid she would have jumped off a tall building in despair.

"So who's the lucky fella?" This had to be the whirliest of whirlwind romances. "And where have you been hiding him?"

"Scotland."

Celia felt the first tingle of uneasiness. In fact, the hairs on her neck actually stood on end. But she told herself she was being alarmist. Just because Ian was a Brit . . . After all, one bad apple didn't spoil the whole United Kingdom.

And the truth was, Celia had a thing for foreign guys. An accent, dark sexy eyes, real estate in a far-off homeland—these were key traits her dream man had to possess. So even though she'd been burned by Ian, she was willing to admit that her friend might be on the way to having herself a winner.

Natalie chewed thoughtfully on her lower lip. "I've got two huge favors to ask, Celia."

"I'll give you a column of course," Celia piped up. "You don't even have to ask."

Natalie looked edgy. "I'm not sure about that . . ."

Natalie Glass saying "maybe" to publicity was like Celia's African gray parrot, Gazpacho, saying maybe to a peanut. Something was seriously wrong here. "Why? Are you marrying a mobster or something?"

Natalie chuckled nervously and nibbled at another piece of bread. "No, but . . ."

No, but? She made it sound worse than marrying into organized crime. Fear spiked in Celia's chest. To anyone who had spent as many hours in front of the Lifetime Movie Network as she had, the notion of a woman unwittingly marrying a good-looking yet crazed Scottish psycho killer was not at all far-fetched. "Okay, Nat. I'm seriously freaked out here. What's going on? Who is this guy?"

"Well, to tell you the truth, I'm not *entirely* certain myself."

"Why not?"

"Because I've never met him."

A waiter came by and littered their table with little plates of mushrooms and sizzling scallops and asparagus. On a normal day, Celia would have pounced on the feast like a Kodiak bear on a baby moose, but today she could only gape at Natalie in amazement. Her jaw was hanging limp. In a reversal of roles, Natalie dove into the food.

Never met him. The phrase kept replaying in Celia's head. How could she never have met him?

After a few moments of chewing self-consciously, Natalie swallowed and flicked an annoyed glance across the table. "Okay, okay, I might as well tell you the whole long story. He's a painter. In Glasgow. Someone I know is trying to get him into the country. We've corresponded over the Internet, and he seems nice. And he's good-looking."

She went back to chewing.

"That's the whole long story?" Celia asked, astounded. "Nat, that sounds more like a thumbnail sketch for a really bad TV movie." This, Celia would know.

Natalie's bony shoulders stiffened. "Of all people, Celia, I expected *you* to be a little more sympathetic. You're alone, like me. Haven't you felt like a complete loser since Ian dumped you?"

Not such a loser that I'm going to start marrying strangers, Celia almost blurted. Thankfully, Natalie didn't give her a chance.

"Oh, I know," Natalie said, almost emotionally. "You probably look at me and think, 'Oh, she's different.' You probably think *glamour.* But the truth is, when I get back to my condo at night, it's like there's this huge vacuum in my life. You must have nights like that, too."

Celia nodded numbly. She knew exactly what Natalie was talking about, all right. After Ian had left her, that same vacuum had made her impulsively go out and buy a hand-raised baby African gray parrot. She'd decided that she would have an intelligent, exotic companion even if it had feathers. At least she would have something to talk to.

Unfortunately, so far Gazpacho hadn't even mastered a piddly hello. The *Teach Your Bird to Talk* CD she'd left playing while she was at work had fallen on deaf avian ears. Thinking perhaps it was English he objected to, she'd started playing him tapes from the many language courses she'd taken. But he was no better at soaking up foreign tongues than she was. Then she'd decided that maybe Gazpacho was more musical than purely verbal. She left a Placido Domingo CD playing round the clock. Still no luck. She'd tried Edith Piaf, Julio Iglesias, and—for one insane week— Swiss yodeling music. Currently she had moved on to lounge singers, which wasn't exactly foreign, but still smacked of second-tier sophistication. Unfortunately, so far Sinatra, Mel Torme, and Sammy Davis, Jr., had all struck out. All Celia's hopes were now pinned on Dean Martin.

"For once in my life," Natalie continued, "I would like to go through a day knowing there's going to be a reason to go home at night."

"Television," Celia said, deciding not to suggest the parrot route. For one thing, she and Gazpacho had a fractious relationship at best. And Natalie absolutely couldn't stand the bird, especially after an unpleasant incident last fall.

But immediately, Celia knew she shouldn't have even suggested TV. Natalie sighed raggedly. "I've *got* television. I've got expanded premium deluxe cable— every stupid channel ever dreamed up by man. It's not enough for me! I want somebody who has to listen to me gripe about my crappy day, or who'll celebrate a good one with me. I want a partner." There was a dangerous quaver in her voice, and she twisted to reach into her purse for a tissue. She honked into it noisily and blurted out, "I want a goddamned husband. Is that so hard to understand?"

Entire tables swiveled to gape.

"Well, no," Celia said, trying to calm her down. The last time she'd seen Natalie so upset was when they had run out of her size at the Nordstrom's anniversary shoe sale. "But shouldn't you wait to find a guy . . . well, the regular way?"

Natalie bristled. "I'll be over the hill if I try to do it the regular way! *You* know the troubles I've had. The men I run into are all self-centered career hounds. If you act the least bit assertive around them, they feel threatened and fall apart."

As her friend described these nightmarish men, it struck Celia that Natalie could have been describing herself.

"These guys are just waiting for the right doormat to come along," Natalie went on. "Well, they can count me out. And I just don't have time to sit around waiting for some man who's the exception to the rule. I'm nearly twenty-eight years old, and I want a normal life. Now."

Celia frowned. "Normal?"

"You know . . . a husband and kids and a house in the suburbs. A real life."

Celia was shocked that Natalie's thinking on this subject was so far ahead of her own. Celia was still trying to get the hang of dating. Kids and suburbs seemed like specks on a distant horizon. "But you've got a great life right now."

Natalie snorted. "How can you say that?"

"Well, you've got your cool condo in the Pearl District—the neatest part of downtown—and—"

"*That* will be the first thing to go," Natalie declared hotly. "I've got to start looking for a real place to live."

"I thought you liked living in Portland, where the action is."

"Oh, sure. It's been great for me. But when I'm married I want to have a real place, around real people."

Natalie was bandying the word *real* about in a way that made Celia uncomfortable. "I'm not sure I understand the difference between a real person and a fake one."

Natalie rolled her eyes. "The Pearl District's fun, but let's face it. It's just twenty-somethings and dinks."

"Dinks?" Celia suddenly felt very slow. "What does that mean?"

"You know—dual income, no kids. D.I.N.K.S."

This was a sociological grouping Celia had never heard of. She was surprised by the disdain Natalie had used when speaking the acronym. "So . . . Dinkdom is a bad thing?"

Natalie chewed the question over for a moment. "Well, it could be worse. I could stay single forever."

A hot flash of panic swept through Celia. That was *her*. Well, maybe she wouldn't be single *forever,* but what if she was? Here she'd thought she was being a responsible adult, getting her ducks in a row, not rushing into anything like her mother had on multiple occasions. Come to find out, she was dooming herself to an unappealing demographic.

And now her friends were all getting married, abandoning her to the ultimate pariah status. She groaned.

"What's the matter with you?" Natalie asked.

"I just realized . . . I'm not even a dink. I'm nothing but a one income, no kids. I'm an O.I.N.K!"

Natalie laughed. But of course, she could afford to, now that she had a husband coming her way. *She* wouldn't be an oink much longer.

"I never knew that I would become part of a demographic other people would want to get away from," Celia said.

Natalie clucked her tongue. "Oh, I'm sure there are plenty of places older single women are welcome." She added, under her breath, "Probably not anywhere you'd actually want to be . . ."

Celia flagged down the waiter and ordered a glass of wine.

"It's like Mother says," Natalie continued, "women

just have this little window of opportunity. And let's face it, our window is about to slam shut on us."

At the mention of Natalie's mother, Celia trembled. Babs Glass was Natalie cubed. "That's just crazy, Nat," Celia told her. "You've never looked so good. It's the first thing I noticed when I walked into the restaurant, remember?"

"That's because you're female. Chanel means something to you. Presentation means something." She gave Celia's Value Village ensemble a disdainful glance. "Well, even if you don't always practice it yourself, you appreciate a well put together appearance when you see it. Any woman does. But men are still the ones who call the shots, and believe me, men have age sensors. It's sick but true. If there's a stunning thirty-five-year-old on one side of the room and a twenty-four-year-old slacker hag on the other, slacker hag wins every time."

Celia sighed. "I think you've been listening to your mother too much."

Natalie glanced at her watch. "Anyway . . . about those two huge favors?"

Celia had almost forgotten about those. "Oh, right. What do you want me to do?"

"Be my maid of honor?"

Celia knew that was her cue to expel a squeal of pleasure, but the reality was her stomach clenched in dread. And it wasn't just because she was tired of weddings.

The last wedding she'd been personally involved in had been a near disaster. Her friend Ellen, a yoga instructor, had married an acupuncturist named Lyle, whom she'd met at an alternative therapies convention in Taos. That had been a whirlwind affair, too— or, as Ellen had put it, an instant melding of souls. For the wedding, the couple had rented an all-too-

rustic wilderness retreat with traditional Indian huts
called yurts. On the appointed day, the weather spiked
up to, uncharacteristically for Oregon, ninety-five hu-
mid degrees. While guests sweltered in the wilderness,
Ellen had come down with cold feet. She kept muttering about the goddess being unresponsive. Even after Celia, as bridesmaid (or as Ellen called them,
female spiritual assistants), had cajoled the bride into
her hemp wedding smock, it had taken another hour
to coax Ellen out of her yurt. A task that Celia wasn't
at all the best person for, because she didn't even like
the groom. Lyle seemed way too controlling, which
was odd in a man who looked as if he had stepped
out of a Birkenstock ad.

Ellen finally decided that the goddess was probably
just tired from the heat and would bestow her blessing
nonetheless. However, the ceremony and its aftermath
had given Celia no optimism about the marriage.
There was nothing like "Morning Has Broken" on
hammered dulcimer, thirty minutes of personal vows
written in free verse by the bride and groom, and a
wheat-free, sugar-free, taste-free vegan reception buffet
to make even a wedding burnout like Celia pine for
time-worn, musty tradition.

Natalie was bound to go a more traditional route,
but still. "I assumed there wouldn't be a wedding ceremony . . ."

Natalie gaped at her as if she'd lost her marbles.
"Well, of course there's going to be a ceremony. That's
the whole point. Dress, big cake, reception—the whole
nine yards. It's going to be so romantic! Besides, do
you think my mother would let me get married without a big party?"

Babs, again. Celia suppressed a shiver. "But you
don't even know this guy."

"We've been exchanging E-mail for a month."

"A month?" This was even worse than she'd thought.

"We've exchanged photos, even," Natalie said. "He's *such* a cutie, Celia. Wait till you see him. He'll look amazing in a tux."

It was as if they were coeds again, talking about some guy at a homecoming kegger. "Nat, shouldn't you know a little bit more about this guy?"

"Please! We've exchanged all kinds of information."

"I'm just worried that this is like the time you thought you were in love with your U.P.S. man."

Natalie rolled her eyes. "Oh, come on. Once the excitement of getting that package delivered from Neiman's had worn off, that romance was all over. This is *completely* different."

"Still, you never can tell about people. I read this book called *Killing Me Softly* . . ."

"Please! I assure you, Angus McDougall is no psychopath."

"Angus McDougall?"

Natalie beamed. "Isn't that great? It sounds so . . . oh, I don't know, so . . . Scottish. Believe me, Celia, I know more about him than most of the guys I've slept with."

Celia didn't doubt this was true. Natalie had never been one for having deep, lasting relationships.

Her friend let out a blissful sigh. "I've always dreamed of a big June wedding."

"June?" Celia gulped. "That's just two months away!"

Those icy blue eyes stared stonily at her. "I know! It's going to be a busy two months—there's so much to do!"

So this was going to be a serious affair—showers, parties, pastel formals. Nonstop Natalie centered activity, orchestrated by Babs, conducted by Natalie at fast-forward speed.

"So will you?" Natalie asked.

Celia tried to feign enthusiasm, even though it felt as though Emily Post was squeezing her intestines. After all, what was the big deal? She'd have to throw a shower for Natalie, but that was just a matter of making up a batch of lemon bars and inviting a few people over. "Of course I will. What could be more fun than being a . . . bridesmaid?"

"Bridesmaid, nothing," Natalie declared. "You're maid of honor, baby. I'm going to be consulting you for everything!"

Right. Like Natalie would actually take Celia's advice.

"Now, about this other favor . . ." From Natalie's businesslike manner, Celia could tell that their thirty minutes were almost up.

"Sure, anything," Celia said. She was numb now anyway.

"Could you meet Angus?"

"Of course I'll meet him. I'll probably be sick of the sight of him by the time the wedding rolls around." She'd certainly been sick of Lyle.

Natalie pinned her with an impatient look. "I mean meet him tonight. At the airport. His plane comes in at six-thirty, and there's *no way* I'll be able to make it."

"You can't make it to the airport to meet your fiancé's plane?"

"The vice president's in town today!" Natalie practically shrieked. "He's got press conferences this afternoon, and then he's speaking to a woman's group in Beaverton at six. How could I possibly get to the airport in time?"

Skip the press conference, Celia considered saying, but just stopped herself.

"I've told you what this means to me," Natalie said. "It might be my big chance to move a rung up my career ladder. This could be my moment."

"Sure, but . . ."

Natalie scowled at her hesitation. "Well, for heaven's sake, Celia, give me a simple yes or no. If you can't, you can't. I'll understand, but I'll need to make other arrangements. I only thought you might want to, after all I've done for you." She paused, and then said with pointed meaning, "After Thailand."

Celia yipped in dismay. Surely Natalie wasn't still holding a grudge about *that.* "You *wanted* to go to Thailand with me."

"I didn't want to get stuck in a typhoon."

"That wasn't my fault," Celia argued. "It's unreasonable to hold me in your debt because of a little bad weather."

"A little? We nearly washed out to sea!"

"Still . . . Typhoons fall under the act of God clause in friendship."

"Okay, but how about the time I drove you and that disgusting bird of yours to the animal hospital last fall?"

Celia fell silent. Natalie *had* been great that night.

"Believe me," Natalie said sternly, "parrot diarrhea isn't easily removed from leather seat covers."

That did it. "All right. Of course I can meet him. But . . ."

"Now, don't worry about a thing," Natalie interrupted. She goggled at her wristwatch and started gathering up her belongings. "I've *got* to run!"

"But—"

"I'll e-mail you everything you need to know, Celia. Airline, flight time arrival, a description of Angus . . ."

She picked up her briefcase, slung her purse over her shoulder, and patted Celia efficiently on the shoulder. "Thanks a bundle! I'll be in touch."

And then she was off.

You'd better be in touch, Celia thought as she watched her friend bolt out the door. *Otherwise, I'll be stuck with your guy.* She leaned back and shook her head in amazement.

She couldn't wait to tell Davis about *this!*

Two

"She's *completely* insane."

Davis looked up from the hot pastrami he was holding aloft over greasy white butcher paper. As Celia tossed her purse onto her desk, he felt a familiar hitch in his chest. Whenever she was around, it seemed as if he was snapping back to life after being on autopilot. "Who is?"

"Natalie!"

"You're just now noticing this?"

Like Celia, Davis was back from lunch, but his had been a working meal. Three days a week he delivered a column on topics ranging from presidential elections to cell phone manners. He gathered "man on the street" insight on these issues wherever people in Portland congregated—coffee shops, the DPS, the steps of Pioneer Square. Today he'd gone to a diner. He didn't like to stuff his face while people were telling him their deepest feelings about politics or mother-in-laws, so he'd just listened—okay, and maybe nibbled a little at a meatloaf plate. Then he'd come back to the Tillamook Deli in the basement of the Times building for a real lunch.

He'd moved to Oregon from Nebraska late last spring, and after a year of this two-lunch system, he wasn't ready for a *GQ* cover, that was for sure. But he doubted he would ever have been a buff ladykiller anyway. It seemed that no matter how old he got, and how far from Omaha he traveled, he just couldn't shake a certain corn-fed farm kid look. He was tall and rumpled, with a mop of blond hair that was still trimmed in the same air force officer's cut he'd been receiving at barbershops since he was ten. In the winter he was doughy; in the summer his skin tended to burn, his cheeks to turn annoyingly pink. His best feature was his eyes . . . but unfortunately, they weren't of the dark and brooding variety. They were blue. Light blue. They couldn't smolder sexily because they were too busy being friendly and twinkly.

Of course, that friendly quality had something to do with his talent for getting people to talk. He was a good interviewer. With men, he was nonthreatening—a man's man. And he was one of those guys women often referred to as *a real pal.* Or *as good as gold.* Or, the one that really made him shudder, *a teddy bear.* God help him.

Women might hang out with teddy bears, and spill their guts to teddy bears, but they didn't fall in love with them. Instead, they wanted to be pals, buddies. Which was great. Terrific. Except when the teddy bear harbored hopes for something more.

Celia flopped into her desk chair across the aisle from him. Wheeling around, she caught a glimpse of his chip bag, which was leaned against a Mr. Pibb can. Davis put his sandwich down self-consciously.

"You've never liked Natalie," she said. "I don't know why."

Davis pretended to ponder the matter. "Hm. Let's see. Could it be because . . . she's crazy?" Celia shot him a disapproving look, so he reminded her, *"You* just called her insane."

"Well, it's okay for *me* to say so," Celia said. "She's my friend."

"Also, she's shallow."

"Okay, but—"

"And vain, and incredibly self-centered." And that was really just the tip of the iceberg.

"You're just hostile toward her because of that time you overheard her saying that you reminded her of a muppet."

True. In fact, his teeth were grinding at the memory.

"Let's face it," Celia said. "Everyone has flaws."

Davis almost sputtered Mr. Pibb across the aisle. "Flaws? Are you kidding? She's a tyrannosaurus masquerading as Paula Zahn."

Celia let out a long breath. "If we didn't forgive each other's faults, nobody would have any friends. Even we nontyrannosauruses."

That was Celia all over. Davis felt his pulse pick up speed again. He just couldn't help being crazy about her.

"Nat's a lot to put up with," Celia went on, "but most people don't realize that when the chips are down there's no better friend. She was great when we were two Oregonians at Mizzou. One time she even skipped her sorority's homecoming blowout because I was stuck in the dorm with a cold."

"Natalie did?" Davis asked, surprised.

Celia laughed ruefully. "I have to remind myself of that fact every time I want to strangle her."

He had a feeling now was one of those times. "Say, I know what will shake those Natalie blues away," Davis said. "Tonight's a Blazers game."

She slapped herself on the forehead. "Damn. I forgot!"

Celia liked to pretend that she could take the Blazers or leave them. She enjoyed lampooning the Blazer-Dancers that entertained during halftime, and coworkers who put Scottie Pippen bobble head dolls on their desks, or guys who tacked up ONE TEAM, ONE DREAM posters in their cubicles. For pride's sake she acted as if sitting tensely through long games at the Rose Garden Arena was just something she did to keep Davis company. But Davis knew better. Celia was a hoops junkie.

It was his ace in the hole. This year for Christmas Davis's dad had given him two season tickets to the Portland Trailblazers' home games. Davis always gave first dibs on his spare ticket to Celia, who made a big show of deliberating before accepting his invitation. Though she'd been deliberating less and less as the season crept toward the play-offs.

Today, however, the hesitation seemed in earnest.

"I can't go," she said.

"What's wrong?"

"It's Natalie!" She let out a bark of frustration. "She's a nut."

"I think we've established that fact."

"This is different. She's going to get married!"

Davis paused to kick this one around for a moment. Natalie's finding some sucker to marry her was bad enough. But apparently she'd had the gall to devise nuptial plans that conflicted with the Blazers game. "Tonight?"

"No, in June."

"I didn't even know she had a . . ." Davis cast about for the appropriate word, but the only one that came to mind was *victim.*

"She doesn't!" She shook her head, sending her sandy brown hair bobbing around her chin. "I mean, she didn't. But now she's got this guy coming from Scotland, and I'm supposed to meet his airplane."

"Wait," Davis said, still trying to make sense of all

this. "You mean Natalie is having a guy shipped in to marry her?"

"Well, what else is she going to do?" No matter how conflicted she was herself, Celia could get a little touchy on the subject of her old college chum. "Poor Nat. People—men, that is—just don't seem to understand her."

Davis smiled knowingly. "Let me guess. According to Natalie, we men are intimidated by strong, successful females?"

Celia crossed her arms. "Wrong. You're intimidated by strong, successful, *beautiful* females." She let out an impatient breath as Davis chortled at her answer. "Anyway, tonight's just a mess. Her fiancé's plane arrives *and* the vice president's in town . . ."

"So naturally Natalie's going to tend to the vice president and make you pick up the bundle from Britain."

"What choice does she have? She's a journalist."

"Right. And you're just an errand girl."

She flicked an exasperated gaze at him and then nodded toward his bag of Fritos. "Aren't you going to eat those?"

"Weren't you just at lunch?"

"Yeah, but I was too stunned by what Natalie was telling me to eat anything."

He forked over the chips. "How are you supposed to know this guy when you see him? And what are you supposed to say to him? 'Sorry, your bride-to-be couldn't be bothered'?"

"I don't know . . ." Celia popped a Frito and turned to her monitor to check her E-mail. The minute her incoming messages popped up, she let out a yelp. "Oh, here we go! This is helpful. Natalie says I can't miss him. 'A dark, brooding Scot.' " Celia rolled her eyes. "Honestly. What's that supposed to mean?"

"Maybe Natalie is marrying Sean Connery."

"Well, at least I'll have his flight number," Celia muttered, scrolling down the message. "But does she think Angus McDougall is going to step off the plane with a label on him?"

"Angus McDougall?"

"That's his name."

"Natalie's going to be Mrs. McDougall?"

"Maybe," Celia said. "If I don't nab the wrong guy at the airport."

This whole setup made Davis uneasy. Celia, of all people, should not be the one meeting this guy's plane. She was still heartbroken from her bust-up with the odious Ian. Who had also been a foreigner.

She had a thing for foreign guys.

"Hey!" he said brightly. "Why don't I go with you tonight?"

"You're sweet to offer, but there's no sense in your evening being ruined, too. You just go and enjoy the Blazers game." Her sigh was practically a moan of despair. "Don't worry about me. This is just the beginning of having my life sucked away by Natalie. She wants me to be the maid of honor at her wedding. In less than two months I'm going to be standing in front of a throng of people in a sickly pastel formal, trying to look happy that my friend is marrying some guy she doesn't even know."

"She might know him by the time the wedding rolls around," Davis pointed out.

Celia sank down in her chair, polishing off the bag of chips as she brooded. "Not to mention, I'm going to have to deal with Natalie's mom, Babs. If you think Natalie's bad, you should meet Mommy Dearest."

"It's hard to imagine Natalie having a mother." But he supposed everyone did. Even the creature from *Alien*.

Celia shook her head. "And the upshot of all this is that I'm going to be the last oink on the planet."

He frowned. "I beg your pardon?"

"That's an acronym for one income, no kids," she told him matter-of-factly. "Which is one huge step down from a dink."

Davis frowned. "I've never heard of oinks before."

"Well, actually, I just invented the term—but I think it's an apt name for what we are. To hear Natalie tell it, pretty soon the oinks and the dinks are going to be living in quarantined areas in the inner cities where no normal married-with-children types would dare to go."

Davis laughed. "Don't worry. As long as there are Starbucks and movie theaters, we oinks will survive."

She shook her head mournfully. "Our numbers are dwindling rapidly, though. Pretty soon I'm going to be the last oink."

"That's a slight exaggeration."

"*All* my friends are married now."

"I'm not."

"Well, no. Not you, of course," she admitted absently as she wadded the Frito bag into a crinkly ball. "I'm already living in dread of this wedding. I'm going to feel like a total oink. And the rehearsal dinner! I'll be stuck two-stepping with Natalie's elderly relatives. Do you know I haven't really had a date since Ian? My professional life is stagnant, my love life is nonexistent, and now all my single friends are abandoning me."

"I'm not."

"No, not you," she said. "Even if you threatened to, at this point I'd have to pay you to stay my friend."

He tapped his chin. "Hm . . . Maybe you shouldn't have told me that. I've been trying to figure out a way to bankroll that book I've been trying to write." The paper clip she tossed missed him by inches. "C'mon, Celia. You always think you're being abandoned."

"And most of the time I'm right," she retorted. "Believe me, a person who had three stepfathers by the age of ten and ended up being fobbed off on her grandparents *knows* about abandonment. I suppose the last straw would be Gazpacho abandoning me."

"Actually, I think that would be cause for celebration." That bird was a menace, and Davis had the scarred index finger to prove it. Gazpacho was the fastest beak in the West.

Celia drummed a pencil against her calendar desk blotter. "I don't want to go through Natalie's wingding alone. But what kind of date can I scrounge up before June?"

"Well . . ." Davis waited a few seconds, just for show. Not that this required any thought. "How about me?"

On the surface, it wasn't such a bold offer. He and Celia attended weddings together sometimes. Every week or so she had to attend a ceremony for her column, and occasionally Davis would tag along for fun. Unlike her, he *enjoyed* weddings. He loved the silly pageantry of them, the cockeyed optimism. He was attracted to the idea of two completely disparate groups of people brought together for a day because of two people's pie-in-the-sky dreams of happily ever after.

Of course, those previous outings with Celia had been working weddings. This was more personal. This would be more like a real date.

Did the difference register with Celia?

She looked at him with her lips parted in wonder, and something in her green eyes melted. Which in turn made Davis feel as if there was a steel band squeezing on his chest. His blood pressure spiked up, and for a moment, he felt light-headed. Reckless, almost.

Heaven help him. In his lovesick woosiness, he was on the verge of blurting out all kinds of things that had been bottling up inside him for a year. Like how the moment he had been installed in the cubicle next to hers, it felt as though his whole life had changed. That he had spent all those months while she was dating Ian holding his breath. That he'd secretly rejoiced when Ian had beat it back to England. That whenever they were together his heart danced joyfully in his chest, Fred Astaire style. That it was hard to concentrate on his work because he was so distracted by Celia's presence right across the aisle. That sometimes the tapping of her fingers on her computer keyboard nearly drove him insane with longing. That he had almost kissed her at the last Blazers game while they were standing in the line for YoCream cones.

That he was ninety-nine-point-five percent certain she was the love of his life. All this information swelled inside him until he was a hairsbreadth from exploding in an amorous confessional.

But Celia piped up before he could utter a single word. "Davis, have I ever told you that you're an incredible pal?"

That word, *pal*, burst his love bubble. A hundred unspoken words gushed out of him in silent disappointment. With Herculean effort he shrugged and pretended that his invitation was just an off-the-cuff thing. As if pal was the most he ever aspired to be. "Yes, you have."

"No, really," she said as she got up and grabbed her coffee cup.

"Really, you have," he assured her through gritted teeth.

"It's just like you to offer to come to my rescue like

that. You're a real brick." She patted him on the shoulder. "But don't worry. Maybe you won't have to go through with it."

Meaning that she was hoping that something better would come along. Better, of course, translated as someone flashier, more exotic.

Less Omaha.

She marched toward the coffee room, leaving Davis to stare blankly at his sandwich. Nobody had to explain to him what had just happened. He'd just volunteered to be Celia's fallback date. The default. The schnook who would do in a pinch.

Was there any way to look at this situation that wasn't completely depressing?

After a short eternity of disconsolately eyeing the congealing cheese and sweaty, wilting lettuce of his sandwich, he attempted to buck himself up. What was the matter with him? He hadn't deliberated this much over making his feelings known to a female since the time when he was eight years old and he'd wanted to invite Dorrie Simpson to see *The Rescuers* with him. Unfortunately, in that case, his desires had been left unspoken, and he'd ended up seeing the mouse movie with Michael, his little brother.

But since that first unfortunate incident, he hadn't had much trouble with women. Taking a tip from his early failure of courage, if he liked a woman, he simply asked her out. No problem. End of story. Until he'd accepted this job and uprooted his life and found himself in this cubicle across from Celia. . . .

Now it was Dorrie Simpson all over again. He was almost thirty years old and afraid to simply tell a woman that he liked her. He'd spent months couching invitations in such a way that Celia could misinterpret them as just-buddy outings.

What was the big deal? The worst that could happen

would be for Celia to say she wasn't interested. And maybe, just maybe, she *would* be interested.

But if she wasn't interested . . .

It was that one *if* that made him cringe. That kept him holding his tongue day after day. That kept him up late nights, turning the thing over in his head. Because if he professed eternal devotion and Celia told him to dream on, there he would be in the cubicle next to hers, day after day, feeling like a complete jerk.

Looking at it that way, staying clammed up was the only way to go. To make a hopeless bid for romance could result in his losing a very good friend. After all, just pals was nothing to sneeze at. Since Ian's blessed departure, he and Celia had spent a lot of weekends bumming around together, hanging out and watching videos or those old made-for-TV movies Celia inexplicably loved so much. Aside from the work weddings, they also attended Blazers games and the occasional concert. They were both road food enthusiasts, so sometimes they would just putter around rural Oregon looking for good diners.

And never in all this time had he detected any love vibes coming off Celia. In fact, the chances were huge that Celia didn't return his feelings. And why should she? Watching Valerie Bertinelli TV movies and hunting for the ultimate grilled cheese sandwich weren't typical foundations for a lasting bond of love.

The day seemed to drag on forever. Davis plugged away at a column he was writing about a proposed new baseball stadium that would lure major league ball to Portland. Sports metaphors and corny baseball jokes churned out of him without conscious thought. His mind was totally focused on Celia, who was typing like a dervish. Though occasionally she would stop to mumble something about Natalie or—even more perplexing—ferrets.

Then, every so often, she would swivel in her chair and toss off disconcerting comments. At first the remarks were in the vein of "Can you believe Natalie? She never even *told* me she was chatting with some guy on the Internet . . ."

Before Davis could respond, she would turn back to her computer screen. Increasingly these asides gave him reason to question her mental state. By midafternoon, she was saying, "Leave it to Natalie to snag a cool guy from Scotland! Does she have all the luck, or what?"

It was the foreign-guy thing that worried him the most.

Celia was always taking Berlitz courses in preparation for having the ultimate holiday romance in an exotic locale, with some Antonio Banderas-like creature sweeping her off her hiking boots. Unfortunately, as far as Davis could tell, most of these vacations ended not in love but in disaster. Last year, a trip to some Mexican ruins had been spoiled when the bus broke down in a jungle somewhere. Celia had come back ten pounds thinner, bumpy with mosquito bites, and harboring a deep-seated fear of howler monkeys. And from what he could gather, earlier trips to Paris and Thailand had also turned into debacles.

But one thing about Celia was, she always kept hoping. She was due to start on Mandarin Chinese in May. Doubtless she was envisioning Chow Yun Fat giving her guided tours of the Great Wall, but considering her travel track record, she should probably be more concerned about the wall's structural integrity. With her luck, the thing was apt to collapse out from under her.

At four-thirty Celia looked up with her brows beetled in thought. "I wonder what I should wear to pick up this hunky Scotsman . . ."

That phrase, *pick up*, unsettled him. *Hunky Scotsman* did nothing to allay his fears, either.

His face must have registered his alarm because Celia hastily clarified, "I want to make a good impression. For Natalie's sake."

"I'm sure anything casual would be fine," Davis said. "It's not like this is any big deal. You're just meeting the guy's plane." He scrutinized her closely. "Right?"

She mulled this over for a moment, then nodded. "You're right. Who cares? All I'm doing is ferrying the guy from the airport to Nat's apartment."

Davis let out an inaudible sigh of relief.

Celia let out a very audible sigh of frustration.

Or was it longing?

"Look," Davis piped up, "why don't I drive you to the airport? This guy is bound to have a lot of luggage, and your Civic isn't very roomy."

"Neither is your Ford."

She had a point. Foiled, Davis swiveled back to his terminal. *Just stay out of this,* the voice of wisdom was telling him. But an even louder voice was chanting *hunky Scotsman, hunky Scotsman* over and over again in a particularly taunting tone.

Celia had been so vulnerable since Ian left. . . .

He tried not to think about what could happen. Because nothing could happen. The man was Natalie's fiancé. Celia would never betray her friend, especially by stealing her man at the airport.

Nevertheless, when Celia got up to go home, Davis bounded out of his chair and nearly beat her to the elevator. "Are you taking off?" he asked casually. "Me, too."

She fixed a curious gaze on him. "You usually don't crash out of here till after six."

This was true. The city of Portland was divided by the Willamette River, and Davis owned a small house with a large mortgage on the east side, across the river from downtown. Negotiating the bridges during rush hour traffic could be murder, but he couldn't resist this last chance to talk to Celia. "I'm bushed," he said. "Guess I didn't get much sleep last night . . ."

Celia looked at him with real concern. "Corky problems?"

"Mm." Davis felt a twinge of guilt for the lie. But maligning his friend Corky was better than confessing what he'd really been losing sleep over lately. Namely, Celia.

And if one had to blame somebody for something, Corky Weatherford was always an excellent candidate. When they were kids, he and Davis had been friends back in Omaha. Then, at age fifteen, Davis had switched schools, and they had lost touch . . . until four months ago when Corky had called him from out of the blue. He said he'd been considering moving to Portland, and out of politeness, Davis had extended an invitation for Corky to use his spare room while he was settling in.

Corky had settled in, all right. Man, baggage, and the complete *oeuvre* of Bruce Springsteen. It had been three months since the fateful day Corky's U-Haul pulled up to Davis's door. Three months that seemed like three decades. Corky had quickly found a job waiting tables during the day, but his forays into the apartment rental market hadn't been as fruitful.

Corky was not an easy housemate to ignore. He was a big, galumphing fellow who was always into something, always in your face. His musical preference ran exclusively to the Boss, whom he played nonstop, at window-rattling volume. He was addicted to the Food Network on television, especially the macho chefs like Molto Mario and Emeril. He always had some project going on—painting or fixing a leaky faucet or making another one of his disastrous home-cooked meals (the kitchen had to be excavated these days just to find a coffee cup). He was completely hopeless at anything he tried. He spilled paint everywhere, he left projects half done, and judging from the dinners Davis choked down out of politeness, all those hours in front of the television were not helping his culinary skills. Corky was no closer to being a chef than Celia's parrot was to being Luciano Pavarotti.

And to top it all off, he liked to reminisce. Davis was as nostalgic for the past as anyone. But there were limits. After three months with Corky, Davis decided he really didn't want reminders of embarrassing questions he'd asked in sixth grade health class (How was he supposed to know that inquiring about something called a dental dam wasn't appropriate on oral hygeine day?). Nor did he want Corky going on at length at parties about the time in elementary school Davis got into a fight because some mouthy kid had called his favorite band, the Village People, a bunch of homos. Youth was unpleasant enough the first time around; reliving it with Corky was akin to going to the proctologist for a recheck.

The trouble was, Corky was just so *nice*. He had no conception of what an irritant he was.

It was impossible to bear him any lasting ill will. It was even more impossible to kick him out of the house. The few times Davis had seriously set his mind to giving him the heave-ho, he'd come home to discover that Corky had mowed the yard. Or taken the old man next door grocery shopping. Or done Davis's laundry.

Celia shook her head in sympathy as the elevator burped them out into the underground parking lot. "You've got the patience of a saint, Davis."

"Not really. I'm just too cowardly to kick a guy out of my house when he has pictures of me dressed as Rambo at a Halloween party."

She gawked at him in amazement. "You made yourself up like Sylvester Stallone? How?"

"With misguided determination and a lot of hair dye."

She clucked her tongue sympathetically. "How awful. I can barely stand to share my apartment with Gazpacho. But at least he doesn't have anything to blackmail me with."

Though, knowing that bird, he was probably working on it.

"Has he said anything this week?"

"No, still silent as the tomb." She dug through her purse for her keys. "At least he's probably going to live a long time. I'll be able to celebrate a fiftieth anniversary with something, even if it is in silence."

Davis remembered something she'd said earlier. "Say . . . You didn't really mean all that stuff about being an oink, did you?" That kind of thinking smacked of desperation, and desperate women. . . .

Well, they shouldn't be picking up good-looking foreigners in airports.

She eyed him with amusement. "Do you think I'm going to do myself in?"

"No, of course not . . ."

She laughed. "You do. I can tell by the look in your eye that you think I'm going to go home and commit old maid *hari kari*. That I'm going to fall on my mascara wand or something." She touched his arm, in a gesture that was supposed to be soothing, he supposed, but of course it wasn't. "Have fun at the game tonight. And when you have a chance, spare a thought for poor me cooling my heels at the airport."

As if he'd think of anything else. All the way home he was haunted by visions of an Ewan McGregor look-alike stepping off the airplane into Celia's open, enthusiastic arms.

On the other hand, this guy, Angus, *was* Natalie's fiancé. Even if Celia found him irresistible, that didn't mean Angus McDougall wouldn't be able to resist her.

Of course, if the guy didn't think Celia was preferable to Natalie, he was a McIdiot.

When Davis finally turned onto his street, his tires sent water spraying. It was as if he were driving in the Columbia River; the street was flooded. *Some jerk*, he thought. *Watering his lawn in spring.* Couldn't people use their common sense?

An idea for a column on water waste flashed in his mind.

The flow down Main grew more torrential the farther up the street he puttered. Finally, up ahead he could see the problem: a geyser of water shooting up at least fifteen feet. A broken water main, obviously. Some idiot . . .

Suddenly, he spied Corky standing in the street.

Uh-oh.

No please, he thought, *don't let it be . . .*

Driving a few yards farther told the tale. Old Faithful was smack in front of his house. And half the neighborhood seemed to be clustering like bugs around it.

Corky spied his car and came loping down the street toward him, splashing water with his boat-sized feet and waving his hands at Davis to flag him down. As if Davis were going to drive right by this catastrophe without stopping.

Though, come to think of it, the idea did have a certain appeal.

Davis slowed to a stop and parked curbside, since his driveway was as navigable as Niagra Falls. He had to remind himself about those Rambo snaps before he was able to step out of the car with any kind of composure.

"Don't worry about a thing!" Corky said quickly. "I've got it all under control."

Obviously. "What happened?"

"I was digging an herb bed." His housemate lifted his hands in frustration. "It was supposed to be a surprise."

"I'm surprised, all right." Davis glanced over to the gusher, which people were *ooh*ing and *ahh*ing over as if it were the fountain at Lincoln Center. The sound of Bruce Springsteen singing "Dancing in the Dark" thumped through the walls of his house. The pulsing drums added to the water carnival atmosphere.

"I've called the city," Corky said. "They're sending someone over right away."

"Good."

"You're not mad, are you?"

Davis looked sharply into Corky's face, which wore a sheepish, apologetic expression, and tried not to succumb to the urge to throttle him. "An herb bed?"

Corky nodded enthusiastically. "Sure. I had it all planned. Oregano, basil, sage—we could even put in a tomato plant or two. For flavor you can't beat a home-grown tomato."

Davis heard the words, but his brain just wasn't up to the task of processing it all yet. He should have stayed back at the office and obsessed over Celia. Now he had this to worry about. How were they ever going to get that thing patched up before tonight? How were they ever going to clean up the mess? Mud and debris were rushing down the street, in which the more opportunistic neighborhood kids were splashing joyfully.

Corky caught his bewildered expression. "The city should be here any minute now. I was looking out for the truck when you drove up." He patted Davis comfortingly on the back. "Like I said, it's all under control."

Davis watched someone's plastic-wrapped morning paper and a Fisher Price tricycle float downstream toward Twenty-fourth Street. Before he could respond to Corky's assurances, he spied two neighbors, Stan and Mike, coming over to greet him. The two men had their jeans neatly rolled up to navigate through the water. Just like Martha Stewart would do if she was out clamming.

"Hey, Davis," said Stan.

"How's it goin'?" asked Mike.

Davis gaped at them. Even given the fact that Stan and Mike were the most happy, unflappable couple he'd ever been acquainted with, did they really have to ask? This wasn't exactly the sort of scenario a person dreamed of coming home to at the end of a busy day. "Jim-dandy, guys."

Stan, the taller man who was balding prematurely and liberally, laughed. "Just a hazard of home ownership!"

A hazard of Corky friendship, Davis was tempted to retort, but he remained diplomatically silent on that subject and instead made introductions. "I don't know if you've met my friend Corky. He's from Nebraska. Been staying with me for—" His brain stumbled past the word *forever.* "A few months."

Corky smiled and shot out his big paw for a shake. "Corky Weatherford."

"Are you the one responsible?" asked Stan, grinning.

"For the water show?" finished Mike.

"Corky was digging an herb bed," Davis explained.

"Oh!"

"Fantastic!"

"We've always wanted an—"

"Herb bed."

"Always! So nice to have—"

"Fresh parsley!"

Poor Corky looked rattled. Though Davis knew these two neighbors mostly from front-yard conversations as they walked their dogs, and a few block parties, he was accustomed to their habit of finishing sentences for each other.

"Right now we're thinking of turning the front yard into a rice paddy," Davis said.

Stan and Mike laughed harder than the lame joke merited and then exchanged secretive glances. "What do you think?" Mike asked.

"Should we?"

"Tell them?"

Stan looked as if he was mulling something over. "Well . . . okay. No sense in being—"

"Coy?"

"Is there?"

For a moment, Davis worried they were here to bear more bad news. "What's the matter?"

Mike burst out laughing. "Nothing tragic!"

"Get that look off your face! We just wanted to invite you—"

"To a party, that's all."

Davis let out a breath he hadn't been aware of holding. "Oh, great. That's great."

Mike and Stan exchanged glances. "Don't you want to guess what kind of party it's going to be?"

He took another breath for patience. He had water

rushing up to his ankles and was a little distracted at the moment for games. "I'm not sure . . ."

"Course not! Why would you?" Stan asked suddenly.

He looked at Mike, and the two of them laughed uproariously. Davis and Corky glanced curiously at the two men, who were having a hard time getting composed again. A tear was actually streaming down Mike's cheek.

"He'll never guess," Stan said.

"We should just tell. Shout it to the mountaintops!"

"Hell, yes." Stan looked at Davis and said in a joyous rush, clutching Mike to his side, "It's an engagement party! We're—"

"Getting married!" Mike finished for him.

"Wow," Davis said. This wasn't something that happened to him every day. And it probably would never have happened back in Omaha. "Congratulations."

No wonder the two guys looked punch drunk.

"Thanks—so will you come? The party's the weekend after next. It's going to be a very short engagement. We're sending out invitations, but we wanted to make sure you knew you were invited."

"Well, thanks," Davis said. "I'll be sure to come."

The two guys glanced at Corky a little uncomfortably. "You're invited, too, of course," Stan said.

Corky's brow was furrowed in puzzlement. "You guys are both getting married at the same time?"

Stan and Mike looked at each other and then burst out laughing all over again. "Oh, you're definitely—"

"Definitely invited!" Stan finished gleefully for him. "Too much funny!"

They looked at Davis approvingly. *"Priceless!"*

Still hooting with laughter, they turned and walked away, kicking up water at each other playfully as they went.

Corky stared after them, then turned to Davis with

a puzzled glance. "I mean, doesn't that seem like an awfully big coincidence?"

"Not if you take into account the fact that they're getting married *to each other.*"

Slowly the lightbulb flickered on over Corky's head. "Oh! Well, that does explain things."

Davis wondered how long it would take Corky to realize that Stan and Mike obviously had assumed that they were more than just roommates.

He felt slightly depressed. Not only did the woman of his dreams not realize he was in love with her, but mere acquaintances now were pairing him up with someone of the wrong sex entirely.

"Well," Corky said with a shrug of acceptance, "they certainly seem happy."

They seemed delirious. Davis felt himself almost becoming jealous of his neighbors. Why couldn't he be that lucky?

Finally he understood a little of Celia's oinky anguish of this afternoon. With every marriage it did seem as though the rest of the world was finding happiness while life was just passing him—and Celia—by.

He needed to do something. Take the bull by the horns. But how? Celia didn't even know he existed beyond being someone to eat lunch and watch Lifetime movies with. She just didn't see him as the bold, exotic lover of her dreams. Someone who could sweep her off her feet.

And why should she? He was about as exotic as a loaf of Wonder Bread. He was a man with a Ford and a mortgage. His house was even located on Main Street. He wasn't given to rash actions. His only claim to exoticism was his friend Antonio, who lived in Argentina. Compared to the men Celia gravitated toward, he was strictly Ward Cleaver material.

He was a man who had to worry about water mains.

He wasn't the type to perform bold, romantic actions. Say, to dash off to the airport to save a woman from falling into the arms of the wrong man.

Was he?

Three

Celia was so worried about getting to the airport late that she ended up arriving a half hour early. Once there, however, she regretted her hyperpunctuality. This was a half hour that she could have been at home eating a real dinner instead of the nuked Hot Pocket she'd scarfed down in the car. A half hour she could have spent productively—for instance, listening to Dean Martin's greatest hits with Gazpacho. Or working a little harder on her appearance.

She'd decided not to go for the jeans look—after all, the man was coming all the way from Glasgow; he deserved *some* sort of reception. So at the last minute she'd punted the denim and comfort shoes and opted for a casual but flirty black dress and a pair of heels. She wasn't Natalie, that was for certain, but at least the guy wouldn't step off the plane only to be greeted by someone who looked as though she was all set to mop floors.

Unfortunately, she thought as she stared glassily at the television hanging in the airport bar, her makeup hadn't been touched up since this morning and now felt like a plastic mask that was glued to her face. Her hair, which never held up well, drooped in wilted hanks over her cheeks.

And not letting Davis come with her to the airport had been a mistake. She needed him. Having him there would have alleviated that used-up, end-of-day feeling. He would have perked her up with a laugh or two. He had a way of being able to take her from the doldrums to delirious laughter in a matter of minutes. Which was why he'd been invaluable after Ian had dumped her. All Davis had to do was talk about Corky, or make a stupid pun, or tell her about the mystery novel he was hatching (which featured a newspaper staff who were being picked off by a crazed style section editor), and her problems seemed to evaporate. Being with Davis made her realize that she could live just fine without Ian. That she didn't need a boyfriend at all to make her happy.

While she sucked down a Diet Coke, she decided that she could put this idle downtime to good use by trying to do a little problem solving. She fished in her pocketbook for the small notepad she'd originally bought months ago to jot down stimulating ideas and wry observations. She had used it twice so far—for grocery lists.

After rescuing the tiny notebook from the sea of old pens and loose Tic Tacs swimming at the bottom of her purse, she flipped to page three. In the upper left corner, she wrote in clear print letters: PROBLEMS WITH CELIA'S LIFE

The primary ill was easy to pinpoint.

1. JOB!!!!!!

She took another swig of her drink and tapped her pen against her chin, feeling pleased that she was finally really tackling some issues. She should have done this ages ago! Once she'd started, the words really started flowing.

2. WEAK BACKBONE (especially in regard to Natalie, the Warden, Gazpacho, etc.)

3. NOTHING INTERESTING HAPPENING (or slated to happen in foreseeable future)

After a moment's more reflection, she added,
4. NO SIGNIFICANT OTHER

As she surveyed her list, she frowned at the last entry. It smacked of the pathetic, twenty-something, single female. Too oinky.

Besides, deep down she was certain her dream guy was at large somewhere, waiting for her to bump into him. Preferably in a foreign country with a temperate climate with no disgusting parasites or menacing nocturnal monkeys. So far there didn't seem to be a biological time bomb ticking away inside her, and unlike Natalie, she didn't harbor fears that a window was about to slam down on her.

Some days, she even felt lucky to be single. The couples she knew certainly weren't studies in ecstatic marital bliss. Especially not her friend Ellen, and she was still practically a newlywed. Every time Celia saw Ellen, a little more of her self-esteem seemed to have eroded. And look at Natalie—so desperate to get married she was throwing herself away on God only knew what. Some unknown, artistic, wildly handsome Scottish guy.

Ridiculous.

She crossed out number four. NO SIGNIFICANT OTHER did not deserve a numbered place on her list. At most it should simply have been a subheading under NOTHING INTERESTING HAPPENING.

Satisfied, she then wrote on the upper right hand of the page: **SOLUTIONS**

At that point, her brain froze.

Her gaze locked on the stricken number four.
NO SIGNIFICANT OTHER.

Who was she kidding. That really was depressing, wasn't it? She hadn't had a real date since Ian went back to England. Despite her best efforts and the comforting presence of Davis in her life, that factoid had been bouncing around her mind all this time. Not that she'd been really obsessed over the fact that she was dumped . . . except maybe on her birthday, major holidays, and weekends. Other times, she barely thought of Ian at all. She'd even practically forgotten what he looked like.

Tall.

Reddish brown hair.

Whiskey-colored eyes.

Adorable dimple on his chin.

Absently, she doodled his name on the page. *Ian. Ian Saunders.*

She'd been dumped. Dumped by the only guy she'd ever really wanted. Or, no, maybe that wasn't totally honest. She'd been dumped by the only guy who fit her ideal of what she wanted (foreign, incredibly good-looking, solvent) and actually loved her back. At least, he'd *said* he loved her. She had patted herself on the back for finding someone so romantic and dashing, but in the end he'd dashed back to England and married his college sweetheart.

Ian, Ian, Ian!

She hardly knew where the time went after that. An Ian funk consumed her. When the loudspeaker in the bar announced the flight from New York, she snapped to and discovered her little notebook page was crammed with Ian's name, along with hearts with little frowny faces on them.

She dragged herself off her stool, jammed a couple of dollars into the tip jar on the counter, and crumpled up the piece of paper, which she decided was evidence more of latent adolescence than true heartbreak. Then she marched out to the area of the concourse where people awaited their incoming loved ones and stood at the front of the gathered throng. One smiling group near her held up a sign festooned with balloons and shiny curled ribbon. *Jean-Claude,* it read.

Why hadn't she thought of that? Instead of getting all misty-eyed over Ian, she could have been doing something useful. She retrieved her notepad and scribbled Angus's name across the page with her felt tip pen, going over the letters several times to make them as bold as possible. It was still a pretty sad little effort next to the one Jean-Claude's people had prepared for him.

A rivulet of travelers trickled forward from the gate area, living proof of a flight's arrival. Then the rivulet became a herd. Celia tried to keep a close eye on the individuals. Some of the people wore openly expectant expressions, casting about for the people who were supposed to meet them. Others rushed through the gauntlet of greeters with preoccupied looks, glancing at their watches or squinting to see directions to the baggage claim and car rental areas. Celia focused on the expectant ones. Once she'd thought she spotted a potential Angus, but when the man had glanced at her scribbled sign, he'd averted his gaze and marched right past her.

The passengers slowed to a trickle again, and finally Celia was the only person still waiting. Maybe Angus had missed his flight. Which meant that she'd just wasted an evening. And now she would either have to hunt down the stray fiancé or else face the wrath of Natalie. Unless Natalie had tried to contact her. . . .

She dug through her purse for her cell phone to make sure the batteries were still working. As she rummaged, an even more distressing idea occurred to her. What if Angus had seen her holding up a sign for him and decided she was a hag? Maybe the man who had eyed her and walked past really *was* Angus. He was probably camped out at the ticket counter now, trying to find out how fast he could get back to Glasgow.

"Nat'lie?"

Celia let out a startled yelp. Her Angus sign fluttered to the floor.

She didn't bother to grab it.

Standing before her was the most incredible looking man she'd ever seen in her life. A god, nearly, if you didn't count the bloodshot eyes. He was tall—not as tall as Ian had been, but much brawnier—with dark hair and eyes that were almost coal black. Heathcliff eyes, she thought dreamily, even if they were red and travel-weary. Those eyes seemed to belong in a gothic story, as did the rest of the package. The chizzled jaw. The broad shoulders. Okay, so maybe the worn blue jeans that fit him like a glove had no place in a gothic novel, but they were nice, all the same.

She felt herself weaving and had to force herself to stand still.

Then she realized that she wasn't actually the one weaving at all. *He* was. And when his confused stare transformed into a grin, a powerful gust of beer breath hit her like a tsunami.

She had to steady herself all over again. "You're Angus?"

Who else would walk up and talk to her in a deep, burry voice?

"Ay, and yer . . ." The smile grew wider. Sexier. "Fair nair as handsome as yer picture, lass."

She gawked at him in momentary confusion as she translated his strange, thick accent into English. Roughly, she came up with, *"You're nearly as handsome as your picture, lass."*

Three things then occurred to her in rapid succession. The first was just a question, really. Did they really call females *lass* over there?

Second, and more disturbingly, came an observation. This man seemed to think *she* was Natalie.

Third—and this was a biggie—Angus was bending down, about to kiss her.

She was slow to react. Slow enough that Angus had pulled her into his broad, rock-solid chest and covered her mouth with his before she was even able to work up a peep of protest. The kiss gave new meaning to the term intoxicating embrace. It was like an alcohol transfusion.

Celia was already a little unsteady and breathless, but Angus's inebriated ardor nearly knocked her off her feet. She was assaulted by several unpleasant sensations. Warm, slobbery lips. Hot, puffing breaths coming out of his nostrils. And way too much tongue.

She banged on his chest, hoping to get his attention.

Still holding her tightly, his ninety-proof lips firmly locked against hers, the man stumbled backward a step. Celia had to grab his shoulders in hopes of steadying him. It seemed to work; they stopped traveling. Unfortunately, Angus translated her gesture as romantic fervor, and a burly growl rumbled in his chest. He dipped her, just like she'd seen in old movies.

She squinted and turned her head against another onslaught of wet Celtic tongue. This simply had to stop. When she opened her eyes again, she found herself looking past the blur of Angus's face pressed against hers, straight into Davis's eyes.

Davis?

She blinked, unsure for a moment whether she was hallucinating. Surely a Diet Coke couldn't have that much of an effect on her. But what would Davis be doing here?

It couldn't be him.

But her hallucination didn't seem to be going away.

"Bending over backward to greet Natalie's fiancé?" he asked in that dry voice she knew so well.

It really was him. Thank heavens! Even given the thunderously disapproving look on his face, she was overjoyed to see him. Rescued!

"Davis!"

She pushed against Angus with all her might. They tottered upright again—momentarily. But once in motion, Angus wasn't able to stop. He kept stumbling backward, taking Celia with him. For a few confusing seconds they performed a crazy tango to regain balance, but it was no use. Angus was huge, drunk, and out of control. He hit a pillar, ricocheted off it, and stumbled into her, knocking her over. She grasped at a bank of plastic chairs, but it was no use. In the next moment she was flat on her back, and Angus was on top of her. Squashing her.

And Davis was still staring down at her like a high school principal who had just caught a litterbug. "Do you intend to tell Natalie about this?"

"Don't be a dope. He thinks *I'm* Natalie." She grunted in exasperation and yelled at Angus. "Get off me, you big galoot!"

In response, Angus let out a hearty, nasal snore.

"Terrific, he's passed out." She looked pleadingly up at Davis. "Would you mind helping me out here?"

He crossed his arms in a sort of angry dad way. "You seem to be doing okay all on your own."

"Oh, sure! I've managed to get myself sandwiched between the floor and a drunken Scot. Would you *please* pull this guy off me?"

His lips twisting into a deeper frown, Davis nevertheless obliged by tugging Angus off enough for her to slip free. She jumped to her feet and wiped her mouth against her sleeve. It was an undignified gesture, but she had too much slobber to contend with to care. What she really needed was a sponge.

Meanwhile, Davis struggled to upright Angus. "He's sort of heavy," he complained.

"No kidding!" Celia positioned herself under one of Angus's armpits while Davis took the other. Together, they staggered toward baggage claim with him. After trudging a few steps, Celia noticed a strange squishing sound. She looked down at Davis's shoes, which were soaked.

"Don't tell me it's raining."

"No, it's not," Davis said, adding, "and that's about the best thing I can say for this evening."

"How did your shoes get so sopping wet?"

"It's a long story."

She fixed a curious stare on him as they maneuvered Angus onto the belt of the moving sidewalk. For a few moments, they were able to lean back and rest. "What on earth are you doing here anyway?" she asked Davis. "I thought you were at the Blazers game!"

"There were complications at home. I meant to get here sooner, but the Max ended up taking forever," he said, referring to the light rail that traversed Portland. "So I didn't get here until it was . . ."

Uncomfortably, he looked away from her.

It was too late, was the implication. As if she had thrown herself at Natalie's drunken fiancé. Maybe he hadn't heard her the first time. "That little scene you came upon was not what you're thinking. I told you, he thought I was Natalie."

Davis eyed her skeptically. "And you just happened to forget to tell him that you weren't?"

"He didn't give me time."

Davis wasn't buying it. He gave her little black dress

a pointed look, and his expression said the ratio of approval and disapproval was dead even.

"Nice casual wear." The comment came out a little snidely.

"Oh, sure—like I asked for it. Blame the victim. For your information, Angus pulled a Valentino on me before I could get a single word out. And then I looked up, and you were there. The whole episode lasted a few seconds, tops."

Not that she had to explain herself to Davis, she thought belatedly and a little resentfully. He probably thought she was really on the make for Angus now. Which was just ludicrous. She shouldn't have started thinking about Ian, or let herself be mesmerized by the whole Heathcliff thing. . . .

The moving sidewalk ended, and they all stumbled onto stationary ground again. If she'd known she'd be lugging a grown man through the airport, she absolutely would have stayed in jeans and sneakers. Wobbling on wedge heels as she lugged Angus's carcass around was no fun.

"I'm surprised American customs just didn't stamp *return to sender* on this guy and ship him back to Scotland," she muttered.

"Maybe he was still sober in New York."

"Couldn't have been. I'm guessing he drank his way across the Atlantic *and* the United States."

By the time they reached the baggage claim area, there were only three lonely bags circling the conveyer belt designated for Angus's flight. They pulled a duffel off with his name tag on it and hauled off a large suitcase of his as well.

"You wait here," Celia said. "I'll get the car."

As she left Davis standing over the pile made by Angus and his luggage, the pickle she'd been in struck her full force. What on earth would she have done if

Davis hadn't appeared? It would have taken her for-ever to get Angus out of the airport. She might have been here half the night!

Truly, Davis was a godsend—even if he did think she was on the make. He had obviously missed the Blazers game to come help her out. If that wasn't friendship, she didn't know what was.

She fetched the car and hurried back around to the arrivals curb. It took some doing to load Angus into the backseat of her two-door Toyota. By the time they were headed back into town, their foreign pas-senger was mumbling. Celia couldn't catch much of it. "Merrit" was mentioned.

Davis listened for a moment and then looked at her curiously. "What's he saying? What's Merrit?"

She cast about in her mind. "Merrit? Isn't that a name?"

"It's a pretty peculiar name if it is."

"It *is* a name," Celia insisted. "The main character in *Where the Boys Are* was named Merrit, wasn't she?"

Davis fixed her with an incredulous stare. "Look, I know I put up with a lot of chick flicks for your sake. Frankly, I've seen more Meg Ryan and Minnie Driver than is probably healthy for a guy. But do you honestly think I've sat through *Where the Boys Are?*"

"I don't see how you could avoid it. It's on televi-sion all the time."

"Not on my television."

"Yes, it is. You get the same stations I do."

"But I don't *watch* the same ones you do."

Just then, Angus's head flopped to the side, bump-ing noisily against the window. Celia looked in the rearview as he mumbled more about Merrit. He had a sexy Scottish burr even when he was slurring drunk. She wondered who this Merrit was. "This is troubling, don't you think? I hope he's not two-timing Natalie."

Davis cocked his head. "Could it be that he's saying *married?*"

Celia gasped at the logic of Davis's guess. "You're right! Oh, what a relief."

"Why relief? What if he's trying to tell us that he's already married?"

"Don't be ridiculous. He's saying that he's *going* to be married."

Davis looked doubtful. "Maybe . . ."

"Do you think he got drunk because he was so nervous about meeting his bride? That would be sort of sweet." Sweeter, at least, than thinking that Natalie's future husband was a hopeless lush with a wife back in Glasgow.

Davis grunted. "If this guy knew Natalie, he might have been swilling something stronger than beer. Like arsenic."

She turned on him sharply. "I know you don't like Natalie; but she's really determined to do this, and I hope it works out for her. I want her to be happy."

Davis sent her an incredulous look. "Does this setup really have the whiff of potential happiness to you?"

"Well, maybe they're off to a bumpy start . . ."

She pulled into the loading zone in front of Natalie's building downtown. Even on a weeknight, the Pearl District showed definite signs of urban life. There were three restaurants on Natalie's block, and the insistent thumping of dance music came from a nightclub across the street called the Torrid Zone.

"I'll get Natalie," she said, glad the ordeal was about to be over with. If she was truthful with herself, Davis's question had made her a little uncomfortable. Despite all the reasons Natalie had given her for wanting to be married, Celia couldn't help feeling that

Natalie was making a mistake. But what could she do? Natalie wouldn't follow her advice. Telling her that her fiancé was a loser would probably just alienate her friend.

Besides, maybe Angus was just one of those people who didn't make a great first impression. Maybe once you got to know him . . .

And sober, he might even be a good kisser.

She buzzed Natalie's place and leaned against the wall, waiting for her voice to come over the speakerphone. It didn't. She pressed the buzzer again and was rewarded by the same silence.

A little knot of dread gnawed at her stomach. She couldn't make herself look at Davis sitting in the front seat. He thought the worst of Natalie already.

She pulled out her cell phone and punched in Natalie's number. The line rang, and Celia got the answering machine. "Okay, I'm assuming you're not there," she said to the machine, hating the way her voice hiked with desperation. "I've got Angus, Nat. I guess I'll try your cell phone number. If you don't answer, I'll take him to my place. Please don't forget to pick him up."

She halfheartedly tried the cell phone, but she didn't really expect Natalie to answer. Not at a press conference for the vice president.

She glanced up at the dark sky. It was past nine now. Could that press conference still be going on?

Not likely. So where the hell was Natalie?

She trudged back to the Toyota, got in, and started the engine without explanation. Not that one was needed. Davis didn't seem at all surprised that Natalie had bugged out.

"Look," he suggested, "why don't we take him over to my place?"

"That's across the river," Celia pointed out.

"Your place is so small, though."

"It'll just be for a few hours, tops."

"You hope," Davis said.

She certainly did.

Her apartment wasn't too far from Natalie's—just a little ways across downtown. Her street was tree lined and very quiet due to the fact that a warehouse from the nineteenth century, now used as an art gallery during the day, stood across from her house.

Her building, an old Victorian mansion in Goose Hollow, had long ago been divided into one- and two-bedroom apartments with galley kitchens. Hers was a one bedroom in the attic. Actually, the bedroom was little more than an alcove with barely enough room for a double bed, which was the only reason she was able to afford to live in such a relatively swank neighborhood on her decidedly unswank salary. Another thing that probably brought the price down on her apartment was the fact that the ceiling slanted severely, which meant that half the time she had to walk stooping over. But Celia was so accustomed now to maneuvering around her place like Quasimoto in his belltower that she barely even noticed that little inconvenience.

As they parked outside and looked up at her building, a new feeling of dread settled over her. It was a long way up to the attic, and Angus hadn't sobered up any. All those stairs. . . .

Davis smiled at her. "Sure you don't want to take him to my place?"

She swallowed. It would be so easy to let Davis haul him away and deal with it. "Thanks, but I told Natalie that he'd be over here. She's bound to come looking for him."

"Are you certain of that?"

"I know she will," Celia declared with more assurance than she actually felt. "Natalie just got held up. You know how these things are."

So they hauled Angus up the stairs—no easy task, especially when he roused himself enough to start singing at the top of his lungs. The song was something about yellow being on the broom, whatever that meant.

"How on earth are Natalie and this guy supposed to communicate?" Celia wondered aloud. "I can't understand half of what he says. And even when I can make out words, I still don't know what he's talking about."

Incomprehensible though the song might be, it was still performed at sufficiently high volume to draw attention. One neighbor—Mr. Zhirbotken, who had the apartment directly below Celia's and always seemed to be annoyed for one reason or another—poked his head out the door and told her, in a thick Eastern European accent, to shut up. This got a rise out of Angus. He started spewing Scottish curses. Celia could make out the words *bleedin'* and *arse*, which she recognized from her Ian days.

Mr. Zhirbotken yelled back something completely incomprehensible except for the words *son of your bitch.*

After letting them spray hose each other with the mixed obscenities of their adopted land and fatherlands, she smiled apologetically at her neighbor. "Sorry, Mr. Z! He won't be here long!"

Mr. Zhirbotken's door slammed shut.

"Nice neighbor," Davis observed.

"He's okay—just easily riled."

When they got to her place and settled Angus on the couch, Davis fell into a chair near Gazpacho's large cage and perch, which was hard to avoid. The parrot's living area took up half the apartment. The large gray bird seemed to be looking at them all with Machiavellian contempt. It was a look Celia knew well. She sometimes imagined that inside that little feathered bird head Gazpacho was plotting to overthrow the entire universe. He certainly had the personality for it—a sort of cross between General George S. Patton and the velociraptors from *Jurassic Park*.

Davis was scrutinizing Angus with open curiosity. "I just don't get it."

"What?"

"The attraction."

Her eyes widened. "What makes you think I'm attracted?"

He shot her a meaningful stare. "You were kissing him."

"Only by mistake. Believe me, I had a better kiss when my grandmother's Irish setter accidentally licked my mouth."

Yet, to be honest, she couldn't help remembering that hungry lurch in her stomach when she'd first clapped eyes on Natalie's fiancé. She glanced back at him again, to see if the magic was still there.

Angus's head was lolled against the couch's back. His mouth hung open, and his chin had temporarily disappeared into his thick neck. The fact was, the man hadn't been at his best since that one moment he'd been standing right in front of her. In the shape he was in it must have taken all his willpower to rouse himself and teeter off that airplane. Or maybe the airline attendants had hauled him to his feet and pushed him toward the terminal. Whatever it was, she would never forget that fleeting glimpse of sheer handsome male—tall, dark, and full of sexy swagger. In that respect, at least, Natalie was one lucky gal.

Of course, Celia had to allow that so far, the send-

ing-off-to-Scotland method of husband hunting was
proving to have a few drawbacks.

"He *is* good-looking," she said in his defense. "You
just can't tell it right now."

"If I were Natalie, I'd worry less about his looks
than whether she can lift him."

"I really hope she isn't making a horrible mistake,"
Celia said, shaking her head. "I can't help thinking
that what Natalie needed, more than a husband, was
a holiday."

Davis's brows twitched quizzically. "Another fun-
filled week dodging typhoons?"

Celia rolled her eyes. Would she never live that
down? "I don't mean a vacation," she said. "Remember *Holiday*, that Cary Grant movie we watched the
other night?"

"Mm." Davis smiled thoughtfully. "I'm always
amazed that a guy can look that good with so much
shiny stuff in his hair."

Celia sighed. Davis just didn't appreciate movies like
she did. "Well, while you were staring at Cary Grant's
hair, you missed the whole philosophy of the movie,
which was that we should enjoy life while we're young.
Go off, have adventures! But here we all sit, a bunch
of malcontents. Natalie wants to have it all. You want
to write a silly book instead of your newspaper column.
I want . . ." She frowned. "Well, I wouldn't mind having adventures. I guess I need to be a little more specific."

Davis interrupted her. "Maybe I'm remembering
the movie differently. I seem to recall there was something about making a fortune first, and then running
off to have an adventure."

"Oh, right." Celia scowled at him playfully. "You
can be a stick-in-the-mud, you know that?"

"I was just stating facts."

"Well, okay—but Natalie *has* a bundle. She could run off and be an adventuress for a while. It would probably do her good. In fact, I don't think she should have moved back home after college. Too close to that mother of hers."

"You can't live Natalie's life for her," Davis pointed out.

"No kidding. I don't think this face of mine is camera ready." She laughed. "You want something to drink?"

"No thanks. I suppose I should get back home and make sure Corky hasn't punctured the heating oil tank or something like that."

Celia frowned at him. Poor guy. He really looked as though he'd been through the mill today. And she'd never figured out why his shoes were such a mess. "Did Corky do something wrong again?"

"He broke a water main. But it's probably all taken care of. The city was there fixing it when I left for the airport."

"You left your house in the middle of a calamity just to help me?"

He shrugged. "Believe me, it was no hardship."

Still, she jumped up, ran over, and gave him a huge hug.

He smiled at her—a long, slow smile that caused an unfamiliar flutter deep inside her.

Good grief! What a night she was having. First she was moping about Ian; then she was kissed by Natalie's imported groom, and now she was fluttering over poor Davis, who had knocked himself out to help her. She really needed to get a hold of herself.

"Davis, you're a saint."

His smile dissolved into an uncomfortable grimace.

That was so like him. He was too modest by half. "I'm not joking," she assured him, giving his arm a firm squeeze. "You're the best friend a girl could ever hope for!"

The compliment only seemed to propel Davis toward the door.

She raced after him. "Wait! I'm going to give you a ride home!"

"I'll catch the bus," he said, not even stopping to turn around.

"But—"

"You'd better stay with Angus till Natalie comes for him."

"Please let me drive you," she said.

"I'll be fine."

"Okay, but call me when you get home," she yelled after him. "You really are an incredible pal!"

He was gone in nothing flat.

Modesty, all right. That was his problem. He just couldn't stand for a fuss to be made over him.

The man was a bona fide gem of a human being. Not to mention, as women in the office so often remarked, Davis was as sweet—and as dependable—as a teddy bear.

Four

The best friend a girl could ever hope for!

Those words gave him chills.

As a bus trundled him home from Celia's, the vision of her swooning in the arms of Angus replayed across his mind. He wasn't sure he bought her excuses about it all happening too quickly for her to resist. For one thing, she wasn't dressed in resistance gear. That little black dress of hers hadn't leapt out of her closet and magically thrown itself on her body. She'd gone to the airport looking delectable, in a sexy outfit that clung to her in all the right places and showed off those great legs of hers.

Also, Angus was just the type she would go for: beefy, swarthy, and foreign. What was it about muscled-up mental zeros like Angus that was so appealing to women? Didn't being a steadfast nice guy count for anything anymore?

Had it ever?

The bus let Davis off not far from his house. As he approached home, he was pleased to see that the water main was patched up. The only reminder of the night's calamity was an angry dirt gash across the previously pristine swath of grass. Davis's feet made sucking sounds against the wet ground as he headed inside.

In the living room, Corky was ensconced on the

couch with a Hamm's beer and a bag of Funyons. The TV blared the news, at the same time that *Nebraska,* Bruce Springsteen's quirky album from the early eighties, wailed away in the background.

Home sweet home.

Corky jumped in surprise when Davis appeared in the living room. "Geez! You snuck up on me!"

Davis crossed his arms. "How can you possibly be listening to the stereo while the TV is on?"

"Oh, well, this album was never my favorite—a little downbeat, you know?" Before Davis could process this disconnect in logic, he went on, "Thank God you're back, man. I've got something incredible to show you. You won't believe it!"

Davis bit back a groan. Corky tended to tape things for his benefit—snippets of *America's Funniest Pet Videos* or the asparagus battle from *The Iron Chef.* "I'm not sure I'm up for anything tonight, Cork."

"But you've got to see this." Corky fiddled with the VCR's remote. "It all happened after you left. There was this TV crew . . . I was hoping you would get back in time to catch it when it first aired . . ."

Davis frowned and settled himself in a chair. "What is it?"

Corky grinned. "Just wait!" He pressed play, and suddenly the news was on again—only this was the beginning of the newscast. Corky fast-forwarded through the national headlines and a commercial and then stopped just as an anchorwoman—who looked a lot like Natalie but who worked for a different station—posed the question, "Is water waste a problem for Portland? Some people in the environmental community think so. For our report, we go to Mike Barnaby live in southeast Portland."

The screen was then filled with water, and oddly familiar shots of children playing. "Some might say this looks like a festive water park," the all-business voiceover said, "but to environmentalists, scenes like this one are nothing to celebrate."

The camera pulled back to reveal a straight column of water shooting out of the ground and the house behind it.

A sinking feeling began to swamp Davis.

Corky grinned at him. "Dude! Check it out—*it's our house!*"

For the next thirty seconds, the reporter explained that Oregon's electricity depended on hydroelectric power, and therefore water wastage was a drain on the state's resources. Pictures of Davis's house were interspersed with footage of dry creek beds, rioting farmers, and beached, gasping salmon.

"I don't believe it," Davis muttered.

Corky gestured with his Hamm's toward the screen. "Hang on, it gets better!"

Davis longed to close his eyes, but they remained wide open and glued to the television set. When the reporter came back from an interview with an environmentalist and Corky's face filled the screen, Davis gasped. "Oh, no." Corky was jawing on about fresh oregano and home-grown tomatoes, and then, to Davis's horror, he added, "But this isn't really my house, you know. No way. You'll never guess who this house belongs to, man—Davis Smith of the *Portland Times.*"

The reporter's face, wearing a world-weary smirk, again filled the screen. "Yes, that's right, Cammie. Davis Smith, who runs the eponymous column concerning topics of the day. Here's a topic Mr. Smith might want to tackle tomorrow: waste. Back to you."

Corky pressed the stop button and looked at Davis proudly. "Was that awesome, or what?"

Davis was dumbstruck.

"You wanna watch it again?" Corky asked.

"No!"

"That Mike Barnaby seemed like a really cool guy." He leaned forward. "And did you notice that little plug I managed to sneak in there for you? Even mentioned your column. Sweet, huh?"

Davis had sunk so far down in his chair that his backbone formed a perfect *C*. "But it made me look like a . . ."

He thought of all those gasping fish, and shame suffused him. *A water waster.*

Corky waved an authoritative hand at him. "There's no such thing as bad publicity. I bet twice the normal number of people read your column tomorrow."

"Sure, to find out who the jerk was that they were talking about on the news last night."

"Hey, you're really upset, aren't you?" Corky's fleshy face collapsed into a remorseful frown. "Gosh, I'm sorry." A thick lock of hair drooped across his forehead like a baby's in a cartoon. Gone was the goofy grin. Back was the earnest, searching, self-conscious expression Davis couldn't stay mad at. Or if he could stay mad, he couldn't do anything about it.

"It's okay," he said.

And as he said it, he realized it was the truth. The news spot might have sent him over the top on a normal day, but ever since Celia had come back from her lunch with Natalie today, nothing had seemed normal.

"There's something wrong, isn't there?" Corky asked.

"Why?"

"Because you look like you want to hurl yourself off the Broadway Bridge. Look, if it's about the water main—"

"It isn't."

"Then, there *is* something wrong," Corky said. "I

knew it. I knew the minute you ran off to the airport that something was going on with you. Hey, I don't want to pry—but what's up? Woman problem?"

"Sort of," Davis admitted, very reluctantly.

"I might have known! Back when we were kids you always did seem to have troubles in that department."

"Back when we were kids I was fourteen. Every male on the planet has girl troubles then." Except men like Stan and Mike, he supposed. Though he doubted adolescence was a cakewalk for them, either.

Corky tapped his beer can and chuckled. "Remember the time when you had that crush on Shelly Murphy? The redheaded girl with the braces? And you were going to toilet paper her house? Remember that?"

"Mm." Here it came—another dropkick down memory lane.

"And then you screwed up the street number of her house and toilet papered her next-door neighbor's instead?" Corky doubled over in laughter. "And the next-door neighbor was a cop! Remember?"

Davis managed a halfhearted smile. "Sure do."

"That was funny, wasn't it?"

"A scream."

At Davis's distinct lack of enthusiasm, Corky sat up straighter and put on a serious face. "Okay, I'm sensing you're not amused. What's the matter?"

Davis's instinct was to keep his problem to himself, maybe to shut himself in his room and work on his book. Get his mind off Celia altogether. But his mouth had other ideas. "I just don't get it," he huffed in frustration. "What do women want?"

Corky sagely wagged a finger. *"That's* a question for the ages, man."

"You know that expression, 'You'll know when the right one comes along'?"

His housemate leveled a doubtful look on him. "Uh huh . . ."

"Well, the right woman coming along is supposed to be a *good* thing, right?"

Corky chortled. "Yeah, although until the right one comes along I'm willing to go wrong a few times."

Davis drummed his fingers as he turned his dilemma over in his mind. "But what if when the right one comes along, she seems to have no idea that she's the right one?"

"Ah." Corky nodded. "I get it. You've got the old unrequited thing going. Just like my old friend Bob!"

The last thing Davis wanted to hear now was that he was just like someone else. Right now it felt as if no guy from Adam to the present day had ever gone through such torment. Why was he talking about this with Corky, of all people? Corky, who was even less sophisticated and more muppety than he was.

"Maybe I should be asking a woman about all this."

"No, no, no!" Corky shook his head adamantly. "That's exactly what you *shouldn't* do. You ask women what they want, and they'll give you some bogus answer like 'a guy with a great sense of humor.' "

"But that's a good thing, isn't it?"

"It would be if it weren't a total lie. I mean, get real. When you look at who women go out with, it doesn't take a genius to see that the funny bone is not the part of the anatomy they're interested in." He snorted. "It's like guys saying they're looking for a woman who's smart."

"But I *would* like a woman who's smart."

Corky sent him a pitying look. "Oh, man. Sounds like you're setting yourself up for some serious misery."

"I know the woman I want," Davis said. "I see her

every day of my life. I just don't know how to make her realize she's perfect."

"Uh huh. Just like Bob," Corky mumbled.

Davis doubted Corky had much of a grasp on the difficulties of his situation. Corky didn't have much of a grasp on anything.

"See," Corky said, "Bob was this really nice guy that women swarmed around like flies. They really went for him—as a friend, though. Oh, he had dates, but all the women he was really interested in seemed to look right past him." Corky grunted disgustedly. "And then they'd come crying on *his* shoulder when their relationships with other men turned sour. Can you beat that?"

All at once Davis was bolt upright, staring at Corky intently. "What happened to this guy?"

"That's the interesting part. See, one day Bob just decided he'd taken it long enough. He was sitting in front of the television watching *Friends* reruns when suddenly he was hit by a bolt from the blue. He discovered this universal truth that *no one* ever mentions. Like, it's a conspiracy of silence or something."

"What?"

Corky leaned forward. *"Most men aren't very attractive."*

For a moment, Davis actually tried to make sense of this. Which just proved to him how desperate he was. "Cork . . ."

"It's true!" Corky tapped a Funyon against his forehead. "Think about it. Can *you* think of a man you find utterly babe-ilicious?"

How? How had his life reached this point? Davis felt as if he were getting a candid glimpse of what was going on in Corky's head, and it was scaring him.

Corky interpreted his silence as agreement. "See, you can't. And you know why?"

"Because I'm a heterosexual male."

Corky rolled his eyes. "Besides that."

Davis was afraid to ask. "Why?"

"Because there's no male standard of beauty." Corky took a swig of Hamm's before continuing his lecture. "That's what Bob figured out. Think about those guys on *Friends*. One's okay looking, but sort of vacant, if you know what I mean."

Davis didn't.

"Then, there's the sort of good-looking one—what's his name. The Vicadin guy."

"Matthew Perry?"

Corky snapped his fingers. "Right." He frowned. "Well, maybe he's good-looking, but kind of short and mousy, when you get right down to it. I mean, if a woman looked like that, would she be considered attractive?"

"I'm not sure I quite . . ."

"No! And then there's that other guy, the one all the women are gaga for. *Ross.*" He said the character's name with distaste. "He's not good-looking *at all*, Bob realized. And I have to agree. He's just a normal-looking guy, when you come right down to it. Kind of puppy doggish."

"Corky, wait. Your friend's theory is full of holes. No male standard of beauty? What about George Clooney and Brad Pitt? They always win those stupid 'sexiest man alive' polls."

Corky rolled his eyes. "Oh, well, sure. Given enough time you can debunk practically anything."

In this case it took all of two minutes. "I'm not sure what all this is leading up to . . ."

"It's leading up to what my friend Bob realized: With men, it's all in the presentation. And for most men, that means muscling up. Looking confident.

That puppy doggish *Friends* guy? Presentation. It's a
snap. You've got to look like you're king of the castle."

Davis was really beginning to wonder about Corky's
sanity. And maybe his own, too.

"I can prove it," Corky told him. "Bob bought himself one of those exercise contraptions that are advertised on the TV all the time. Pretty soon he was buffed
up like a movie star—practically a babe magnet—and
the next thing you know he was married. The very
next year, in fact."

"Exercise machine," Davis muttered. "The most
dreaded two-word combination in the English language."

Corky shook his head. "No, that would be erectile
dysfunction."

Davis had bought a rowing machine once, and it
had sat in his living room unused for three years until
finally he'd tripped over it. He'd had to go to the
emergency room with a chipped ankle bone. He'd
sold the rowing machine at a garage sale for a fraction
of what he'd paid for it and swore he'd never buy
another piece of exercise equipment.

It was a rule he intended to stick to, no matter what
oddball theory *du jour* Corky was espousing.

"Maybe I'll join a gym."

"Gym's no good," Corky declared unequivocally.
"It's expensive and inconvenient. Besides, it's easy to
be intimidated by those muscle-bound gym lizards.
What you need is an exercise machine. Then you buy
yourself some snappy new clothes, get a forty-dollar
haircut, a little expensive aftershave, and believe me,
you'll be cooking with gas." He swigged down the last
of his Hamm's and belched loudly. "King of the castle."

Davis got up. "I'll give it some thought."

But of course he didn't actually intend to. Following

Corky's advice to the lovelorn would be like a paranoid turning to Ted Kazynski for tips for a happier, more well-adjusted personality.

Celia's doorbell buzzed insistently, rousing her out of sleep. She turned bleary eyes toward the glowing green numbers on her alarm clock. It was two A.M.

The doorbell buzzed again.

When her brain began to function, Celia remembered last night. Angus! Slobber! *Natalie!*

Careful to duck lest she bang her head on the ceiling, she jumped up and threw on her robe, then dashed out of the apartment and down the three flights of stairs. When she opened the door, Natalie was tapping her foot impatiently.

"I've been out here forever." Natalie brushed past her and started up the staircase. "You must have really been conked out! Me, I don't think I'll be able to sleep for weeks now. I feel like I'm floating!"

She sort of looked like she was, too. At least to Celia's bleary gaze. It was the middle of the night, and Natalie, still in her fabulous blue dress, looked as fresh as a daisy. Not a hair was out of place, and her makeup was still camera perfect. Lipstick glistening. Eyes bright.

How the hell did she do it?

"You would not *believe* what happened tonight!" Natalie said.

"I've got a lot to tell you, too," Celia said.

"Oh, really? Well, wait till you hear who I spent the evening with—it'll knock everything else out of your head."

It apparently had already done that trick for Natalie, who had not as yet breathed a word about her fiancé.

Celia would have thought she'd be a little more curious.

"Don't tell me," she guessed, "you're going to be our country's newest second lady."

Natalie laughed. "Ha! He's already married. And anyway, you're not even close."

They reached the top of the stairs, and Celia lifted her hands in surrender. "I give up."

"Peter Jennings! The suavest of all anchormen, and *I* had drinks with him."

"Wow."

"And it wasn't just drinks. He was doing a special interview with the vice president after the banquet—and I got to watch!" She sounded like a schoolgirl who had been taken backstage at a Backstreet Boys concert. "And afterward we had coffee in the bar of his hotel—the Benson, natch—and he told me all sorts of stuff about Henry Kissinger and Sam Donaldson and, oh, just everybody. He knows *everybody!*"

Celia tilted her head. "Wasn't this a little weird? I mean, just you and him?"

"Oh, there were other people there, too." Natalie laughed. "What? Did you think there was some hanky-panky going on between me and Peter Jennings?"

Celia struggled with the tricky lock on the door and finally managed to coax it open.

"Besides," Natalie continued, "the man's *ancient.* Fifty if he's a day. Also—" Her words cut off abruptly. Her hands raised to her cheeks, and she stared with awe at the recumbent figure on Celia's couch.

Then Natalie looked at Celia with wide blue eyes, as if she'd just been given a present. "Is that him? Really?"

Celia nodded.

Natalie tiptoed over to the couch and ogled her new acquisition. "Oh . . . my . . . God."

"What do you think?"

It was hard to gauge what was going through Natalie's head. For one thing, Angus was still not at his best. He was stretched out on the couch, but he didn't exactly fit. He'd kicked off the afghan she'd placed over him, and now one of his legs draped over her coffee table. His right arm was dangling off the couch, too. His dark hair was smashed every which way, and his mouth gaped open. The stale stench of beer still clung to him, but since Natalie glided through the world in a permanent cloud of Chanel Number Five, she probably didn't notice.

She turned bright eyes on Celia. "He's a hunk of heaven, isn't he?"

As long as you don't get too close to those lips, Celia thought.

Actually, she was unaccountably relieved by Natalie's reaction. Maybe she'd been afraid Natalie would refuse delivery, now that she'd broken bread with Peter Jennings.

"Did he give you any problems?"

She shook her head, deciding to gloss over the kiss. It hadn't really been intended for her anyway.

"He seems to be a sound sleeper."

"Well, he's a little . . . drunk," Celia confessed.

Natalie put her hands on her hips. "What did you give him?"

"He arrived this way," Celia explained. "I was just lucky that Davis came by and helped me out with him, or I might never have gotten him home."

Natalie's brows arched with interest. "Fozzie Bear was at the airport with you? That was convenient!"

"Yes, it was." Because of the dig at Davis, Celia couldn't help adding, "Davis is a dependable friend."

The words bounced right off Natalie. She wasn't affronted or impressed. "The things you say about people, Celia. Dependability is something you look for in tires."

Now that fatigue was wearing off, indignation was setting in. "Natalie, didn't you get my message? Davis and I brought Angus by your place, but you weren't there."

Natalie blinked. "Of course I wasn't. I just told you. I was with Peter Jennings."

"But I didn't know that four hours ago."

"Well, no. How could you?"

Hopping up and down and yelling like Yosemite Sam would have felt so good just then. The woman had no shame, no conception of how her actions might inconvenience someone. But Natalie didn't take criticism very well, and Celia didn't want to start a screeching argument at two in the morning. Mr. Zhirbotken had been forbearing enough for one night.

Besides, Natalie had met Peter Jennings. Celia supposed a person who had had a brush with media superstardom deserved a little forbearance. "Does he really say 'aboot'?"

Natalie's eyes glistened. "He really does."

Damn. Some people had all the luck.

Celia looked back down at Angus. Okay, maybe not *all* the luck. She wondered how long it would be before Natalie realized her Scottish import was not such a prize.

"He's all yours now," she told Natalie. "If you can carry him."

Natalie pursed her lips and sighed. "My building has an elevator, thank God, but I'll need some help getting him down your stairs."

Ugh. Celia was still sore from carrying him up.

Natalie sensed her hesitation and turned on some congeniality. "Please, Celia? My oldest pal?"

What choice did she have? Natalie rarely lifted anything heavier than a bottle of Evian. It was either help or have a guy passed out on her couch for heaven only knew how long. "Wait here while I get my sneakers on," Celia told her. She padded off to her bedroom, grumbling to herself.

After tonight, the debt for the parrot diarrhea would definitely be wiped clean.

There was barely a spare minute to talk to Celia the next morning. Davis was too busy answering angry E-mails and fielding phone calls from people who wanted to call him a flagrant water waster. But when Celia got up to take her midmorning swing by the coffee machine, he gratefully fled the computer and the phone and fell into step right beside her.

"So what happened with Angus?" he asked.

She lifted her shoulders. "Natalie came by for him." A little bitterness crept into her tone when she added, "At two A.M."

He *tsk*ed sympathetically. Or as sympathetically as he could while envisioning Angus enfolding Celia in his brawny arms. The mental picture almost made Davis give investing in an exercise machine a second thought. "So . . . Did he ever come to?"

"No, he was out like a light the whole time."

Davis was ashamed to say that he felt immense relief to hear this. But he couldn't forget the position he'd discovered them in at the airport.

They swung into the coffee room, where Olga Jarvis, the resident advice columnist, was stirring sweetener into the industrial-strength sludge that passed for coffee at the *Times*. Davis grinned at her while Celia busied herself pouring coffee. The two women hadn't gotten along very well since last year's office Christmas party, when Olga had spilled a glass of eggnog on

Celia while Celia was standing among a group of carolers.

Celia maintained the sabotage had been on purpose, though Davis seriously doubted this.

"Hi, Davis," Olga said, smiling back at him. With less enthusiasm, she tossed over her shoulder, "Hi, Celia. What have you been up to?"

As Celia dumped nondairy creamer in her cup, she mumbled a diffident response. Something about watching out for falling beverages.

One thing that didn't help Olga's popularity—at least with the female staff—was the fact that she was breathtakingly beautiful. Like Cameron Diaz sent from heaven to the male drones of the *Times*. In fact, she was the most beautiful woman Davis had ever laid eyes on outside of a multiplex. She was nearly six feet tall, with luxurious honey blond hair and large, slightly slow, sleepy blue eyes. She had a sexy, husky voice, skin like Catherine Deneuve's, and she carried herself like a queen. And, strangest of all, she was *nice*. Or at least Davis thought so.

Celia said she didn't trust her.

"How can you say that?" Davis had asked her once.

"If you'd had the experience of singing 'Jingle Bells' one minute and then getting an eggnog hair rinse the next, you wouldn't have to ask."

"That was just an accident."

The suggestion had caused a shrill rebuttal. "I was *standing up!* How could she accidentally dump a mug of eggnog if she was just walking by?"

That was always the sticking point. He and Celia had whiled away more time speculating about the trajectory of that spilled eggnog than they spent on most of their columns.

"Granted, the woman is an Amazon, but she still

would have had to reach up and dump over that mug," Celia always concluded.

"You're just being paranoid."

What reason could Olga have had for purposefully dumping eggnog on Celia's head? It just didn't make sense.

"I saw your house on the news last night," Olga said now.

Celia pivoted toward Davis. "Your house was on TV last night?"

He nodded and told Olga, "I saw it, too. My roommate—that mug you might have noticed in the news report—taped it for me."

"*Corky* was on the news?" Celia wore the stunned look of a Rip Van Winkle freshly awakened. "You didn't tell me!"

"I didn't know myself until I got home," Davis answered.

Olga looked mildly amused as she waited for their back-and-forth to peter out. "You've got a really nice house, Davis."

"Thanks."

"Is it a rental?"

"No, it's mine—lock, stock, and mortgage. I bought it last fall."

Olga looked impressed. "Arts and crafts style, isn't it?"

Davis nodded.

"When was it built? 1920s?"

"1911."

"Wow. *Very* nice."

"Well . . . I bought it when the market had dipped," Davis said modestly, but a little king of the castle crept into his tone. The truth was, he loved his house. It was just a one-story affair with two bedrooms and one bath, but it had style, including high ceilings, a large front porch and cool beveled glasswork on the windows and doors.

"Smart," Olga said.

Davis restrained himself from sounding like a real estate ad by reeling off the house's better attributes. But he still had the proud glow of home ownership when Olga turned and left the coffee room with her slinky, catlike gait.

Celia stared after her, shaking her head. Her lips turned down at the corners. "Shameless!"

Davis looked at her, waiting to hear Olga's latest sin. "What's wrong?"

"Didn't you catch the way she was flirting with you?"

He laughed.

"I'm serious."

"She was just complimenting my house."

"She was trying to *sound* like she was just complimenting your house. But believe me, she was flirting. She got a load of your 1911 craftsman bungalow, realized that you were a wise investor, and decided to ingratiate herself to you today."

"That's the craziest thing I've ever heard of. She was just being nice."

At his linking Olga and the concept of nice, Celia just rolled her eyes. "You always say she's nice."

"So?"

"What you mean is that she *seems* nice. Why shouldn't she? With looks like hers, she's probably never had a problem in her life. It's effortless for her."

"And your point is . . . ?"

She gaped at him as though he were hopelessly naïve. "Effortless nice isn't the same as nice for the rest of us. Most people have to work at it. Olga's brand of nice hasn't been tested, so it isn't as reliable. What she was really doing was flirting with you in the guise of being nice."

"You're crazy. Olga flirting with me would be like Julia Roberts flirting with Pat Sajak," Davis insisted.

"Don't think it couldn't happen," Celia shot back. "She married Lyle Lovett, didn't she?"

Davis shook his head. "Well, even if Olga was flirting, what of it?"

"I don't want her to take advantage of you."

He grinned. "I don't know if I'd mind it so much."

Something between a howl and a squeal came out of Celia. "And you don't trust me to have Natalie's fiancé parked in my house! *You're* like a babe in the woods!"

He braced himself for a sip of coffee. The stuff could dissolve the enamel off teeth. "Are you doing okay today? You sound a little on edge."

She leaned against the counter. "I guess I'm still a little miffed with Natalie and the stunt she pulled last night. But the worst part of it is, I'm jealous."

Alarm bells clanged in his head. "Why? Because of Angus?"

She huffed out a breath. "No, it's not that. Do you know who Natalie was out with last night?" She was so keyed up she didn't wait for an answer. "Peter Jennings!"

"So?"

She flashed him an astonished gaze. "*So?* Nat's got this fast-track career while I'm still plugging away at obituaries. It's depressing!"

"Your career's doing fine. You've got a byline. And look at it this way. To have Natalie's career, you would probably need to have a little of Natalie's personality. At least you don't have to send away for men who will marry you."

"Maybe I should."

His panic meter spiked. Maybe it was best to stay away from the topic of marriage. "Anyway, what's the matter with your job? It's not so bad. You have a lot of autonomy."

"Only because Marie knows I could edit obituaries and wedding announcements in my sleep now."

"Well, if you feel so down on your work, why don't you start looking for another job?" He jabbed her playfully with his elbow. "You're not married to this one, you know."

She sent him a deadpan stare, though her eyes sparked with grudging appreciation for his dumb joke. "What I should do is stop whining and try to use a little initiative."

"That's the spirit," he said encouragingly.

"I need to try to figure out something that will make Marie see me as someone who can break out and do something more."

"There's no reason why you can't. You're more talented than most of the writers on staff already."

She looked at him gratefully, if a little disbelievingly. "Thanks. Which reminds me, I haven't told you today what a—"

"Don't mention it!" he said, trying to stave off another testament about what a pal he was. "I'd better get back to my desk."

"Yeah, me, too." They headed back to their cells. "Oh!" Celia said, remembering something. "I can't make it to lunch today. I've got to go out with Natalie. She's registering."

Davis felt his brow crinkle as he attempted to puzzle this one out. "Registering as a dangerous person with the department of mental health?"

Celia rolled her eyes. "Registering for wedding gifts."

"Oh, right." He was having a hard time picturing

Celia playing bridal vizier to Natalie. It sounded like something he didn't want to miss. "Mind if I come along? I wasn't going to do lunch today, anyway."

His words stopped her dead in her tracks. And it wasn't even his wanting to go shop with Natalie that had stunned her. "You're skipping lunch? Are you sick?"

He chuckled self-consciously. "No, nothing like that."

She eyed him skeptically.

"I ate a huge breakfast. Corky made waffles." Inedible, rubbery waffles. But doing without breakfast had given him an idea. Maybe if he couldn't shape up by exercising, he could reduce another way. Like by skipping lunch. At least one of them.

The explanation made Celia sag with relief. "For a minute there I thought . . ." She laughed. "But I know *diet* is the one word that would never cross your lips."

He chuckled along with her, fearing he was going to have to flat-out lie to her. Fortunately, Marie barreled down the hallway toward them. She halted right in front of Celia and clapped her on the arm.

"I think I've solved your problem, Snowden!"

Celia blinked. "What problem?"

"That column of yours," Marie explained. "My thinking cap has been firmly planted on my head, and I've figured out a new name for your column. Something that gives readers a taste of the real meaning of marriage."

Celia smiled expectantly. "Great! What is it?"

" 'Welcome to Inertia.' "

Marie continued down the hall, cackling gleefully at her own joke.

Five

"Do you think it's too . . . oh, I don't know . . . plebian?"

Celia, who had been off in another world since she and Davis had left the office, barely heard Natalie's question.

"Celia?"

Davis coughed pointedly, causing Celia to jump as if poked. She focused on the display she'd been gazing at unseeingly. The Limoges pattern Natalie had chosen was eye-poppingly expensive. As was the crystal she'd blithely picked out for her bridal wish list.

"What's the matter with you?" Natalie asked impatiently. "Even Davis is being more of a help than you are."

Natalie hadn't been too pleased when Celia arrived with Davis in tow, but so far she'd been able to refrain from calling him Fozzie. For that Celia should have been thankful. On the surface, at least, all was calm. So why did she keep feeling the urge to look over her shoulder?

"I've got a funny feeling."

"You don't like the pattern?" Natalie asked worriedly.

"No, it's not about the china. I know this sounds crazy, but I have a creepy feeling."

"That's the feeling I always get here, too." Natalie

peered suspiciously around the packed housewares department of Meier and Frank. "Too much rubbing elbows with the masses. I *wanted* to register at Saks, but Mother said too many of our relatives would feel pinched."

Davis gaped at her in feigned shock. "Don't tell me *you* have poor relations."

Natalie frowned unhappily. "Mostly on my dad's side, but since he is paying . . ." She lifted her eyes up to the acoustic tiled ceiling. "I suppose I should be grateful Mother didn't make me register with Club Wed at Target."

"I like Target," Davis said.

Natalie sent him a pitying look.

"Maybe I'm insane," Celia said. She'd barely been following their conversation. "I feel like we're being followed."

Davis frowned at her, making her feel a little foolish. She tried to shake off her odd mood. "I'm sure it's nothing."

"I hope so," Natalie said. "I'm pressed for time already, and with you zoning out, we'll never get through this."

Celia managed to stay on task long enough to okay Natalie's pattern—not that her disapproval would have changed her friend's mind. Natalie hadn't invited her along as an adviser so much as an entourage. She wondered why Natalie hadn't brought Angus, too.

"Where's the fiancé?" she asked.

"Sleeping in," Natalie replied. "He's got a touch of jet lag, I'm afraid."

Celia and Davis exchanged looks. A touch of a hangover was more like it.

Dutifully, they trotted after Natalie as she perused more aisles of stuff. Celia had expected Davis to be bored out of his mind, but instead he seemed to study each shelf and display as though he were an anthropologist taking notes of a newly discovered civilization. One would think he'd never been in the housewares section of a department store. Objects kept snagging his attention. Celia caught him eyeballing a cheese plate.

"This is one wacky butter dish," he said, lifting the square, sloping cover.

"It's for cheese."

He looked surprised. "How come you know that?"

"How come you don't?"

He laughed. "You're right. I was impressed by the breadth of your knowledge when I should have been embarrassed by my own ignorance."

"You have to remember how many weddings I've been to. Three of them were my own mother's." She felt her lips tighten into a flat line. "Quite a few of these cheese wedge dishes passed through our house."

"You mean your mother had a big wedding every time?"

"The first two. Three was kind of rushed and small. By four, she eloped to Las Vegas. People in town were pretty fed up buying wedding gifts by that time anyway. I think they were getting suspicious."

"Right," Davis joked, "the old wedding registry scam."

A smile came back to her face. "Well, she *did* send the gifts back after husband number three. Though she didn't get many, naturally. She was filing divorce papers before most of our family friends had even had time to traipse out to Sears to buy something."

"Which husband was number three?"

"Wade." Celia had only a dim memory of him. She'd been in sixth grade at the time and was hell-bent on being a cheerleader the next year. To that end, she'd spent months hopping around her front yard, trying to learn something called a herkie. Her cheerleading ambitions, short-lived and unsuccessful as they were, still managed to outlast her mother's marriage. "Wade and my mom had this incredible love at first sight experience. One night he came into the restaurant where she was a waitress, and the next night he was back again, pledging eternal love. They were married two days later."

"Wow," Davis said, duly impressed by her mother's stupidity.

"Wade moved into our house, and it really looked like the marriage was going to work out, until they were watching the news a month later and Mom figured out that Wade was a Libertarian. That ended that."

Davis looked dumbstruck. "She kicked him out because of his political affiliation?"

"I think it would have been all right if he'd been a Republican or a Democrat," she explained. "It was just the Libertarian thing that threw her. She said third parties seemed sneaky."

"No wonder you're so jaded about marriage."

"Not marriage—weddings. The size and elaborateness rarely has any correlation to how successful a marriage will be."

Davis put the lid back on the cheese wedge dish. "Maybe that's my problem. My family didn't have enough divorces, so now I'm cursed with being a hopeless romantic."

She had never thought of Davis as a hopeless romantic. Sure, he liked weddings, but she always assumed that was just because he'd been underexposed to them. But romantic?

If anything, he seemed the pragmatic type. The kind of guy who would consult his stack of *Consumer Reports* before buying a wedding ring. But maybe she just perceived him that way because she'd never witnessed him head-over-heels in love with anybody.

Which was strange, now that she thought about it. As far as she knew, he hadn't even gone out with a woman since moving to Portland. How could that be? With all the whining single women floating around this city, you'd think someone would have pounced on him by now. Davis wasn't bad looking. Not Adonis, that's for sure—but he possessed that cuddly teddy bear quality. And he had a great sense of humor.

She opened her mouth to pry into his love life, but Natalie interrupted. She was impatient to hit another area. "Come on, guys, I don't have a lot of time, and we haven't even *thought* about flatware yet."

"Tally-ho," Davis said dryly.

A half hour later they emerged from the department store onto the busy downtown street across from Pioneer Square. It was just after noon, and a marimba band was playing in the public area, where a throng of people had gathered to eat lunch or just lounge and listen to the music. The rhythm of the music was upbeat and infectious, and the air was cool and clear. No rain. Perfect loafing weather.

"Days like this were made for playing hooky," Celia said.

Davis pivoted toward her, smiling. "Are you trying to tempt me?"

Natalie shifted restlessly. "I can see it's just as I suspected—I have a truly rare work ethic."

"Long lunches spent shopping excluded, I suppose," Davis said.

"Shopping is a necessity," Natalie explained. "If I didn't go shopping during the day, I would be thinking about it at work all the time. Then how productive could I be?"

They headed for their cars, but they had only

walked ten feet from the store when a man in a baggy fatigues ran up and started hurling water balloons at them. He lobbed them quickly and mercilessly. Everything was suddenly pandemonium. Celia was too shocked at first to react. There was water everywhere. The missiles exploded on the wall behind them and on Davis's chest and at his feet; two rubbery projectiles made direct hits on Natalie. She let out a screech that sounded like a wounded bunny.

"Hydro-hog!" the man shouted at Davis.

Then their assailant took off running.

Davis sprinted after him, and Celia followed, but she saw in a flash that they would never catch the guy. He was already on the next block by the time they had reached the corner. Davis gave chase for another block before giving up.

Natalie, on the other hand, was still frozen in the exact spot where she'd been hit. Posttraumatic stress had already set in. "What the hell was that!" she yelled. "Has the world gone completely insane?"

"It's okay, Natalie," Davis said. "The guy was aiming at me."

"Why? What did you do?"

He wrung out the front of his shirt, sending a stream of water to the sidewalk. "My water main broke last night. The people on the news said I was a water waster."

"What news?" Natalie demanded.

"Um, Channel Four, I think."

She rolled her eyes in disgust. *"Those* idiots!"

"I wish we could have caught him." Celia was still breathing hard from her short sprint. Maybe three nights at the gym were simply not enough.

"It's no big deal," Davis said.

Natalie's eyes bugged. *"No big deal?* I was just assaulted by some ecoterrorist! I've become a victim of ecosabotage!"

"We were assaulted, too," Celia pointed out.

"But at least Davis was guilty of something. And you two work together. *I* was just an innocent bystander, and I was eco-taged right here in broad daylight." She glared up at the Meier and Frank building, as if it were somehow the fault of the department store. "I knew I should have gone to Saks! This is outrageous!"

"Nat, it's just water."

The water bomber had not gone unnoticed by the public at large—nor had Natalie's histrionics. They were drawing a crowd, and Natalie was showing all the grace of a wet cat. A hank of hair hung limply, and the front of her suit was soaked. She flicked her wet hair unhappily.

A middle-aged guy with a windbreaker and a Mariners baseball cap stopped and squinted up at Natalie. "Say . . . Aren't you that woman from the news?"

Realizing she was being watched, Natalie gasped and straightened. She tossed back her wet locks and shot the man a winning smile. "Yes, I am."

"I thought so!" The man waved a few of his buddies over. "Hey, guys, lookit here—it's that news lady. Jane Something-or-other . . . Jane Rizzo. Right?"

Natalie's smile turned glacier frosty as the men encircled her. Even the fact that he'd gotten Jane's name wrong didn't soothe her. "No. I'm Natalie Glass."

In unison, the men's brows puckered in confusion.

"Oh!" the first guy said. "I thought you was the other lady. The six o'clock lady."

His words pelted Natalie like verbal spears. She suddenly looked wet and beaten, and Celia felt terrible for her. This was the icing on the cake of her misfortune.

Then, in a show of support that nearly knocked Celia off her feet, Davis took Natalie's arm. It was as if he was physically bucking her up as he helped her face her tormentors. "You guys mean that *older* lady, Jane Russo?"

The men mumbled among themselves briefly and exchanged befuddled looks. "Yeah! That's right."

"Right. She's older."

"Sure," the first guy said. "Got her face all over the place. Get sick of the sight of her sometimes."

Elbowed by Davis, Natalie managed a tight smile. "If you're ever up at six A.M., turn your sets to Channel Seven. It's the best news show in town."

"Will do," the man said, sending her a salute as he and his friends shuffled away.

Davis steered Natalie down the street, and Celia fell in. Even though Natalie had recovered somewhat, Celia could still practically hear the gnashing of teeth.

"That's *just* what I needed!" Natalie fumed.

"They were just schmucks," Celia said.

Natalie took no comfort in that fact. "So? Most of our viewers are schmucks! And who do they like? Jane Russo!"

Davis shook his head. "You're overreacting."

There was no comforting Natalie. "I've never been so humiliated! First I'm an innocent victim of eco-tage, and then those idiots come along." She huffed indignantly. "I wish I'd told that water bomber what an asshole he was. Who cares if people waste a little water? It rains here all the time!"

"It's a matter of supply," Davis explained, still trying to calm her. "In a dry year . . ."

Natalie bristled. "Spare me the guilty liberal crap! We're not in a state of emergency. What difference does it make if somebody wastes natural resources, as long as they're not hurting anyone?"

Davis and Natalie squared off. Celia feared they were about to start throwing punches.

"Guys!" She stepped between them before they could come to blows. "For heaven's sake. If you two don't stop squabbling, I'm going to have to hold peace talks, like Jimmy Carter."

Davis snickered. "Natalie would make a great dictator."

Natalie was hopping mad now. *"Dictator? Me?"*

Celia took a deep breath. So much for peace brokering. "It's okay, Nat."

"Did you hear what he said?"

"Davis and I need to get back to work. The Warden's probably watching the clock right now."

Natalie frowned. "Oh, okay. I need to go home and change. I hadn't expected to be eco-taged today." She shot a look at Davis. "Or lectured by Ralph Nader, Jr., here."

As they watched her flit off, Davis shook his head. "That woman is a nut."

Celia frowned. "Did you have to call her a dictator?"

He appeared only slightly remorseful. "I was trying to be nice before then."

"I know. I couldn't figure out why."

His blue eyes twinkled down at her. "Can't you guess?"

Celia took a stab at it. "Temporary insanity?"

He shook his head, and she could have sworn there was disappointment in his eyes. "Because she's your friend."

She waited for a punchline, but it never arrived. "Oh." Suddenly, something in his expression made her feel off balance. She swallowed. "Well, thanks."

"Don't mention it." He put a hand on her shoulder as they walked the rest of the way to the car, and she felt a strange flip in her stomach that made her cheeks become warm.

Shouldn't skip lunch, she told herself, chalking up the strange light-headed, wobbly sensation to hunger. She *hoped* that was what it was.

"How's it goin' with the mystery gal?" Corky asked, slurping down some gummy fettuccini as they watched the latest installment of *My Country, My Kitchen.* It wasn't one of Corky's favorites, so he didn't mind talking during the program. The E Street Band wailed through the house, though, which made it necessary to shout at each other across the living room, much as they would have done in a blizzard.

"Not so good."

At one point, Davis recalled, he'd been rather fond of Bruce Springsteen. If he heard him on the radio, he wouldn't change the dial. Now he feared that if he ever found himself in Asbury Park, New Jersey, he couldn't be held responsible for his actions.

"Exercise machine," Corky declared loudly. The subject was now a certified bee in his bonnet. "I'm telling you, it gets results."

Davis was beginning to realize that his troubles with Celia went beyond whether or not she found him good-looking. They were simply on different wavelengths. The more he hung around her, the more she seemed to think of him as the perfect pal.

Corky drummed his fingers. "Or maybe you're going to have to resort to direct action."

Davis dreaded the answer, but couldn't help asking, "What would that be?"

"Slip her the old tongue. Maybe she'll come around."

Why did he keep discussing this with Corky? The guy had the sensibilities of Homer Simpson. He was the modern woman's nightmare—insensitive, uncouth, unclean, and domicile challenged. No wonder he was approaching thirty and still single. What woman in her right mind would go out with him?

Of course, Davis was also still single. Which put him in the same boat as Corky.

If he pondered *that* too long, he'd end up in a padded cell.

Davis skulked off to his room. Sitting at his writing table, he could almost shut out the noise from the rest of the house and think. Unfortunately, he couldn't think about his book. He was five chapters into his novel. Was it good? He couldn't say. He'd always wanted to write a mystery, like the Nero Wolfe books. But right now the biggest mystery in his life was Celia.

What was he going to do?

Corky's suggestion sounded like a recipe for disaster.

He considered doing something less outlandish. Bringing her flowers, for instance. But how could he do that? Sneak flowers onto her desk before she arrived at work? Knock on her apartment door and present them to her?

The only thing that he'd done that seemed to make an impression was his little attempt to buck Natalie up. But he couldn't keep helping Natalie. Especially since most of the time, he wanted to strangle Natalie.

But if he could figure out a way to help Celia . . . help her at work, maybe.

Was it possible to work your way into a woman's heart with good deeds?

"Elton's supposed to meet us here," Natalie told Celia. "I want him to give me his visual assessment of this place as a possible wedding and reception site."

They were standing among a riot of blazing pink

azaleas in the yards of Pittock Mansion in west Portland. Set high on a steep hillside, the yard offered a breathtaking view of the city of Portland and Mount Hood rising up on the horizon beyond it.

"I don't think you need anyone to tell you that this place would look fabulous." Though the price they were quoted to have a wedding there was outrageous.

"Well, no, but . . ." Natalie sighed. "Well, poor Elton. I think he wants to be involved."

"Who is this Elton guy?"

"I told you. He's the videographer-photographer."

"What does he have, four hands? A person can't videotape and take pictures at the same time."

"He has an assistant named John," Natalie said. "Get it? Elton-John."

Celia moaned. "Do they run around in big hats and sequins?"

"Oh, Celia—even the real Elton John isn't that tacky anymore. Besides, apart from cashing in on the name thing, Elton has nothing to do with the singer. In fact, he couldn't be more different. Oh, I should warn you, he's got a tongue stud."

Celia narrowed her eyes. "A tongue stud?" She couldn't believe it. Natalie was usually repulsed by people with body piercing—she called them staple-faced cretins.

"I know, it's gross," Natalie said. "Just don't stare."

Most of the time piercing didn't bug Celia, but it was her firm belief that people should leave their tongues alone. "It's so unsanitary. When you think of all the bacteria and—"

Natalie laughed. "Oh, I was thinking about the other aspect of it."

"What other aspect?"

"You know . . . the reason people put these tongue studs in . . ."

"Because it's cool?" Celia guessed.

Natalie sent her a how-can-you-be-so-dense look and lowered her voice. "My God, Celia—don't you know? It's supposed to enhance pleasure during oral sex."

Celia blinked. "Really?"

"Sure, we did a segment about it last year. Guys do it all the time. Women, too—especially lesbians."

Celia didn't want to go there. *Just when I thought I understood everything* . . . "So you're going to let a staple-faced cretin videotape your wedding?"

"No," Natalie said, "I'm going to let the stepson of the Channel Seven station manager videotape my wedding. So please behave."

Celia took offense. "You must think *I'm* a cretin."

"No, but this guy is . . ." Natalie let out a breath. "Well, never mind. I'm sure he's a very able photographer and everything will work out fine!"

Natalie's saying everything would be fine struck an ominous chord. Optimistic bliss was very un-Natalie. But this was the first time she and Natalie had been alone together since Angus's arrival, so she hadn't really been able to gauge her friend's mental state before now.

"You seem different today," Celia said. She seemed almost . . . nice.

Natalie straightened her shoulders and lifted her chin and declared in a rush, "Celia, as of today, I'm a changed woman. In fact, from now on, I'm really going to be nice."

Celia shot her a skeptical look. "What's happened?"

Natalie released a long, gushing sigh. "Love!"

"Love," Celia repeated.

"What else?"

"I didn't know you were in love."

A trace of the old Natalie irritation shadowed her

smile. "Well, of course I'm in love. I'm getting married, for God's sake."

"Yeah, but you and Angus . . . Well, you haven't known each other for that long . . ."

She stared at Celia impatiently. "Haven't you ever heard of love at first sight?"

"Sure. I've heard of it blowing up in people's faces." And if Celia remembered correctly, Natalie's first sight of Angus had been of him passed out on her couch. Maybe Natalie meant first sober sight. "So . . . I guess you two really hit it off?"

Natalie grinned slyly. "Oh, yes. In a big way—and I do mean big. Angus is *quite* well equipped." When Celia gawked at her, she tossed back her head and laughed. "Don't look so shocked! We're engaged."

"Yeah, but . . ." Celia had worried he and Natalie might have gotten off to a rocky start.

Natalie stretched like a happy feline just getting up from a nap. She was wearing a sheath dress made of a white silky material that fluttered in the light spring breeze. She really did look like a woman in love. "I've never had such a masterful lover."

"Really?" Celia couldn't keep the amazement out of her voice. But perhaps Angus had toweled off his tongue.

Or maybe Natalie just had higher saliva tolerance.

"He's a real man—not like most of the newsroom eggheads I've wasted my youth on. Angus has given some real thought to how to please a woman, not just to how to take his pleasure and expect a woman to tell him how great he is afterward. I've had it with egomaniacs!"

Celia nodded. "It sounds like he's really . . . something."

"He is! He's got a great sense of humor, too."

"Well, that's the most important thing."

Natalie frowned. "Well, actually, I can only catch about every third word he says. But he *sounds* funny. And did I tell you that he already has friends here? There's a whole community of foreigners around here that we know nothing about. Angus has already been invited out Sunday morning to play soccer. Though, of course, he calls it football. He's even promised to teach me. Isn't that cute?"

Celia was trying to form a mental picture of Natalie decked out like Mia Hamm. It wasn't working.

Natalie sighed again and hugged her arms around herself. "I think being nice might be good for me, I really do. For instance, did you notice what a snobby jerk the guy at that hotel was this morning when he said their wedding reception area was all booked up for June?"

Celia thought the guy was just being matter-of-fact, but she nodded anyway.

Natalie lifted her head proudly. "And did you notice how calm I was about it all? How I didn't point out to the man who *I* was and all the publicity that I could bring to his shabby little hotel?"

"You were the soul of restraint."

Natalie snapped her fingers as if she'd just performed a magic trick. "It's the new Natalie! I didn't argue with the odious little jerk, and I feel a thousand times better for it. I'm probably extending my life expectancy, too, by not letting my blood pressure spike up whenever a self-important prick gets in my way."

"Good for you, Nat."

She crossed her arms. "And did you get a load of the price he quoted for renting that place? Eight thousand—*not* including the bar!"

"It's outrageous." But all the prices they had been quoted as they had scouted around town were outrageous. Pittock Mansion was completely out of the question, of course, though it at least offered a truly majestic setting. But these other places—chain hotels and restaurants that really weren't any great shakes— seemed ready to rob people blind. It was usury, plain and simple. Someone should shame these people.

And then it came to her, like a voice from the heavens.

Why not you, Celia Snowden?

As if suggested by a booming voice from above, an incredible idea occurred to Celia. *She* wrote about weddings all the time—so who better to write an exposé on the high cost of weddings? Someone should point out to prospective brides that they could easily let what should be a happy celebration turn into a debt-incurring nightmare. A whole industry of shops and magazines and advisers turned on the vulnerability of prospective brides to extravagance. Normally frugal people would cater and wet bar themselves into the poorhouse.

Natalie was a perfect example. She made good money and liked to appear rich, but Celia had seen her haggle with a waiter over a twenty-cent overcharge on an eighty-dollar tab. And now here she was traipsing around Pittock Mansion as if she was really considering renting the place.

"Here he is!" Natalie smiled and waved at a man coming down a flight of stairs.

Celia used the word *man* liberally. Elton might have been in his mid-twenties, but he still had the awkwardness of a teenager. A teenager who had become trapped in a nineties gothic time warp. His black pants were frayed at the knees, and his black Marilyn Manson T-shirt hung on his bony torso like a shroud. Massive black boots looked like they would be too heavy for his legs to lift, but he somehow managed to shamble along.

From the general slackerness of his appearance, it was obvious how desperate Natalie was to curry favor with her station manager.

"Elton!" Natalie gushed. "This is the woman I was telling you about. My maid of honor, Celia Snowden."

Elton grinned. "Hi, Thelia."

In spite of her assurances to Natalie that she would be able to handle this tongue piercing thing like a grown-up, Celia found herself struggling. She had expected the silver stud she spied when Elton smiled at her, but she hadn't expected the lisp.

"Hi," she finally managed, shaking his hand. Elton's arm was so thin and pale that the long blue strings of his veins hovered right below the skin. Celia was reminded of that TV show guy, Mr. Body, the man who ran around in the leotard with all the internal organs depicted on it. Mr. Body and Elton had one thing in common: they both gave her the creeps.

"You two wait here a sec and get acquainted," Natalie ordered them. "I have to go ask about awnings in case of rain." She scampered off in a flutter of white.

Celia felt like running after her.

Elton's sad eyes had dark bags under them, like a Saint Bernard's. They were eyeing her now with a little embarrassment. "You probably notithed my lithp."

Her smile froze. "Oh . . . well . . ."

"It'th not natural. My tongue's thwollen because I jutht got my sthud."

"That must be . . ." She cast about for a word. "Painful."

"Yeah, but it'll be pretty cool when I get uthed to it."

"Mm."

He took a step closer to her and grinned. "Tho . . . I gueth we're going to be thrown together a lot now."

She fumbled for words. "Looks that way."

"Do you have a boyfriend?"

Could she possibly lie? "Well, no. Unfortunately." Realizing how mean that sounded, she quickly tacked on, "I mean, unfortunately my boyfriend went back to England six months ago."

"Thix months? That'th about when I lotht my job."

"Really? What did you do?"

"I was a forenthic photographer."

"A what?"

"I worked in a morgue," he translated.

"Oh!" Instinctively she felt herself backing away. "That must have been interesting. I mean, I love Patricia Cornwell books. All that forensic stuff is so—" She stopped. Maybe it wasn't wise to sound too interested. "Well, it's sort of ghoulish, actually, but I'll bet you know a lot about . . . corpses . . . and photographing them . . ."

His voice dropped to a froggy croak, and he sidled up to her. "After thix months, you mutht be lonely."

"No!" Her mouth pulled into a tight, lip-splitting smile. "Actually, I find being alone very refreshing, don't you?"

"What makes you think I'm alone?"

She gaped at the Manson T-shirt, the pale, bony body, the infected tongue. "Well, aren't you?"

"Luckily, yeth." He beamed at her so that his stud glinted in the sunlight. "I'm footlooth and fanthy free."

Celia felt paralyzed. The words *oral thex* had lodged in her brain and refused to be rooted out.

"No awnings!" Natalie bellowed.

Celia had never been so glad to see anyone in her life. She turned and had to restrain herself from falling on Natalie's neck in gratitude. "No awnings!" she repeated with more sympathy than was really necessary.

"Can you believe it?" Natalie asked in disgust.

Elton shrugged. "Well, I thtill think it would be very nithe here . . ."

Natalie snorted. "Nice?" She made a sweeping gesture to the beautiful scenery all around them. "In two months all these azaleas are going to be dead. The last thing I want is to have a bunch of brown flowers in all my wedding pictures."

"So much for needing a photographer's input," Celia muttered.

As if recalling she was supposed to be nice, Natalie threw Elton a brief, apologetic glance. "It just won't work, and it would be too expensive in any case. Sorry to have wasted your time."

Elton turned that winning smile of his again on Celia. "I don't conthider it a wathte."

Celia practically tugged Natalie back to the car, where Natalie fixed a disappointed frown on her. "Honestly, Celia! I knew you were worried about all that oink stuff, but really. I turn my back for five minutes, and you start flirting with my photographer!"

Celia nearly lost it. "He was flirting with *me*. How could you leave me alone like that?"

"Well, for heaven's sake. I thought for sure I could trust you to act like two professionals."

Celia frowned quizzically. "What would my profession be in this scenario? Professional bridesmaid?"

"You know what I mean," Natalie said. "I don't want any emotions mucking up this wedding. Everyone needs to concentrate on making my day a success."

"You don't have to worry about me. But that Elton—"

"I'm sure you're exaggerating, Celia," Natalie said

dismissively. "The important thing now is to find a venue. *Nothing* is catching my fancy."

An idea occurred to Celia. It was a long shot, but it was worth a try. Maybe it would save her from more of these outings—and more contact with Elton. "You know what? I told Ellen I would have lunch with her soon. You should come along."

Natalie looked horrified by the suggestion, which reminded Celia that whenever Natalie and Ellen got together, it didn't worked out so well. Natalie sneered nonstop at Ellen's vegetarian, earth-friendly, knee-jerk liberalism, and after their last encounter, Ellen had pronounced Natalie "out of balance." Which, for someone as peace loving as Ellen, was the equivalent of a withering put-down.

"You want *me* to break bread with Miss Macramé?" Natalie asked.

How much simpler would life be if the people she knew would just get along with each other? "I've told you, she doesn't do macramé."

"Then, why did we have to spend a whole afternoon in a bead shop with her?"

"Ellen makes jewelry," Celia said. "Just as a hobby. And it wasn't an entire afternoon. It was barely forty-five minutes."

"The universe expanded while I was standing in that place," Natalie said.

Maybe it was best to get off the subject of the bead shop. "Anyway, Ellen got married last year and went through all this stuff you're going through now. She might be able to give you some ideas on venues."

Natalie hooted. "Wasn't she married in the boondocks?"

"Well, yes," Celia admitted, "but she looked into a lot of other places. I was thinking we could meet Saturday and—"

"Saturday's impossible," Natalie said. "Mother and I are going to pick out my engagement ring."

The statement threw Celia. "Your mother? Shouldn't you be doing that with Angus?"

"Please! You think I would trust a jewelry purchase like that to a man? This is a job for Babs."

None of my business, Celia thought. She cleared her throat. "Okay . . . Maybe next week. Or even Saturday after you and your mom have finished."

To her surprise, Natalie actually appeared to be mulling it over. "Well . . . It couldn't hurt. Okay."

"Okay?" Celia was amazed. Maybe Natalie *really was* working on being nice.

"Anyway," Natalie continued before Celia could praise her for her new self, "I'd *love* the chance to show granola girl how fabulously happy I am."

"Marie, I've got a great idea."

The Warden tapped her pencil impatiently against a stack of papers in front of her for a full ten seconds before deigning to look up at Celia. "Is it going to win a Pulitzer Prize?"

"Well, no, probably not . . ."

"Will it increase circulation?"

Celia stifled the urge to sigh. On the way back from lunch she had been so pumped about her expensive wedding exposé, she had forgotten what a hard sell Marie was. Fearing the wind was about to completely die out of her sails, Celia flopped down into the chair opposite Marie's desk and leaned in to plead her case. "It's about weddings," she said, trying to recapture some of her excitement.

Marie's brows rose. "Could you be a little more specific?"

"The high cost of weddings," Celia continued. "You

wouldn't believe the amounts brides are willing to spend these days. I've got a friend, and she's estimating it's going to cost fifteen thousand dollars. Did you know a dress alone can cost the average bride up to two thousand dollars? And that's not at all outlandish. It's nuts. People are spending on weddings what parents used to save for their kids' college tuition!"

"Uh huh."

"And it's not just brides and their families that would be the focus of the piece. They're just the victims of trend, as far as I'm concerned. The real focus should be on the merchants who take advantage of these people. I mean, really, people pay hundreds of dollars just for a wedding cake. But how much can a cake really cost to produce?"

Marie nodded.

Celia translated that as encouragement. "It could be a three-part series. I even have a title. 'The Price of Love.' "

Marie leaned back, eyeing her steadily. She tapped her pencil against the arm of her chair. Then, after several minutes' thought that left Celia hanging uncomfortably in suspense, she announced her verdict.

"Are you insane?"

Celia's face, which had been tense with expectation, fell. "You don't like it?"

"It stinks! Snowden, you write the wedding column. Remember? *W-e-d-d-i-n-g c-o-l-u-m-n.* People read your Sunday feature because they *like* to know about people spending outrageous sums of money for a single goofy ceremony. That's the whole point. If people weren't going berserk, readers wouldn't give a rat's ass about a bunch of nobodies getting hitched."

Marie's voice carried like a foghorn. All sounds of work in the cubicles behind them had died. Keyboards had fallen silent. No one seemed to be on the phone.

The whole office was listening to Celia be exposed as an idiot.

Still, she soldiered on. "But it's investigative journalism."

"And this is a business we're trying to run here. Haven't you ever noticed who advertises in the *Today!* section? Those department stores that sell the expensive dresses you intend to complain about. The restaurants that cater those usurious receptions. You'll kill us. You might as well pour lighter fluid all over the fifth floor here and put a match to us!"

Celia's lips twisted into a wry smile. "Don't hold back. I'd like your honest opinion."

"What you're suggesting is suicide."

"Are advertisers dictating what we can write about now? People are getting ripped off."

"No one's got a gun to their heads. They want to be ripped off."

Celia squared her shoulders stubbornly. Marie was the one who was always saying that reporters had gotten soft and lazy. This was a chance to spice up the lifestyle section a little. "Not everyone does. This could be a wake-up call—"

Marie groaned and dropped her head into her hands. Always a bad sign.

But Celia wasn't ready to give up yet. "I'm sure people didn't want to hear about problems in meatpacking plants, but that didn't stop Upton Sinclair."

Marie peeked at her through her fingers. "That was a century ago, Snowden! And it was a matter of public health!"

"And this is a matter of the public spending their life's savings on a party. And it's happening every day."

"You're really determined to do this, aren't you?" Marie asked.

"I just think it could be interesting. And anyone who follows my column would want to read it."

"And you want to do the legwork?"

Celia nodded enthusiastically. "I can even do the photos myself, like I do for the 'Unions' column."

Marie shook her head, but it was a shake of resignation, not refusal. "Okay. Here's the deal, Snowden. I'm still not convinced that this isn't a stinker. But see what you can come up with."

Celia didn't dare savor triumph now. Instead, she hopped up and escaped before Marie could change her mind and tell her to scrap the whole idea. She scampered back to her desk before she even allowed herself to smile.

Across the aisle, Davis was leaning back in his chair, grinning. He gave her a thumbs-up.

"It wasn't much of a victory," Celia said.

"I think it's a good idea."

She tilted her head. "Do you really?"

"Sure."

"But *you* like elaborate weddings."

He nodded. "That's the beauty of it. People always want to know about how much money other people are spending. This will highlight that expense for them. It's doesn't take away from their enjoyment—it enhances it."

Celia frowned. Enhancing people's enjoyment wasn't precisely what she was aiming for. She leaned back, drumming her fingers on her desk.

"And you know what?" Davis asked.

Celia grunted.

"While you were at lunch I had this brainstorm— you know, because you'd just been talking about being bored with your job. What if you covered a different kind of wedding?"

"Different how?"

"Something most people don't think about."

She sighed. "This weekend we're going to the wedding of some historical reenactors. They're going to have an Oregon Trail wedding. Real nutcases. What could be more different than that?"

"The wedding of two men."

Celia frowned. That didn't sound like something "Unions" column readers would be very enthusiastic about. In fact, she wasn't wild about it, either.

"That's brilliant!"

They both looked up to see Marie standing not ten feet away.

"It is?" Celia asked.

"Hell, yes!" Marie said. "If you want a little edge to your column, Snowden, that's the angle you should go for."

Celia could feel her face contorting in displeasure. "But gay marriages aren't even legal in Oregon. Maybe if we were in Vermont . . ."

"Sure it's not legal," Davis said, "but these ceremonies are happening every day. And to the people involved, they're every bit as meaningful as a 'real' marriage."

Marie snapped her fingers. "Terrific!"

Celia nodded halfheartedly. She didn't want to seem belligerent. "The trouble is, I don't know any gay couples who are going to be married . . ."

Davis smiled. "I do. I can introduce them to you. They're neighbors of mine."

"Great. That's it," Marie declared. She turned to Celia. "Jump on this one, Snowden."

Then she turned and went back to her desk.

Celia tried to avoid looking at Davis. She should have thanked him for giving her an idea. The trouble was, she wasn't thankful. In fact, she was a little miffed. Marie had liked his idea better.

But that was silly. A truly petty thought.

But it was there.

She turned to Davis with a stiff smile. "Thanks."

He looked puzzled. Hurt, almost. "Did I do something wrong?"

"No, no. I just wasn't expecting it. You could have brought it up with me first."

"I was trying to. I didn't see Marie standing there."

Celia realized he was right. Maybe she was just still fuming from being cut down to size by Marie before. That wasn't Davis's fault, either.

She decided she was getting way too cranky. Maybe she needed to spend a quiet evening at home listening to Dean Martin with Gazpacho—an activity that would undoubtedly make her appreciate human beings more.

"You know what tonight is, don't you?" Davis asked.

She glanced at him. "No."

"Blazers. Timberwolves. The Rose Garden Arena."

She hesitated. She shouldn't go. Sports were such a waste of time, really.

More of a waste than teaching a bird to sing Dean Martin songs?

"What time?" she asked.

"Seven-thirty."

"You're on."

Six

The Blazers were down by twenty-one, so doomed they might as well be called the Portland Martyrs, but the raucous crowd was still in denial. Davis was too much of a realist to fully enjoy the halftime festivities. He was also too distracted by Celia, who always seemed to revel in this portion of the evening. She licked her Yo-Cream cone and chuckled at the antics on the court two tiers below them, where kids were lined up, blindfolded, trying to make free throws.

"That kid can't be more than five." She pointed at a hopelessly small child in the line. "He can barely lift a basketball, much less throw it."

Sure enough, the kid managed to toss the ball only a few feet. Nevertheless, the crowd roared enthusiastically. Then another kid came up. Miraculously, the ball he threw sailed right into the basket, nothing but net.

The Rose Garden went nuts.

"Put *him* on the team!" a spectator in front of them hollered through cupped hands.

Celia turned to Davis, laughing. "Sure you don't want a Yo-Cream?"

"No thanks." A chocolate-vanilla swirl on a waffle cone was their halftime tradition, but tonight he was abstaining. For the past two days he'd eaten only one meal a day and spent the rest of the day snacking on vegetables whenever he was hungry. He'd lost—and he'd had to step on the scales five different times to make his brain absorb this figure—four pounds. The figure still astonished him. That was two pounds a day! If he kept this up, in a month's time he would not only be trim, but he would be hospitalized.

The glance Celia sent him contained more than a drop of suspicion. When it came to sweets, abstinence wasn't usually his bag. He added quickly, "I wouldn't want to miss the BlazerDancers."

This excuse seemed to satisfy her. Sneering at the BlazerDancers was their other tradition. At halftime and whenever there was a long time-out, a crew of shapely twenty-somethings burst onto the court and wiggled and writhed to pop hits played at ear-splitting volume.

As if on cue, the lights dimmed, Britney Spears blasted from the central speaker, and the Blazer-Dancers popped onto the court. Davis and Celia darted sidewise glances at each other.

She leaned closer to him, close enough that he could smell her hair. That all-purpose flowery shampoo scent had never seemed so intoxicating. "Do you think there is such a thing as a BlazerDancer groupie?"

"Why? Are you thinking of changing professions?"

She practically doubled over. "Oh, sure. That would work out great. I've got the rhythmic abilities of an aardvark."

"I was thinking more in terms of your becoming a groupie, actually."

She shook her head. "Couldn't do it. I'm afraid it would involve taking a pay cut."

The loud guy in front of them cupped his hands to his mouth and screamed over the music, "Wish our damn team could play half as well as these girls dance!"

Davis watched closely for the way Celia's nose always wrinkled slightly when she was trying not to laugh. A wave of desire washed over him, and he gritted his teeth, trying to shake it off. Halftime during an NBA game was not the moment to become carried away with lust.

He needed to get a grip. To say something witty and intelligent that would make Celia finally realize in one crystalline moment that he was the man of her dreams.

Most of all, he needed to banish Corky's words *slip her the old tongue* from his head.

"Davis?" Celia's face was scrunched up in concern. "Are you all right?"

Okay, buddy. This is your cue. Something brilliant. Witty.

"You sure are pretty," he blurted out.

The words leapt from his lips before he could stop them. Now they seemed to jangle discordantly in the air. Even Britney Spears couldn't drown them out.

After her expression turned from surprise to confusion to disbelief, Celia laughed. "You should have gone for a Yo-Cream. The lack of sugar is affecting your brain."

"I meant it."

"Oh." She appeared befuddled. "Well, thanks." She faced forward quickly.

None of the players on the court had thrown a bigger brick tonight than he had. His compliment had completely missed the mark. But then, everything he did seemed to backfire. Certainly this afternoon his suggestion about Stan and Mike's wedding had gone over like a lead balloon. If he'd thought *that* would win Celia over, he'd gotten a rude awakening when she'd looked at him as if he'd betrayed her.

And now he'd done it again.

He searched for a way to recover some normalcy between them. The usual status quo might drive him crazy, but it was better than stiff silence. "So . . . I guess you won't have much time for yourself this spring, what with the wedding and everything."

She shrugged. "After it's all over, I think I'll start planning my trip to China."

Davis felt his lips curling into a frown. "Do you think that's wise?"

"Why not?"

"Well, with your travel history . . ."

She groaned. "Now you're starting to sound like Natalie!"

"I wasn't thinking about the incident in Thailand. Although now that you mention it . . ."

She waved her hand to dismiss the subject. "Please! Getting laid up with the flu in Paris that week was just a fluke."

"What about the hookworm you picked up in Jamaica?"

"You just have no sense of adventure," Celia admonished. "No sense of wanting to discover different cultures."

"Yes, I do," he said.

A brow darted up skeptically. "Since when?"

"Since a long time ago. For your information, my family sponsored a foreign exchange student in high school. I can still speak passable Spanish."

She drew back in surprise. "Get out."

"Es verdad."

At the sound of a foreign language coming from his lips, she drew back in shock. "Where was this exchange student from?"

"Argentina. I still keep up with Antonio—he's a

doctor now. He's always inviting me to come stay with him."

Celia's chin dropped to her chest. "Where in Argentina?"

"Buenos Aires."

She seemed to be on the verge of fainting. "You mean you've got a doctor hidden away in the coolest city in South America and you never told me about him?"

"It's never come up."

"Of course it's come up! I talk about taking trips all the time."

"For some reason, I never thought of Antonio as a travel destination for you."

"Is he single?"

Davis quickly began to regret this conversation. "Oh . . . I guess so."

"You *guess* so?"

"Yes, he's single."

Her eyes were glittering with interest now. "You've got to show me a picture."

"Don't tell me you're considering pulling a Natalie."

"Of course not." She clucked at him in mock disgust. "I'd definitely want to meet him before I could commit to lifelong wedded bliss."

Davis faced forward. The dancers were gone, and Britney Spears had finally shut up. Players were congregating again, but Davis's heart wasn't in the game.

What lunacy had made him bring up Antonio? He'd been bragging, of course. As though knowing someone in a foreign country would make him more appealing to Celia.

Instead, it had just made his friend sound appealing.

"He's not Antonio Banderas," he bit out.

She laughed. "I'm not *that* picky."

In frustration, he added, "I thought you'd given up on Spanish."

Celia swallowed her last bite of waffle cone and licked a little spot of chocolate off her lip. The dainty little flick of her tongue nearly made him lose it. How could she be so unconsciously sexy? "I could always take it up again."

Davis suddenly felt the urge to eat ten Yo-Cream cones; but now the game had started, and he was six seats away from the aisle.

Celia clapped when the Blazers sank a three, then poked him to get his attention. "Don't look so glum, Davis. We're only eighteen points down now."

He tried to keep his mind on the game, but for the rest of the evening all he could think about was Celia swooning in the arms of Antonio. His friend. Now he was unreasonably jealous of a friend an entire continent away, who didn't even know of Celia's existence.

Davis had picked Celia up in his car, so after the Blazers went down in defeat, he drove her home. She seemed awfully chirpy to him on the way back over the river. She was humming *Guantanamera*.

"So how well do you know Dan and Mike?" she asked him.

"Stan," he corrected tersely.

She frowned. "Who?"

"That's his name. Stan. It's Stan and Mike."

She laughed. "Okay. Is something wrong? You sound a little bit tense."

"Sorry."

He could feel her eyes on him. He tried his damnedest not to look at her, into those eyes that tended to make him lose his reason. He needed to calm down, stay cool.

"Look," she said. "Is this about this afternoon? Is that why you've been acting so wigged out all night?"

He didn't even know what she was talking about.

"I know I was snippy about the gay marriage idea," she said. "I shouldn't have been. You were just trying to help me out. I apologize."

She was apologizing to him, when he was the one who was acting moody. All because he was terrified that she would someday just slip away from him, before he seized the opportunity to tell her how he felt.

So tell her now, a little voice commanded him.

Right! In a car. That would be real smooth.

"Davis?" He jumped. "You were a million miles away," she said. "Is something bothering you?"

"No," he lied.

"I had a great time tonight. It was fun, wasn't it?"

Opportunity number two. This was his chance. All he had to do was say, *Any time I spend with you is fun. That's because I'm in love with you.*

The words choked in his throat. The most that he was able to manage was a croaky, "Yeah."

Good Lord. Was it any wonder he was a writer when he possessed such powers of expression?

Too soon, he was driving down Celia's street. He pulled up to the curb next to a fire hydrant—the only free spot on the entire block.

"See you tomorrow," she said.

Tomorrow. It was just another work day. Davis nodded.

She frowned in concern. "You'd better get some rest—you don't look so hot."

And then she was gone.

Davis sat facing forward, braced against the steering wheel, and suddenly all the things he should have said overwhelmed him. He felt like a balloon that had too much air in it. If he didn't let something out, he was just going to pop.

Without thinking, he yanked up the emergency brake and jumped out of the car. He didn't even take the time to kill the lights or pull the keys out. He just ran. He caught up to Celia as she was turning the key in the lock, and when he skidded to a stop behind her, she turned and shrieked.

When she realized who it was, she sank against the door in relief. "Davis! You scared the crap out of me!"

He felt as if he was gulping for air.

She tilted her head. "Did you want something?"

He nodded and swiped his cowlick back over his head.

"What is it?"

"I . . ." He swallowed. "I wanted to make sure you knew."

She squinted at him. "Knew what?"

Words came out in a rush. "That I think you're just about the most wonderful person I've ever known. I mean it. I—"

It was a little difficult to go on now. Celia's face had sagged in shock, as if it were imprinted on Silly Putty and someone had pulled it like taffy. In other words, she didn't seem exactly ecstatic.

His verbal momentum ground down, and he finished, less than spectacularly, "I . . . think the world of you, Celia."

They stood there for an eternity, she with her Silly Putty face and he with egg all over his. What should he do now? She already looked as though she needed smelling salts, but he couldn't just disappear. Some gesture seemed called for.

He didn't know where the impulse came from. He would always wonder. As if he'd practiced it a million times, he reached out, grabbed her shoulders, and hauled her against him as if he were some other being entirely. A tough guy. Vince Vaughn.

But when his lips touched hers, it didn't matter who he was. What mattered was that he convey everything he possibly could in this one kiss—all the longing, all the months of wanting her, all the times he'd wanted to do this before. Celia lifted up on her toes, and he slanted his mouth to kiss her more deeply; but it was impossible for him to even pretend that he was in control. All he could do was react to the sweet warmth of her mouth, the surprising thinness of her shoulders, the way her body, still rigid with surprise, fit against his.

If she was shocked, he was possibly even more so. He'd been dreaming of this moment for months, but come to find out, he hadn't gotten it right at all. He hadn't dreamed that her mouth would taste faintly of chocolate, or that her hands would grip his shirt, or that he would suddenly be so full of love for her that it was as if all his feelings for her over the past twelve months had intensified a million times.

Knowing that if he didn't stop soon, it would be torture to have to stop at all, he dragged his mouth from hers. Her green eyes, dilated in shock, were luminous in the yellowish light from the streetlamps. Her lips were slightly parted, and it was all he could do not to dip his head and kiss her again.

With a mighty effort, he managed to step back and smile. "Night."

He unhooked her hands from their frozen clawhold on his shirt. Then he turned on his heel and strolled away, imitating composure he certainly didn't feel. He knew she was watching him. His legs were shaking. He might be trying for Vince Vaughn on the outside, but the way his heart was beating was pure jackrabbit. Not to mention, his head, bombarded by doubts, was pounding.

He had the excruciating feeling that he'd just blown it.

Celia locked herself in her apartment and collapsed against the door before she would allow herself to even think about what had just happened.

Had Davis actually *kissed her?*

She was shaking like a leaf. It was ludicrous. But it had all happened so fast, like an earthquake. Her head had just been adjusting to what was happening when suddenly it was all over.

Despite the fact that in a matter of one short week, Angus, and now Davis, had kissed her, this wasn't the sort of thing that happened to her. Angus didn't count anyway, since he'd thought she was someone else. Usually when a man kissed her, it was something she had been anticipating, even plotting, for months. But this kiss had come out of the blue, like kisses did in movies. Yet she and Davis weren't movie stars by any stretch of the imagination. They were friends. Two co-workers who had just watched a basketball game. This was real life.

Only suddenly it all seemed very unreal.

Gazpacho squawked at her. Glad for the distraction, she fetched him a peanut and braved putting her hand inside his lair to let him climb on her arm. She'd left Dean Martin on continuous play while she was gone, but she could tell by the stubborn look in those eyes of his that Gazpacho hadn't soaked up a single note. He was no closer to crooning than he'd been to operatic arias or yodeling.

He was one ornery bird.

Needlelike claws jabbed her as he climbed onto her

forearm and made uncomfortable tracks up her sleeve until he could finally dig into her shoulder. This was his favorite place to eat a peanut. She assumed that was because he took sadistic pleasure in having to dig his talons into her extra hard to stand on one foot while the other was involved in hulling the nut.

Wincing in pain, she went over to the window and peeked through the miniblinds to the street below.

Davis's car was gone.

The sight of the empty space in front of the fire hydrant affected her strangely. It was almost as if she were disappointed. But that was demented. She hadn't really expected Davis to still be there, strolling up and down the block singing "On the Street Where You Live."

Then again, she'd never expected him to kiss her, either. But he had.

She recalled the exact warm pressure of his lips against hers. Who would have thought the guy in the cubicle next to hers, the guy who had been taking her to greasy spoons for nearly a year, would be such an incredible kisser?

The moon was shining through the window, and she hummed along with Dean for a moment. "Ain't Love a Kick in the Head," he was singing.

Well, yes, it was. Or at least, whatever had just happened on her stoop felt like a kick in the head. One moment she was terrified that she was about to be mugged, and the next, Davis had started sputtering out . . .

What had he said?

I think the world of you. . . .

Or something to that end. She'd been so stunned she hadn't even been able to listen properly. Was that a declaration of love? And if it was, why wasn't her heart singing with happiness?

Because she didn't love him back, was the obvious answer. How could she? She'd never even thought about him that way. When she needed a bud, that was when she thought of Davis. He was the greatest person in the world to go to games with, or the movies, or watch *The Sopranos* with. When she felt like spending a Saturday afternoon combing musty thrift stores, Davis was her man. But as a boyfriend?

What was she going to do?

She moved away from the window and began to pace, which made Gazpacho hold on that much tighter. He was yanking her hair with his beak, too—another of his tricks. Times like these she wondered why she hadn't done like any normal lonely single woman and adopted a sweet, fluffy kitten or puppy.

But of course she knew the answer. A parrot had seemed more unusual. The exotic angle had appealed to her. As did the idea of coming home at the end of a long, hard day and having something to talk to—especially when that something could only reply with words she'd taught him.

Finally reaching her threshold of pain, she put Gazpacho on the perch on top of his cage. He spent a few moments gnawing on the thick wood and eyeing her suspiciously with his almost lizardlike eyes.

If she were a puppy dog type of person, Celia mused, she would probably go for Davis in a big way. Davis himself was loyal, steadfast, domestic. His hair was even sort of golden retriever blond, now that she thought about it.

She tried to sift through the past year to figure out any misleading signals she might have sent him. But she couldn't think of any. They were friends. Good friends. It didn't make sense that he would suddenly go berserk and make a move on her.

She sank onto her sofa and tried to think through

those confusing moments that had gone by with lightning speed. She'd now spent ten times as much time obsessing about the incident than it had actually lasted. And doing so hadn't cleared up her confusion one iota.

In fact, she was more flustered than ever. Did Davis really mean that he wanted to have a relationship with her? Because she liked their relationship just as it was. He was practically her best friend now. With Natalie getting married so soon, she'd be lost without Davis.

But how could they go on as before now that he'd . . . he'd . . .

She leaned forward, tapping her chin with her forefinger. What was it that he'd done, exactly, that was so awful? He'd just kissed her. Was that any reason to freak out?

What a dope she was being! Maybe he hadn't even meant anything serious by it. What if it had just been curiosity that made him kiss her?

The doorbell rang, and Celia flew off the couch, her heart drumming against her ribs. She whirled toward Gazpacho. "Who could that be?"

He blinked at her in disgust, as if to remind her that despite all her efforts, he was a nonverbal bird.

She glanced anxiously at the door. Had Davis come back?

Maybe he wanted to apologize for acting so weird. Maybe he was going to tell her that he hadn't gotten much sleep the night before, and in his near delirium from fatigue, he'd suddenly had the uncontrollable urge to behave as if he were in a Merchant-Ivory film. Which would have been as reasonable an explanation as any she could come up with.

In fact, any old lame excuse would be welcome. They could just shrug off the incident and pretend it had never happened. They could go back to business as usual.

She hurried to the door, threw the dead bolt, undid the chain latch, and opened it wide with a conciliatory smile. But the man she was facing did not appear the least prone to reconciliation. In fact, he looked as mad as hell.

Also, he wasn't Davis.

Mr. Zhirbotken from downstairs stood before her in his pajamas and bathrobe, which was a shiny purple paisley affair worn with a mismatched green terrycloth belt. He looked rumpled, rattled, and maybe even a little bit insane. His bloodshot eyes were glowering at her, and his hands, tensed to the point that ropy veins were popping out on them, were making strange clawing gestures around his Albert Einstein-like hair.

"Mr. Z!" She was surprised to see him. He'd never been up here before. "Is something wrong?"

He growled angrily at her. She caught only the words *music* and *pizza pie.*

She squinted in concentration. "I'm sorry?"

"The music! The music!" He yelled as if the English words were exploding out of him. "All night I hear the moon hitting the eye like a pizza pie! All night I hear the 'Volare'! The Jerry Lewis! I go mad with your music!"

She straightened, and suddenly realized that the volume on her stereo was up higher than normal. She must have forgotten to lower it before she left for the basketball game, which had been early in the evening, before her downstairs neighbor was even home from work.

And when she'd arrived home, she had been distracted by other matters, to say the least.

"I'm so sorry!" she exclaimed, understanding his eye-popping rage completely. "I'll turn it off at once."

She lunged for the stereo's remote and hit the stop button.

Unfortunately, there wasn't a stop button to Mr. Zhirbotken. The music was gone, but he was in her apartment now, still raving. "The 'That's Amore'! The 'Ain't That a Kick in the Head'!" He was spewing Dean Martin hits—all in the order they appeared on her CD. The poor man had probably heard it fifteen times through.

She cringed in guilt. He must have thought she was purposefully tormenting him, though, of course, if she'd wanted to do that, she would have tried to have Gazpacho emulate Eminem.

"I just left it on for my bird, you see. I'm very, very sorry."

He was grabbing hanks of his hair now and pulling. " 'The Evening in Roma'! The 'You Belong to Me'! The 'That's Amore'! How can I forget now these things?"

Apparently apologies weren't what he wanted. He wanted full Dean Martin brain erasure. She clucked at him soothingly and tried to nudge him back out the door. "It's okay, Mr. Zhirbotken. Everything will be all right now. The 'That's Amore' will go away, you wait and see. Give it time."

His eyes were tearing as he turned back to her. "Please to play no more the Dean Martin, okay?"

"Okay. I'm very sorry," she reiterated.

He held his arms outstretched in a plaintive gesture. "At least no more the same songs!"

"Don't worry—Gazpacho wasn't soaking up Dean, anyway." Though apparently Mr. Zhirbotken was. "I promise you."

"Okay! Okay!" he raved as his white hair disappeared down the stairwell.

Celia went back into her apartment and sighed heavily.

She needed to go to bed before anything else weird could happen to her today.

But as she squeezed into her bedroom and slipped beneath her cool sheets, the trouble that had been temporarily jogged from her mind by Mr. Zhirbotken came back full force. And she was left staring at her slanty ceiling and remembering that kiss. What was she going to do?

Davis was so *nice*. A gem of a friend. She was even flattered that he would think her worthy of kissing. But she didn't want to lose him as a buddy. And she feared she would, especially if she made some hackneyed speech about how she cherished him like a brother. That would just be too embarrassing for both of them.

And after all, they still had to work five feet away from each other. It was a situation that called for the highest diplomatic skill. Frankly, given her confused mental state, she wasn't entirely certain she was up to the task.

Which all seemed to leave her and Davis with the same problem Mr. Zhirbotken had. How to make the "That's Amore" go away.

Davis had never driven so recklessly. But he'd never felt such a desperate need to flee before.

What had he done? He'd told himself that making a confession would be the worst possible thing to do. And sure enough, after he'd told her how he felt— after he'd kissed her—poor Celia had stared at him like a deer caught in headlights.

Everything had felt great while they were kissing. Now he felt like some kind of masher.

When he screeched into his driveway, he was relieved to find all the lights in the house off. He just wasn't up to dealing with Corky right now. He supposed he should also thank his lucky stars that there didn't appear to be any new disasters visible from the yard. His insides might be churning, but at least his house seemed calm. For one night in his life, he would be able to drop off to sleep without a lullaby from the Boss.

He turned the key quietly in the lock and tiptoed inside, keeping the lights off so he wouldn't draw Corky's attention to the fact that he was home.

Halfway through the living room, he walked right into a large steel structure. His head hit a metal pole just as his shin butted an entirely different protrusion. Davis yowled in pain and jumped to the side to escape whatever it was that was blocking the middle of the room, but in so doing he whapped his temple against something else hard and metallic. He stumbled across the floor, groaning, and managed to topple backward over the coffee table.

Both his body, the table, and a half-empty bowl of popcorn fell to the floor with a crash. The glass bowl broke and disseminated tiny glass shards and popcorn kernels across the hardwood floors.

From his ground position, Davis tried to take stock. He was all in one piece, at least.

What the hell had he banged into?

He turned to try to focus on whatever contraption had mysteriously appeared in his house while he was at the basketball game; but as he was turning, the lights flipped on, and he was suddenly squinting up at Corky.

"Did you see it?" Corky asked. He looked as excited and eager as a kid on Christmas morning. As if to make matters even jollier, his roommate was wearing nothing but a pair of bright green boxers with Daffy Ducks all over them. His thick torso was pale pink and flabby; his pot belly flopped over the waistband of his shorts.

Davis pushed himself up to a more comfortable sitting position. "See what?"

"The Omni-Flex!"

Davis turned. And gaped. Taking up half the room was a giant exercise machine like he had seen advertised on television. Only on television, the salesperson never explained that the simple machine that could change your life for just twenty minutes a day was the size of Godzilla. And about as attractive. It had a long bench seat attached to a huge rectangular post. Along this metal spine, the creature sprouted innumerable pullies and handles, cables and padded Nautilus-type weights. On the back, two steps protruded. Davis assumed this was so a person could practice stair climbing without actually having the inconvenience of finding a staircase.

"It's a total workout package!" boomed Corky. "Isn't it something?"

Davis began to silently count to ten for patience, but he only made it to six before Corky interrupted his numerical therapy.

"Hey, what's the matter? Why are you sitting on the floor?"

"I fell!" The retort came out more sharply than he intended.

Corky looked at him cautiously. "Well, it's no wonder, wandering around in the dark the way you were."

Davis heaved himself onto the couch and buried his aching head in his hands. He could barely bring himself to look at Godzilla, though he did notice that the behemoth effectively blocked the view from the couch to the television. That was handy. "Where did it come from?"

Corky stepped forward, positively atwitter. "You'll never believe, man! Isn't this weird? We were talking about Bob just the other night, and today as I was walking home from work, I passed this place that specializes in used sporting goods. Well, naturally I made a beeline for the exercise equipment. And what was the first thing I clapped eyes on? This! And I got it for a song! Can you believe it?"

"There are a lot of things I'm having a hard time believing right now."

"These things cost an arm and a leg new," Corky informed him. "Somebody must've shelled out the big bucks for this fine machine, then sold it off for a song. Who the hell would do something like that?"

Remembering his rowing machine, Davis shook his head. "Some sucker."

A la Carol Merrill, Corky began demonstrating the weights. "The great thing about this is everything's adjustable. The guy at the store showed me. It even comes with the original instruction booklet. Isn't that incredible?"

"Incredible."

Corky frowned. "You're worried about how much I paid, aren't you? Well, don't bother your head about it. I figure for all the hospitality you've shown me, I owe you ten machines like this."

"One's more than enough," Davis assured him.

Corky laughed. "You'll thank me for this. Pretty soon you'll be set for life, just like my old pal Bob."

Recalling his blunder tonight with Celia, Davis was pretty sure it would take more than a few minutes of exercising to fix his problems.

"Why don't you try 'er out?" Corky asked.

"Not right now."

"C'mon, I'll show you what the guy at the store told me."

Sighing, Davis stood and gingerly approached the monster. Their first meeting hadn't given him any confidence. Corky busied himself pulling out cogs and adjusting the bench level and then showed Davis a few exercises. Sweat popped out on his brow, which surprised Davis. What Corky was doing didn't look all that tough.

Davis finally took his turn, and after twenty minutes he was completely bushed. Moreover, he realized he hadn't cringed in shame over kissing Celia since banging into the exercise machine. Maybe the machine would serve a useful purpose after all.

Corky lifted his brows. "Say, I forgot to ask. Did the Blazers win?"

The Blazers. That seemed so long ago, Davis actually had to give the question some thought. "No, they got smeared."

Corky clucked in sympathy. "No wonder you looked so done in. Must have been a pretty disappointing evening."

Davis's lips twisted into a rueful smile. "You don't know the half of it."

Seven

On Friday morning, Celia bought a coffee from the Tillamook Deli and took it to her desk with her. She'd hoped this would help her avoid an awkward scene in the coffee room with Davis. But as she rounded the corner from Marie's desk to her cubicle, Davis was already at his computer, busily typing away.

On the corner of his desk sat a to-go cup from the Tillamook Deli.

Was he hoping to avoid *her*?

Maybe she was reading too much into a coffee cup.

He glanced up at her, then did a double take, as if surprised to see her here at work, of all places. "Hi! How you doin'?" His tone was even more than his usual Nebraska friendly.

"Fine." A wave of heat slammed through her as she remembered his lips on hers. "You?"

"Oh, you know." He chuckled. "The usual."

The usual? After last night?

Her lips froze in a flight attendant grin. If she'd worried there would be a scene, she could apparently rest easy on that score. Davis seemed no more eager than she was for an awkward heart-to-heart.

Naturally she was as pleased as punch to avoid the subject of last night . . . except it left an eight-hundred-pound gorilla in the aisle between them. Usually she liked the camaraderie of the open wall between her and Davis's desks, but today it felt as if they were breathing down each other's necks. Every squeak of a desk chair, pencil tap, or cough was occasion for an uncomfortable glance, a stiff smile. Minutes dragged like hours. Neither of them made their usual pilgrimage to the coffee room, but instead sipped listlessly at their expensive lattes.

By midmorning, it seemed more awkward *not* to talk about last night.

Just say something, she thought. She'd practiced all sorts of speeches as she dressed for work this morning. Little monologues about how much she enjoyed his—platonic—company. Apologies if he felt she had led him on. Pat homilies about how precious friendship was.

She picked up her ringing phone and was actually relieved to hear Natalie barking at her. "We simply *must* go shopping!"

Celia was already lunging for her purse. "Great!"

This was research now, she thought, justifying breezing out of the office at ten-thirty to shop. She could gather information for "The Price of Love." *And* she could escape the palpable tension between her and Davis.

Natalie had picked a large bridal store in the suburbs for her first foray into the world of wedding dresses. "I want the ultimate dress," she told Celia on the drive to Beaverton. "I'm not going to settle for something second best, so you need to keep your eyes peeled. I want something unique and completely me."

At the store, Celia gazed helplessly across the racks of dresses that, face it, were all long and white. She felt as if she'd seen all of them before on one bride or another. But for Natalie's sake, she gave the hunt the old college try. After sifting through two racks, she picked out a gorgeous-looking creation and held it out. It was simple, fitted, and had elegant beading that she assumed justified the sixteen-hundred-dollar price tag. "What about this?"

Natalie skewered her with a glance. "Are you insane?"

Celia looked again at the dress, more doubtfully this time. "What's the matter?"

"Oh, nothing," Natalie answered acerbically. "Except that if you tore off the ridiculous sash and the cap sleeves and changed the color by a few shades of beige, it's *exactly* the dress Catherine Zeta-Jones wore when she married Michael Douglas. I'm not going to prance down the aisle looking like a movie royalty wannabe."

"Oh, I didn't know . . ."

Natalie sighed impatiently. "Of course you knew what Catherine Zeta-Jones wore on her wedding day. You haven't been living under a rock for the past five years. You just need to concentrate."

So much for the new, nicer Natalie.

Celia quickly stuffed the hanger back on the rack, feeling foolish and a little headachy, much as she had in third grade when she hadn't grasped division the first time through.

She soon learned that to present dresses to Natalie was simply begging for her friend's scathing assessment of her lack of fashion savvy. So she began taking notes on prices and talking to sales clerks instead. "Three hundred dollars for a veil? And that's modest?"

"Well . . . We have cheaper veils," the clerk, an older woman who looked as though she'd seen about a million brides, assured her. "Are you working with a more modest budget?"

"Oh, I'm not getting married," Celia answered.

"Tell me, do you display cheaper fashions as prominently as more expensive ones?"

The saleslady tilted her head. "Well . . ." The woman's dark eyes narrowed on her. "Are you in sales?"

"No, actually I write for the *Portland Times.*"

Suddenly, the clerk's face broke into a smile, and she was very cooperative, until she managed to figure out that Celia was interested in doing a story on the high price tag of weddings. Then the woman clammed up.

"We're simply trying to serve our customers, of all income levels," the clerk insisted.

Uh huh, Celia thought. Dodging responsibility.

Moments later she was installed on a settee in Natalie's dressing room with a glass of sparkling wine. The first dress Natalie tried on had a lace bodice and full, tulle skirt. Natalie plucked unhappily at the skirt, fluffing it. "What were you talking to that clerk about?"

"I'm doing an article on how expensive weddings are."

Natalie threw an unhappy glance at her. "No wonder the clerk looked like she couldn't wait to get rid of you!"

"Did she?"

"I hope your research doesn't take long. You'll get us kicked out of every dress shop in town." She wrinkled her nose at the mirror. "Doesn't this look like something you'd see in a Disney on Ice show?"

Celia nodded regretfully. "A little bit."

Natalie puffed out her breath and began the laborious task of getting out of the dress again.

As she helped her with buttons, Celia asked, "What's Angus been up to?"

"Today he's resting. Still jet-lagged, poor thing."

She picked out the next dress, a loose, silky sheath with a beaded overdress.

"Does he have any ideas for the wedding?" Celia asked.

Natalie laughed. "No, thank goodness. I tell you, he's the perfect man. Won't even have any relatives at the wedding, so I don't have to worry about in-laws. It's going to be my show completely."

"That's good . . . I guess."

"Well, except that it leaves *everything* up to me. And the time crunch is murder! Angus wants to apply for residency as soon as possible, though. I suppose if anyone can plan a wedding in just over two months, I can, but it's still a lot of pressure."

The words *city hall* were on Celia's lips, but she dared not utter them.

Natalie frowned into the mirror. "I look like a refugee from Masterpiece Theater, don't I?"

"I was thinking Little Miss Muffet, actually."

Natalie quickly removed the dress and tried on a more traditional, fifties-type number. "Just wait till you have to go through all this, Celia."

"I don't think I'll ever get married," Celia said. "Let's face it. My life revolves around my job, a few friends, and a parrot." She clapped a hand over her mouth as yet another unpleasant realization dawned. "My God, I even have a lonely-old-lady pet!"

Natalie shook her head. "No, that would be a canary. And believe me, a canary would be an improvement over that disgusting creature you've got."

"Gazpacho's my baby!" Celia said with the defensiveness she always felt when anyone besides herself insulted her bird. Then, as Natalie eyed her pityingly, she added, "I mean, he's not so bad."

"I doubt very much that you have to worry about

being a lonely old lady," Natalie said. "Not while Fozzie Bear's around."

Celia bolted upright and eyed Natalie suspiciously. It seemed very odd that she would mention Davis after what had happened last night. "What's that supposed to mean?"

Natalie chuckled. "*Surely* you've noticed that the Foz likes you!"

Good grief! How could something that had managed to pass under her radar have been picked up by Natalie of all people? Natalie had the sensitivity and perceptiveness of a bowling ball. Had Davis been that obvious? "Why would you say that?"

"Because he's *always* around you."

"Of course. We're friends."

"Please! I just don't buy that men-and-women-being-just-friends crap. Not unless the guy's gay, which I assume Davis is not." She narrowed eyes on Celia. "He's not, is he?"

"No," Celia said, her face pinkening.

Natalie's mouth popped open. "Celia, *what* are you not telling me?"

"Nothing!"

Natalie planted her hands on her hips. "Don't give me that."

"I swear, nothing has happened. Nothing that I can really talk about."

Natalie gasped. "What can you not talk to me about? I've told you every sordid detail of my love life for the past decade."

"But that's just the problem. Nothing sordid's happened. I'd feel silly even mentioning it."

"Mentioning *what*?" Natalie asked, her thirst for gossip now at a fever pitch. "Don't hold back. Even if it's only phone sex, I want to know."

"It wasn't any kind of sex!" Celia explained. "It was just"—her words lowered to a mumble—"a kiss."

Natalie's brow puckered in confusion. "A what?"

"A kiss. He kissed me."

"When did this happen?"

"Last night."

"Last night?" Natalie practically screeched. "You mean you've known this guy for a year and he never has made one move on you till *last night?*"

Celia flapped her hands to try to get Natalie to tone it down. "I told you. We're friends."

"You don't find it insulting that a nongay man could hang around you all that time and not show the slightest interest?"

"He shows interest. Friendly interest. We hang out."

Natalie looked dumbfounded, as if such a thing had never occurred to her before. "Oh!"

"Platonic friendships, Nat. They happen."

"Not all that successfully, apparently. Sounds like your platonic friendship just hit the skids," Natalie pointed out. "What did you say to Fozzie after he pulled you into his arms for a steamy embrace?"

"It wasn't steamy," Celia said quickly. Then she amended, "Not *too* steamy."

Natalie's blue eyes glittered. "So . . . Is he a good kisser?"

As she flashed back to those few moments on her stoop, Celia felt her body go boneless on her again. She flopped back against the settee. "Yes!"

Natalie clapped her hands. "This is *too much.* So he kissed you . . . and then what did you say?"

"Nothing, really. He didn't give me a chance. He just walked off. And today we seem to be trying to pretend that it never happened."

Natalie's smile disappeared. *"That's* not good."

"Why?"

"Because if he's not saying anything more, maybe he's having morning-after regrets. It could mean he's changed his mind and has decided to punt you."

At those terrible words, Celia felt an instinctive shudder move through her. Surely not! Davis would never abandon her.

But maybe Natalie was just talking about abandoning her as a romantic interest. "But that would be okay. I like being just friends with him. I didn't mean to encourage anything more. You know he's not my type."

Natalie laughed. "That's where you're wrong. He's so your type you two could almost be twins. He's just not what you want."

Celia had never looked at it that way before. "How weird. I think you're right."

Natalie shot her a look that said, *Aren't I always?* Back to business, she took a last glance in the mirror. "I sort of like this one—it has a little Grace Kelly flair."

"I thought you didn't want to look like a movie royalty wannabe," Celia pointed out.

"Grace Kelly's different. She was movie royalty *and* real royalty." She smoothed out the full skirt and sighed. "I'll have to think about it, of course."

"Mm." Celia was still lost in thought. Could Davis really be closer to her dream man than, say, Ian? And if he was, why would it take Natalie, of all people, to point it out to her?

"Did you look at the bridesmaid dresses here?" Natalie asked.

Celia shook her head.

Natalie, surprisingly, seemed unfazed by her dereliction of duty. "Never mind. I gave them a quick once-over myself, and all they have are these bright, eye-popping colors that are so overdone nowadays."

Celia nearly vaulted out of her chair. "Really? Well, if you want me to take a look . . ."

Natalie waved a hand to stop her. "I was hoping for something more mellow."

"Pastel," Celia said flatly.

"But cheerful," Natalie assured her. "Believe me, I realize that with your looks we'll have to be careful not to get anything that makes you appear too wan. On the other hand, we don't want the bridesmaids to draw attention from me."

As if Celia could, even if her dress was made of neon.

When Celia dragged back to the office with a Thai takeout, she and Davis were still on cordiality over-drive. One would think they had only met that morn-ing. Celia tried to avoid eye contact all afternoon, but every once in a while she couldn't stop herself from tossing a sidewise glance his way.

Was Natalie right? Were she and Davis really suited? And yet, if even Natalie had noticed . . .

Of course, it didn't really matter if Davis was her dream man or not, since they were barely talking.

"I'm going home," she announced at five to no one in particular, though, of course, Davis was the one who heard her.

"See you tomorrow," he said.

"Tomorrow's Saturday."

"Right. I'll see you tomorrow morning." Seeing that she was drawing a blank, he said, "The Oregon Trail wedding. That's tomorrow, right?"

She all but smacked herself in the forehead. "Oh, right!" He still wanted to go with her to that?

His eyes widened, and he looked slightly embar-rassed. "Or if you wanted to go by yourself . . ."

"No!" she said quickly. It would be too awful to

uninvite him at this point—and it wouldn't make
sense. They were just friends.

Friends who had shared a moment of lip-to-lip in-
timacy.

Sheridan-Jones

The bride wore pale pink calico and a fetching
bonnet trimmed with daisies. Paul Jones, her
groom, wore a woolen suit and a nervous expression as he waited for her next to the black-cloaked
parson. The weather was boiling hot for late April,
and the wedding reporter was about to collapse
from sunstroke. . . .

Celia deleted the last line from her mental compo-
sition. Anyway, the heat wasn't bothering her so much
as the tension. It had been a long morning. She and
Davis had driven for an hour and a half, barely speaking the whole time.

This was getting crazy, she thought, only half listening as the bride and groom finally started exchanging
vows in front of their rustically dressed guests.

The ceremony was conducted in a field in a state
park where many thousands of nineteenth-century set-
tlers had ended their journey on the Oregon Trail.
Since the bride and groom were history buffs, at-
tempts had been made to make the setting look
authentic. The reception would take place by a covered wagon where the refreshments were kept. Guests
not outfitted in their own nineteenth-century garb had
been provided with parasols, stovepipe hats, long kid
gloves, and other props that would disguise their
anachronistic appearance.

Celia and Davis, who hadn't been spared the couple's period zeal, stood in the back of the crowd. She snapped a few pictures with the camera she'd had to argue to be able to use. But unlike most of the weddings they had attended together, they didn't exchange glances at things they found amusing. They didn't whisper to each other, or even look at each other.

This had to stop. She'd been practicing her love-you-like-a-brother speech again this morning, and the way things were going, she might have to use it. The spiel might sound condescending, but on the other hand, if she didn't say something, she was going to lose Davis's friendship anyway.

After the ceremony, she decided. She would tell him then. Get it over with.

Of course, it might be wiser for her to wait till they were in the car again . . . say, about a quarter hour away from home. That way, if there was going to be a scene, it would be a short one. The downside of that appealing if cowardly plan, though, was that it left so much more time for them to have this awkward thing hanging over them, unspoken.

The rings were being exchanged, and Celia snapped to attention. This was the part that always got her. The do-or-die moment when two lives were being inextricably joined. As many weddings as she'd been to, it never ceased to amaze her that so many underwent this same solemn, hopeful moment.

When it was all over and everyone was congratulating the bride and groom, Celia turned to Davis and caught him gazing at her. Hard. *Oh, no,* she thought. *It's going to happen again.*

Quickly, she opened her mouth to speak, but he cut her off.

"Please—"

"Wait," she said at the same time.

He suddenly looked so anxious, Celia had a sinking feeling in the pit of her stomach. This was killing her. She didn't want to hurt Davis's feelings. If only she could—

"I want to apologize," he said.

She blinked. "Pardon?"

"Apologize," he said more slowly. "For the other night."

"Oh!" She was going to attempt to pretend that she hadn't thought a thing of it. But of course that was ridiculous.

"It was an idiotic mistake," he said. "I don't know what got into me."

"Oh, well . . ." She looked into his eyes, which actually did seem sorry.

Idiotic mistake?

"See, I guess all your talk about feeling like a . . ." He snapped his fingers. "What did you call it?"

"An oink."

"Right. I guess that was getting to me, too." He shrugged. "I don't know—I just had this romantic impulse, but it was completely foolish."

"Gosh!" she said. And she hadn't said gosh in at least five years. She yanked off her bonnet and fanned herself with it.

"You won't have to worry about a repeat performance of my Don Juan act, I assure you." He smiled ruefully, and suddenly, she saw him transforming back into the old Davis. Her buddy. *Just joshin' you!* he might have said.

She felt like a dope. And for a bizarre moment, she wanted to channel the Don Juan Davis for just a few more minutes, so she could really talk to him. Had it really been an idiotic mistake, or had there been an honest impulse there?

"So . . . You do forgive me, don't you?"

She nodded quickly. "Of course!"

He laughed. "Good, because I don't think I would have been able to stand another two hours of silence in that car. I was considering hitching a ride home by covered wagon."

For the rest of the reception, she smiled and mingled and interviewed guests so that she would have a few cute personal anecdotes about the bride and groom for her column. Davis, as usual, managed to look as if he was having the time of his life. Striding about in his stovepipe hat and black jacket, he found something to talk about with everyone there. And after three fiddlers came out to provide the entertainment, he practically never missed a dance. The most amazing thing was, he even looked like an expert square dancer.

Who knew?

Toward the end of the party, he came over to her and bowed jokingly. "Feel like cutting a rug?"

She tilted her head. A waltz. She could handle that. The other dances the wedding party had been doing—reels and schottisches and whose elaborate steps she couldn't decipher—were beyond her.

Davis took her hand and led her onto the dusty patch of ground that served as the dance floor. She felt a strange lurch inside as their skin touched, much as she had the other night. But that was just a physical thing, she told herself. Like the urge to eat candy when it was sitting out in a dish. It didn't indicate real hunger.

And the minute Davis grinned down at her, she knew the world had been put to rights again. They were just friends.

Funny, though, that she'd never realized quite how tall her friend was. And though they had occasionally danced at weddings before, she'd never been so acutely aware of having his arm around her waist. Or clasping hands. Or having her hand on his shoulder, which felt surprisingly solid beneath his black coat. She'd given so little thought to Davis—except to think of what a comforting presence he was in her life— she'd always assumed that he would be sort of pillowlike. Instead, her hand pressed against normal firm muscle. She was tempted to poke at it, to see if there wasn't marshmallow filling underneath.

"Something the matter?"

She glanced up at him guiltily. "No, why?"

"You were looking at me funny," he said; then he laughed. "But I guess you're not used to seeing me dancing around in an Abraham Lincoln outfit."

"Hm, I was thinking you looked more like an undertaker. But you are quite a twinkle toes. I never knew."

"When I was twenty-three I fell madly in love with a woman named Kiki Swann. She ran a dance studio."

Celia blinked at him. "Kiki Swann?"

"I don't think it was her real name, but she actually was sort of swanlike."

Celia cleared her throat. It was hard to get used to the idea of Davis and someone named Kiki. "If she ran her own studio, she must have been pretty . . . mature."

"She was. That was part of her allure, I think. She had that 'older woman' mystique. Thoroughly unattainable. She was twenty-six."

Celia pursed her lips. "If this dance instructor was so unattainable, how did you learn all those moves?"

"I was in love, and she wouldn't give me a second look. So I took dance lessons for six solid months. I can waltz, tango, rumba, and fox trot. I even haunted the senior citizens' center where she had a folk dance session every Friday night."

"So what happened?"

He sighed. "It was no go. My ardor died of natural causes about the time we were learning the cha-cha."

"Hm."

He frowned at her. "What?"

"Nothing. I'm just a little surprised, that's all. You never mentioned this great love of your life."

"Because it's ancient history. I don't like to whine about the past."

Unlike you, he might have said. "I told you all about Ian. Was that whining?"

"That was happening while I knew you. You never told me about guys you went out with in college, for instance."

"College doesn't count. But you said Kiki was post-college," she pointed out. "So by that reckoning you should have told me about her."

He laughed. "But I told you, Kiki was never even my girlfriend."

"You said you were in love with her."

"But it was insignificant compared to other relationships."

"And you never told me about those, either!"

They were no longer moving. Instead, they were standing in the middle of the field arguing while couples swirled all around them. Celia looked around. So did Davis. They were drawing stares.

They glanced back at each other and laughed.

"Okay," he said, swinging them back into motion again. "Next week after work we'll go out for coffee. I'll bring my list and you bring yours. We'll swap stories and get all caught up. Would that satisfy you?"

She was too curious now to turn down that invitation. "You're on."

"Good, maybe you'll simmer down now!" The glimmer of humor in his eyes belied his cranky tone. It was just the sort of conversation they had always had—lighthearted, laughingly exasperated with each other. It was comforting to fall back into their easy patter.

Comforting, and a little frustrating, too.

Eight

Celia had met her friend Ellen when Ellen was leading a yoga class at her gym. Natalie always cited this as the reason that she would *never* take yoga.

Basically, Ellen was Natalie's nightmare. She possessed long, wavy brown hair which had never been touched by mousse or hair spray. Her favorite color was tie-dye. In the summer she wore Birkenstocks; the rest of the year she wore Birks with socks. Ellen was a determinedly positive person. She saw only the best in everyone. Meat had not crossed her lips in decades.

Whereas Natalie's ambition was to poke her spike heel into Jane Russo's skull as she clamored her way to the top of the TV journalism heap, Ellen's ambition was to achieve perfect inner peace. Unfortunately, Ellen had a sensitivity meter that quivered constantly toward the edge of hysteria, so peace was hard to come by. She tended to burst into tears over things like the melting polar ice caps. Celia had seen her get sniffly staring at the lobster tank at the grocery store.

Today, she seemed especially tense. Either something was wrong or she had skipped her tai chi this morning.

But then, Natalie looked a little on edge, too. Manic, even. Something didn't seem right—a hunch that was borne out when Natalie gave the waiter her order.

"I'll have a cheeseburger," she said.

Celia laughed. Surely this was a joke. It had been years since she'd heard Natalie order anything more substantial than a Caesar salad, and even then she usually made a show of picking out the croutons.

Then Natalie smiled at the waiter and added, "With fries. And could you please ask the chef not to skimp on the cheese?"

Celia nearly fell out of her chair.

"What?" Natalie asked her.

"All those fat grams!"

"So?" Natalie said, poking her menu back toward the waiter. "I'm hungry."

Ellen's long bead earrings swayed mournfully as she shook her head. "You're a journalist, of course," she told Natalie, "so I suppose I don't have to tell you what the beef industry is doing to Mother Earth, especially to her rainforests."

"I know, I know." Natalie fixed an irritated gaze on her. "Somewhere Deepak Chopra is boo-hooing over my food choices."

Lunch was off to a great start.

After Ellen had asked for a tempeh stir-fry over brown rice, Celia ordered a garden salad, feeling that she was keeping the lost spirit of Natalie alive somehow. But fifteen minutes later she felt deprived as she watched Natalie devouring her greasy burger while she was stuck picking at a plate of romaine lettuce.

"Okay," Natalie said to Ellen, "Celia tells me you have all sorts of information about where to have a wedding reception."

Ellen, having recovered from the Deepak Chopra comment, nodded. "I brought my list. Congratulations, by the way," she told Natalie as she pushed the piece of paper across the tablecloth.

"Thanks," Natalie said absently. She snatched up the paper and studied it.

"When do I get to meet your guy?"

Natalie shrugged. "He wanted to come to lunch today, but I think he's still a little jet-lagged."

"He should try ginger tea," Ellen said.

"Without scotch," Celia added.

Natalie's perfectly plucked brows rose imperiously. "What's *that* supposed to mean?"

"Nothing," Celia said quickly.

Natalie plunged a French fry into a puddle of ketchup and returned to the matter of the list. "Some of these places you have here are ones I've discussed with my mom."

"Really?" Ellen asked, apparently shocked that she might be of use.

"We're going to check out a bunch of them tomorrow," Natalie said. "You don't have anything near the water down, though. Mother heard about renting out a barge on the Willamette River."

"That sounds *so* romantic!" Ellen gushed.

It sounded like a disaster, Celia thought. For one thing, what if it rained? That wouldn't be pleasant.

Ellen was gazing dewy-eyed at Natalie. She seemed to look at her with new respect. "I just think it's so great that you're embracing joy now, Natalie. I really do."

Celia snickered. "I think all this has more to do with embracing Angus than embracing joy."

It was the wrong thing to say. Natalie, who had been just barely keeping her tartness bottled up, finally came uncorked. "Everything's sex to people who aren't having any," she snapped at Celia. "Or has Fozzie Bear turned up the heat?"

Celia felt stung. "I was just joking, Nat."

Ellen's eyes were owl round. "Did something happen with Davis?"

"No, not really."

Natalie cackled. "Davis kissed her."

"Oh!" Tears welled in Ellen's eyes. "I think that's sweet."

As Ellen lowered her head, Celia reached across the table. "Are you okay?"

She nodded. Then, seized by trembling, she shot out of her seat and ran to the bathroom. "I'll be right back!"

Natalie and Celia stared at each other in amazement.

"Granola girl is going psycho," Natalie said.

"You shouldn't have said that about Deepak Chopra," Celia scolded her. "You know how she feels about him."

"Oh, please. Who knows what upset her? She probably looked at my hamburger and thought of a baby moo cow somewhere losing its mother."

Celia stared at Natalie taking a big bite of burger and felt a pang herself. Unfortunately, it was a pang of hunger.

"Or maybe she's pregnant," Natalie suggested. "That would account for her twenty-yard dash to the bathroom."

"She seemed to get upset when I mentioned kissing Davis," Celia said. "Do you think there's something wrong with her marriage?"

"How could there not be? She married a New Age nut."

"It's hard for me to be objective about Lyle," Celia confessed. "I've never liked him."

"The only time I met him was at that party at your apartment. He cornered me and gave me this long lecture about how the media ignores the views of practitioners of transcendental meditation."

"He can be a little overbearing."

"A little? Are you kidding? I wanted to wad up his hemp shirt and gag him with it." Natalie leaned in. "This was right after the wedding, if you'll remember, and frankly, Ellen didn't seem that much in love. More like under his spell."

"She had her doubts about marrying him . . ."

Natalie sighed pityingly and popped another fry. "Some poor women just don't know when they're rushing headlong into a disastrous marriage."

"But it's been less than a year." Could a relationship head south that quickly?

Then again, look at her and Davis. In ten seconds a few nights ago, their whole friendship seemed to teeter on the brink of disaster. Thank heavens they had manage to salvage it.

Natalie scarfed down her last bite of hamburger and pushed her plate away. "Well, I know I'm going to be dying of curiosity about Ellen all day long, but I simply must run."

"Wedding stuff?"

Natalie leveled a quelling stare at her. "After our experience at the bakery, I'm not sure I should tell you the next time I run wedding errands."

Celia's mouth dropped open. "What did *I* do?"

"You insulted the man."

"No, I didn't. I just added up the cost of the ingredients and compared it to what he was charging for wedding cakes."

"You can't *do* things like that. It's like telling Picasso that the value of his work is whatever he spent on canvas and paint tubes."

Celia had to admit she had a point. "Okay, next time I'll factor in the cost of artistic expression."

Natalie tossed up her hands. "If you don't stop accosting these people with your damn notepad and your calculator, there won't be a next time. Merchants will bar the door when they see us coming. I might as well have asked Mike Wallace from *Sixty Minutes* to be my maid of honor."

The comparison held a certain appeal. And she was very eager to start investigating florists. "Well, *are* you going shopping?"

Natalie sighed. "No, I just have to get back to work. I can't allow myself to slack off for a single second now that I've got Angus living with me."

"But he's going to get a job, right?"

"Well, eventually. But he's an artist. He can't do just anything."

This seemed awfully tolerant of Natalie. But then, given that Angus was mostly a trophy husband, it shouldn't have surprised her.

Natalie clucked her tongue regretfully as she looked at the dessert menu, then scooted out of the booth. "See you soon."

A few minutes later, Ellen scuttled back out from the ladies' room and slipped into her place. She looked curiously at the void where Natalie had been. "What happened to Natalie?"

"She had to get back to work."

"Oh." Ellen forced a smile. "You know, sometimes she's really not such a bad person."

Like when? Celia was tempted to ask. But she decided it would be more diplomatic to change the subject. "Are you feeling better?"

"Oh, sure. Fine." Despite her words, Ellen looked thoroughly embarrassed and miserable.

"No, you're not. There's something wrong."

"No there's not. Except . . ." Ellen's face crunched

up, and her shoulders began quaking. "Except my life is falling apart!"

Celia leaned forward. "What's happened?"

"Nothing! Nothing except that I'm a wreck!"

"Is it Lyle?"

In response, Ellen barked out a single syllable that Celia interpreted as a yes.

"Did you two have a fight?"

"No, of course not. There's nothing to fight about." The laugh Ellen emitted was as bitter as Celia had ever heard from her. "Lyle is always right, and I'm always wrong. Period."

"He always did have a sort of . . . controlling personality."

Ellen nodded. "You know those little plastic silverware holders that fit in a drawer?"

Celia was jarred by the unexpected question. "With different dividers for knives and forks and spoons."

"Right. Well, last night I accidentally put a teaspoon in with the soup spoons."

"Wait," Celia said, trying to comprehend this. "Are you saying Lyle got upset by some misplaced cutlery?"

"Upset? He completely *freaked out*. He spent the whole night cleaning out all the kitchen cabinets and putting them back together again."

Celia absorbed this for a few moments. "Ellen, that's seriously messed up. That's like something out of *Mommie Dearest.*"

"I know . . ."

"How long has this been going on?"

"Eight months."

"Eight months? That's how long you've been married!"

Ellen was silent for a moment. She looked truly astonished. "Is that all it's been?"

Celia groaned. No wonder she was such a nervous wreck. "Oh, Ellen. This is terrible."

"I know. Poor Lyle!"

Celia nearly flipped her lid. It was so like Ellen to bend over backward to see things from another person's perspective, but this was ridiculous. "Poor Lyle?"

Her friend shrugged. "Back when we were dating, I just thought he was a neatnik. But he's really sort of . . . well . . ."

Celia gladly supplied the word. "Insane." She didn't know what else to say. The man was obviously an obsessive-compulsive, but she wasn't sure she could counsel Ellen to leave him just for that. "He needs therapy."

"I've told him that."

"And what does he say?"

"That there's nothing wrong with him. That it's me not doing things the logical way that causes all our problems."

Celia considered the situation, then looked her friend in the eye so Ellen would know she was making a sincere offer. "Look, I can't give you marital advice, but if you need to, you can come stay with me. Any day, any time. For as long as you need."

"Thanks, Celia." Ellen sniffled. "But that sounds really awful."

Celia laughed. "Is it me, or Gazpacho?"

Ellen lifted a hand to her lips. "I'm sorry, that's not what I meant. You're really nice to offer. I only meant that it would be like being homeless. I'd be starting from scratch."

"Sometimes a fresh start is just what a person needs."

Ellen shook her head. "You don't know how I envy you! You're so alone, so solidly single."

Celia managed a tight smile. "I'm afraid that might be my life's crowning achievement."

"Is there something wrong with your neighbor?" Davis asked Celia as she let him into her apartment. "As I was coming up the stairs he cracked open his door and gave me a sort of creepy stare."

"He's probably just making sure you aren't smuggling in any Dean Martin records."

"Why?"

"We had an altercation a while back. Actually, I think he's about ready to kill me." She gave him an up-and-down look that made him self-conscious. "Say, what happened to you?"

"What do you mean?" He knew what she meant, though. He was wearing a new shirt. To get away from that gaze aimed straight at his chest, he strolled over to Gazpacho's cage and said, in his best accent, *"Hola,* Gazpacho."

The parrot blinked at him contemptuously. Davis contemplated petting the bird's head, but decided against it. He was a writer. He needed his fingers to type with.

"You ducked my question," Celia said. "Where did you get the spiffy shirt?"

"I picked it up on Twenty-third Avenue yesterday."

Her brow puckered. "Twenty-third Avenue? You mean you went into one of those trendy little shops and bought it yourself?"

He grinned. "I'm twenty-nine years old now. I've learned to dress myself."

He noticed that she hadn't dressed up for their meeting. She was wearing her most worn-in weekend jeans, the ones with the fraying patch at the knees. An old, gray T-shirt layered under a checkered purple-and-white shirt were apparently intended to complement the workman look. Ancient high-top sneakers completed the outfit. The effect was sort of a hybrid between Debbie Reynolds in the *Tammy* movie and Josephine the plumber.

The hell of it was, she was still gorgeous to him. Just looking at her made his chest tighten and his breathing feel shallower. He wanted to pull her Salvation Army-clad body into his arms and bury his face in her unwashed hair. Maybe it was the Nebraska in him, but he would rather see her like this than dolled up in a thousand-dollar evening gown. Or a skimpy bikini. Or a sexy negligee.

Okay, maybe he'd opt for the negligee. . . .

"Davis?"

When he snapped to, her head was tilted, and she was eyeing him as a nurse might watch a particularly unstable mental patient. "Sorry. What were you saying?"

"Are you going somewhere after this?" She was watching him sharply.

"No, why?"

"Oh . . . you know, the cool shirt. I thought maybe you had a date or something."

Would it never occur to her that *this* was his date? He tried to keep from sagging against Gazpacho's cage. It was important to play this cool. "I just bought this new shirt, so I thought I'd break it in." He chuckled listlessly as he gave it a second glance. It wasn't anything outlandish, just a burnt orange shirt of a rough cotton-silk fabric. "Guess it's a good thing that I did. It obviously makes me stick out like a new haircut."

"I didn't say that." Celia crossed to her little kitchenette. The tiny apartment was filled with the welcoming scent of coffee. When Celia had suggested meeting at her place, he'd jumped at the offer. Portland was a city second only to Seattle in its proliferation of coffee shops, so that it seemed almost subversive to actually stay at home and make a pot themselves. Also, it gave him a chance to be in a more intimate setting with her.

Much good it was doing him.

Yet he was determined to soldier on in his quest. His first foray into romance with Celia had been an abysmal failure, of course, but he tried not to be too discouraged. They had patched up their friendship. If he just stayed the course, maybe another opportunity would present itself and he wouldn't botch it.

Or maybe he'd make a fool of himself all over again.

"I always pegged you for the type who had drawers overflowing with clothes given to you as gifts from your parents," Celia continued. "Manly plaid shirts from Sears."

He chuckled uncomfortably. "What have you been doing? Going through my drawers?"

She squinted in concentration. "In fact, I don't think I've seen you shop for anything besides stuff before."

"Clothes are stuff."

"No, they aren't." She handed him a steaming mug. "Stuff is CDs. Towels. Second-hand chairs."

He took a fortifying dose of caffeine. "It's just a shirt. I wouldn't have worn it if I'd known it would set off all these bells and whistles."

Of course, the shirt was supposed to draw attention. Only right now it didn't seem to draw good attention—it just gave Celia an opportunity to dwell on his usual ordinariness.

Soldier on, he thought.

"It looks good on you," Celia said, a compliment which would have been appreciated more if it had come five minutes earlier.

"Thanks." Time to change the subject. "What have you been up to?"

She frowned. "Not much. I had lunch with Ellen and Natalie yesterday."

"Referee duty. How did it go?"

"I think Ellen's having trouble with her marriage. It really makes me wonder."

"About what?"

"Marriage. It seems like all my friends are rushing into doomed marriages. Look at Ellen—and now Natalie!"

"Not so long ago you seemed to envy them."

"I know. I even felt that way a few days ago, when Natalie looked so happy. But then I started thinking . . . She never mentions Angus unless I ask her about him. I haven't seen him since I helped haul him down to her car the night he arrived. And all the reports of him have been how he's still adjusting. The man could get into *The Guinness Book of World Records* for the longest case of jet lag."

"Natalie's a big girl. She can more than take care of herself."

"That's what we all said about Ellen, too. We all disliked Lyle, but we said she was an adult, she said she was in love, she knew what she was doing . . ."

"You can't police people's relationships. Especially people as difficult as these friends of yours." He noticed a sheet of paper on the counter between them. "What's that?"

She looked at the sheet and then back up at him, startled. "The list."

"What list?"

"You know . . . the *list.*"

He vaguely recollected the conversation from the wedding when she seemed upset that he hadn't enumerated the women in his past for her. As if he wanted to talk about other women with Celia. "Oh. I thought you were just sort of kidding around."

Though, of course, he couldn't help eyeballing her list. One of the four names written there, a sportswriter from the paper, elicited a stunned reaction. He goggled the name in utter stupefaction. "You went out with *Kevin Muldoon?*"

"Two years ago," she said.

"Yeah, but . . ."

She blinked up at him. "I don't see anything terrible about Kevin."

"He's not your type!" Davis said.

"What are you talking about? He's got that twinkly Irish charm."

"Yeah, like a leprechaun. Not to mention, the little guy is the biggest lech in the building."

"I know that!" she said defensively. Then she had to add, sheepishly, *"Now* I know that."

"And your list is so short! Four measly names, and one of them is Kevin Muldoon!"

"It's just a rough draft." She snapped the paper out from under his nose. "It's no fair looking if you don't have your own list."

"Don't worry, I've seen enough." She'd gone out with Kevin Muldoon and given *Davis* the cold shoulder? That was beyond depressing.

Celia took another sip of coffee. "The whole point of this exercise was for me to see your list. You're the one who's the mystery man."

He laughed. Some mystery. Apparently he didn't have as much mystique as Kevin Muldoon.

The doorbell buzzed. Celia's brow drew into a frown. "I'm not expecting anyone."

"Maybe your downstairs neighbor wants you to put on some music."

"Very funny." She grabbed her keys off the kitchen counter.

She was gone for only a few minutes—the duration of which he spent looking at Kevin Muldoon's name and cursing the man. When Celia reappeared, he had every intention of bringing up the subject of the sportswriter again, but one look at her panicked face and he knew he wouldn't get around to it. There was trouble.

She stepped inside and was followed by Natalie, and then an older woman who looked like Natalie except about twenty-five years older. "Davis, I don't believe you've ever met Mrs. Glass, have you?"

The formidable woman, who was wearing a salmon pink pantsuit with black piping and black slings that made her tower over even Davis, marched toward him, hand outstretched. She wore a tight smile. Next to her, Natalie looked almost meek, and definitely nervous. Davis had never seen the newswoman so lacking in self-confidence before.

He shook Mrs. Glass's hand, which was cold, thin, and strong. Like metal. "How do you do, Mrs. Glass?"

"Please!" the woman boomed. "Call me Babs." She seemed completely out of proportion in Celia's apartment. As she looked around the place, her nose wrinkled as if someone had left a rotting fish under the couch. She gave Gazpacho's cage an especially disdainful once-over. "You're right, Natalie. This will *never* work."

Celia and Davis exchanged puzzled glances.

"I beg your pardon?" Celia asked.

"For the shower," Babs said, sweeping through the apartment and peeking into doors, as if trying to see if there was more of it.

Celia followed her with her gaze. "What's wrong with it?"

Gold bracelets jangled as Babs planted her hands on her slender hips. "Not a thing, dear, if you were hosting a reunion of the Lollipop Guild. But stuffing forty-six shower guests in here would be impossible."

Celia's gulp could probably be heard in Canada. "F-forty-six?"

"That's all *I* could come up with," Babs said. "No, we'll definitely have to try to find another place to have the shower." Her gaze honed in on Celia. "I don't suppose you've worked anything out yet?"

"Well . . . I was going to make my grandmother's lemon bars." She chuckled nervously. "Guess I'll have to double the recipe."

Babs let out an impatient sigh and pulled a legal pad out of her handbag. "Well, that's one more thing we'll have to tend to."

Natalie looked at Celia almost apologetically. "I'm sure we'll work out the details on the shower . . ."

"Well, it's a cinch the details won't work themselves out," Babs told her daughter. "Honestly, Natalie, I can't believe how lackadaisical you are."

Celia choked on her coffee. "She is?"

"There are a million things yet to do." And Babs's tone strongly indicated an intention to do at least a few hundred of that million here and now.

"Davis and I were just having coffee," Celia said.

Babs gazed disapprovingly at their mismatched mugs. "That sounds very *restful*. Natalie and I were taking in reception venues today."

Celia was beginning to look trapped. Then she grinned. "How nice! Unfortunately, since Natalie was just telling me that she didn't want to take me shopping anymore . . ."

Natalie clawed at her in despair. In fact, she looked as if she might cut off the circulation on Celia's left arm. "Couldn't you come with us?" she pleaded.

"Please? Mom and I have been together *all morning*. We could use another person's opinion."

Relenting to her friend's obvious desperation, Celia glanced apologetically at Davis.

He jumped up. "Sure, let's go."

Babs, however, seemed hesitant to have him along. In fact, she seemed to view him as some kind of gnat she would have dearly loved to swat away.

"Oh, but we'd bore you, I'm sure."

"No way," Davis said. "Nothing I'd like better. In fact, I was going to suggest hitting a really great place I know." He held the door open for them as they piled out.

Babs eyed him doubtfully. "What place is that?"

"Target. I hear they've got this great program called Club Wed . . ."

Babs responded with a frosty silence, but he heard Celia and even Natalie snicker as they clopped down the stairs.

"You don't have to do this," Celia muttered to Davis as they slid into the backseat of Babs's Volvo.

"Are you kidding? I wouldn't miss it for the world," he responded in a low voice. "How often does modern man get to witness an outing with mother and daughter tyrannosaurs?"

Celia looked over at those twinkly eyes and felt a pang of tenderness well up in her. At least, she *hoped* it was just tenderness. She certainly didn't want it to be anything more, now that Davis had assured her that he thought their kiss on the stoop had been just a major blunder on his part.

Just an idiotic mistake.

She had to admit, having Davis along as they trooped through many of the same places that she'd been to with Natalie already made the whole day more bearable. And the day was a long one. They sped from hotel to hotel, searching for the perfect place to hold the wedding and reception. After what seemed like hours, they stopped briefly to grab something to drink.

Babs pulled out that legal pad again, which had a page jammed full of names; she presented it to Celia. "Those are the names I've come up with so far. I've included phone numbers, of course, and addresses. Naturally, you'll need to get the invitations out ASAP. We can pick some of those out today." She shot Natalie a look. "Put that down in your day planner, won't you? It might slip our minds otherwise."

Celia swallowed. "Oh? Are we doing other stuff today?"

Babs looked as if she might fall off her chair. "Are you mad? We're just getting started! We've got materials to look at."

"Materials?"

"For the bridesmaid dresses."

"Mother decided we should have them made," Natalie informed her. "That way my cousin in San Francisco can make her own."

Celia felt a moment of panic. "You don't want *me* to sew a dress, do you?"

Davis laughed. "Celia was ready to take a dress back to Goodwill rather than sew a button that had fallen off. I had to convince her that she didn't need a sewing machine for the task."

Babs's eyes narrowed on Celia. "You bought a dress at Goodwill? To wear?"

Celia nodded.

Natalie explained, "Celia's into thrift."

"Mostly because my employer's into thrift," Celia said. "It's a matter of a lowering tide beaching all boats."

Babs blinked at her. "Oh! I see. You're joking."

Celia and Davis exchanged confused glances. "Well, sort of," Celia said. "I'm not one of the hundred neediest cases. I can afford a bridesmaid dress."

Babs sagged with relief. "Thank goodness!"

Their first stop after the break was the river, where Babs was inspecting a barge she'd heard was available for renting. Barge Bonanza ran tours along the Willamette River and rented the boats out for parties. Babs had read about them in a magazine and had decided it would be perfect for the rehearsal dinner.

"Excellent!" Babs declared, clapping her hands together as she inspected the long, narrow boat. Natalie tripped after her, nodding. "This could be *very* elegant."

Celia didn't see it. The thing wasn't a yacht as much as a flat-bed tug. The gray weathered wood did not inspire romance. The boat didn't provide much protection from the elements, either. "What if it rains?"

Babs turned on her. "It wouldn't *dare.*"

Celia and Davis looked at the ropes tying the vessel to a dock. "Once those ropes are freed, we'll be captives," she whispered to him.

Davis laughed. "Don't kid yourself. We'd be captives on dry land, too. I'm already beginning to feel like my will has been broken by Babs."

Celia was laughing as Natalie rushed up to them. "I think this could be great, don't you? If you imagined lights, and a band, and maybe polished the thing up a bit . . ." Her voice trailed off, and she sent them a pleading look. "Don't you think?"

"It would different," Celia allowed.

Natalie looked as though she would grasp at anything so long as she could stop running around with her mother. "That's right!"

The final stop, after they discovered the stationer

was closed and they couldn't order shower invitations, was the cloth store. By this time Davis, bless his heart, did look as if he might go insane with boredom. Luckily, he was given something to do when Babs decided he would make a perfect stand-in for Angus to model material.

"Is Angus going to sew his own tux?" Davis asked.

Babs pursed her lips. "No, we're making him a kilt."

"A *kilt?*"

"Isn't that a *great idea?*" Babs gushed. "It will look so authentic!"

Unfortunately, they discovered McDougall plaid was rather dull. So Babs decided that a more colorful Buchanan plaid would serve just as well. "Maybe it's not technically the right little pattern, but who will *ever* know the difference?" she asked, draping fabric around Davis.

While they were busy, Natalie and Celia perused bolts of bridesmaid dress fabric.

Natalie seemed to have a homing device inside her that went directly for pastel taffeta. Fingering a particularly nauseating color called pale puce, she nodded toward Davis. "What happened to our muppety little friend? He looks different."

Celia swung around and stared at Davis, who was being swathed in wool by an enthusiastic Babs. Maybe it was the distance, or the new shirt he was wearing. He *did* look different. More angular. As though he'd thinned out. She wouldn't call him buff, exactly. Just less Pillsbury Doughboyish.

"Has he been sick?" Natalie asked.

Celia couldn't make her brow unfurrow. "I don't think so . . ."

"Must have been," Natalie insisted. "Probably that stomach bug that was going around a few weeks ago."

Celia shook her head. "I don't think so . . ."

Natalie fixed her with a level stare. "Celia, you're repeating yourself, and you're certainly not being informative." She looked at Davis and nodded. "I'm right. He's losing his Fozziness. Plus he was very sweet to come along and put up with my mom this way."

Celia felt that tug in her chest again. "I just don't understand him," she said in frustration. "I thought we were such buddies, but I keep finding out odd things about him. Stories of old girlfriends are starting to pop up, and he's being secretive."

Natalie's eyes lit with interest. "Ooo, about what?"

Celia remembered the list incident and bit her tongue. Nevertheless, considering the way Davis had sneered at her head count, what might his have been if he'd brought his own list? His dodginess made her wonder whether he'd left a whole trail of broken hearts all the way from Omaha to Portland.

"He's just been acting a little odd lately."

"Odd, how?"

"Well, look at that new shirt. He looks almost . . ." She could hardly make herself spit out the word. *"Spiffy."*

"Hm." Natalie tilted her head and smiled at her. "Has it occurred to you that he might have been trying to be spiffy for *you?*"

Celia exploded in a laugh that turned several heads. "Not likely! Did I tell you what he told me at the wedding?" She didn't wait for Natalie's go-ahead. "He told me that kissing me had just been *an idiotic mistake.* His exact words. That he liked me too much as a friend to ruin that relationship. That it definitely wouldn't be repeated. He's hardly been what you would call amorous since then."

"That's good."

Celia shot her a quizzical glance.

Natalie's eyes widened. "Well, you said you just wanted to be friends, right?"

"Sure."

"Then, it's good that he's not trying to make passes at you, which, as you said yourself, is not very friendly behavior."

"Well, yeah, but . . ."

Celia didn't know why she was arguing. Natalie was right. She'd gotten what she wanted. They were back to their old relationship . . . except that Davis just wasn't his old self, somehow.

And even though she didn't want him to be in love with her, it wasn't exactly flattering that he found it so easy *not* to be in love with her.

After spending the day chasing Natalie and her mom, they decided to wind down by going to a movie. They had a little extra time, so Davis buzzed them by his place. Too late—right as he was unlocking the front door, in fact—he remembered the exercise machine lurking in the living room.

"What *is* that?" Celia said moments later, circling the thing in his living room.

Davis felt suddenly as if he'd left his dirty laundry out. "It's an exercise machine."

"Corky's?"

"Well . . . not exactly."

She tapped her finger against her chin as she regarded him. "So *that's* what's going on! Natalie noticed that you looked a little different. She said so. Said you looked good."

Natalie had noticed? But not Celia, apparently.

She was very curious about the machine, especially the little steps on the back. She climbed up and began doing the stair exercise. "This hurts," she said with approval, as if pain were a good thing. Then she turned and looked him up and down. "So you've lost weight?"

"Ten pounds."

She stopped stepping. *"Ten pounds?"*

He nodded.

She eyeballed the machine with renewed admiration. "And you've been using this thing for how long?"

Davis was torn between pride and agonizing self-consciousness. "Oh . . . about two weeks, I guess."

She laughed dismissively. "No, really. How long?"

"Two weeks," he answered. "Really."

Her face went pale. "Wait just a minute. You're telling me that you've lost ten pounds in two weeks?"

"Thereabouts."

She hopped down from the machine and stood rigid before him. "What have you been doing? Working out every night for five hours after you get home?"

"Not really. I just do about twenty minutes a day."

It was *the wrong* thing to say. The next thing he knew, Celia was almost wailing in despair. "Twenty minutes a day! You've got to be joking!"

"I don't see what the big deal is."

"No, you wouldn't. Because *you* haven't spent the past eight years going to aerobics and tae-bo and pilates three times a week, not to mention yoga classes. For an hour! Have you ever done a box step class for an hour?"

He didn't even know what a box step class was.

"It's exhausting!" she raved. "Not to mention, they make you listen to old Spice Girls songs in these places. I've been slaving away in misery at the exercise racket for years and years and *nothing's happened*. I haven't lost any weight. Not a single pound."

"That's because you don't need to lose weight," he pointed out.

She gaped at him as if he'd gone mad. And suddenly she was coming at him, sidling crabwise and pinching a section of her outer thigh through her jeans. "Look at that! Just look! Do you know how long that hunk of flab has been living there on my leg?"

He would have laughed, but he was afraid that would really set her off.

"Ten years! Ten years I've been dragging these around with me. And *you* do twenty measly minutes a day for two weeks and suddenly, *presto*, you're Charles Atlas!"

A throat cleared, and she and Davis turned to find Corky in the doorway, staring at them with a perplexed expression. "Um . . . Am I interrupting something?"

"No, come on in," Celia said. "I was just showing Davis my saddlebags."

Corky smiled excitedly. "Did Davis show you the new machine?"

As if she could possibly have missed it. "Yes."

"I found it two weeks ago," he boasted.

At the mention of the time frame, Davis was afraid Celia was going to explode again. Instead, she flopped onto the couch. "I hate men."

Davis and Corky looked at each other.

This was not the reaction Davis had been hoping for.

Nine

"Two weeks!" The next day, Celia was still ranting. "Can you believe it?"

"Well, he *does* look better," Natalie said, scooping a blob of banana cream pie onto her fork. Celia had been a little surprised when Natalie had suggested meeting at Papa Hayden's, an old restaurant known for its decadent desserts. But apparently Natalie had been craving sweets.

"*I* can't believe it," Celia grumbled.

Her mouth full of custard and meringue, Natalie said something that sounded like *war way*.

"*What?*"

Natalie gulped down her load with effort. "Water weight. First-time dieters always drop weight fast at first. It's a cinch." She shoveled in another piece of pie. Twenty-four hours after her day with Babs, she looked as if she couldn't consume calories fast enough.

Celia, on the other hand, could only pick at her éclair.

"Plus, men have it easy," Natalie continued. "They're just made more efficiently."

"I guess so."

"It's true! We've talked about that lots of times on the morning show." She licked meringue off her fork.

"Diet stories are always ratings gold—so many poor slobs in this world, I guess!"

Celia sighed. "I never would have pegged Davis as a guy who would suddenly become weight obsessed. He's not vain."

Natalie's lips twisted into a smirk. "This is America. Everyone's weight obsessed. That's why I'm glad I found Angus. He says he doesn't like bony women. He says he likes a woman who has something he can hang on to."

There was something very creepy about that phrase. Although maybe it explained why Natalie wasn't so worried about calories these days.

Her friend chuckled as she shoveled in another bite of pie. "Can you believe it? He says I'm *too* thin. As if there could be such a thing!"

"Where is Angus? Didn't he want to come along?"

"I think he's out with the guys this afternoon." Natalie smiled. "Isn't that cute? I think it's great that he has so many friends and is assimilating so well. And to think, I was worried that Angus would have a hard time adapting to life in America, that he'd be a burden. But really, he barely seems to need me at all."

Celia wasn't sure having an absentee fiancé was anything to sing about. "This is good?"

"I don't want some clinging vine who's going to be jealous the moment I want to step out of the house," Natalie said, "or a guy who's forever bugging me at work. Angus and I are able to give each other space."

Celia looked at the happy glow in Natalie's newly filled-out cheeks and felt a pang of envy. Maybe Natalie was right. At least she had *someone.* She wouldn't approach old age alone. Or with only a cranky parrot.

"Celia, what's the matter with you?"

She shrugged. "Nothing."

Natalie narrowed her gaze on her, concerned. "You aren't mad because of my mother and I barging in on you yesterday, are you? I swear to you, I tried to cut her off at the pass, but she insisted on going to your place."

"It's not that."

"Well, then what?" Natalie asked her. "You're acting very strangely. And you're not eating your éclair."

She lifted her hands in a gesture of hopelessness. "I just can't stop thinking about Davis. I wonder if he's going through a midlife crisis."

Natalie rolled her eyes. "At twenty-nine?"

"These strong mid-Western types mature faster than the rest of us."

Natalie laughed. "You're right. He probably seemed middle-aged by the time he hit puberty."

Celia nodded. "Maybe his twenty-nine feels like thirty-nine."

Natalie tapped her fork against her pie crust impatiently. "You've *got* to stop dwelling on this guy, Celia. You never gave him a second thought until he kissed you, for heaven's sake."

"Yes, I did," Celia said. Then she realized, no, she hadn't. Not a romantic thought, at least.

Was she thinking about him that way now?

"I'm just concerned," she said to assure herself as much as Natalie.

Natalie frowned in concentration for a moment, then brightened. "Look, Angus has all sorts of buds I can try to set you up with. His soccer crowd is perfect for you—very international."

Celia tried to perk up at this news, but it was a struggle. Who was she kidding? She was no soccer moll. She had to force herself to go to the gym three times a week. "I don't think I'm the jock type."

"I'm offering to introduce you to a bunch of muscled-up foreign babe magnets, and you're not interested?"

"Well . . ." Look what a few muscles on Davis had done to her. Thrown her for a loop. And she couldn't help thinking that she probably wouldn't have that much in common with Angus's people. "What would we talk about?"

Natalie looked at her as though she had finally gone around the bend. "Since when do you care about that?"

Since . . . She wasn't sure. She hated to think that everything was being dated from the moment Davis kissed her. But it was beginning to seem that way.

Natalie frowned at Celia's untouched éclair. "Aren't you going to eat that?"

Celia shook her head.

Natalie pulled the plate across the table and dug in.

At the end of the next weekend, perhaps in a state of madness, Davis confessed to Corky that Celia was his dream woman.

At first, Corky was horrified. "*She's* the babe you've been losing sleep over? *Celia?*"

Celia and Corky didn't exactly get along like a house afire. Still, Davis was a little surprised, and defensive, at his roommate's reaction. "What's wrong with Celia?"

"Well . . . nothing. But the way you were carrying on, I was expecting somebody hot. Jennifer Lopez." Corky shook his head. "This . . . This is something else entirely. This is a delicate problem you've got here."

"I know."

"This is like, falling in love with your best friend or something."

"I know."

Corky's expression was uncharacteristically grave. "And I hate to tell you this, buddy. But when a woman starts showing you her fat deposits, it's not a good sign."

"I know." It was so obvious Celia thought of him as nothing but buddy material. "I feel like I'm deceiving her now. I've got the hots for her, but I'm lying about it."

"You're not lying. You're just not telling her."

"But I tried to tell her, and it didn't work. I botched it. Now I'm just trying to pretend to be her friend."

Corky propped his elbows on the table and steepled his fingers in a fatherly way. "Let me get this straight. You've been hankering after this woman for nigh on a year. Then you told her you were in love with her?"

"Well, not exactly. I kissed her."

Corky moaned. "Oh, man. What a mistake!"

Davis glowered at him. "Just a few weeks ago you were saying things like 'slip her some tongue.'"

"Yeah, but you didn't tell me it was *Celia*." Corky shook his head, pondering this new angle. "Okay, I see what we're working with now, and I'm ready to help. You kissed her, and *then* she said she just wanted to be friends."

"Well, not in so many words . . ."

"But she made it pretty darn clear. Am I right?"

Davis nodded. Having the situation spoken aloud made his hopes grow as dim as the flicker of intelligence inside Corky's brain.

"You want my advice?" Corky asked him.

Davis feared he'd taken too much of Corky's advice already—and where had it gotten him?

Unfortunately, Corky didn't wait for his permission to speak. "Give up."

Davis's heart sank. In fact, it felt as though it might have hit bottom. "Give up?"

"Why waste your time? Why chase this impossible dream, tilting at windmills like Don Whatsawhosit, when there are plenty of fish in the sea? Hey, Portland's crammed with beautiful women." He grinned. "And I mean beautiful, not just girl-next-doorish things like your little friend."

"What are you talking about? Celia's beautiful."

"Okay, okay. You've got a weak spot there that's going to be hard to remedy. The point is, you need to get back into circulation again. You're in a rut. You're rusty. Not to mention, you must be horny as hell."

Davis shook his head. "I'm not ready for cruising bars."

"Why not?" Corky asked. "It's tons of fun, and I guarantee that I can take you to some places where you'll meet a woman who'll take your mind off Celia."

"That would be a miracle."

But Corky was as good as his word. Two hours, three bars, and three whiskey sours later, Davis was feeling no pain and seated at a table with an acquaintance of Corky's named Kyra. She was very pretty, with streaked blond hair, light brown eyes, and a slender body that given the skimpiness of her outfit, she was obviously proud of. Her top didn't cover her midriff, and the only word Davis could think of to describe her skirt was *insufficient*.

The trouble was, he could barely think of a thing to say to this pretty young thing. Maybe because his brain was in the early stages of pickling. He strained to come up with an opener.

"So, Kyra, what do you do?" he finally yelled over the music.

"I dance."

"Ballet?"

She cackled. "Not exactly. You go to basketball games?"

"All the time."

"Well, heck!" Kyra's face brightened a few hundred watts. "You've seen me, then. I'm a BlazerDancer."

Davis's smile was a frozen slash on his face. After months of conditioning by Celia, just hearing the word BlazerDancer gave him a knee-jerk urge to laugh. And yet, he couldn't. Kyra seemed very nice. And maybe she was talented. He'd never really paid that much attention to the expertise of the BlazerDancers, now that he thought about it. Who could see them from the second tier? It was more the *idea* of them that he and Celia had chuckled about.

"That's great," he finally choked out.

"I enjoy it lots—but it's pretty hard work. We have to work our butts off practicing our routines all the time."

"I'll bet." She certainly had the butt to back up that assertion.

She leaned on her elbows and grinned up at him. "And what do you do, Davis?"

"I write for the *Portland Times*."

Her brows knit together. "News stories?"

"No, I write a feature three times a week. Stuff about people's opinions on topical issues."

She gasped. "Oh, my God. I knew you looked familiar! You're Davis Smith, as in *Davis Smith?*"

He nodded, a little taken aback. He rarely got this kind of extravagant reaction. Kyra was beaming at him as if she'd just discovered he was Mick Jagger, as in *Mick Jagger*.

"This is so incredible! I read you *all the time*. You're, like, famous!"

"No," Davis said modestly.

"Yes! *I* knew who you were. That makes you famous in my book." The gaze pinned on him was so bright and unblinking that it made him a little uncomfortable. "Your columns are so fun! I read them right after Ann Landers and my horoscope."

"Thanks, that's flattering." It *was* flattering; he had to work to not show how much. "You must be recognized a lot, too."

"Nah." She shrugged. "You know how it is. The lights dim, the strobes come on. We hop around really quick, then run off the court. We're more, like, a unit than individual stars. *You* didn't remember me, did you?"

He felt guilty now. "Not exactly."

She smiled knowingly, and not at all bitterly. "Try not at all." She looked at him for a moment and laughed. "Hey, I know what! Next game, why don't you meet me courtside during halftime? You and Corky. You can see things close up, and then maybe after we can go out for a drink."

"Sure, sounds fun," he said.

It wasn't for another few minutes that he realized that he'd sort of agreed to go on a date. And it wasn't until later that night, when he was back at home brushing his teeth, that he realized what had seemed so strange about the way Kyra had looked at him. That bright intensity in her eyes.

She liked him.

In a rare switch Monday morning, Davis was scurrying in late, while Celia had already proofed Tuesday's wedding announcements and was now perusing the latest memo from the Warden.

She nodded toward the identical sheet of paper on his desk. "Big fun at the office this week."

The memo, which had a cheesy clip-art clown next to the *Portland Times* letterhead, announced that the next employee group birthday party would be held on Thursday. Marie couldn't stand the idea of her staff taking time out to celebrate every person's birthday individually, so every three months she would dip into her department's budget to spring for a sheet cake from Safeway. With one eye on the clock, Lady Bountiful would allow precisely one hour of merriment during lunch hour on the appointed day. Typically these affairs had all the sparkle and gaiety of a forced march.

Davis pointed to the clown. "She went all out this time."

Celia nodded. "Not only that, but I've begged her for an extra few dollars to go out and buy a half pound of good coffee with. We're really going to live it up this month."

"Those April-May-June birthday people have all the luck." Davis collapsed into his chair with a laugh.

He looked tired to Celia. "I was a little worried about you," she confessed. "You didn't call after *The Sopranos* last night."

He slapped his desk in disappointment. "Damn! I forgot to tape it."

"Tape it?" *He hadn't watched it?* Neither one of them liked to miss an episode.

"Yeah, I went out for a little while. Corky and I cruised bars."

Celia laughed. "A little research for a column on barflies?"

He turned to her with a dead-serious look in his eye, despite the fact that his lips were turned up in a smile. "No, just socializing."

"Oh." She strained to banish the avid curiosity from her tone. "Have a good time?"

"Yeah, I did. We ended up at this place on the east side called O'Reilly's. It was kind of nice."

And with that, he got to work.

So did Celia. Except every once in a while, she would suddenly discover she was tapping her pencil eraser on her desk and mentally combing through everything Davis had said. What puzzled her was the lack of details. Davis never scrimped on descriptions of evenings he'd had before. He was always willing to talk about Corky, if nothing else, and the dumb things that Corky inevitably did. She imagined bar hopping with Corky would have afforded plenty of opportunity for him to witness his roommate at his bone-headed best.

And yet, what had he said? He'd said he'd had a good time. That the bar was kind of nice. Not very descriptive.

Socializing? To her, *that* had definitive connotations of rubbing elbows with the opposite sex. Why was he being so vague?

She scribbled down the one detail he'd mentioned—a place called O'Reilly's. A pub, she guessed. It sounded like a man's kind of place. Maybe a sports bar. Though, of course, women could have been there, too . . .

She felt a sharp stab in her gut, almost like betrayal. How could it be that her dependable best friend was turning into a bona fide man of mystery?

Celia never was able to squeeze any more information out of Davis about his night on the town. As the week wore on, their talk was the usual: shop talk, Corky talk, Natalie talk. Strangely enough, Davis didn't

mention the Blazers, even though there was a big
game coming up against the dreaded Lakers.

She was hoping to get a chance to talk to him again
about his Sunday night socializing during the office
birthday party. The event was held, as usual, at Marie's
desk, where on top of her usual stack of papers and
proofs and memos, the Safeway sheet cake bore the
cheery icing message, *April-May-June: Time Marches On.*

Celia shook her head as she stared at the thing.
"Good to see you're not holding back on those warm
fuzzies, Marie."

"What do you think this is?" Marie asked. "A kindergarten?" Then she clapped her hands—much like
a kindergarten teacher, Celia noted—and called the
party to order. "Okay, folks, let's get the ball rolling
here. We don't have all day."

Most of the office shuffled over and surrounded the
desk. Davis wasn't there, and his absence made Celia
uneasy. He was usually front and center at office get-
togethers. But nothing about Davis was usual these
days. He'd shown up at work this morning in a brand-
new shirt-tie combination, looking as though he'd
stepped out of a Helmut Lang ad.

After all assembled rendered a lackluster performance of "The Birthday Song," the birthday people
blew out the candles. Then, with the swift precision
of a samurai, Marie hacked up the cake. Celia could
tell her boss was already getting impatient; even as she
handed out slices, her brain was probably tallying up
wasted man hours.

Celia's purchase of the half pound of dark roast
Hazelnut turned out to be a rousing success. The first
pot had disappeared seconds after the last bit of water
had dripped through the filter. People sucked at their
mugs as if they had never tasted real coffee before.

"See, I told you they'd like it," Celia boasted to her boss.

Marie pursed her lips. "Wimps! Back in my day we drank Folgers."

Celia almost quipped that back in Marie's day women were wobbling around on platform shoes, until she realized that she herself was wearing a pair right now. And before she could come out with another quip, maybe about Tony Orlando, Marie was already barking orders at her again.

"Snowden, didn't you buy enough of that Hazelnut stuff for two pots?"

"Three, if you don't mind it on the weak side."

"Well, I do. Go brew some more, and make it strong." Marie surveyed her worker bees, who were now gathered into little clumps at various desks, scarfing down cake and gossiping. "The natives are getting listless. We need to do something to counteract the cake. I don't want the entire department to be in a sugar coma this afternoon."

Celia saluted and marched off to the coffee room. As she hurried through the door, she nearly ran smack into Davis and Olga, their heads bowed together in conversation—apparently humorous conversation. Laughter died abruptly when Celia entered the room. The silent treatment gave her a decidedly fifth wheel feeling.

So *this* was why he'd skipped the party, Celia thought.

"Sorry for interrupting," she said. "I have orders from the Warden to make sure the office doesn't fall asleep on the job after her birthday spectacular." She took the little bag of coffee out of the refrigerator and measured it out as carefully as gold dust into a new filter.

"Doesn't Davis look sharp, Celia?" Olga asked her.

Celia gave his new outfit a second glance. "Sharp as the pins in my Marie Warden voodoo doll."

"No, I really mean it," Olga said.

As if I didn't, Celia fumed. Did Olga think she was the only person around here who appreciated Davis? Even if her tone had been a little flippant, Davis knew she was sincere. She and Davis sniped at each other all the time. It was just good mean fun. Life would be very dull if all she did was deliver simpering comments to Davis like Olga was doing. Dull for her, at least. Davis might enjoy it.

In fact, he looked as though he was enjoying Olga's company very much. Celia tapped her foot as she waited for coffee to brew. She could have left the room and given them some privacy, but for some reason she stubbornly planted herself in front of the sink.

"Anyway," Olga said when it was obvious that Celia was not going to budge, "I know a place where you can buy a really cool leather jacket."

Celia snorted. Davis in a leather jacket? "Are you going to start trying for the Hell's Angels look next?"

Olga eyed her as if she were some sort of monster. "Good quality," she told Davis, as if Celia hadn't spoken at all. "My ex-boyfriend used to work there."

"Ex?" Davis asked.

"Didn't you *know?*" Olga asked the question as if her life had been splattered all over the *National Enquirer.* "Eddie and I split up."

"I'm sorry," Davis said. "I hadn't heard. I guess I've been preoccupied lately."

Celia zeroed in on that word. *Preoccupied.* What—or whom—had he been preoccupied with? And how recently was lately? Did this have to do with Sunday night and his missing *The Sopranos?*

"It wasn't too bitter, I hope," Davis told Olga.

"Well, Eddie's sort of bitter, I guess."

Celia had to work hard to keep her guffaws down. Naturally, Olga would believe that her ex would be the person broken up about the split.

When Olga left—and it seemed she would drone on about Eddie forever before she finally did leave—Celia shook her head. "Incredible."

Davis grabbed his mug off the drying rack by the sink, giving Celia a whiff of musky cologne. Not soap, she registered very definitely, but cologne. Calvin Klein.

"What's incredible?" he asked as he poured himself a cup.

"Olga!"

He sent her a mystified glance. "What was the matter with her?"

Celia rolled her eyes. "She was flirting with you, Davis. Flagrant flirting, I would call it. Don't tell me you didn't notice."

"No, I didn't."

Celia was happy to interpret for him. "And all that stuff about Eddie was just meant to pull at your heartstrings."

Davis busied himself pouring coffee. "She was just telling me about her breakup because that's what's on her mind. Naturally that's what she would talk about."

"The point is, why would she talk about it at such length *to you?*"

"Because I was listening?"

"Very attentively, I noticed." Celia tilted her head. Did Davis have a thing for Olga? Was that what was brewing?

Davis smiled in a sort of far-off way as he stirred his creamer into the good coffee.

"So," she asked, glad to change the subject, "do you think the Lakers are going to whup up on us tonight?"

His face darkened to a deep crimson color. "Oh, I . . ." He sipped at his coffee. "Celia, I don't know how to say this, but . . ."

Not that he had to.

He had given the spare ticket to somebody else.

The realization doused her in disappointment, but she managed to laugh breezily. "Davis, I certainly don't mind if you take somebody else to the games. You've been awfully generous, but I know you've got other friends."

"It's just Corky," he explained quickly.

Her good-loser smile froze on her face. "Corky?" He was taking *Corky* instead of her? Corky—the irritant—now rated higher than she did?

"Yeah," he stumbled on. "See, it was a last minute thing. We're meeting some people there, and . . ." He smiled at her, relieved. "I'm so glad you don't mind. It's been bugging me all week."

"Of course I don't mind," she forced herself to say. As if that wasn't lie enough, she took it one step further and told and out-and-out whopper. "I wish you'd told me earlier. See, the thing is, I promised Ellen I'd go out with her tonight, so I've been feeling a little uncomfortable, too."

He reached out and patted her arm. Sort of like her third stepfather had at her college graduation. It was a relieved, you're-on-your-own-now-kid sort of pat. "You're a good sport. I'll give you a play-by-play tomorrow over lunch."

"Sure. Have fun."

"Thanks," he said.

They parted ways as if they weren't going to be spending the next four hours five feet away from each other. And suddenly Celia wished they weren't. Of course, she meant what she'd said to Davis about it being good for him to share the wealth of his season tickets. She wasn't his only friend by a long shot.

But for some crazy reason, she felt spurned.

The fact of the matter was, she was going insane. Her apartment walls seemed to be closing in on her, and after a quick call to her grandmother—who, she was reminded, was having a perfectly busy life without her—Celia actually got into an argument with Gazpacho. He almost gobbled down her finger as she was giving him a peanut. She yelled at him, and he squawked back. When he petulantly tossed his peanut across the room, she thought they would come to blows. Then she felt almost melodramatically contrite and spent five minutes assuring Gazpacho in a cooing voice that his mommy would never lay a hand on him in anger.

That was when she decided she *really* needed to get out of her apartment. Immediately. Just as she was about to pick up the phone, it rang. She lunged for it as if it were a lifeline. She didn't care if it was Natalie calling to debate wedding cake options. She would be grateful to hear from anyone.

"Hello? Is this Thelia?"

Well, almost anyone.

"This is Elton Nedermeyer."

"Elton. Hi." She tried to inject some friendliness in her voice. "What's up?"

"Oh, nothing."

"Your voice sounds better."

"Yeah, my tongue's practically back in working order." He chuckled as Celia fought off a shiver. "I was calling to thee if you wanted to go out."

"Oh, sorry, I'm busy," Celia blurted out.

"But I didn't tell you when."

"This weekend's crammed for me," she explained.

"But I thought we could go out tonight."

"Oh, no." She could have kicked herself as the impolite words flew out of her mouth. "I mean, oh, damn—I've already got something going on tonight."

"Oh." There was an extended pause while Elton tried to discern whether she was lying and she tried to figure out whether she'd gotten away with it. "Well, okay. Just thought I'd check. I know it's incredibly last minute, but a client gave me these Blazers tickets . . ."

Her breath caught. "Oh!"

"But if you're busy . . ."

"Oh, well—"

"Maybe thome other time."

After he'd rung off, Celia collapsed in a chair. She didn't know what made her feel worse—lying to Elton, or realizing that she was such a depraved basketball junkie that she would possibly gone out with Elton if she'd known in advance that he had tickets. She was one step removed from being a complete hoops whore.

"This is ridiculous," she muttered. There were a million productive things she could be doing. She looked over at her bookcase and decided tonight was the night to alphabetize. She set diligently to work on her fiction shelf.

She dawdled forever over her six Jane Austens. What was the appropriate way to arrange them—by date written? Alphabetical order? Order of preference? That last option created a whole new conundrum. Which did she like better, *Pride and Prejudice* or *Persuasion?*

The phone rang again when she was five chapters into the latter book. She jumped, startled, and stared at the phone. Should she get it? It might be Elton. A half second before the machine was due to pick up, she gathered courage and dove for it.

She was in luck. It was Ellen.

"What are you doing?" Ellen asked.

"I'm . . ." She almost said cleaning, but then she looked at the shelf she was supposed to be tidying up, which was virtually unchanged. Except that now her Jane Austen collection was strewn across the floor. "Actually, I need to get out of the apartment."

Ellen had obviously needed to get out, too, because she acted as if they couldn't meet soon enough for her taste.

"Where should we go?" was all she wanted to know.

"Well . . ." Celia felt silly for even thinking it. Devious, actually. But she couldn't help herself. "I've heard of this place on the east side called O'Reilly's . . ."

"Great!" Ellen said.

"Have you ever been there?"

"No, but it sounds great."

Ellen was already parked at a table, nursing a drink, when Celia got there. O'Reilly's was a dark-paneled, Americanized version of an old Irish pub. The big TV over the bar announced that the place catered to sports nuts. The air was a little smoky, and everything seemed to be coated with a film of grease. Ellen, who seemed to be holding her breath and was wearing something that looked like a gauze turban around her head, managed to appear even more out of place than she usually did.

"The snake charmer look," Celia said in greeting. "I like it."

Ellen grinned up at her. "I was so glad you were free. The minute I hung up the phone I dashed out the door."

Celia took in the room again. It brought to mind

drunken poets on their last legs. "This might not be your kind of place," she said, satisfied now that she had checked it out that Davis had just come out here on a lark . . . or maybe Corky had talked him into it.

"That's okay!" Ellen chirped. "I'm enjoying myself."

As much as she could without breathing, maybe. Celia wiped off a bench seat with a napkin and sat down.

An elfin-faced waiter came over and asked them what they wanted. Celia looked around for a menu. There wasn't one. "What do you have?"

The elf sighed impatiently. "Fish and chips or burgers."

"Oh." She looked anxiously at her friend. Ellen was out of luck.

Or so she thought. But Ellen was already piping up, "I'll try fish and chips."

"Ellen, no!" Celia cried, horrified. She looked imploringly at the waiter. "Don't you have anything with some nice fresh greens? Or tofu?"

The waiter looked at her as if she'd gone insane.

Remembering Ellen crying in front of the lobster tank, Celia started to sling her purse over her shoulder. "We'll go somewhere else."

"That's okay, Celia. I *want* fish and chips."

"But you can't!"

"It's okay," Ellen assured her. "I eat meat sometimes."

At that startling revelation, Celia felt as if the earth were rumbling beneath them. "Since when?"

Ellen cut an uncomfortable glance toward the waiter. "Aren't you going to order, Celia?"

Celia ordered a beer. She'd lost her appetite completely now. When the waiter was gone, she asked Ellen, "When did you fall off the wagon?"

"Oh . . . I have a few times, actually," Ellen confessed. "Sometimes after Lyle's gone to sleep, I'll sneak out to Burgerville."

Ellen, scarfing down burgers on the sly? Fast food?

Her friend eyed her anxiously. "Do you think I'm a terrible hypocrite?"

Celia gulped. "No . . . Well anyway, *I* can't throw stones. But . . . Why?"

Ellen lifted her shoulders. "I don't know. I just get so nervous sometimes, and something comes over me."

"It's Lyle," Celia guessed. "He's turning you into a closet carnivore."

Her friend sighed sadly. "We had a terrible fight over the laundry today."

"The laundry?"

"He doesn't like me to do it. Everything has to be just so. Socks go in one load, shirts in another. I accidentally threw a pillowcase in with the towels, and Lyle went berserk. He just started raving about how incompetent I am. Then I think he felt guilty, because he told me that I'm indecisive and that I let people step all over me."

Apparently, he didn't have qualms about stepping all over her himself.

"Maybe I *am* a little passive-aggressive," Ellen allowed. "I know I should be a stronger person . . ."

Just strong enough to gather up the gumption to leave your husband, Celia thought, biting her tongue. "Don't start criticizing yourself, Ellen. You're living with an anal retentive. He needs to go to therapy."

"Oh, Celia!" Ellen cried in frustration. "You're so lucky to be single still. I wish I were!"

"This is a switch. Natalie tells me I ought to be panicked that I'm not married."

"Oh, no," Ellen assured her. "Being alone, life is so much simpler. I wish . . ."

"Ellen, you've got a strange look on your face. Like Farrah Fawcett before she kills her husband in *The Burning Bed.*"

Ellen chuckled uncomfortably. "You just don't know how fortunate you are, Celia. You've still got a chance to meet someone normal and a have a little family with someone you love."

"So do you."

She shook her head mournfully. "No, it's all over for me. I'm through with love—it's just brought me grief. Besides, to meet someone normal you have to be normal, and I'm afraid I just don't qualify." She had tears in her eyes. "Oh, I wish I'd listened to you, Celia!"

"To me?"

Ellen sniffed. "The day of my wedding you told me that if I had any doubts, I should call it all off. Remember? You said that Lyle was a controlling jerk and that I'd be just as well off, if not better off, without him. You said I was letting myself be bullied into something *he* wanted, not what *I* wanted."

"I said all that?" Celia was stunned at how right she'd been. How wise. It happened so rarely.

But now, for Ellen's sake, she wished she'd been dead wrong.

"And the terrible thing was," Ellen continued, "I knew it was all true at the time. It was just that everything was set, you know? I had the beautiful hemp dress my friend Rumela had worked on for months, and the incredible food, and all my family from all over the United States were there. I just didn't have the guts to admit I'd changed my mind."

"It sounds like you've changed your mind now."

Miserably, Ellen nodded. "I guess I have. I just don't

know what I'm going to do. Sure, it's easy to say, 'Leave your husband,' but it's not that simple. I'd be leaving parts of me behind. Not just things I own, but pieces of me who fell in love with Lyle in the first place. I'm afraid of being a divorcee, I guess. It sounds so . . . used."

Celia felt as if she were swimming out of her depth. "If you need help . . . anything I can do . . ."

"You're a great friend!" Ellen said, obviously trying to switch emotional gears. She wiped her eyes and blew her nose into her napkin and plastered on a determinedly cheerful smile. "I haven't even asked how *you've* been."

Celia wasn't sure how to answer the question honestly, so instead, she informed Ellen of how Natalie was, and about how work was, and even about how her grandparents were. She told her about trying to write about the incredible expense of weddings.

Ellen frowned. "My wedding wasn't expensive."

"Well, maybe not *too* expensive . . ."

Ellen shook her head. "Not expensive at all. Rumela made my dress, I prepared most of the food myself, and since Lyle's a shutterbug anyway, we didn't have to hire a photographer."

"Yeah, but then you ended up with wedding pictures with no groom in them." It had made for a peculiar wedding album—Ellen and all the attendants in front of the yurt, Ellen feeding herself the taste-free wedding cake, Ellen dodging bird seed as she dashed toward the VW Microbus to begin her honeymoon. Anyone would think she was some sort of psychotic who had staged a wedding for herself.

Sort of like Natalie, Celia realized with a shudder.

"Lyle just didn't trust professional photographers to get it right," Ellen said. "And it *did* save us money." She frowned. "But how can you really talk about the price of something like a wedding? People see it as a great event, a once-in-a-lifetime thing. It's a beautiful part of life."

Wasn't this the woman who was just saying that she should have never left her yurt and married creepy Lyle? Had *that* been such a great event?

Celia opened her mouth to respond, when all at once Ellen's gaze focused on the door behind her. "Look who's here!"

When Celia turned to look, it felt as if the breath had been sucked out of her lungs. She was staring at the door, wondering if what she was seeing could possibly be a mirage. Davis was holding it open for Corky and two women. Young women. Pretty women.

And they were dressed like BlazerDancers.

Ten

He was betraying Celia.

That was the way Davis had felt all night, even when he was watching the basketball game with Corky. It just hadn't seemed right. For one thing, Corky ate all the wrong foods during the ballgame. No Yo-Cream cones for him. Instead, during the first quarter he had scarfed down an awkward boat of nachos that he had to balance on his knee. The second quarter he downed two Budweisers, and then brought back from the concession area a vat of buttered popcorn that kept spilling everywhere whenever he clapped, or worse, cupped his mouth to yell down at the court.

Davis found himself shooting Corky annoyed sidewise glances, wishing he would somehow magically transform into Celia.

And though Davis felt an odd twinge of anticipation every time the BlazerDancers took to the floor—he could pick out Kyra only from her hair—he couldn't help remembering all the times he and Celia had shared laughs at the dancers' expense. Now he felt guilty for ever having laughed. On the other hand, he felt equally guilty for not laughing now.

He just felt guilty.

But this was crazy. He and Celia were just friends—she'd made that abundantly clear. He needed to get the message through his thick skull and get on with his life. Go out with Kyra. End of story.

That was what he'd decided five minutes before he stepped through the door at O'Reilly's and came face-to-face with Celia. She looked flabbergasted, hurt. . . .

Betrayed.

What is she doing here? As he stood in suspended animation, Davis's heart pounded against his ribs. He felt absurdly embarrassed to be seen with his perky, pretty date in her flared black spandex pants and low-cut, midriff-revealing sports bra with the Blazers logo on it. Also, he felt the ungenerous urge to push Kyra back out the door or throw a bag over her.

But it was too late for that. He'd caught Celia doing a double take at Kyra. After a series of elaborate facial contortions, she managed to put on a big grin and waved.

Davis smiled, too, and elbowed Corky in the ribs. "Look who's here."

Corky glanced over and muttered, "Oh, no. This is the last thing you need, bud." As his gaze scanned the other person at the table, Corky's forehead pinched into a mass of lines. "Lord have mercy! What's that thing in the turban?"

"That's Ellen, Celia's friend." If anything, his spirits sank lower. Even he had difficulty dealing with Ellen sometimes; a conversation with her could be like being smothered by a cloud of good karma. She and Corky would be a train wreck. "She's very nice . . ."

Corky smirked. "She'd have to be, with a wardrobe like that."

Kyra tugged on Davis's sleeve. "Is something wrong?"

"No," he said quickly. "Why?"

She nodded in the direction of Celia and Ellen.

"Aren't you going to go say hello to those women who are grinning and waving at you?"

Should they sit with Ellen and Celia? Just stop by the table briefly? Go somewhere else as fast as they politely could?

As Davis sank into a quagmire of indecision, Corky called an audible, "Here's the deal—we sit with them for a second, then bolt, okay?"

"Okay," Davis said, glad to have the decision making taken out of his hands. Then another wave of guilt hit him full force. He never thought the day would come when he'd want to shun Celia. It seemed disloyal.

Still, as he stumbled toward Celia's table and caught the look in her eye, he saw the wisdom in Corky's plan. Oh, Celia was all friendly smiles. But amusement was just beneath the surface as her gazed flicked over Kyra's black spandex outfit and her long hair with glitter dust in it. No doubt she was witheringly assessing Kyra as an airhead.

"What a surprise!" Celia's voice was so aggressively friendly it nearly blew them backward.

"Hi!" Kyra boomed back, obviously seeing nothing out of the ordinary in Celia's manner.

Davis suddenly felt as if he were throwing a bunny rabbit into a coyote den. He opened his mouth to say hi, too, but instead, he heard the curt words, "Celia, what are you *doing* here?"

"You told me about this place, remember?" she said. "So Ellen and I decided to check it out."

She introduced Ellen to Corky. Corky mumbled introductions for his date, Stacy, and Kyra. Ellen slid toward the wall on her bench seat. "Why don't you all sit down?"

While Corky and Davis blanked out in an etiquette

panic, Kyra and Stacy plopped right down next to Celia. "Sure! I'm just *dying* for a burger," Stacy said.

"Me, too," Kyra chimed in. Then she turned to Celia and explained, "We're dancers."

"I guessed that," Celia said. "BlazerDancers, right?"

Was he mistaken, or was that brow of hers subtly arching his way?

"All that moving gives me a *ferocious* appetite," Kyra said.

"Mm," Celia said. "I've seen you in action."

Kyra glanced up at Davis and Corky. "Aren't you guys going to sit down?"

Corky and Davis reluctantly scooted in over on Ellen's side.

Davis was now boomeranging between embarrassment and resentment. Didn't it just figure that Celia would insinuate herself into the first date he'd had in a year? As if being in love with her weren't obstacle enough to his dating other women—she had to physically show up and ruin everything. As soon as Kyra finished her hamburger, he was whisking her out of there.

"I've heard a lot about you," Ellen said to Corky.

"Really?" Corky's tone revealed minimal interest. Probably he was eager to get Stacy, a luscious redhead, out of there, too.

"Celia was telling me that you love to cook."

Celia had probably been telling Ellen that Corky was a disaster in the kitchen, but Ellen's sweet voice and clear blue, friendly eyes made it seem as if Corky had a *cordon bleu* reputation.

"I'm mostly just self-taught," he admitted modestly. "But someday I wouldn't mind making a career of it. Right now I just wait tables."

"I'll bet that's a great way to learn the business,"

Ellen said. "Especially if you want to open a restaurant someday."

Corky's breath caught. "Well, see, *that's* my dream. To own a restaurant. Maybe not too different than this place, as a matter of fact."

"I like this place," Ellen said.

"Do you? I want mine to be like an Irish pub, only more Italian, maybe. You know, like an Italian pub."

"Are you Italian?"

"Well, no," Corky admitted, "but Italian food's my forte. Not that I mean to brag or anything. Do you ever watch the Food Network?"

"I don't have television," Ellen said. Then she added quickly, "But there's a cooking show on public radio now."

"Really? I'll have to check that out."

Davis almost lost it. Corky, listen to public radio? He probably thought *All Things Considered* was a quiz show.

"You should have a big dinner sometime," Ellen suggested enthusiastically, "and invite everyone over to see what you can do. I would love that."

"Would you?" By this time, Corky was so enthralled with Ellen that he didn't seem to hear the groans coming from Celia and Davis. Or the glare Stacy was shooting Ellen's way.

Celia quickly attempted to change the subject. "Why don't you tell us all about yourself, Kyra."

Kyra looked at her quieter friend self-consciously. "Well . . . There's not much to tell."

Just enough, it turned out, to get them through waiting for their food and eating it. About an hour, Davis calculated. An interminable hour of watching Celia, with that polite, slightly amused smile on her face, nod patiently as Kyra took them through the saga of her life year by year. Through grade school and the

Brownies and her first moments on stage in her school's Thanksgiving play. Through junior high school, during which she excelled at social studies and twirling. And then, of course, the miraculous day she signed up for dance instead of P.E. in high school—the day that changed her life. From then on her existence had been a whirl of classes, competitions, intensive summer camps, and auditions, auditions, auditions.

As each minute ticked slowly by, Davis sank a little farther on the bench seat. He sucked down two beers and began to have churlish thoughts. Why couldn't Kyra stop jabbering and eat her stupid hamburger so they could get out of here? Why didn't Celia say something to cut this short, instead of sitting there looking fascinated?

Oh, he knew what Celia was really thinking. She thought he was pathetic. Kyra was only twenty-two—practically jailbait! He hadn't even known that much of her biography before tonight. In fact, he couldn't remember now what they had talked about Sunday night that had made him want to see her again.

Which made it all the more surprising when Kyra's narration wound down and Celia said, "Well, it sounds like you and Davis have a lot in common!"

"We do?" Davis couldn't help blurting out.

Celia gazed at him evenly. "Dancing."

Kyra gasped and turned on him with a playful huff. "You didn't tell me you're a dancer!"

Celia feigned amazement. "Davis is a ballroom champ from way back."

Kyra's expectant smile faded slightly. "Oh. *That* kind."

"Don't you like ballroom dancing?" Celia asked.

"Well, I'm more into jazz and hip-hop. And I took a little ballet, of course. It's not really the same thing at all. And that ballroom stuff—well, it's kind of old-fashioned, don't you think?" She glanced at Davis. "No offense."

"No, of course not." He felt like an antique.

Finally, finally, they all decided it was time to leave. Unfortunately, just as they were about to get up, Kyra decided she needed to take a slightly disgruntled Stacy—who had been completely ignored by Corky—to the powder room for a pow-wow. Which left just the four old folks at the table. Corky and Ellen had moved on to cultural topics. Corky was telling her about *Xena, Warrior Princess.* They were so absorbed in each other that Celia and Davis might as well have been alone.

"Okay," Davis said, turning to Celia. Better to get her scathing summing-up of his date over with. "Let me have it."

Celia frowned. "Have what?"

"Tell me what you think of Kyra. I know you want to."

She shrugged. "She's very nice."

She sounded sincere, but she often did before she hurled a verbal dart. "And?"

"Well, aside from being a little long-winded, I found her sort of frank and funny."

"You did?" Davis asked, confused. Frank and funny wasn't an insult. Her tone sounded genuine. Maybe she was just waiting for his guard to be down before she zinged him.

"Oh!" Celia straightened as if something just occurred to her.

Here it came. The whammy. Davis braced himself.

"She's also very pretty," she said.

"Pretty," he repeated dully.

"But I guess you noticed that."

"Well, yeah . . ."

She laughed. "You look disappointed, Davis. Do you want me to say that I didn't like her?"

"No, of course not."

"Good, because I think you two make a cute couple." She winked at him. "Maybe you can teach her to appreciate your old-fogy way of dancing."

When Stacy and Kyra came back to the table and they all stood up to leave, Davis felt slightly off balance. The beers, he told himself. But he knew that wasn't really it. What had thrown him for a loop was Celia. How could she say he and Kyra made a cute couple?

Depression swamped him. To think he'd felt guilty—almost as if he was betraying Celia. But Celia obviously didn't give a hoot. Since that first smirking glance at Kyra—which could have just been a matter of surprise—she hadn't shown so much as a twinge of jealousy. But what did he expect? This was why he was out with Kyra in the first place.

He drummed his fingers uneasily.

Even her saying she liked Kyra only served to make Davis all the more critical of his date. Frank? Try tactless. Funny? What had Kyra said that was funny?

What was he doing with this woman?

"What is he doing *with that woman?"*

Ellen didn't answer. She looked as though she was in a stupor of some kind.

But Celia's question was merely rhetorical. She knew what Davis saw in Kyra—a fantastic, twenty-two-year-old body. Of course, Kyra seemed nice . . . but not exactly Davis's type. What could they possibly have in common?

Ellen continued to somnambulate toward Celia's

car. She looked like a good candidate to get run over by a bus.

"Earth to Ellen."

Her friend turned to her with dewy eyes. "Bruce Springsteen . . . He's country western, isn't he?"

Ellen tended to be culturally illiterate about anything that wasn't mentioned in *Mother Jones* magazine. "No, he's rock," Celia explained. "Corky has a sort of fetish about him. It's really irritating."

"Irritating? I can't believe that—he seems like a very positive type of person."

"Yes. Positively irritating. To put it in your language, if Corky were ever reincarnated, he'd come back as a sore tooth."

Ellen's brow furrowed in disbelief. Then, as they closed in on the car, she hesitated. "Would you mind if I went home with you, Celia? Just for a nightcap or something?"

Celia frowned. Nightcap? Her apartment wasn't exactly the Stork Club. She didn't stock much liquor besides a bottle she had designated her desperation vodka. If Ellen wanted a drink, they could go to a bar. But since they had just left a bar, she assumed that what Ellen really wanted was to spend the night on her couch. When she had offered her home as a refuge to Ellen, it wasn't an empty gesture.

"Sure, hop in the car."

"If it's too much trouble, I'll just go home," Ellen said.

"And face Lyle the laundry freak? Screw that. It'll be fun to have a little company."

Clomping footsteps sounded behind them, and they turned to see Corky running down the sidewalk. "Hey!" He stopped next to them. His face was flushed, and his breath came out in gaspy puffs.

Ellen snapped back to life. "Well, hi!" she said, as if they had been separated for months.

He sent her a dopey grin. "I thought maybe I'd take you home. You know, in case there's any trouble with Lyle."

"You told him about Lyle?" Celia asked, amazed. They really must have gotten acquainted. Of course, they had had plenty of time, since they had gabbed straight through Kyra's "A Dancer Prepares" monologue.

As she gazed up at Corky, Ellen looked as though she just might swoon from gratitude. "That's so nice of you! But it's okay. I'm going home with Celia."

Disappointment crossed Corky's face until a light bulb blinked on over his head. "Say, I know. I could go with you guys."

Ellen turned to Celia. "You said you wanted company."

Not that much company, she almost retorted. Besides, there was the matter of Davis. What if he intended to take Kyra back to his house? If there was ever a time Celia wanted Corky in Davis's house being a nuisance, it was now.

"Aren't you forgetting about Stacy?" she asked him.

"Oh, yeah." Disappointment settled over him, and he shrugged. "Well, it was just a thought. Maybe some other time."

"Bye, Corky," Ellen said, her tone wistful.

"Bye, Ellen."

This two-ships-passing-in-the-night tone was too much.

"Good night, Johnboy," Celia muttered, giving Corky a gentle shove back toward his real date.

As they watched him shuffle off, Ellen was all admiration. "Isn't he something?" she gushed. "He seems so . . . so *normal!* Don't you think so?"

Celia shook her head. "No, I don't. But I do think Cupid's arrow has pierced a significant number of your brain cells."

One week later, Ellen was still in Celia's apartment. Instead of going home, she'd simply gone to the thrift store down the street and picked up clothes. The woman was bringing the art of avoidance to new heights.

"Don't you think you ought to *tell* Lyle you've left him?" Celia asked her one night as they watched a rerun of *A Woman of Independent Means*. Celia was hoping that Ellen might take a few tips in developing backbone from Sally Field.

"Why?" Ellen asked.

Apparently, Sally Field wasn't working.

"Well . . . Maybe it would give your marriage some sort of closure."

Ellen pinned her with those big, innocent eyes of hers. "You're tired of having me here, aren't you?"

"No."

And the strange thing was, it was the truth. Sure, the apartment was a little crowded. But it was sort of nice not to be alone when she got home in the evenings.

Ellen nodded thoughtfully. "Okay. Maybe tomorrow I'll call Lyle and tell him I'm staying with you for a while."

Celia frowned. She wasn't sure she liked the sound of that.

"A short while," Ellen said.

"I don't care how long you stay," Celia insisted, "but don't you think it should be a clean break? Something more definite?"

"I'd rather give it to him in stages," Ellen replied.

"Maybe this way, it won't really occur to him that I've actually moved out for good. And after he's been in the house alone for a while, with no one moving things out of place, maybe he won't even want me back."

In other words, she was hoping to do a slow fade.

The hardest part of this new arrangement, Celia found, was mornings. Two people getting ready for work in the tiny apartment was sort of a squeeze, so one morning Celia tried waking up with the birds and trooped off to work early. She grabbed a bagel at the deli and found herself at work just after seven.

She'd never been to the office this early. There were actually a few people around the building, although on her floor it was just her and Marie.

Did the woman really never go home?

Spotting Celia coming out of the elevator, Marie practically fell out of her chair. "Stop the presses! Snowden arrives early!"

Celia groaned.

Her boss straightened up and eyed Celia suspiciously. "What's the matter? What are you doing here?"

"I just decided to see what went on at a paper at the crack of dawn."

Marie smirked. "Seven-fifteen is *not* the crack of dawn."

"It's as close to it as I ever want to be."

"Okay, so you're not here to win any attendance awards. Could you actually be planning to get work done?"

Celia had never missed a deadline, and Marie knew it. She even had this week's "Unions" column, covering two people who met during jury duty at traffic court, sitting in her in-box. "No, I'm going to do something even more shocking. I'm going to sit down and read our newspaper."

She went to her cubicle and flopped down into her desk chair.

The trouble with a newspaper, she decided as she skimmed the headlines and munched on her bagel, was that it delivered so much bad news. One was supposed to read the paper first thing in the morning, but was it healthy for people to start their days reading about child molesters and wars and tornadoes ripping through peaceful rural towns? By the time she finished the front page, she already felt like crawling back home to bed.

"Hey, Snowden!" Marie hollered at her through the partition. "How about this for a new name for your column—'We Give It Six Months, Tops.' "

"Very funny."

"Or this—'Future Litigants of America.' "

Ignoring her boss's heckling, she flipped to *Portland Today!* and read Ann Landers, then her horoscope. Then, for chuckles, she gave Olga's column a look-see. Olga was sort of like Ann Landers, except that instead of in-law conundrums, almost all of the questions Olga fielded were about sex. Which was probably why she was so popular. She had the best-read local column on the paper, behind Davis's.

Celia expected to give the letters and Olga's answers little more than a critical glance, but her attention was snagged by the second letter on the page. She read it several times, trying to make sure it wasn't a figment of her early morning imagination.

It wasn't.

Dear Olga: I'm afraid I have made a terrible mistake. Recently I met a beautiful young woman (I'll call her "Kellie") and started dating her. We are involved, and the sex is dynamite. Moreover, I think Kellie is in love with me. But now I've realized that I am in love with a woman at work (I'll call her "Inga"). She's gorgeous and friendly and funny, everything I've ever desired. For a long time I've worshiped her from afar, but she was living with another man. Now they've broken up, and I want to make my feelings known to Inga. But what should I do about Kellie? I don't want to hurt her feelings. Am I being hasty? Maybe I should wait to find out whether Inga will go out with me before I give Kellie the heave-ho. I'm eagerly awaiting your answer!—Confused Casanova

Celia's arms went limp, and the newspaper slid to the floor. She bent down to pick it up immediately. Her eyes felt crossed from reading and rereading the letter, but she went over it one more time, just to make sure she hadn't been hallucinating.

Wasn't the name "Kellie" suspiciously similar to Kyra? And then, the other woman—Inga! That was so close to Olga as to be practically transparent.

Could Davis have written this? The time frame fit perfectly.

The thing that shocked her was that this man said he was having sex—*dynamite* sex—with *Kellie*. When she'd seen Davis and Kyra together, they didn't seem that intimate. Of course, that could have been because they were sitting at a table full of people. Nevertheless, Corky and Ellen had seemed more intimate than Kyra and Davis.

Then again, her perception on intimate relations like this wasn't the sharpest. While Ian was hopping a jet back to England, she was at home getting dressed to see the touring production of *Stomp* with him. She'd missed any number of signals—including the Dear

Jane note Ian had cravenly left on her pillow in lieu of dumping her in person.

She'd also missed *Stomp*.

But even if Davis and Kyra were having *dynamite* sex (was this antique Jimmy Walker word the best description he could come up with?), the real stunner was the bit about *Inga*. It had to be Olga. Had to be. They worked together, she was gorgeous, and she'd just broken up with her longtime boyfriend. She'd even been flirting with Davis. The only reason to believe Inga wasn't Olga would be because it was too obvious. Anyone with half a brain in the office would be bound to figure out who Confused Casanova was really talking about—even Olga herself.

And then it hit her. That cagey devil—he *wanted* Olga to figure it out. This wasn't just a letter seeking advice; it was practically a declaration of love. She read the last line over again . . . *eagerly awaiting your answer!* Most of these pathetic letter writers signed off with words like *Help!* or *Please advise!* But this guy was begging for *her answer.*

And what had the wise Olga answered?

Dear Confused: You did not make a mistake; you have merely fallen in love with someone else. By all means, pursue your dream woman.

Of course, Olga *would* say that, Celia thought huffily. If she knew she herself was Inga, it was just blatant self-interest. Olga shouldn't have even answered this letter; a more honest person would have abstained. Wasn't there any system of ethics for advice columnists?

But by stringing Kellie along as you romance Inga you would be trying to have your cake and eat it, too.

Couldn't she have come up with a better cliché than that?

> If you want Inga, you must cut yourself off from the dynamite sex with Kellie. Be a man and do the deed. Do not worry that you will hurt her, because you probably already have. Surely she's noticed that the love in your relationship is one-sided.

"Whatcha readin'?"

At the sound of Davis's voice, Celia levitated about two feet out of her chair and slammed the style section into the top drawer of her desk. Then, gathering her composure again, she whirled on him. "Davis! What are you doing here?"

He looked confused. "I work here, remember?"

"But it's so early."

He nodded toward the large clock above Marie's desk. "It's eight o'clock."

"Oh." She'd been staring at that stupid letter forever.

Davis chuckled. "You're bright-eyed and bushy-tailed this morning."

As if to prove she really was, Celia made a show of performing her getting-to-work ritual: turning on her computer, flipping open a notepad, selecting a pencil with a noneroded eraser (for tapping against her desktop), positioning her coffee cup at the perfect angle from her arm for optimum sipping efficiency. Unfortunately, even with care, she could only stretch these activities out to last about three minutes.

Then it was back to sitting at her desk and having to think. But all she could think about was that stupid letter in her top drawer. She darted a furtive glance

at Davis. Would he really call himself Confused Casanova?

Of course, only to someone like Davis would the
conquest of two measly women at once amount to
Casanova-type behavior.

"Celia?"

She started and turned toward him. "What?"

"What's wrong? You looked completely disgusted
about something."

She gave herself a mental slap. "Oh, I was just
thinking about . . . a friend."

"Ellen?" Davis asked.

"Yeah, Ellen," she said quickly.

"Is she still staying at your place?" To Celia's nod,
he added, "Because Corky's been asking about her. I
think he wants to pay her a visit."

"He wants to see Ellen?"

Davis laughed. "I know—I was amazed, too. It's like
Brit Hume falling for Shirley MacClaine."

"I thought Corky was seeing that Stacy person."

Davis shrugged. "Yeah, but I don't think it's serious.
At least not on his part."

"You mean he wants to dump Stacy and pursue Ellen?" Celia zeroed in on him sharply, watching for signs
of discomfort as she asked, "Isn't that very *Casanova*-
type behavior?"

She studied his reaction so closely that she might
have been seeing him in successive freeze frames. First
his brows knit in thought. Then, in the next frame,
his face contorted into a puzzled frown. Then he
looked over at her, and his eyes widened. "I'm worried
about you, Celia."

So. He was going to dodge questions now. "Why?"

"Well, for one thing, you're looking at me like a
bug under a microscope. Is having a roommate driving
you crazy? Are you getting enough sleep?"

"I'm fine," she answered. "Maybe we should set up a meeting between your roommate and my roommate. Sort of like parents arranging a play date."

Davis chuckled. "He was really taken with Ellen. I was sort of surprised, but it's all he's talked about for a week. He's even started to watch a yoga show on television that conflicts with Emeril. This could be serious."

Celia crossed her arms. "And how's *your* love life? How's Kyra?"

He seemed to squirm a little at the question. "Oh, you know."

"Are things *dynamite*?"

"Dynamite?" He squinted at her. "Why would you ask that?"

The answer was all there in his reaction. Suspicious. Defensive. She chuckled, even though she suddenly felt very shaky. "Never mind—just me being nosy."

"I'm worried about you, Celia. You seem a little fuzzy-headed."

She shook her head. "Actually, I think I'm seeing things very clearly."

Davis had *Confused Casanova* written all over him.

"I don't think you can tell much from one word," Natalie told her.

They were in yet another dressing room, in a position Celia was growing used to. Natalie was standing in front of the three-way mirror trying on a dress— only this, supposedly, was *the* dress. It looked like a lot of the other dresses she'd tried on—a silk, floor-length, backless fitted sheath with an elegantly short train. Sort of like a dress that a certain movie star wore on her wedding to Michael Douglas, though Celia stayed mum on that subject.

"Have you sent out the shower invitations?"

Celia nodded. Her fingers still felt cramped from addressing fifty-three invitations with the thin calligraphy pen Babs had insisted on her using. But at least it was done. And it was going to be held at Natalie's condo, so now all she had to do was buy some balloons and bake the lemon bars.

"What about your dress? Have you had your fitting yet?"

"Tuesday," Celia said. It was going to be a moment to dread. The dress Natalie had picked out for her bridesmaids (which now included two cousins), managed to look both uncomfortable and juvenile. It was strapless with ruffles at the bustline and a floor-length A-line skirt. And the material Natalie had picked was pale lavender taffeta. It looked like a dress a geeky sophomore would wear to a prom.

In fact, it practically *was* the dress Celia had worn to the prom when she was a sophomore.

But it was hard to get too bent out of shape about the dress now. Not after her discovery about Davis. Celia was seated on her usual settee, with a bag of Oreos she'd brought for lunch. She'd also brought Olga's column as a show-and-tell. She kept compulsively consuming them both.

"It's such a goofy word. *Dynamite*. Nobody uses that word except motivational trainers and aw-shucks people like Davis."

"So? There are a lot of people like Davis," Natalie said, twirling so she could see how the train turned.

"Okay," Celia admitted. "But what about the names Kellie and Inga?"

"Could be coincidence."

Celia groaned in frustration. It was so rare that she faced off with someone more skeptical than herself. Now she knew how door-to-door evangelists felt. She definitely had grabbed on to this letter business with an evangelist's zeal. "But look at how Casanova describes his dream woman: gorgeous, friendly, and funny."

Natalie tugged at the dress's top. "How on *earth* am I going to keep my breasts up in this thing?"

Celia frowned. "Who besides Davis would describe his dream woman as *friendly*?"

"We're going to have to do some extreme foundation garment shopping."

"I mean, does *friendly* seem like a typical dream woman descriptor to you?"

"Celia!" Natalie said, twirling on her ferociously. "You're completely off topic." Her gaze zoomed in on the Oreos. "Not to mention, you're going to make yourself sick eating that stuff. Can I have one?"

"Sure," Celia said, offering her the package. "Want some wine?"

Natalie twitched her nose distastefully as she bit into her cookie. Whole, Celia noted. Natalie didn't bother to separate the halves, or perform any elaborate licking ritual. But she probably hadn't had enough sandwich cookie experience to perfect a technique.

At least the sugar seemed to calm Natalie's temper a bit. "Okay, maybe it *could* be Davis."

Celia felt a jolt of triumph. And then an equally violent jolt of despair. Did Davis really think he was in love with Olga? Was he really having *dynamite sex* with Kyra?

Natalie took another cookie. "My question is, do you care?"

Celia looked up at her. "Of course I care."

"You sound like you're jealous," Natalie said.

"I'm not jealous. It's just that neither of these women is right for him."

"Who is?"

Celia's face felt hot, and she sputtered as she tried to come up with an answer. "I-I don't know. I just think he's making a terrible mistake. Is it so wrong to care?" But she had to admit, her uneasiness about the whole situation ran deeper than that. "It's the idea that Davis suddenly has this whole other life—old girlfriends, dates with BlazerDancers, a secret crush on Olga. He keeps appearing in new clothes! I hardly know him anymore. It seems like just yesterday he was my old trustworthy pal, and now he's Casanova!"

Natalie turned back toward the mirror and primped some more. "Believe me, no one is more surprised than yours truly at the change in the Foz. My God, the man's practically a babe."

Celia frowned. "Do you really think so?"

"Well, he needs a better haircut." Natalie sighed. "But that's just life, Celia. People change. A month ago would you have thought I would be engaged to a dashing Scottish hottie? That I would be trying on wedding dresses?"

"No." In fact, she still couldn't believe it.

"So there you are. We're just evolving." Natalie drew back her shoulders and announced with finality, "This is the one. Don't you think it's perfect?"

"Yes." She'd thought so when they had seen one like it weeks ago.

"Good," Natalie said; then she frowned as she tugged at the material at her hips. "Only this sizing of wedding dresses is simply outrageous. I've never had to wear a size ten in my life!"

Celia murmured sympathetically.

Maybe Natalie was right. It was just a little social evolution happening. But the depressing thing was, Davis was evolving *away* from her.

Eleven

"What do you think would be better for a first date: *The River*, or *Greetings from Asbury Park, New Jersey?*"

Corky, who was sitting in lotus position as he sipped his Hamm's, was staring at Davis as if he actually expected him to answer this question. Davis wished he could think of something positive to say. But it didn't seem likely that his roommate would find much success wooing a yoga lady with Bruce Springsteen. "I think Ellen is more the Enya type."

"Enya? What's that?"

The relationship was doomed.

"Are you sure Ellen is the right woman for you, Cork?"

Corky looked offended. "What's that supposed to mean?"

"It just doesn't seem like you two have a lot in common. Ellen's so . . . well . . ."

Corky crossed his arms. "Oh, sure. Come on out and say it. You don't think I'm sensitive enough for her."

"I didn't say that . . ."

"But it's what you meant."

"Corky, she's *married.*"

"Separated."

"Sort of separated. I just don't know if that's a situation you really want to get involved in."

"But what about Ellen? You think I can just leave her there, stuck with that tyrant?"

"You're not the marines, Cork. You can't storm in and rescue her."

"I'm not going to. It's up to her. But I want her to know there's someone who is ready to step in and take care of her."

Davis let out a long breath. He didn't know what more he could say to dissuade his friend from getting involved.

Of course, he wasn't in a great position to give advice to the lovelorn. In his despair over Celia, he'd inadvertently gotten entangled with a woman he wasn't even interested in. And now he didn't know what to do about that. In his life, most of his relationships had simply dissolved from lack of interest. But Kyra was simply too nice to leave dangling. He felt as if he needed to make an honest break.

But once he did that, he'd be back to his unrequited love for Celia. And Celia seemed to be getting nuttier every time he saw her. Now she was speaking in code, as if she were harboring some secret about him. He didn't know what that was about.

"I think we'd all be better off as monks," Davis said. "I should turn my house into a retreat. The Main Street Monastery."

"Oh, no," Corky said. "Monks have to wear those hot, very unhip robes all the time. It would be like walking around with female repellent."

"That would be the point," Davis said.

"Oh." Corky stared at him with growing concern. "That would be awful! What's the matter with you? Having problems with Kyra?"

"No. I just need to break up with her."

"You're tossing away a perfectly good babe? Why?"

"Because I'm not in love with her."

Corky looked at him as if he were crazy.

"What about you and Stacy?" Davis pointed out. "You gave her up."

"Yeah, but I've got Ellen."

"No, you don't. She's married."

"Yeah, but she likes me." Corky looked at him and shook his head sadly. "I can tell you're thinking about Celia, but I gotta tell you, from what I saw the other night, she didn't seem too interested."

"I noticed that."

"I can't believe it myself. You got my friend Bob's strategy down pat."

Davis sighed. He had turned himself around—lost twelve pounds now. He had a few muscles, even. "It's done me zero good."

"I wouldn't say that," Corky pointed out. "You look better, and heck, you're probably healthier. You might live another ten years."

"Great. Ten more lonely years tacked onto my life. Thanks, Bob."

Corky laughed. "You can't give up yet. If Celia doesn't appreciate you, that doesn't mean someone else might not. Look at me. I was wandering around as happy as a clam, and then *bang*, there was Ellen."

Davis had already had his *bang* moment, but apparently Celia hadn't felt so much as a tremor.

He felt restless. "I think I'll go out for a while."

"To do what?" Corky looked at him closely. "You're not depressed, are you?"

"No, just stir-crazy."

Or just crazy, period.

Immersion in Mandarin wasn't all that Celia had hoped. Her fellow classmates were the usual assortment of adult education types—oinks all. Sad. People who weren't finding fulfillment in their jobs or relationships and so were desperately grasping at straws to make their lives seem exotic or worthwhile.

For the first time, she hadn't been able to pay attention in a language class and didn't even seem to care that she had no idea what Professor Li was trying to teach them. She felt she was ready to jump off this Berlitz hamster wheel.

She wanted to evolve.

As she trudged up the steps to her apartment after class, she heard a strange, steady thumping coming from the top floor. *Her floor.* Frowning, she began to take the steps more quickly. She couldn't scoot by Mr. Zhirbotken, however.

"Miss Snowden!" he yelled at her as he poked his head through the door. "Why the music again so loud?"

"I don't know," she said, hurrying by. Ellen was usually maddeningly quiet.

The wild-haired man jabbed a finger toward the ceiling. "All night this I hear! I call landlord. Next will I call police, yes?"

Oh, Lord. Would he really call the cops on her? "No! Please don't call the police. I'm sorry—I'll take care of it!"

The poor man, she thought. What torment she seemed always to be putting him through. He probably wished he'd never left the fatherland.

She opened the door to her apartment and found Corky and Ellen together on the couch. *Very* together! Bruce Springsteen was blaring "Born to Run" on the stereo, and Gazpacho was flapping his wings. He looked as agitated as Mr. Zhirbotken had.

She shut the door loudly, causing the lovers to spring apart.

"Celia!" Ellen exclaimed, beet red.

Corky didn't seem half as embarrassed as Ellen. But then, he didn't have a husband across the river. "Hey, Celia! What's cookin'?"

Celia ran to the stereo and turned it down. "My neighbor. He's burning mad."

"Say," Corky told her, "that reminds me. Some guy named Halsman's been leaving messages for you."

Ellen smiled at her apologetically. "I haven't been picking up the phone, in case it was Lyle."

Celia tapped her foot. "Halsman is my landlord."

"Oh, okay." Corky nodded. "He kept saying that people were complaining about you, which I thought was really weird, since you weren't even here."

"Not about *me*," she said, her voice strained. Was there ever a guy so dense? What was Ellen thinking? "About the music! Mr. Zhirbotken downstairs doesn't care for Bruce Springsteen. At least not at ear-piercing decibels."

Corky looked as if she'd just blasphemed. "You just can't mute the Boss."

On his perch, Gazpacho flapped his wings and squawked out a very unmelodious noise. In fact, it almost sounded as if he had spoken.

Celia stared at the African gray in shock. "Did you hear what he just said?"

"Cute bird," Corky said. "We're pals already."

She ran over to the perch and tried to squawk back at him. He tensed, spread his wings unsteadily, and said in a shrill, Pee Wee Herman voice, "Ruuuuuuun!"

Her guests gasped.

"He said run!" Corky exclaimed.

Ellen hopped excitedly. "Isn't that great, Celia? He finally spoke!"

Celia had to grip the perch to keep herself upright. She was overcome. He'd spoken! Her little bird, whom she'd nurtured and patiently taught all these months, had finally broken his silence. For a split second it was as if Helen Keller had just spelled water into her hand.

Then, in the next moment, her Annie Sullivan elation turned sour.

Ellen beamed at her. "You must be so proud!" But as the moment stretched into prolonged, tense silence, Ellen's smile melted into concern. "Are you all right?"

"Noooo . . . I am *not* all right!" Celia jabbed a finger into Gazpacho's feathered breast. "I've been working with beak face here for months and months, exposing him to exotic beautiful music in multiple languages. I wanted him to be quirky and exotic. And who did this ornery bird finally choose to emulate? A rock singer from Jersey!"

"Sweet!" Corky said. "You should rename him Bruce."

"I should strangle him."

Ellen held her back. "Now, Celia, don't be upset. Maybe he just *sounded* like he was singing 'Born to Run.' "

Hearing his tune, Gazpacho proudly shrilled, "To Ruuuuuuuuun!"

Corky's head snapped back in amazement. "Listen to that—he sang more of it. That is one awesome bird!"

She groaned and sank into the chair next to the perch. "Great. Corky comes over, and now I'm going to have to listen to chunks of 'Born to Run' for the next fifty years."

"Maybe he'll learn some other songs now, too," Ellen said, trying to inject Celia with a little optimism.

"Yeah, how about 'Glory Days'—I really like that one," Corky said.

Celia shook her head. "Everyone told me I should just get a cat. Why didn't I listen?"

Now that he'd found his voice, Gazpacho was on a tear. He spent the next ten minutes crowing out his two words. With each repetition, Ellen cringed and looked anxiously toward Celia. But Corky seemed all the more charmed.

Celia tried not to sink into despair. After all, at least her parrot was now speaking. All the training manuals said that was a big step. If she could just get Springsteen out of his pesky bird brain and something else in. . . .

Maybe she should go back to Chinese class so she could question Professor Li about reeducation methods during the Cultural Revolution.

Gazpacho finally shut up, and silence fell over the room. Celia noticed Corky and Ellen mooning into each other's eyes again. She felt like the annoying chaperone. "What's Davis doing tonight?" she asked Corky.

"I think he went out with Kyra."

Celia frowned. She had to hand it to Gazpacho. For a little while, at least, she hadn't been thinking about the Davis-Kyra-Olga question, and that damn letter. "Actually," Corky said, "I think he may be putting an end to that relationship."

Celia was suddenly rigid with attention. "He's dumping her?"

"Well, yeah."

So he'd done it. He was following Olga's advice. Which meant his next move would be . . . Olga herself.

She suddenly felt very, very tired. "I think I'm going to turn in," she said, pushing herself out of the chair. She put Gazpacho back in his cage and covered it. He was now a disembodied voice screeching "to run" through the house.

Friday morning Davis wore a new pair of pants to work. When she saw them, Celia nearly wept.

"They're just pants," he said, mystified by her reaction.

She sniffed. "I know."

"Then, why are you suddenly reaching for the Kleenex?" She'd been acting so strange lately. What was her problem?

"Never mind." She looked as though she was pulling herself together until her gaze moved up to his face. She sucked in her breath. "Davis! Your hair!"

He ran a hand over his recently buzzed off hair. He'd gotten a severe trim; it was pretty severely short on the sides and a little longer on the top. He'd even run a little gel through it this morning. "What's the matter with it?"

"It's spikey, and it's got stuff in it. It's Ben Affleck's hair!"

He laughed self-consciously as he sank down into his chair. "Really? What's Ben Affleck doing for hair now?"

She groaned. "Oh, never mind."

"Are you worried the Warden won't like your piece on weddings?" He knew she'd planned to give it to Marie early this morning. He doubted she would have heard one way or the other on it yet, though. Marie liked to let people sweat for a few hours before pronouncing judgment.

"No, I'm not worried about that," she said. "In fact, I feel pretty confident. I changed the whole slant, so she won't have to worry about it pissing people off." Her shoulders went proudly rigid, and she collected herself enough to give him a sober up-and-down glance. "You look nice, by the way."

"Thanks."

She shook her head sadly. "You really are evolving, aren't you?"

He regarded her cautiously. "Evolving?"

"Everybody is. Natalie, Ellen, you—even Gazpacho has taken up interests I'm not any part of."

Davis frowned. He'd heard about Gazpacho's first words, of course, but he didn't think that was the core of the problem here. But he did have an idea of what was really troubling Celia. It wasn't her parrot or his pants. It was his roommate. "Okay, it's Corky that's bothering you, isn't it?"

"Corky?"

Davis ran his hand through his newly barbered hair and felt a wave of remorse. "He's spending so much time at your house. It's been a little break for me, of course, but I should have known how difficult it would be for you. Believe me, when he first started staying with me, I wanted to weep, too."

"Corky's fine," she said. "He changed a lightbulb in the hallway last night and didn't even need a ladder."

Poor thing, she was trying to put on a brave face. He wished he could give her some glimmer of hope that Corky would go away. Unfortunately, once installed, Corky had the sticking power of Super Glue.

He fixed his face in a bright, upbeat smile, hoping to cheer her up. "Hey, I went by Stan and Mike's last night. They've got a tent up in their backyard for the reception."

"That's right," she said. "Saturday's the big day."

"They're really doing it up. They're going to have a mariachi band."

"Really?" She didn't seem overly enthused.

"They're going to Mexico on their honeymoon, so they said they wanted to give their poor guests a little taste of the fun."

"I'll have to remember that for the write-up." She smiled limply and shot him a quick glance before looking away. "So . . . Are you taking Kyra to the wedding?"

At the mention of Kyra, all the cheer drained out of him. "Oh, well, no."

Her desk chair spun, and suddenly she was giving him that eagle-sharp look of hers. Just as she had the other day when they had been talking about Kyra. "Why? Did you break up with her?"

"Not exactly."

"What does that mean? Things aren't so dynamite anymore?"

There was that word again! *Dynamite.* It was as if that word was supposed to have a double meaning. "Not really. I guess I should break it off, but it's not so simple . . ."

"So you'll be solo at the big wedding?" she asked.

"Yeah, I guess so," he answered, "although technically I suppose Corky is my date."

Her eyes bugged. "Corky?"

"Stan and Mike invited us together. Probably the whole neighborhood thinks we're gay."

She leaned back in her chair and shook her head. "Then, there's no telling what *my* neighbors think now."

He laughed. "Probably that you're a kinky threesome."

"It's no joke. I'm afraid the guy below me is going to detonate one of these days."

"That is a problem."

She stared at him closely. "Maybe I should write a letter to 'Ask Olga.' "

"Actually, that's not a bad idea," Davis replied. "I think she gives pretty good advice."

Celia whirled back to face her computer monitor with lightning speed, so he couldn't read her expression. But he should have known she wouldn't appreciate a kind word for the advice columnist. Celia was always a little nutty when it came to Olga.

Actually, Celia had put an idea in his head. Who better to ask about his own little problem than Olga? She would surely know the best way to handle the sticky Kyra situation. Maybe she would even give him some advice on how to deal with a woman who had rejected him once. Should he try again? Give up? Keep biding his time?

He shook his head, disgusted with himself. He even *sounded* like one of those letter writers of hers.

He waited until Celia had gone to bug Marie before sneaking away to Olga's cubicle. He didn't want Celia getting wind of the fact that he was seeking advice to the lovelorn. In fact, this whole situation was very delicate. Because if Olga figured out who in the office he was talking about, and then word got around . . .

Olga, once she had him installed in the spare chair in her quiet corner cubicle, was very no-nonsense. "Dump the girlfriend you don't like. Pronto. Don't be mean, but there's no sense dragging this out. And as for the friend who you *want* to be a girlfriend . . ."

She thought for a moment.

Davis squirmed.

"Stay cool," she said.

"Cool?"

Olga ran a manicured hand through her long blond hair. "You have to understand what we women go through, Davis. Men are just hitting on us *constantly*— in bars, at work, even in grocery store checkout lines.

It's *such* a nuisance. So when a woman has a true male friend, to have *him* turn around and hit on her . . ."

This was not what he wanted to hear. Any hope he had of an easy resolution to his problem was dashed once and for all. "Bad?"

"It's like a betrayal."

He sank down into his chair. "Oh." No wonder Celia had looked so stunned and uncomfortable after he'd kissed her.

"You have to be a friend first," she said. "And then, if anything happens to come about naturally . . ."

"How can anything come about naturally if I'm busy being her buddy? If anything, I'm just back to where I started."

"You have to accept that maybe nothing will happen. But at least Celia will still be your pal."

Davis looked at her sharply. "How did you . . . ?"

She laughed. "How could I not guess? She's your best friend, isn't she?"

Davis nodded. And apparently, to keep his best friend, he was going to have to stay on the treadmill of sexual frustration.

Marie finished Celia's exposé on weddings and slapped it down on her desk. Then she let out a long breath.

She's trying to think of a way to let me down easy, Celia worried.

Then she remembered whom she was dealing with here. "Softening the blow" was not a fully formed concept in Marie's head.

At last, her boss made her pronouncement. "It's okay."

Celia's jaw dropped. *Okay* was practically a ringing endorsement from Marie. "You really liked it?"

Marie crossed her arms and twisted her mouth in barely leashed amusement. "Don't start dusting off your Pulitzer Prize acceptance speech. But yeah, this will do. I like the way you showed several examples of less-expensive weddings. The cheapskate brides lessen the sting of the piece."

"You mean it waters it down."

Marie's lips turned down. "No, it makes it seem less black-and-white. Of course, for you youngsters raised on *Star Wars* and *Rambo,* nuance and shades of gray probably don't have much appeal. If you'd been in the business when Watergate was going down—"

Celia nearly choked. "Watergate? I've heard of that." Though it was hard to make a connection between "The Price of Love" and the downfall of the thirty-seventh president. She was resigned now to the fact that a piece in the style section was never going to change the world.

"The point is, *you* might think the piece is watered down, but this way people can read it and not think everyone getting married is a dupe."

"Just the stupid rich ones."

"Right. The rich are always fair game." Marie thought to herself for a moment, then laughed. "By the way, where did you dig up that screwball who got married in front of the yurt?"

"Oh . . ." Celia had tried to disguise Ellen's odd-ball tendencies a little. Apparently she hadn't entirely succeeded.

"Well, never mind," Marie said. "Weddingwise, I guess you've seen everything."

"When will this run?"

"Pretty soon. It's getting to be wedding season."

As if Celia needed to be reminded. Natalie's wedding was bearing down on her. She'd already ducked three calls from Babs this week. The woman would give her an ulcer. "Well, I'm glad it's okay."

Marie gave her a thumbs-up as a dismissal, then picked up the story again and tossed it on a disturbingly large pile of papers in a file box at the corner of her desk. To Celia that pile suddenly looked like the land of lost exposés, but she decided she shouldn't push her luck by bugging Marie any more. Celia went back to her desk with a bounce in her step. She wanted to save her celebratory moment for when she saw Davis, but when she rounded the corner, his chair was empty. His coffee cup was gone, too.

She grabbed her own mug and breezed over to the coffee room. When he wasn't there, she filled up her cup and headed out again to hunt him down. He wasn't with any of the usual suspects.

Then she heard him laughing.

She glanced in the direction of Olga's cubicle. The partition blocked her view of what was going on inside there.

All her elation about the article seeped away. Her throat felt dry. So far, Davis had been following the Confused Casanova script pretty closely. And the next step was . . .

Olga.

She told herself she was acting like a jealous girlfriend. She told herself it was none of her business whom Davis was talking to. She told herself to go straight back to her own cubicle and do something productive, for God's sake.

Unfortunately, she wasn't listening to herself.

The hallway leading to the bathrooms was just beyond Olga's cubicle. She could pretend she was headed for the ladies' room. Nothing suspicious about that.

She started walking, but her steps were heavy. The

closer she came, the more she felt like a stupid character in a slasher film, headed for the door to the closed-off room where doom obviously awaited. But like the stupid character, there was no stopping her.

Until she heard Olga's husky laughter as she drew even with the cubicle. Seeing Davis and Olga huddled in conversation, she felt paralyzed.

"Hi, Celia!" Olga said brightly. She gave Davis a little punch in the arm to alert him to Celia's presence. He straightened. When his gaze caught Celia's, he looked like a bunny staring down a gun barrel.

"Don't mind me," Celia said quickly. "I was just passing through."

She sped toward the bathroom and locked herself inside a stall. What *had* those two been talking about?

Come to think of it, maybe she didn't want to know.

Twelve

The grooms wore tuxes by Armani—classic black with black bow ties, snowy white shirts, and white rosebud boutonnieres. Celia usually took note of these details in the most ho-hum manner. But for some reason, at the wedding of Stan and Mike, all the little touches stood out in relief.

She didn't know what she'd expected from this ceremony. Or, unfortunately, she *did* know. She'd expected an extended gay joke. Stan or Mike in a frothy white wedding gown. Decorations *a la* Liberace. A priest who would throw off his cassock in the middle of the ceremony and start belting out "Everything's Coming Up Roses." Every campy cliché in the book.

But the setting at the Crystal Springs rhododendron garden was so tasteful as to be almost disappointing. Martha Stewart could have taken tips from these guys. A bower of white roses had been set up on a hill near a picturesque duck pond. The friends and relatives of the grooms clustered on the small hillside, most of them standing throughout the short ceremony, which was performed by a suit-clad Unitarian minister who appeared to have no intention of doing Cher impersonations.

Celia had already spoken to Stan and Mike, learning their history, hearing stories from their relatives gathered for the big event. She'd heard how they had met when Stan was starting up Golden Video, a movie rental store for both new and hard-to-find titles, and Mike had been finishing up a degree in art history. They had broken up when Mike ran off to Florence to study; but he'd come back, and they had become good friends. When Mike was diagnosed with Hodgkin's disease, Stan had sold his house to help pay for the medical bills and had been at his side during every terrible hospital visit. Mike, who now worked at the Portland Art Museum, had just celebrated his fifth cancer-free year. The two men now shared a house and the custody of two Welsh corgi dogs, Buffy and Angel.

Like all couples, they had their differences. Stan was good with money, while financially Mike enjoyed flying by the seat of his pants. Mike adored Stan's family, while Stan usually headed for the hills when Mike's clan descended upon them. But they seemed truly happy and amazed and thankful that they had each other.

Perhaps that was what made the ceremony, which was as staid and boring as any Celia had listened to, so damn moving. She'd been to scores of weddings where she'd thought the bride and groom were well suited. But she'd never witnessed a marriage of two people she felt one hundred percent sure *would* stick together through thick and thin. They had already done it.

As they exchanged vows, Celia came to the shocking realization that she envied them. They had a ten-year history. They had proven their devotion to each other in so many ways. There was no doubting how strong their bond was, stronger than anything she'd ever experienced. Or maybe ever would. Stan and Mike would never abandon each other.

By the time they were exchanging rings—simple

platinum bands, Tiffany's—Celia was weeping more profusely than Mike's mother. After the minister pronounced the couple honorably joined in matrimony, the family and guests surged forward to congratulate the ecstatic couple. Celia busied herself digging through her purse for a Kleenex.

Davis grabbed her arm. "Are you okay?"

"F-f-f-f-fine!" she gulped in on a sob.

"My God, Celia, it was just a wedding service. You've seen tons of them."

She blew her nose. "I know!" She hesitated to look at Davis when she knew her eyes would be rabbity and red and her mucous membranes were going berserk. "I was thinking about Stan standing by Mike while he h-had c-c-c-cancer and how they f-f-f-ell in love all over again, and their d-d-dogs!"

Davis, who usually was the sentimental one of the two of them, clearly thought she'd snapped. And maybe she had. She couldn't add, of course, that what she'd *really* been thinking about was how no one would probably love *her* enough to sit in an oncology ward for months on end.

"You know what *I* was thinking?" Corky asked.

Celia had almost forgotten he was there. But then, she was becoming so accustomed to being around Corky that the man barely made any impression on her at all anymore, except as a slight annoyance.

"W-what?" she hiccuped.

Corky's brow furrowed into a contemplative expression. "Well, I was thinking, when two guys tie the knot, does that mean there's two more available women floating around for the rest of us?"

Celia clucked contemptuously.

"I mean, hey, everybody gets so twisted out of joint about this gay marriage business," Corky went on, "but actually, this sort of thing really helps us out, if you think about it."

"How can you be so crass about something so moving?" She couldn't imagine what Ellen saw in him, except maybe that he wasn't Lyle.

Corky's eyes widened in surprise. "I thought I was making an important sociological observation."

While the ceremony was disappointingly staid, the reception more than made up for it in Mexican flamboyance. The backyard at the house on Main Street was done up in bright, garish colors. A Mexican combo played sambas in one corner while nearby a bartender in an aqua ruffled-sleeve shirt ladled out drinks from a vat of sangria. It looked as if everyone the two men knew, plus the entire neighborhood, had been invited. Kids wearing sombreros ran underfoot. Waiters hefted trays practically sagging with little empanadas and stuffed jalapenos and other spicy south-of-the-border treats.

Celia, who had recovered her composure and fixed her makeup, stood in a huddle with Corky as Davis mingled with practically everybody in the tent.

"Nice dress," Corky told her.

"I'm glad *somebody* noticed."

She'd bought the dress on a whim—a rare full-price retail buy. Her Visa card had groaned, but she hadn't been able to resist the impulse. The magenta dress had a low neck and was fitted down through the hips, where it then flared into a flirty skirt that came just above the knee. It was bright and sexy and springy.

But until Corky, it hadn't garnered the attention she'd hoped for. Davis hadn't uttered a peep about it.

"Actually, I saw the Nordstrom's bag on your bed yesterday," Corky explained, "so I figured you'd be wearing something new. Ellen told me you could probably use a compliment."

"Oh." So now she was reduced to pity praise.

"But I probably would have noticed it anyway," he assured her.

Suddenly, she felt a tap on her shoulder. It was Davis, grinning. If this had been a month ago, she would hardly have recognized her old friend. His hair was short, his face had thinned out so that his jaw was sharp and strong, and his blue suit looked like something out of *GQ*. But that smile—he couldn't disguise that grin of his, or those light blue eyes.

Only why hadn't she ever noticed before how sexy light blue eyes could be?

Her heart did a quick flip, and she hugged one arm around her middle, as if she could hold herself upright.

"Care to dance?"

"Maybe in a little while," she said.

He looked out at the little patio, where plenty of couples were shaking booty to the exotic rhythm. "We wouldn't be the only mixed sex couple out there, so you wouldn't have to worry about looking weird."

"I wasn't worried about that," she said tightly.

"Then, what . . . ?"

"I *can't* dance," she told him, "because I don't know the cha-cha."

He laughed. "Why didn't you say so? I can teach you."

"Not likely. I have two left feet."

"You're a good dancer," he said. "And I should know, I've danced with you before."

"Correction. You've *waltzed* with me. It's the only dance I know, and I've been practicing it since I was a flower girl at my mom's second wedding."

"The cha-cha is easier than the waltz. Any dope can do it."

"I can't," Corky said.

She arched her brows at Davis. "See?"

"Any dope besides Corky," he assured her.

Not about to take no for an answer, he grabbed her hand and tugged her out to the little dance floor. She tried to ignore the warmth that seemed to radiate through her just from his simple touch. When it proved impossible, she chalked up the flushed, weightless feeling she had to the two glasses of sangria she'd gulped down in quick succession.

"All right, Arthur Murray," she said when they had stopped and were facing each other. "Do your worst."

He took both her hands now, and she was grateful that she could stare at her feet. Otherwise he might be able to look into her eyes and see a foolish simper.

What was wrong with her? She needed to get a hold of herself.

"This is so easy you're going to think I'm joking," he instructed. "All you do is step, step, cha-cha-cha." He demonstrated the combination so easily that it seemed like child's play.

But Celia wasn't fooled. "The band is cha-cha-cha-ing a lot faster than you are."

"You'll get the hang of it," he said. "Now try."

Feeling about as agile as an elephant in quicksand, Celia forced her feet to follow his lead.

"See!" he said, beaming at her. "You're Ginger Rogers!"

"Davis, we're about to be mowed down by everyone else on the dance floor."

"Okay, so we'll speed it up now. Just remember to count to yourself."

Celia concentrated so hard her brow was practically popping with perspiration. *One, two, cha-cha-cha!*

"Great!" said Davis. "Now try moving your feet without moving your lips."

She did as instructed. Still, in her head she repeated relentlessly, *One, two, cha-cha-cha! One, two, cha-cha—*

"You know," Davis said, "I can't remember when I've seen you look so gorgeous."

As the husky sound of his words sank in, her third *cha* turned into a trip. She stamped down on Davis's foot.

"Ouch!"

"I'm so sorry!" she said, stopping.

He winced. *"Don't* stop or you'll lose your rhythm. One, two . . ."

Cha-cha . . . gorgeous? That wasn't a word that got used on her very often. Pretty, occasionally. Ian had called her lovely—though, to be honest, Ian had called everything lovely. *"A movie—what a lovely idea!"* he'd say. Or, *"Bagels—how lovely."* In retrospect, the lovelies between her and the bagels hadn't differed all that much.

But this was her first gorgeous. She gawked at Davis in amazement.

"Keep moving!" he coached sharply. She stumbled back into step. "That's an incredible dress."

Since she was concentrating hard, she didn't lose rhythm. "You didn't say a word when you first saw it."

"That's because Corky was standing right there. I was hardly going to break into raptures in front of him."

Raptures? Over her?

"Cha-cha-cha," he reminded her, causing her to hop for a moment to get the rhythm back on line.

It was harder to get her thoughts back. Part of her wanted to pursue the raptures comment, but she didn't want to press her luck. "Do you think Corky might really be falling for Ellen?"

"I'm afraid so."

She stiffened slightly. "It's Ellen I'm afraid for. It's

not enough that Corky corrupted my parrot. Yesterday he and Ellen were eating bacon-and-peanut-butter sandwiches. It was the weirdest culinary combination I'd ever seen—and Ellen was scarfing it down like manna."

"Well, *they're* a weird combination."

Weirder than he and Kyra? Or he and Olga? She stumbled again, and he caught her this time, taking her by the elbows. "Sorry," she mumbled. Heat flared in her cheeks.

He was holding her arms. They were so close she could feel his breath. See the dark flecks in the light blue of his eyes. Smell the sharp scent of Obsession.

"Celia . . ."

Her feet weren't moving anymore. Neither were his.

Her head felt light, almost dizzy. She drew in a deep breath with difficulty. "I told you I wasn't a quick study."

His dark blond brows drew together, and he squeezed her arms a little tighter. *No wonder Kyra went for him,* she thought. Olga probably would, too. He wasn't the old Davis anymore. He was sexier, more sure of himself.

Or maybe he had always been that way, and she'd just never noticed.

"Let's get out of here," he said.

Her pulse leapt like a filly at the starting gate at Churchill Downs.

She swallowed. "I'm supposed to be working."

"You have enough for your column already," he said. "It's a great day, and it's been ages since we've been able to just go hang out together."

"Hang out?" she asked, feeling a base drumbeat of disappointment begin to pound in her head. *Just* hang out, he'd said.

He nodded, and when he smiled at her, he *was* the same old Davis. "You know, like pals."

Pals.

Hearing that word was as though being doused with a bucket of cold water. She'd been feeling sexy, reckless—but *he* was just thinking of her as his buddy.

Of course! What did she expect? The man wasn't short on women who wanted to be more than buddies with him. Confused Casanova wasn't looking for another conquest. He was probably relieved to be able to take a rest from his little romances. And who better to rest with than old reliable Celia? She was the comfortable old sweatshirt he could pull on when he tired of his snappy new clothes.

The thought made her feel inordinately frustrated.

Her chin jutted forward. She pulled her arms away from him. She hated the wounded pride that surged through her, but she couldn't help it. "I don't think I'm in the mood."

He looked surprised. "We haven't spent much time together lately. I would have thought . . ."

Maybe a flash in her eyes kept him from finishing the thought. Heat fired through her body. Her face was probably color coordinated to her dress now. "You would have thought I'd be desperate for company?"

He laughed. *Laughed!* "Not exactly."

"My life isn't so empty that I need friends to make quality time for me."

He blinked in surprise. "I never said—"

"I'm not waiting by the phone for your calls. I know you've had Kyra . . . and other things going on."

He reached out to grab her arm, but she jumped back as if his hand were a hot poker.

"And what with *your* roommate living in *my* apartment now, what I would like more than anything is time to myself. Which I might as well go home and take advantage of right now."

Reeling from how foolishly hot-headed she must sound, yet unable to cool off, she spun on her heel and fled the dance floor. And once she was moving, she decided it might be wise just to leave the reception before she made even more of an ass out of herself. She sounded like an embittered nut. A jealous shrew.

"Hey, Celia!" Corky shouted after her. "Stop, drop, and roll!"

Celia groaned and sped away as quickly as possible. She would have done anything to be able to take her words back.

After Stan and Mike took off for the airport in the traditional spray of birdseed, Davis crossed the street to his house. Instead of going inside, however, he got in his car. Without thinking, he drove straight to Kyra's.

"Oh, hi," she said, opening the door for him. She was dressed in jeans and a big T-shirt. "I thought you had some wedding to go to today."

"It's over," he explained.

"Great. Have a seat."

He looked at the couch, which was strewn with magazines. *Harper's Bazaar, Glamour,* and *Cosmopolitan.* Mariah Carey was cranked on the stereo.

"I'm sort of glad you came over," Kyra said, sitting down next to him. "I've been needing to talk."

He felt a pang of guilt. "I've had something I've wanted to tell you, too."

Her eyes widened. "Maybe I should go first."

"No, I wanted—"

"I don't think this is working," she said, cutting him off.

He blinked, not certain he'd heard correctly. "What?"

Her shoulders rounded, and she reached to the coffee table for a fortifying sip of Diet Pepsi. "I'm sorry, Davis. I've wanted to tell you this for a while. I like you, but not, like, a boyfriend."

"Oh."

"Please don't take it hard."

He frowned. This was a good joke on him. He'd been worried about how to let Kyra down easy. Apparently it was he who should have been worried about soft landings.

Luckily, this was what he wanted. Relief surged through him, but he was puzzled.

"I don't want to lose you," Kyra told him. "As a friend."

"Oh, well, no. No reason for that."

"Good. Then, would it bother you if I called Corky?"

"Why would you want to do that?"

"You know . . ."

It took him a moment to understand. "You mean, you like *Corky?*"

Her head bobbed enthusiastically. "That's why I was hoping we could stay friends, Davis. I'd really appreciate it if you'd put in a good word for me with him." Her nose wrinkled, and she giggled. "Don't you think he's cool?"

"Cool?" Davis asked in disbelief. *"Corky?"*

He couldn't believe his ears. It wasn't just the blow to his ego that had him reeling; it was the way the world seemed to have suddenly switched directions. Celia had flipped her lid at the reception. Corky had announced that he was in love with Ellen the earth mama. And now this.

He wondered if he should tell her the bad news

about Corky and Ellen now or let her find out for herself.

"I know it sounds weird," Kyra explained, "but Corky's sort of different from the guys I've always hung out with—he-man wannabes. You know."

"I'm not sure . . ."

"But Corky's not like that at all. He's sort of lumpy and cuddly, you know? I've never been around a guy from Nebraska before."

"I'm from Nebraska."

She frowned at him. "Really?" She shook her head, clearly mystified. "Maybe it's not that, then. I guess it's just that Corky . . . Well, he's like a big old Teddy bear. You know what I mean?"

Evidently, for some women, Teddy bear was a *good* thing. Davis just hadn't found the right woman. And now, apparently, along with twelve pounds he'd lost his Teddy bear status.

By the time he had driven back to his street, he was in the middle of a full-blown identity crisis.

He pulled into his drive and gave his place a clear-eyed inspection as he headed inside. His yard was tidy; there was barely a scar from the water main incident. Everything was in its place. He went into the house and looked about him with a critical eye. His couch was navy blue. His rugs were beige. His walls were off-white.

He was living in a Pottery Barn catalog.

No wonder Celia thought he was boring. He *was* boring.

He sank down into a white-and-beige-striped chair and took stock. The most wild and crazy thing he'd ever done was move to Oregon, but that had been because he was offered a job. He'd graduated from college and gone right to work. He had a mortgage. He had a good steady job. He was so buttoned down he was practically in a straight jacket. *Who did that appeal to?*

All this past year, he'd thought Celia's pining for exoticism and adventure was odd. He thought her pie-in-the-sky idea of punting everything and running off like Cary Grant in some damn movie was endearingly absurd. He knew she was just reacting to a rural upbringing, living with her grandparents, dreaming of bigger things, and would probably grow out of it. He thought he understood it all, but was above it.

Now, as he looked around his place, he *really* started to understand. The whole place felt as if it was chaining him down to his blah existence. The closest thing to adventure he'd experienced in the past year was driving to Sisters, Oregon, to search for the ultimate French fry. He'd never had a real adventure in his life.

Suddenly, he wanted to break loose.

Even if it meant breaking loose from Celia.

Thirteen

Celia fled straight to the office to write up the wedding while it was fresh in her head.

Unfortunately, what was really on her mind was whether there was a quick test one could take to detect schizophrenia. She'd told Davis she'd wanted to be his *friend*. She'd told everyone that was what she and Davis were. She was scared when she thought they *wouldn't* be friends, and had been horrified the one time he'd hinted he wanted more. But now she wanted . . .

What did she want?

Davis?

She tried saying it to herself. *I want Davis.*

Davis-n-Celia.

But the words rattled uneasily inside her head. Davis Smith? He was *not* part of her life plan. He wasn't her ideal man at all. He didn't look like Antonio Banderas or even have Ian's dash.

Of course, Ian had dashed clear back across the ocean to get away from her. And none of the men she'd met who looked anything like Antonio Banderas had shared—or even put up with—her love of road food and made-for-television movies. They hadn't had endless capacity for talking about either life's biggest mysteries or nothing in particular.

And none of them had made her pulse skitter as it had when she'd been dancing with Davis.

How could this be?

Maybe Davis just looked appealing now because he had other women interested in him. That wasn't a worthy impulse, but at the moment it was the only explanation that made some sort of psychological sense to her.

Saturdays at the *Times* there was only a shoestring staff. Wanting to avoid irritating conversations, Celia crept by the Warden. She was hoping to get her column knocked out fast because she'd promised Ellen she would go by Lyle's with her later and pick up some more of Ellen's things. Which meant she wasn't going to have time to breathe until tonight. And tomorrow? Tomorrow she got to go buy lingerie for Natalie's trousseau. When one discovered chunks of free time set aside for shopping for somebody else's underwear, it was time to give the old social life an overhaul.

She shot a look over at Davis's cubicle, remembered stomping out of Stan and Mike's, and felt belatedly repentant all over again. Should she call him and apologize now or wait till she got home?

Her phone buzzed.

If she'd been hooked up to an EKG, she would have flat-lined. *Could it be Davis? Do we have some kind of psychic connection?*

She lunged for the handset. "Celia Snowden!"

"Hiya, babe!"

Celia groaned. It wasn't Davis—it was Art Carney, her persecutor. She'd almost forgotten about him. He hadn't pestered her in weeks.

"How'd you like to spare some time for some real union action, Miss Hotshot reporter?"

"Don't you have a life?" she snarled into the phone.

Of course, anything she said only encouraged him. "Atta way, babe. Real men like 'em feisty."

"The only real thing you are is a real asshole!" She slammed down the phone.

Why, Lord? Why was she a creep magnet?

Trying to regain some composure, she mentally switched gears and turned back to her wedding story. As she was poking over one paragraph, hunting for the exact words to convey how moving the ceremony at the rhododendron garden had been, Sara, the receptionist, peeked over her cubicle wall. *"Hey!"*

Celia jumped. The woman had lungs of steel, so that even her urgent, confidential whisper sounded like a bellow.

"Have you heard?" Sara asked.

"What?"

"The latest."

Celia shook her head. "If it's about me, I don't want to know."

Sara looked perplexed. "Who would ever gossip about you?"

She laughed in spite of herself. "Good question. So what's the scoop?"

"It's Olga." At that name, dread flashed through Celia, but Sara apparently mistook her silence for rabid interest. "You'll die when you hear this. Somebody in this building wrote to Olga's column asking her advice about a love problem. Maybe you read it— Confused Casanova?"

Celia feared she was going to be sick. How could juicy gossip have developed so quickly? She'd just seen Davis, and he hadn't mentioned Olga to her.

Then again, maybe she needed to stop taking lines of communication for granted. Her mother hadn't hinted to Celia when she was about to leave her at her grandparents' house for, oh, about a decade. Ian had fled to England without so much as a peep of discontent. Natalie hadn't told her when she was

E-mailing back and forth with a guy she thought she might actually marry.

"Confused Casanova? I might have read that one . . ."

"Well!" Sara scooted around to the interior of Celia's cubicle and plopped herself down in the little chair in the corner. "Get *this*. Confused said he was in love with someone at his office he called 'Inga,' but it was really Olga he was talking about."

"How do you know?" Celia heard herself asking. "After all, a name . . . It could be just a coincidence."

"Oh, come on. *Inga? Olga?* A whole bunch of us figured *that* out." Sara's brows knit together. "But what we couldn't figure out was who the guy was. Then last night, guess what?"

"What?"

"I saw them together at a club!"

Oh, God. She didn't want to know.

But she absolutely *had* to know. "Olga and . . . ?"

"Kevin Muldoon!"

Celia's jaw dropped, and all at once her enthusiasm for the gossip reached heights that would satisfy even Sara. "Kevin Muldoon?" she squeaked in disbelieving glee. Her creepy old flame . . . and Olga. For a brief moment, she felt that if she opened her mouth, she might be able to hit a joyful high C, like Ella Fitzgerald in the old Memorex commercials.

If Sara had nodded any faster, her head might have flown off. "Can you believe it? That lech!"

Celia laughed and gripped the arms of her chair to keep herself from floating right out of it. "I never would have guessed. It's a match made in heaven!"

Could this possibly be the explanation for the egg-nog drop at the Christmas party? Perhaps Olga had had her eye on Kevin Muldoon even back then and had heard some ancient office scuttlebutt . . . And then, *sploop*, took out her jealousy on Celia's hair.

Sara looked at her suspiciously. "Wait. Didn't you go out with Kevin once?"

"Don't worry. She's welcome to him."

The receptionist, making a mental note of it for future dissemination, nodded. "I better get back to the phone. I'm on until two. I just had to come spill, though."

"Thanks."

Celia leaned back in her chair and luxuriated in this news. What an idiot she'd been! That stupid letter. It had nothing to do with Davis. And she'd . . .

Her smile faded. And *she'd* been sneaking around the office, spying on him. Not to mention, she'd been tossing barely veiled accusations at him all week, making references to phrases in the letter to see if he would crack. He must have thought she was insane!

And now . . . Now she could hardly apologize for acting so weird without tipping her hand and letting him know that she'd felt jealous of Olga.

All the elation she felt faded. It would be a miracle if Davis even wanted to speak to her anymore. And if he did, she swore she would never do anything dumb to jeopardize their friendship again.

The phone would not stop ringing. Celia peeled one bleary eye open and noted the time. One-twenty-six A.M. Already she'd ignored two calls. Normally, her answering machine would have picked up, except they had turned off the machine to avoid messages from Lyle, who had finally realized that his wife was no longer living with him when Celia and Ellen had shown up at the house and started carting away boxes of Ellen's belongings.

This could be Lyle harassing them now. Ellen had said the man had very regular sleeping habits, but Celia knew better than anyone that being abandoned could induce some wicked insomnia.

Or it might be her grandmother calling her. That thought brought her bolt upright. What if something was wrong at home? She felt a pang of guilt, because she hadn't been home since her grandfather's birthday in March. That was almost two months ago now. Grandpa had looked all right during that visit, but . . .

She threw the quilt back and jumped out of bed, tripping over one of Ellen's boxes. She knocked her head against the ceiling and let out a muffled yelp. Holding her head, she padded quickly out into the living room, picking her way around Corky, whose body was wrapped sausage-style in an afghan on the floor. A long snore honked out of him. Ellen was conked out on the sofa. From inside his shrouded cage, Gazpacho was muttering snatches of "Hungry Heart" to himself in a sleepy parrot voice.

How could they not have heard the phone?

When it rang again, she snatched it off its cradle and ducked into the bathroom, shutting the door for privacy.

"Oh, Celia, thank God you finally picked up!" Natalie's voice sounded strange. Constricted. She sniffled. "I need help."

The phone nearly slid out of Celia's fingertips. A cry for help? From Natalie? She sounded almost . . . vulnerable! "What's wrong?"

The sound of a nose blowing blasted across the line. "I can't explain it over the phone."

"But, Nat—"

"It's too complicated. You'll have to see . . . Anyway, could you come over here?"

"Of course!"

Natalie let out a muffled wail of relief. "Oh, thank heavens! You're the best, Celia. I'll never forget this."

"Just sit tight, Nat," Celia instructed her. "I just have to throw on some clothes."

"You don't know what I've been going through!"

"I'll be there as fast as I can."

Celia punched the phone's off button and splashed cold water on her face. Her hands were actually shaking. But hearing Natalie like that—so panicked, needing help, reaching out to her. This had never happened before.

She scurried to her room to throw on the clothes she'd worn yesterday to haul Ellen's boxes—a pair of jeans and an old Missouri sweatshirt with a tiger on it. What could be wrong with Natalie? Had Angus done something? With all the wedding plans, Celia had almost forgotten about him. She tried to picture what could be happening at Natalie's condo. Angus definitely seemed to have a drinking problem. What if he was uncontrollable? Or violent? She'd have to call the police. Though, of course, Natalie would never allow that. She'd be too worried about how the publicity from such an event would affect her shaky career.

Maybe she should wake Corky. Or better yet, call Davis. Davis was more dependable. He'd know what to do in any circumstance.

She had her hand on the phone, but hesitated. It was late. But maybe since it was a Saturday night . . .

On the other hand, after Stan and Mike's wedding, he might want to stay as far away from her as humanly possible. And he was certainly no pal of Natalie's.

But he at least might be able to put her mind at ease, or give her advice. He was always good at that.

She dialed.

He picked up on the third ring. "Hello?"

"It's me," she said in a rush. "I'm sorry to bug you,

but I think something really bad's happened over at Natalie's. She called here and sounded really upset."

"Did she say what was wrong?"

"No, but she was crying. She sounded really shaken. I'm going over there now—"

"I'll be right behind you."

She sagged with relief. She should have known he would help. She would never forget this. Never.

She broke practically every traffic law on the books in her haste to get to Natalie's, where she was buzzed up immediately. It occurred to her as she mounted the stairs two at a time that maybe she should have brought something with her. Of course, she didn't own any firearms; the most threatening weapon in her house was an electric bread knife her grandmother had given her for Christmas. But she doubted an insane, drunken Scotsman would be intimidated by a wedding journalist wielding a bread knife.

As Celia reached the top of the landing on the third floor, Natalie threw open her door. She was wearing lavender silk shorty pajamas—no rips on them, Celia noted quickly—and matching slippers with feather boa tufts on the toes. In her hand was a family-size bag of Cheetos. Aside from being a little tense and puffy, her face looked fine.

Angus hadn't been physically abusive, at least. In fact, as Celia stepped into the apartment and saw Angus zonked out on the couch surrounded by empty Guinness bottles, she realized that he wasn't in a condition to do much of anything.

"You certainly got here fast," Natalie said. "You want something to drink?"

At Natalie's casual tone, Celia's heart slowed its furious beating. "No thanks."

"Sure?"

She tried to catch her breath, which was still labored from running up the three flights. "I thought you were having a crisis over here."

"I am!"

"I mean, an emergency."

Natalie gestured toward her elegant glass-topped dinette, which was strewn with little baskets and cellophane wrapped packages. "What would you call *that* if not an emergency?"

Celia didn't know what to call the peculiar pile of junk. "What are those?"

"Reception favors. I forgot about them completely, and now I'm totally stumped about which to choose."

"Favors," Celia repeated numbly.

"I've *got* to decide. The wedding is just weeks away, Celia, and if items are going to be personalized, I have to order them *yesterday.*"

What was the best way to tell your friend that she had a mental health problem?

How about this? "Natalie, you have a mental health problem. Do you know how scared I was? I called Davis. He's on his way over right now."

"Davis?" Natalie's face screwed itself into a puzzled frown as she popped a Cheeto. "What does *he* know about reception favors?"

"Nothing! I thought you were dying over here."

"I *am* dying, Celia. You don't know what pressure I'm under!" Her friend collapsed into a chair. Cheese doodle dust spilled down her silk pajama top. "Maybe this all seems trivial to you, but just you wait till you're in my shoes."

Celia grunted. "By the time I find some guy who'll marry me, my shoes will be orthopedic granny oxfords."

"Could you please put your cynicism aside for once and try to help me out here?"

Celia dutifully inspected the junk on the table. "Is

this stuff really necessary? I'm not Letitia Baldridge, but not all the weddings I go to have reception favors. Frankly, I believe it's enough to simply thank all your guests for coming. Provided you ply them with champagne, of course."

"But that's so cheap!" Natalie huffed. "If I'm going to have a wedding, I damn well want people to remember it, even if they have to haul home a bunch of monogrammed Hershey bars they'll never eat."

Hershey bars would certainly be more practical than some of the items on the table. Like the coaster and glass gift set. Who would want to *take home* coasters with somebody else's name on them? Or the accordian picture frames, which Celia assumed would be filled with pictures of the bride. Even coming from Natalie, that seemed a little overly narcissistic.

"I've simply got to decide." Even though she wasn't finished with the first one, Natalie snatched a new bag of Cheetos off the counter and tore it open so forcefully that they showered through the air. "It's driving me *out of my mind!*"

Obviously. "Nat, get a hold of yourself. You'll live through this."

"I'm not so sure! I've got all this wedding stuff to take care of. My mother keeps nagging me about every little detail. *'Natalie, do this. Natalie, did you remember? Don't forget, Natalie!'* Do you know what it's like to be twenty-eight and have your mother pestering you a million times per day?"

"My mother didn't even pester me when I was thirteen."

"Not to mention," Natalie continued, much as if she were talking to herself, "my work life is falling apart. The station manager is interviewing people for my job, I know it. Even after I hired that creep Elton!"

"How do you know?"

"Because I saw a knockout blonde go into the head producer's office today. Somebody told me she's from a station in Idaho. She's a dead ringer for Jane, and she stayed in the producer's office for an hour and came out smiling. Then he gave her *a tour of the building.*"

"Okay," Celia said cautiously, "so maybe they want her for an evening anchor position."

"But that should be *my* job!" Natalie wailed. "They should be promoting *me*, not trucking in some Barbie doll from Boise!" She stuffed a fistful of Cheetos in her mouth.

"But maybe what's happening is they're going to promote you and put her in your place. That would be a good thing, wouldn't it?"

"That would be a miracle, and I don't believe in those." Natalie looked so dejected, slumped in a kitchen chair with an orange ring around her mouth, that Celia almost felt sorry for her. "Did I tell you I got a call from a station in Eugene?"

Celia shook her head.

"They're looking for a new anchorwoman to boost their ratings. Six o'clock spot."

"The evening news? Just what you wanted. That would be great!"

Natalie rolled her eyes. "Eugene, Celia."

"So?"

"It's the hinterlands."

"I've heard it's a cool place to live."

"Give me a break. *Cool?* That just means it's full of old hippies!" Natalie shuddered. "I'd be taking a step backward in my career *and* a step backward in time, living with a bunch of flower-power throwbacks."

The doorbell rang.

"That'll be Davis," Celia guessed.

Angus mumbled and flopped over on the couch,

and Natalie went to the door and buzzed Davis up. Moments later he rushed into the apartment carrying a first aid kit and a baseball bat. He was unshaven, and his outfit was a sight—khaki pants with hiking boots, a black T-shirt, and a knit cap.

Celia looked at him eyeing the living room like a cinema commando and felt her heart swell.

Natalie laughed. "Sorry to disappoint you, but I'm still in one piece."

Davis slowly surveyed the apartment until his gaze landed on Celia. She lifted her shoulders in an apologetic shrug, but tried to convey her thanks to him silently, with her eyes. "It wasn't that kind of an emergency."

"Oh." Davis took a moment to let the adrenaline settle. "Good."

"Cheeto?" Natalie asked, holding out the bag.

He shook his head as he tried to absorb the situation. "No thanks." For a moment, Celia wondered if he was going to snap. After all, he'd been dragged out of bed for nothing. She'd been a hairsbreadth away from throttling Natalie herself. But finally, Davis smiled. "Do you have anything to drink?"

Natalie visited the fridge and came up with a can of soda. "As long as you're here, do you know anything about reception favors?"

"Reception what?" Davis asked.

Natalie sighed. "Well, take a whack at it anyway," she said, pointing him toward the table. "You're *bound* to know as much as Celia."

For the next half hour, they debated the merits of picture frames versus little baskets of designer chocolates, or little baskets of cookies, or little baskets of monogrammed soaps, or the Hershey bars that would have the name McDougall in the block letters of the company logo. Natalie pronounced the chocolate bars "too ordinary," even though neither Davis nor Celia had ever seen them before.

In the end, they took a vote. Davis chose the basket of cookies. "But those you wouldn't even have to order from anybody," he told her helpfully. "Heck, chocolate chip? You could just make 'em yourself."

Natalie leveled her most withering you've-got-to-be-joking look on him. "Do I look like Fannie Farmer to you? Do I look like some bubbly dope who's going to inflict tacky homemade favors on her guests?"

Taking a cue from Natalie's reaction to Davis's choice, Celia opted for the little baskets of soaps, monogrammed with Natalie's and Angus's names and the wedding date.

But Natalie was even more displeased with that recommendation. "That is my *least* favorite."

"What's the matter with it?"

"Please! It looks like something you'd find in the bathroom at a La Quinta."

"Well, which would you choose?" Davis asked.

Natalie replied without hesitation. "The accordian picture frames."

Davis and Celia exchanged vexed glances.

"When you think about it, it's the most practical," Natalie explained. "Everyone who comes to the wedding will naturally want a wedding picture, and this way they'll have one—actually several—immediately." She frowned. "Of course, this means I'll *really* have to get Elton on the stick. Oh, and alter the dress! Did I tell you that even the size eight is squeezing me around the hips? I might have to go to a ten!" She drained the last of the Cheetos directly from the bag into her mouth.

When Natalie finally released them back onto the street, Davis and Celia simply stood for a moment, blinking at each other in the dim lights of the street lamps. Then they lost it.

It was just a few chuckles at first, but the mirth escalated rapidly into full-fledged hysteria. Once she was laughing, Celia felt as if she might not be able to stop. All she had to do was look at Davis in his yuppie commando gear, and the laughs just kept peeling out of her. Her stomach began to ache.

"I'm sorry I got you into this," Celia said when she could finally speak again. "But I'm so glad you showed up. Now I have a witness to exactly what a lunatic my friend is."

"I thought someone was trying to kill her," Davis said.

"*I* considered doing just that when I walked in and saw that all she was upset about was her reception favors."

Davis looked at his watch.

With that one impatient gesture, their shared mirth seemed to dissipate into the wet night air. It all came rushing back to her. Kyra, Olga. She'd been so overcome by Davis rushing to the rescue, by laughing with him just like old times, that she'd forgotten everything that had been happening. She'd forgotten what an ass she'd made of herself at the reception.

"Is it too late for a nightcap?" she asked, wanting to make amends.

He hesitated. "I don't . . ." He didn't finish the sentence, but it was clear he didn't want to go anywhere.

She nodded quickly. "I understand. How could you possibly want to go out with me after I acted like such a jerk?"

He frowned. "When?"

"At Stan and Mike's!"

He shrugged. "Actually, your walking out like

that . . . well, and some other things . . . made me think."

She wished she could sink through the pavement. "I should explain about that. Or, no—correction—I can't explain it. I just spazzed. But I do apologize."

"It's okay."

"No, it's not. I feel terrible. I acted like such a nut—and all because I thought you . . ." She shrugged. "Well, for some idiotic reason I thought you pitied me."

"Take off the hair shirt, Celia. It's okay."

"Well, I suppose it is, if it achieved the feat of making you put your tater into high gear. So did you have any revelations? Come to any great conclusions?"

"I did, as a matter of fact," he said. "I'm thinking about leaving."

The muscles in her face went slack. "Leaving the *Times*?" Was he going to finally take time off to write that book he was always talking about? She'd always thought that was sort of a joke.

He shook his head. "Leaving Portland."

It was as if someone had walluped her upside the head.

"You'll be proud of me. I'm going to grab a chance at an extended leave—like Cary Grant in that movie. At least for a little while." He smiled ruefully. "But it's still up in the air, depending on how long the paper will let me go. And of course, I'm not as rich as Cary Grant . . ."

She studied him for a moment, then attempted a smile. Naturally, Davis would be tentative. He even approached spontaneity with baby steps. "That doesn't sound very definite. Where do you think you'll go? Off to the Oregon coast for a while? Back to Nebraska for a visit?"

"No, I'm going to Argentina."

Fourteen

"Celia!"

Celia tried to snap to attention as she faced Natalie over the racks of the wispiest, most transparent lingerie Saks had to offer. "What's the matter with you?"

"Sorry. Late night."

"Well, I *know* that. We all had a late night."

Not that late, Celia thought as she yawned. She'd barely slept a wink after Davis had delivered his bombshell. Instead, she'd stayed up until the wee hours wondering how it could be that Davis—*Davis* of all people!—was going to flit off to Argentina just when she most wanted him here. She had hoped they were going to have some sort of reconciliation, and maybe a second chance kissing on her stoop. Instead, Mr. Homebody had told her that he was running off to Antonio in Buenos Aires. It was the sort of thing *she* was supposed to do! Only now she didn't even want an Antonio anymore.

She wanted Davis. *Celia-n-Davis* was beginning to sound a little less weird to her today. But repetition and a little time usually tended to make things seem more credible.

Unfortunately, even though *I want Davis* didn't sound as weird as it had yesterday, it was still every bit as unrealistic.

He was leaving her. Abandoning her. And the worst part was, he didn't even seem to know it.

Last night she had sifted through the conundrum over and over. She couldn't very well tell Davis *not* to go. For years she had been if not the poster child for, then at least one of the biggest advocates of the foreign. Now that she finally had a disciple, she could hardly discourage him. What could she say? *'Wait, I've decided I want you here now?'*

When daylight finally had beaten its way through her window shades, and Gazpacho was screeching for his breakfast, and the lovebirds were twittering back to life, she was no closer to a solution to her problem than she'd been hours before. Gorging on Corky's rubbery pancakes did little to make matters clearer. Around ten in the morning she'd collapsed back in bed in a sugar coma and slept fitfully for two hours until Natalie had come to drag her out on this shopping expedition. Now she felt equal parts jittery and exhausted.

And the fact was still racing around her tired brain—Davis was leaving her. Davis, Mr. Dependable. Just when she'd expected to be celebrating the fact that he wasn't having some hot and heavy fling with Olga. South America!

She moaned. "I shouldn't have gotten up this morning."

Natalie lifted up a thong and scrunched her face into an uncomfortable mask. "Morning? It was already noon when I dragged you out of bed. Besides, we have to buy you a merry widow if you're going to wear that strapless we picked out." She nodded over to a wall filled with sturdy, corset-type contraptions. Some of them looked bullet proof. "I don't want my maid of honor's breasts sagging like an old orangutan's. That would be *too* distracting."

Celia heard an insult, but her head was still too muzzy for her to rouse herself to self-defense. "Hmph."

Natalie put back the thong and scowled at her. "What's the matter with you today? We've got so much to do, and you're *so* glum!"

Celia wished she could curl up in a heap in some inconspicuous part of Intimate Apparel. "It's Davis. Last night he told me he's thinking of taking a leave of absence and going to visit a friend in Argentina."

Natalie's blue eyes telegraphed alarm. "A woman friend?"

"Not unless Antonio has turned into a gender neutral name without my knowledge."

"Oh! Well, then, what's the problem?"

Celia was astounded. Wouldn't the crux of the matter be obvious, even to Natalie? "The problem is Davis is leaving. He says he wants to broaden his horizons."

"So? Isn't that what you always tell people *you* want to do? Why do you take all those stupid language courses and pester people at travel agencies? Isn't that why we spent that wretched, life-threatening week in Thailand?"

"I swear no one told me that it was the typhoon season," Celia said for the hundredth time since their leaky hut nearly washed away with them in it.

Natalie's expression revealed that this was a subject best put off for another day. "My point is, why are you so upset about the guy spreading his wings?"

"Because he's spreading them without me!"

Natalie pounced on Celia's pronouncement with the gusto of a cat on an overturned bug. "Aha! So admit it. You *do* have a thing for Davis."

"Well, of course I do. Isn't it obvious?"

Her friend sent her an impatient stare. "To *moi?* Of course. It's all as clear as Saran Wrap to me. But

I understand behavior, and I was never shunned by you. Our ex-Fozzie, on the other hand, still living under your stinging rejection, is probably trying to think of you as something verboten to him now, like Twinkies."

Celia contemplated a nightgown that was as modest as a fish net would have been. Natalie's observations seemed depressingly and surprisingly astute. "But what can I do now? I can't chase him."

"Why not?"

"Because . . ." How could she explain it? "I'm just not like that. Some women are Scarletts, some are Melanies. I, unfortunately, am a Melanie."

"Bullshit," Natalie said, rifling through the sleepwear. "Who really sympathizes with Melanie? The woman spent her life married to a drip, and then she died. Is that what you want to happen to you?"

Celia opened her mouth to refute this interpretation of *Gone With the Wind,* but then stopped, puzzled. Come to think of it, maybe Natalie had a point.

"Your trouble is, when it comes to relationships you just float along. You need to take some initiative, like I did. When it comes to catching a guy, you have to be a little cunning, like the tigress stalking the wildebeest."

Celia rubbed her temples and realized how woefully unprepared she was for Natalie's laws of the jungle, or the savannah. Tigers? Wildebeests? "I think you've got your continents mixed up."

"Whatever."

"Besides, I don't think I'm capable of thinking like a tigress just now."

But Natalie was already off tigresses and wildebeests. Sort of. "Mother wants us to nail down the shower decorations today, if we can. And while we're out today, we should try to hunt down some shoes for you, too. You'll need to practice walking in them."

The implied insult finally roused her. "I'm twenty-seven. I can walk in adult shoes."

Now that she'd circled the department and made her inspection, Natalie started snatching up lingerie with lightning speed. "Can you stand for hours in four-inch heels? Can you *dance* in them?"

"Four inches?" Celia squeaked. By the end of the day she'd be crippled.

"You're so short, Celia. We have jack you up so that you're at least a few inches taller than the flower girl."

That did it.

Celia's head felt as if it were about to explode. Arms akimbo, she drew up to her full five-foot-three and glared up at Natalie. "That's it!" The words were a staccato battle cry; Celia didn't care how many underwear shoppers turned to stare. She felt like Ahab finally facing off with the white whale. Nothing now could have stopped her from throwing her harpoon. "I have about had it!"

Natalie whirled, her eyes wide blue saucers. "What's wrong?"

"What's wrong? *What's wrong?*" Celia's voice looped up an octave. "I'm exhausted, that's what's wrong. In case you've forgotten, I was yanked out of my bed at two o'clock in the morning to help you decide on reception favors!"

"You said you wanted to help," Natalie said, all innocence.

"Sure I did. Or I would have, if you'd just been honest and said what you were really calling about."

Her friend looked almost hurt. "I didn't think it would matter."

"Maybe it wouldn't have. But I would have liked the opportunity to have decided that for myself. Instead, you got me all panicked. I even called Davis to come help. Which was fine. He was a good sport about it. But don't you think you could have thanked us?"

"I did." Natalie's brow drew into a frown. "I thought I did."

Celia crossed her arms. "Ever since you sprang this engagement on everyone, you've been completely absorbed in these plans of yours."

"Well, naturally I've been absorbed," Natalie said. "What's the matter with you?"

"Everything, apparently! I'm too wimpy to catch a man, too feeble-minded to entrust with wedding shower plans, too ignorant to advise you on dresses, too short, too orangutan breasted! My God, Natalie, if you think I'm so inappropriate, why couldn't you have picked another person to put through this hell? Why me?"

As Celia spoke, Natalie's face reddened to a deep crimson. She grasped her chosen lingerie to her bosom and flinched at Celia's words. Then, when Celia stopped, she began to quiver. Her face melted like a rubber mask. Faster than you could say "bridal breakdown," Natalie was sagging against a rack of panties and bawling her head off.

Really bawling her head off.

And she didn't seem inclined to stop anytime soon.

Celia darted a few self-conscious glances around them. A stern, gray-haired saleslady at the crowded cash register glared at her accusingly—a look that said there would be hell to pay if that panty rack went over.

Celia dashed over to keep it upright, and Natalie went from sagging against the stainless steel panty tree to sagging against Celia. She nearly buckled as her friend's dead weight crashed on top of her. "Uh . . . Nat?"

Through tears, Natalie said something that sounded like, "You're mebested."

"What?"

Natalie dragged her arm across her nose and sucked in an uneven breath. "I said"—she sniffed, looking straight into Celia's eyes—"you're my best friend, Celia." She blinked and hiccuped, then dissolved again. "That's why I wanted you to be my maid of honor. Even though Mother tried to talk me out of it, nothing could have made me choose anyone but you. You're the best friend I've ever had! In fact, you're practically the only person who's ever really liked me."

She broke down sobbing again.

All these years, Celia had assumed that she was the needy, subordinate one in the relationship; that she was just someone Natalie barely managed to squeeze into her busy life. An afterthought. An amusing leftover from college days. She'd thought that the friendship meant more to her than to Natalie. To learn that this wasn't the case, and that they were *both* clinging to the relationship like pathetic codependents, nearly bowled her over.

Given her exhaustion, given the fact that Davis was about to bail on her just like Ian and every other person she'd ever cared about had done, having anyone declare her to be her best friend was nearly her undoing.

Celia's eyes went misty, and she had to sniff back a sob herself. At least Natalie would never leave her!

Natalie blew her nose into an as-yet-unpurchased peach camisole. "You don't have to be my maid of honor, Celia," she said pitifully.

Celia's emotions were too shaky for her to leap at the dreamed-of reprieve. "Of course I want to be your maid of honor. I just get tired of being sniped at."

Natalie stepped back, nodding and sniffling like a recalcitrant child. "I know. I'm so sorry. I don't know what's come over me. For a while there I was *really* trying hard not to be a bitch."

"Well, you need to renew your efforts."

She was afraid Natalie was going to collapse on top of her again. "You're such a good friend, Celia. I honestly mean that."

"Right. I'm such a good friend I'm causing you to have nervous breakdowns in Saks."

Natalie chuckled as she dug into her bottomless purse for a Kleenex. "I want to take you out to lunch."

Celia was so exhausted now she didn't think she would be able to sit up for that long. "Oh, that's okay. I think—"

"I will *not* take no for an answer," Natalie said, recovering control. She rattled off her afternoon plans as if she would brook no argument. "We're going to buy you some four-inch heels and a merry widow brassiere and then eat a light seafood brunch at Jake's, and that's that!"

Celia staggered home that afternoon, weighted down with shopping bags and full after Natalie's fried calamari feast. Natalie had packed away the greasy seafood as if she were a longshoreman. And all through the meal, she'd reiterated that Celia should be more tigresslike toward Davis.

Unfortunately, she didn't say how this was to be accomplished.

Maybe the answer wasn't to beg Davis not to go. What she needed to do was make him want to stay.

But how?

She passed a bookstore and ducked inside. Much as she hated to admit it, she needed guidance from the self-help aisle. She was making a beeline for the relationship books when her gaze snagged on something completely different in the bargain bins. She picked up an oversized cellophane-wrapped book entitled, *Shall We Dance? Ballroom Dancing in Ten Easy Lessons (CD included!).*

Celia gawked at the thing, amazed by her offhand discovery. It was as if fate had lured her into this store and then zapped her with a lightning bolt. Dancing? Her mind flashed back to Davis giving her the cha-cha-cha lesson at the wedding reception. Until she'd started thinking about Olga and had gone temporarily bipolar, the dance had been great. Intimate. Sexy.

This was exactly what she needed! She could learn a few steps and show Davis that she was really interested in being able to go out and cut a rug with him. Maybe by the time of Natalie's wedding, she would be able to impress him with her swanlike grace and prowess. She could sweep *him* off his feet.

Her tired feet flew the rest of the way home, and she sailed up the stairs to her garret. Just having the book and CD in her possession was already making her feel almost twinkle-toed.

Her apartment was blessedly empty—and even clean. Gone was any residual mess from the pancake breakfast. On the refrigerator was pinned a note: *C: We've gone to the movies. Back tonight. C&E.*

What luck! She had the apartment to herself. The first thing she did was yank Bruce Springsteen out of the CD player and pop in her new dance music. The Blue Danube waltz came on, in an excruciatingly slow learner's tempo. Well, at least there was one lesson she could skip. She hummed along with the remedial Strauss as she flipped on lights and threw open the windows to freshen the place with the cool evening air. Then she went to her bedroom with her new purchases.

Much as she hated to do it, she decided she needed to try on that horrible bra Natalie had forced on her. Against every principle her grandmother had tried to instill in her, she'd bought the thing without having it fitted at the store. She just couldn't have faced it, especially with Natalie breathing down her neck. Now, trying it on in privacy, she realized her grandmother's wisdom and her own mistake. The primitive thing was tighter than it had appeared, so that fastening it required the muscular wherewithal of Stone Cold Steve Austin.

Finally bolted in, expecting at any minute that her limbs would turn blue, she tottered breathlessly across the hall to the bathroom, where there was a full-length mirror. What she saw horrified her. The Victorian contraption was supposed to lift and shape. But what it really did was pinch and mold. She looked like Cloris Leachman as Nurse Diesel in *High Anxiety*.

Frantically she ran back to the bedroom and shoved on the towering Blahniks Natalie had insisted on. After all, maybe if she were taller . . .

Teetering back to the mirror to test that dubious theory, she nearly twisted her ankle. Shoot! Maybe Natalie was right. She *did* need practice walking in these horrible things. Distracted by her feet, she wobbled across the living room a few times pretending that she was balancing a book on her head.

Abruptly, the music on the CD changed. Celia recognized the rhythm. It was a cha-cha. The dance Davis had taught her at Stan and Mike's reception. Closing her eyes, she lifted her arms to mime an imaginary partner about Davis's height and concentrated on remembering the steps.

Step, back, cha-cha-cha. Step, step, cha-cha-cha.

Without another person, it was very simple. She added a little Latin wriggle of the hips, aiming for Rita Hayworth sexiness.

She wouldn't have even noticed that something sailed just past her head, except that it crashed against the wall behind her. *That* she couldn't miss. Gazpacho squawked loudly.

At first, frozen in shock, Celia thought she must have imagined that something had just torpedoed through her open window. But then she turned and saw a brick lying on her floor. Actually, it was only half a brick, with twine wrapped around it several times to hold down a piece of paper.

Approaching the missile as cautiously as she would a land mine, she carefully eased the paper out and unfolded it. On it was scrawled a simple message in block capital letters. YOU'LL BE SORRY, BABE!!

For the second time in less than twenty-four hours, Davis raced across the Willamette River, emergency adrenaline pumping. It was difficult to keep his foot from flooring the accelerator.

He left the baseball bat at home this time, but only because Celia had assured him she would call the police the minute she hung up the phone with him. Her voice had sounded tight with panic, and even though she'd attempted to laugh about someone lobbing bricks with menacing messages through her window, she wasn't fooling him. She was shaken up.

The thought of her being frightened sent one hundred percent raw fury coursing through him. Who the hell would be throwing bricks through Celia's window?

He was glad to see a police cruiser parked outside Celia's building. He ran up the three flights of stairs to the attic and was about to dash into the apartment when an arm held out at chest height stopped him. A young policeman with buzzed-off red hair, a square jaw, and a liberal coating of freckles glared at him. "Wait a minute."

"It's okay," Davis assured him.

Square jaw turned. "Hey, Tray—we got a visitor."

Celia looked up from where she was talking to a slightly older, stockier dark-haired cop. Her face broke into a beaming smile that made Davis's heart do elaborate acrobatics. Which wasn't at all appropriate, he decided, when he was supposed to be coming to her rescue . . . or whatever it was he was doing. Celia was still in the same Mizzou sweatshirt she'd worn the night before and looked as frazzled as she'd sounded over the phone. "Davis!"

She launched herself at him.

"Wait a minute!" the cop named Tray said.

"It's okay," she assured him.

As Celia clung to him like a barnacle, Tray and his partner exchanged looks that clearly indicated that they found Davis suspect. "Uh, Celia . . ."

She pulled back. "Thanks for getting over here so fast!"

"Very fast," Tray noted.

Celia laughed, guessing the cop's line of thinking. "Oh, no—*he* didn't throw the brick. This is my friend Davis. Davis, this is Tray, and the officer who met you at the door is named Marty."

Tray and Marty? Their nametags said McLean and Remnick. Celia was already on first-name basis with these guys?

Marty looked from Davis to Celia. "What is he? Your boyfriend?"

Celia and Davis blinked at the cops, and both started stammering out denials.

"N-no . . ."

"Friends, we're friends."

"Right," Celia said, her mouth clenched tightly. "Friends. Anyway, Davis couldn't possibly have hurled that brick, because he was at home on the eastside when it happened. I called his cell phone number right after the brick came through the window."

"You called him before you called the police?"

Celia's brows lifted. "Anything wrong with that?"

"Nope," Tray said, jotting something down on a little notepad. Davis could swear the guy was still looking at him suspiciously.

He crossed to the kitchen counter, where the offending brick was. Next to it was the note Celia had told Davis about. YOU'LL BE SORRY, BABE!! It was just as she said. Only she hadn't told him about the red indentation on the wall opposite the window, where the brick had obviously hit. He stared at the spot in growing anger. What if that had hit Celia?

Moreover, how could someone have thrown a brick up to the third floor? He squinted through the window. The brick thrower couldn't have been on the ground. That would have taken a vertical curveball beyond even the talents of Roger Clemens. The brick must have come from across the street, where there was an old warehouse that now housed an art gallery. The top of the building was about even with Celia's apartment.

"Okay, so this brick just came sailing through your open window," Tray was saying.

Marty, apparently bored with what was obviously not an emergency, strolled over to look at Gazpacho. The gray bird was flapping his wings in agitation and muttering something in his unintelligible birdspeak.

"That's right," Celia said.

"And the apartment was just like this?" the cop asked. "Windows open, lights on?"

She shrugged. "I guess."

"So whoever it was who lobbed the brick could probably see it was you."

Celia's face paled. "What?"

Davis decided to put in his two cents. "He's right. If the guy was standing on the warehouse roof, he probably could see in."

"It's a narrow street, and you had the lights on, so he probably had good visibility," Tray added.

Celia was now changing colors like a mood ring. Her face went from white to red to green in a matter of seconds, and she let out a sickly moan.

Tray squinted at her. "What's the matter?"

She shook her head. "N-nothing. I just hadn't thought the person could see me."

"So the guy saw you in here and hurled a brick," Tray said. "And you immediately hopped on the horn and called David here."

"Davis." He put an arm around Celia for moral support. "Are you okay?"

She nodded dully. "Just creeped out. *Really* creeped out."

"Okay," Tray went on, noting their arm-in-arm stance, "so you hopped on the horn and called Davis just-a-friend here. And *then* you called the police."

"That's right."

"Didn't you first run to the window to see if whoever tossed the brick was still around?"

"No," Celia said.

The cop's brows darted up. "Wouldn't that have been the logical thing to do?"

"Not under the circumstances," Celia insisted.

"Why not?"

Davis frowned. Why was the cop riding her like this? Couldn't he see she was upset? "What if the guy had tossed another brick and bonked her on the head? You'd be standing here calling her an idiot."

"No, I would have thought it was a *natural* reaction. Also, it would have helped us figure out who we're looking for. Male, female . . ." He turned to Celia. "Sure you didn't see anything?"

"I'm sure."

"Not even out of the corner of your eye?"

"I'm sorry, I wouldn't have run to the window—in fact, I ran away from it."

"Why?"

How dense could a guy be? "Because she didn't want to get beaned with a brick," Davis said.

But at the same time he was speaking, Celia was piping up, *"Because I didn't have any clothes on."*

Davis pivoted in surprise. "Nothing?"

Colorwise, she could have given a hot tamale a run for its money. "Well . . . nearly nothing."

As her words sank in, the deeper Davis's frown became. He swallowed. Then he swallowed again. Scantily clad Celia. He should not be thinking about this.

The cop gave her sweatshirt and jeans a once-over.

"I put these on *after* I made the phone calls," she explained.

"Okay, so you were . . . well, never mind," Tray said. "Do you know of anyone who would want to do you any harm?"

"Of course not!" Celia said.

Davis turned to her. "Wait a minute. What about the guy downstairs?"

"Mr. Zhirbotken?" She hooted. "No way!"

"Last time you mentioned him, you said he was ready to kill you."

She chuckled. "Oh, right."

"There's a guy downstairs who wants to kill you?" Tray asked.

"Not really. He was just a little peevish because I was teaching my parrot to sing Dean Martin songs."

"Really," Tray said, sending a glance over to the parrot perch as if for confirmation.

Marty shook his head. "This parrot is *not* singing Dean Martin."

"Well, no," Celia huffed, "he's not."

"He's saying something, though . . ." Marty leaned in closer to the bird—dangerously close, in Davis's opinion.

Celia didn't try to hide her exasperation. "He sings Bruce Springsteen."

As if they had been zapped, Marty and Tray froze, their eyes bulging. They gaped at her almost reverentially. "The Boss?"

"Get *outta* here!" Marty cried enthusiastically. "He's my fave, man."

"Gazpacho can sing snatches of several of his songs now." Celia added, not without grudging pride, "Off three different albums."

"Cool!"

"But 'Born to Run' is still his favorite," she said.

Marty clucked disgustedly, as if this should be a given. "Well, yeah."

Celia looked like a mother who was beginning to wonder if her child who had just pulled apart the vacuum cleaner wasn't a prodigy. She warmed up to the cops. "He'll break into song any minute now, but you can't be watching him. He's like a cat—absolutely will not perform on cue."

Davis cleared his throat. "Um, Celia, don't you think we ought to be talking about the brick?"

Tray swung on him and shot him a look as if he were the biggest wet blanket in the world. "Oh, right. The brick."

"I *really* doubt it's the guy downstairs," Celia said.

"For one thing, the sentence in the note is far too coherent. Mr. Zhirbotken would have butchered even a four-word message."

"Well, we'll drop by and talk to him, just in case," Tray said.

"Also, *babe* is not a Zhirbotken kind of word." Celia tapped her forefinger against her chin in thought, then sucked in a breath. "Omigod, I forgot!"

"What?"

"Art Carney!"

Tray shook his head. *"Art Carney?"*

"I call him Art Carney." Celia turned to Davis. "You know, that guy who's always harassing me at work?"

"A coworker?" Tray asked.

"No, he's just some drunk guy who thinks it's funny that I write a wedding column called 'Unions.' His schtick is to call me up and ask me to put something about labor disputes in the column. You know, *unions*. Ha-ha."

Tray sent her a steady look. "What was the tone of your last conversation with this guy?"

Celia frowned. "I think it ended with me calling him an asshole and slamming down the phone."

The cop watched her closely. "And is this the first act of violence perpetrated against you recently?"

"Recently?" Celia asked. "Try ever." She glanced at Davis. "Unless . . ."

"What?" Davis asked.

"Well, I was with Davis when a guy hurled a few water bombs at him, but I'm certain that act of violence wasn't directed at me."

"No," Davis explained to the cops. "That was directed at me. Because I was a hydro-hog."

Tray looked completely clueless, so Celia got him up to speed on the details of the water main incident. Then she pursed her lips. "The water balloon guy *looked* the type to call women babes. More than Mr. Zhirbotken, that's for sure."

Tray was about to ask another question when suddenly there was a clatter on the stairs. Everyone tensed.

Natalie flew into the room and launched herself at Celia.

"Oh, Celia! What an emotion-packed day we've had! I *zoomed* over here as soon as I'd finished touching up my nails!"

Celia, buried in Natalie's now almost ample bosom, grunted. "Thanks, Nat."

"Who's this?" Tray asked.

When it came to dealing with Natalie, "Who's this?" was the wrong question to ask. The newswoman pushed Celia aside and turned on the policeman with an imperious stare. "I am Natalie Glass of Channel Seven news. My question is, who are *you*? And what are you going to do to ensure my friend's safety?"

"You recognize Natalie Glass from the earlybird show, I'm sure," Celia prompted the cop. "I called her right after I called Davis."

"Before you called the police."

Celia shrugged. "What can I say? A girl needs friends in times of crisis."

Natalie dug into her huge Louis Vuitton tote. "Well, never fear. I've got the suspect list right here with me." She brought out a hefty notebook.

"You have an idea who did this?" the cop asked.

"Didn't you tell them?" Natalie asked Celia. At Celia's nonplussed expression, Natalie turned back to Tray. "Celia's a journalist who has been working on a very inflammatory article on wedding prices. I'm sure this brick incident is someone's crude way of sending a message."

"What's that?" the cop asked, pointing to the notebook.

"My wedding planner. I'm getting married at the beginning of June, and Celia's my maid of honor. And during the course of our shopping trips she started investigating—"

"Uh, Nat . . ." Celia said.

Natalie turned to her. "You *know* how mad some of those proprietors were with you."

"I doubt angry caterers are tossing bricks through my windows."

"Well, who else would?" Natalie asked.

"That's what we're trying to figure out," Davis told her.

Natalie blinked up at him. "Oh! *You're* here!"

"I called Davis first thing," Celia said.

"Good for you!" Natalie exclaimed.

Davis shared a puzzled look with the cops.

" 'Boooorn in the U.S.AAAAAA.!' "

A collective gasp rose in the room and everyone turned toward Gazpacho.

"Awesome!" Marty exclaimed.

Celia shook her head sadly. "That's a new one. I should murder Corky."

"Who's Corky?" Tray asked.

"He's the guy that taught those songs to my parrot. He lives here . . . sort of."

Tray looked around the room again, taking in the boxes. Marty was trying to coax Gazpacho into doing another number.

"He's supposed to live with Davis," Celia continued, "but he sort of hangs with Ellen. She kind of lives here, too."

The cop shook his head. "Wait a sec, there are *three* of you living in this place?"

"Sort of."

Tray's eyes narrowed. "Where's this Corky guy now?"

Celia shrugged. "He and Ellen went to the movies. I haven't seen them all afternoon." She caught the suspicion in his eyes, then laughed. "But Corky's not your man."

"Then, what about Ellen?"

"Ha!" Celia exclaimed. Davis and Natalie joined in. "She's never done anything hostile in her life. She hates scenes. Which is why it took me so long to convince her . . . to . . ."

Her words petered out, and her face drained to a pasty white. "Oh!" she exclaimed.

Davis figured it out at the same time. "Lyle."

Fifteen

"It *can't* be Lyle," Ellen insisted.

She and Corky had come back a little while after the cops had politely told Celia to call if any more bricks came through her window. When the moviegoers heard what had happened that afternoon, they were stunned. Ellen was even more shocked to hear that they had come to the conclusion that the brick had been lobbed by her husband.

"Lyle wouldn't do that," she said flatly.

They were all sitting in the crowded living room now, debating who had done it and what to do next. To Celia, still stunned to find herself the victim of this bizarre crime, the situation felt surreal. As if all her friends had morphed into inept detectives. They still didn't get along with each other, but now they had something meaningful to argue about. Should they confront Lyle? What if it wasn't Lyle? Should they wait and see?

They certainly couldn't go after Lyle without Ellen's agreement, but with stubborn irrationality, Ellen was embracing the angry caterer theory, which now even Natalie had abandoned.

Natalie, who was slumped in an armchair with a bowl of M&Ms, had joined the Lyle-as-brick-lobber camp (which included everyone except Ellen). "Of course it was your hubby," she told Ellen. "You officially moved out on him yesterday, and now he's enraged by your abandonment. *And* you said he sometimes calls you babe."

"But only in a kind, slightly ironic way," Ellen argued, "not a menacing or patronizing way."

"It's always patronizing when a guy calls you babe," Natalie said.

"Wait a sec," Corky said. "People say babe all the time."

Like a college professor about to make a point that should have been learned in grade school, Natalie released an impatient breath. "Of course people call other people babes—that's a compliment. But no guy with any appeal says, 'Hey, babe, get me a beer.' "

Corky looked perplexed. *"I do."*

Natalie folded her arms. "I rest my case."

"Oh, and what does your Celtic wonderboy call you?" Corky shot back at her. "Your Highness?"

Davis bravely leapt into the fray. "Calm down, guys. Maybe we shouldn't put too much importance on a single word."

"Besides, the police said that the brick thrower could probably see into the apartment," Ellen pointed out. "Why would Lyle have lobbed a brick at Celia if the message was meant for me?"

Every time it was mentioned that the brick thrower might have seen her, Celia felt queasy. This meant the assailant—Lyle?—had seen her dancing around in her underwear. Why did everything in her life have to come with an embarrassing little spin? Next time she was parading around in next to nothing, she definitely needed to be more careful about pulling down the shades.

But how could she have guessed there would be a psycho on the warehouse roof?

Davis was staring at her anxiously. And no wonder. Though he was too much of a gentleman to ask her straight out, he was probably wondering why she'd been running around her living room with no clothes on.

But the fact that he had been practically the first person on the scene, and that he seemed more than typically concerned for her welfare, made her feel perversely light-headed. It was the first time in her life that she'd felt watched over. Once when she'd had a crank caller pestering her, she'd called Ian hoping he'd suggest she come over to his place to stay the weekend. Instead of running to her side to play Galahad, he'd told her that if she had a brain in her head she would have gotten caller ID before then.

"Lyle wouldn't hurt a flea," Ellen said.

"What are you talking about?" Natalie grabbed up a whole handful of candy. "The man makes a living sticking pins into people."

"But that's to *alleviate* pain."

Corky looked at Ellen, faintly annoyed that she would be so vociferously advocating for Lyle. "Honey, you of all people should know that the man is unpredictable."

"He is not," Ellen countered. "He's *very* predictable. To the point of mania."

"There!" Natalie said.

"Besides," Ellen insisted, "that isn't his handwriting on that note."

"He could disguise his handwriting," Davis said.

"Why are you defending this guy?" Corky asked Ellen.

Celia cleared her throat uncomfortably. Poor Ellen looked miserable. She hated to think the worst of anybody—even a guy who had made her a nervous wreck for eight months. "Ellen's just being judicious."

"She's just being a dope," Natalie said.

For once, Corky was in agreement with Natalie.

"This is no time to try to win any Gandhi awards. The guy is a nut."

Natalie nodded. "Think about it, Ellen. What have Celia's Lifetime movies taught us? *The husband can never be trusted.* Just think about Sally Field in *Not Without My Daughter.*"

This was so true. Celia certainly couldn't think of a more logical suspect than Lyle at this point. There was just one thing that bothered her. "But Lyle could surely tell that it was me and not Ellen standing in the middle of the living room."

"Maybe he wasn't wearing his glasses," Corky said.

"He *always* wears his glasses," Ellen insisted.

If they didn't drop this soon, Celia feared Corky and Ellen's budding relationship would be a casualty of the brick. "It doesn't really matter, guys. What are we supposed to do? Storm over to Ellen's house and confront Lyle? All he has to do is deny, deny, deny."

Davis cleared his throat. "One thing I think we should do is move everybody over to my place for a little while. You'll all be safer."

Celia's heart flipped. He wasn't calling her a jittery ninny. He really was wonderful. A true Galahad. The anti-Ian.

Corky bristled at the idea of running. "We'll be okay over here. I can protect Ellen." As an afterthought, he tossed in, "And Celia, too, I guess."

Much as Celia wanted to play damsel in distress at Davis's, she had to agree with Corky. As long as they kept everything locked, they would be fine. No reason to swarm over to Davis's house. She smiled at him gratefully. "Thanks, but we'll be okay here."

An M&M thunked her upside the head. "Oh! Sorry!" Natalie exclaimed.

Celia picked the candy off the couch cushion. What was that about?

Natalie darted a glare at her. "Are you sure you really want to stay here, Celia? You might be more *aggressive* in avoiding danger at *Davis's* house."

Celia squinched her face in puzzlement. It took her a long time to interpret what Natalie was doing, and when she did she felt herself cringe. Good Lord! Did she have to be so *obvious?*

Now, with bricks flying through her window, was not the time to worry about being a tigress. Besides, even if she did take Davis up on his offer of a safe house (a scenario ripe for seduction, she had to admit), Ellen and Corky would have to come along, too, and she could hardly act slinky and catlike with them around. "We'll be okay here," she repeated, to Natalie's obvious disappointment.

"Besides," Corky said, "who'd take care of my main man Gazpacho if we left?"

Davis looked painfully torn. "You could bring him," he finally said.

The offer nearly brought tears to her eyes. Offering her a safe house was one thing, but extending the invitation to Gazpacho, who had nearly taken off his finger once, was true gallantry.

But to move Gazpacho was a major operation involving the transporting of cage and perch. To say nothing of what it would take to move herself, Corky, Ellen, and all their impedimenta. The thought was just too tiring. Celia had had so little sleep today she was just running on fumes. Besides, whoever was bothering them, she didn't want that person to have the satisfaction of knowing he'd run them out of their apartment.

"We'll stay here," she insisted with an assurance that came more from exhaustion than bravery.

* * *

As soon as Celia slipped into her office chair at seven minutes past nine the next morning, Marie was tapping her on the shoulder. "The eighth floor in ten minutes. Be there."

"Personnel?" Celia croaked. "But I'm only seven minutes late . . ."

Marie pursed her lips. "This isn't a slap on the hand for tardiness, Snowden. It's the big boys who want to see us. As in, Caselli."

"Mr. Caselli? The owner? Wants to see *us?*" Celia tried to think of some bone-headed thing she'd done at work lately and for once came up blank. "Why?"

"Read your E-mail."

Celia sank down in her chair and turned nervously to Davis. He was smiling at her encouragingly. His twinkling at her reminded her of yesterday, when he'd offered to rescue her. Which in turn made her feel as though her insides were turning to mush.

"You okay?" he asked.

"I was just dandy till now. I've never been to the eighth floor before. What's going on?"

"Your piece about Stan and Mike has flooded this place with E-mail and phone calls."

She hadn't even had time to pick up the paper yesterday, so she'd forgotten all about her column. "Oh, no," she groaned.

She flicked on her computer to survey the damage. There were two hundred and seventy-three new messages awaiting her, and a quick perusal told her that most of them fell into one of two categories. A typical example of one type of letter read:

Bravo! Finally, the journalistic establishment is beginning to open its eyes to the wonderful di-

versity of this city. Congratulations to Stan and
Mike!

While the other half went more along these lines:

You call this journalism, Ms. Snowden? I call it
sicko liberal propaganda. It's people like you who
are ruining this country. . . .

And as she discovered upon further study, *that* was
one of the more kindly phrased of the negative
E-mails. At least that reader hadn't called her moral
pond scum.

Celia lowered her head to her desk. "I'm not certain whether I'm ready to deal with this today."

Davis wheeled over and patted her on the back, a
simple physical contact that hit her system like three
cups of espresso. "Don't let it get to you. You can't
please everybody."

"Am I a dolt? I thought the story might be distaste-
ful to some, but *ruining the country?* With a silly article
in the style section of the newspaper?"

"Apparently some people didn't find it so silly."

No kidding. Ten minutes later, she and Marie were
standing in front of Hal Caselli, the owner of the *Portland Times,* and Martin Donaldson, the paper's editor
in chief. Both of them looked as if something had just
died.

That something was probably her career.

Caselli, who had the immaculately groomed appearance of a man who had never done time as a drone
at a news desk, folded his hands on the polished wal-
nut expanse in front of him. "Well, you've created
quite a stir."

Celia stiffened at the slightly condescending tone.
She almost expected him to tack on "little lady" to

the end of his statement. She squared her shoulders, looked the man in the eye, and replied, "I saw it as just another wedding."

Caselli guffawed uncomfortably. "Your 'just another wedding' has just cost us a little under two hundred subscriptions."

"I'm sorry about that."

"Sorry?" Martin, the second in command, squealed. "Do you know what subscribers mean to us right now? They're like gold, Snowden. We're not only competing with television and other print media, we've got to fight the free news coverage on the Internet. People who actually want to *pay* for a newspaper should not be taken lightly."

"I didn't say I take them lightly," Celia said, "but what should we do? Issue an apology for simply covering something that happens in the world?"

"Celia . . ." Marie muttered in warning.

Celia understood that she was in danger of digging herself even deeper into trouble, but she couldn't help popping off. "Are we supposed to see only what a certain segment of the population wants us to see?"

The men blinked at her. Marie gaped at her as though she had lost her mind.

Maybe she was so shaken after her exhausting weekend and having someone throw a brick through her window that she didn't care whether or not she courted danger. Or perhaps there was a part of her that wouldn't have minded being booted back out onto the street, where she and her slightly tarnished resumé could make a new start. The truth was, she didn't feel like kowtowing or apologizing.

"Look," she went on, "the *Times* has featured a wedding a week for almost a decade now. That's five hundred and twenty, approximately. So once in ten years we toss in a story that's not quite to the taste of our mainstream readers. One out of five hundred and twenty. Is that really a reason to get our panties in a twist?"

A gurgling moan stuck in Marie's throat.

"It's the readers who are in a twist," Caselli said sharply. "We're talking dollars and cents."

"Half of the feedback I received was positive," Celia said. "Maybe some of those who weren't subscribers before—because the *Times* is an old, stodgy publication that can't compete with the Internet and the free weeklies—might consider subscribing now."

"That's a big maybe," Martin argued.

Marie finally jumped into the fray. She straightened, allowing her shoulder pads to rise to the occasion. "Snowden's right about the positive feedback, Hal. The ratio of my mail was about fifty-fifty, too."

Caselli and Martin looked at each other. "Well, all right. We'll leave this for now," Caselli said. "But for God's sake, the next time something like this is in the works, will someone please send up a red flag?"

Martin and Marie practically saluted before they turned and scurried out, tugging Celia along with them. "Jesus, Celia," Martin said when the three of them had stopped to huddle outside in the hallway. "I didn't know you were so fond of living on the edge."

Celia rolled her eyes. "Did you hear what he said? 'Send up a red flag.' That means send him a warning so he can squash the story next time."

Marie didn't even seem to care about the substance of the meeting. "I can't believe you said *panties* in front of Hal Caselli."

Martin laughed and jabbed a thumb in Celia's direction. "She's got spunk. What's she doing covering weddings?"

Celia felt herself draw up with pride. It wasn't every

day that somebody told her she had spunk. To have it said in front of Marie, who thought she was a numb-skull, was particularly gratifying.

Celia even sensed the Warden reassessing her a little on the elevator back down to the fifth floor.

"So what happened?" Davis asked when they were back in their department.

"Well, my head is still attached to my shoulders," Celia said.

Davis drummed his fingers on his chair. He seemed worried. "While you were gone, I was reconsidering yesterday's incident."

"The brick?" At least her Stan and Mike article mess had allowed her to forget about *that* for thirty minutes.

Marie, who had followed Celia all the way back to her cubicle, looked confused. "What brick?"

Davis filled their boss in on the events of yesterday. Happily, no mention was made of the fact that Celia had been naked in her apartment (for unknown reasons) when the incident occurred. Maybe Davis had forgotten that part . . . or maybe he was just being kind. The story seemed to shock Marie enough without its most salient detail.

"So you've got some wacko husband harassing you?" Marie asked Celia. "Why don't you tell wifey to go find her own place? Kick her out on her tail."

That Marie. She was all heart.

"But I'm not so sure it was Lyle now after all," Davis said. "Think about it. Your Stan and Mike article came out yesterday morning. Look at the vitriol it created."

Celia considered the possibility for a moment. "I suppose that would explain why somebody would throw a brick at me. Because it still seems weird that Lyle would toss the brick at me with a message for Ellen."

Marie shook her head. "All I know is, after seeing Snowden tell Caselli not to get his panties in a twist, nothing would surprise me."

Davis grinned at Celia. "You said that?"

"I sort of shot off my mouth."

Marie slapped her on the back. "Kid, you did good."

When Marie had returned to her desk, Davis and Celia exchanged amazed glances. "Did you hear what I heard?" he asked.

"That actually sounded like a compliment. In fact, Marie's been incredibly calm about this whole Stan and Mike fallout. Do you think someone's been spiking her coffee with Prozac?"

Davis laughed before his expression turned worried again. "So . . . Was everything okay last night?"

She looked into those blue eyes and felt his waves of concern wrapping around her. "We muddled through." Her heart seemed to swell to ten times its normal size. Maybe he was just being friendly, but she was feeling something much stronger than that.

How could she ever have thought her dream man was anything other than a cautious worrywart?

That night, Celia was in the middle of making up the place cards Natalie insisted on for the shower. As she worked, her mind ricocheted between the two subjects fighting for prominence in her head: the upcoming wedding and the brick. She definitely wasn't standing anywhere near open windows these days.

She was avoiding her phone, too. Natalie seemed to pester her almost hourly about wedding details. Whether Celia had liked the mushroom puffs a caterer had given them samples of. Whether they should decorate Natalie's balcony for the shower. Whether she should go for a jazz combo or an oldies rock band for the Barge Bonanza rehearsal dinner.

Natalie's nerves were fraying at the edges, but now it seemed *everyone* Celia knew was coming apart. This impression was reinforced when Ellen returned home. The poor woman was trembling so that the Cocopelli figurines dangling from her ears jangled audibly.

"I talked to Lyle!" she blurted without preamble.

"What happened?"

"I told him that I want a divorce. That's what we talked about. I didn't mention the brick. He didn't either." Ellen sighed. "Though I guess he wouldn't have—if he were the culprit."

"You need a drink?" Celia asked her.

"I sure do! I was thinking about making some ginseng tea. You want some?"

Celia laughed. "I thought you might like something stronger. We can break into the emergency vodka."

Ellen shook her head. "No thanks. I think Corky wants to go out anyway when he gets back from the restaurant."

Celia hesitated, but curiosity won out. "How did Lyle take it?"

Ellen shrugged. "He said he expected as much when I came to collect my stuff."

Celia frowned. "He didn't try to talk you out of it?"

"No."

"Did he yell?"

"Oh, no." Ellen's brow pinched in concentration. "All he said was, 'Are you going to stay with Celia forever?' And I said, 'I don't know.'"

It didn't sound like the behavior of a man who would have been hurling bricks at people just the day before.

"Oh, and the other thing he said was, 'You left your old robe, a box of candles, and several books.'"

"You mean he wants all evidence of you erased?"

"I guess so." When Celia looked up at her, Ellen's lower lip was trembling. She sank onto the armchair. "I'm going to be erased!"

Celia pushed her place cards away and put an arm around Ellen's shoulders. "I'm sorry, I should have used a different word."

Ellen sniffled. "N-no, erased is just right."

Celia handed her a box of Kleenex that was sitting on an end table. It seemed as if she'd been going through a lot of those lately. Her life had never so closely resembled a daytime drama. *All My Neurotics,* she could call it.

Ellen blew her nose and let out a mirthless laugh. "You must think I'm crazy, getting so upset over Lyle wanting to erase me when *I'm* the one who left him."

"No . . ."

"Plus, I've got Corky now, who's so wonderful."

"Well . . ."

"He *is* wonderful, Celia. He's opened up a whole new world to me."

"Right. The rarified world of ESPN and *Emeril Live.*"

Ellen tossed her long hair, which was French braided into a long ponytail, over her shoulder. "It's new to me."

"But Corky . . . Well, he's not your type. Not what your whole life has been about. Are you sure it's not just the newness that's reeled you in?"

Ellen shook her head. "I don't know what you mean."

"It's just that you guys are opposites. Maybe Corky seems a little exotic to you." Just saying the words *Corky* and *exotic* in the same sentence was a tongue-straining exercise.

"It's more than just the thrill of the new," Ellen said. "I feel a real connection between us."

Celia was flabbergasted. "Really?"

Ellen nodded. "It's like something spiritual, almost. You must have felt that before."

Celia wasn't sure whether she wanted to guffaw or to weep. Corky and Ellen were having a meant-to-be spiritual thing? It was hard to digest. Why did lightning strike other people, but never her?

Instead, she just seemed to flounder from one ill-fated relationship to the next. And now she was so confused that she was turning to her best friend, who had hit on her once—put ideas into her head—and now didn't even seem interested.

"Do you think I'm terrible?" Ellen asked. "I mean, feeling guilty about Lyle when I've got Corky . . ."

"You probably wouldn't be human if you didn't feel guilty. The man's your husband."

It seemed she had just given Ellen permission to open the floodgates, because she began crying in earnest.

Corky's history, Celia decided, shaking her head. Ellen would never survive this breakup with Lyle.

But in the next moment, Corky walked through the door, took one look at Ellen, and ran over to her. He gathered her up into his arms.

That was it. They didn't speak. Didn't move. He was just there for her.

Celia watched them, dumbfounded.

How could she be wrong about so many things? How could a person live for twenty-seven years and manage not to be able to read people at all?

Celia stood. "I think I'm going to run to the store for a moment."

Ignoring her, Corky kissed Ellen's forehead, then the tip of her nose, then her lips.

"I might take in a movie, too," Celia added as she snatched up her purse.

But she doubted either of them actually noticed her leaving.

Celia made it to work on time the next day, despite the fact that she'd been out past midnight. She'd sat through the same movie twice—a sweeping romantic drama with Ralph Fiennes. Which she supposed was better than walking in on a sweeping romantic drama in her own living room.

Her ears were still ringing with syrupy soundtrack music as she got on the elevator to go up to the fifth floor. The car was crowded, and when Celia thought for a moment that some of the people were staring at her longer than was polite, she put the suspicion down to sleep-deprived paranoia.

But there was no denying the smirk Andy from circulation gave her when *he* got on the elevator.

And Sara was not at all subtle as Celia walked by the reception desk. *"Go home,"* the receptionist commanded.

Celia stopped in her tracks. "What?"

Sara's face was grim. "Don't ask. Just turn around and march back into that elevator. Believe me, if you don't follow my advice, you'll regret it."

Celia's stomach lurched. Was this about the Stan and Mike article? "Has somebody from the eighth floor been down here?"

Sara was as unenlightning as she was insistent. "Go home, Celia. You were never here this morning. Call in sick. Don't come back for a week."

A week? Jesus. Now she was too curious to go home. She turned in the direction of her cubicle.

"Fool!" Sara yelled after her.

Celia moved fast, but she couldn't help noticing that as she passed each cubicle, all activity ceased.

Voices died midword. Every step she took only widened the wake of awkward silence she was leaving behind her. As she scooted down the final stretch toward her own desk, eager to dive into the semiprivacy afforded by a few gray partitions, Davis let out a cry of alarm.

She let out a responding bleat. "What *is* it?"

"I was hoping you wouldn't come in," he said.

Celia dropped into her chair and whirled on him. *"What? What is going on?"*

"Check your mail."

The directive sounded ominous. "My E-mail?"

"Snail mail," he said in a clipped yet sympathetic voice. "Yellow envelope."

With pounding heart, Celia inspected the little pile of letters on her desk. Sure enough, there was a letter-sized yellow envelope there. She picked it up and opened it gingerly, as though it contained explosives.

It contained worse.

As she unfolded the piece of heavy glossy paper inside the envelope, her ears began to ring. Her face caught fire, and the rest of the world became a spinning blur. "Oh . . . my . . . God . . ."

There, in living color, was a picture of herself, wearing nothing but her Nurse Diesel bra and bikini panties, doing the cha-cha in her apartment.

Only you couldn't tell it was her apartment. The background was blacked out, so it was just her. Her and the bra. She could have been dancing at a gentleman's club or in the middle of Pioneer Square. That bra, which, now that she looked more closely, she realized with growing horror didn't cover as much as she'd thought. Her pointy breasts were practically spilling out the top. And the panties . . .

She was too horrified to inspect her lower torso any closer. She glanced back up to her face, but there was no consolation there, either. The photographer had caught her in a particularly bizarre expression—she might have felt like Rita Hayworth at the time, but she looked more like a female impersonator doing Charo.

Oh, why hadn't she taken Sara's advice? She wished she could sink through the floor, disappear. After all, if Sara had seen the picture, then obviously others had, too. Some vicious type—she already suspected Olga—might have gotten their mitts on a copy and posted it on the coffee room bulletin board.

There was an incredible racket in the office, which she finally realized was the sound of her own gasping breath. She was hyperventilating.

She slapped the picture facedown on her desk. She couldn't look Davis in the eye. "Did *you* get a copy of this?"

"Mm."

She took that as an affirmative. "Did anyone else?"

"Mm."

"Who?"

At that moment, Marie's computer blared out a downloaded MP3 recording of Offenbach's *La Vie Parisienne*. Can-can music.

Naturally, no one could tell *what* dance Celia was doing in the picture.

Tittering laughter emanated from the surrounding cubicles.

Celia's body toppled forward till her head hit her desk top. "Who else?"

"Everyone got it," Davis said regretfully.

"Our whole department?" Celia moaned.

"No, all eight floors."

Davis whisked her away to their favorite restaurant across the river in Vancouver, Washington. Pete's Hide-a-way, a great old diner with vinyl turquoise booths, had a comforting name for a time of crisis and the best crinkle-cut fries around. They ordered a plate as soon as they were seated.

"Better make that a double," Celia told the waitress.

She was still obviously shaken. She sat in a mortified stupor until some coffee arrived.

This wasn't what he'd wanted to do today. He'd been hoping to tell Celia all about Argentina. His travel plans had changed a little, and he didn't want her to feel that she was out of the loop. But she'd had so much to worry about . . . and now this.

"The picture wasn't _that_ bad," Davis said. He'd been trying to convince her of this for the past half hour.

She barked out a laugh. "Not that bad? How could it have been any worse?"

"Well . . ." Davis wracked his brain. "You could have been _completely_ naked."

"I'm not so sure. A naked person is a naked person. A nut dancing around in her apartment in a Nurse Diesel bra has no claim to dignity whatsoever."

Davis stared into his coffee cup. He knew he should be tactfully trying to steer the conversation toward a different topic, but his curiosity got the better of him. "What _were_ you doing in that picture?"

She shuddered. "Dancing."

"Well, yeah, but . . ." He hesitated. "By yourself?"

"Yes, by myself."

"Half-dressed?"

"Yes."

"Why?"

Her eyes flashed. "I was doing the cha-cha, okay? The dance _you_ taught me!"

"Oh." He frowned. "Why?"

"For practice!" She sighed. "I bought this book . . .

Well, it's history now. The way I figure it, I've got two problems. The first is that everyone in the office now thinks I'm a wacko who spends my weekends pretending my apartment is the Moulin Rouge. The second is that there's somebody out there who is really creeping me out now. How the hell did he take that picture?"

"He must have had a camera set up on the roof of the old warehouse building across the street."

"He must have had a telephoto lens."

"He must *really* dislike you."

Their French fries arrived. Celia blobbed a huge puddle of ketchup on the plate and dug in. The comfort food seemed to hit the spot within seconds. She let out a long breath. "That's better. The world wouldn't need psychiatrists if everybody could just have a plate of these."

This whole incident had shaken him nearly as badly as it had her. It wasn't just that someone was out to publicly humiliate the woman he loved; what if this escalated into something different, something violent? The brick had been bad enough.

"I think you need to show the picture to the police."

Celia nearly choked on a fry. "Not on your life! That picture's been seen by enough people."

"But they told you to call them if anything else happened to you."

"What would they do with my picture? Besides pass it around the station house for a good laugh, I mean."

Unfortunately, Davis's knowledge of police procedure began and ended with what he'd learned from *Adam-12* reruns. "Maybe they could fingerprint it?"

Celia sputtered into her coffee cup. "Oh, right. They didn't even really look interested in taking the infamous brick with them to analyze and catalog as evidence. Let's face it. These guys have to deal with murders and riots and the grand opening of the newest Krispy Kreme. I've had two sort of weird things happen to me. I'm small potatoes."

"That brick could have hit you."

"But it didn't. Anyway, from the looks of those guys, I'd say we have as good a chance of figuring out who's doing this as they do."

He had to admit she had a point.

She munched a fry contemplatively. "At least we know we can rule out Lyle."

"Why?"

"Because we now know that brick was aimed at me, not Ellen. Besides, from what Ellen said after talking to him about a divorce, he didn't even sound that upset. Just told her to get the rest of her stuff out of the house."

Davis frowned, remembering someone Celia had been telling him about a while back. "What about that creepy guy you told me about once . . . the photographer . . . What was his name?"

"Elton Nedermeyer." She bit her lower lip as she worried over this possibility. "But he's so anxious about drumming up jobs—why would he do something stupid to a friend of a client?"

"The person who did it would have to have some knowledge of photography. It was a pretty good picture."

"What?!"

"Technically," he explained quickly. "I mean, it was very . . . clear."

She fell back against the booth with a moan. "I'm never going to live this down. How can I possibly go back to work after this? I wonder if the Warden would let me telecommute from now on."

"Fat chance. She likes to keep her eye on people."

She let out a long breath. "What am I going to do?"

"Concentrate on figuring out who it is. I still think Elton should be a suspect."

"God knows, the guy *looks* creepy enough to do something like this," she admitted. "And I might have hurt his feelings. He called me to go out once, and I sort of artlessly put him off."

Davis nodded, and they both digested the possibilities in silence for a moment.

"I've been thinking about your angry reader theory," she finally said. "The article about Stan and Mike certainly struck a nerve with a lot of people."

"And the timing would be right."

"But why wouldn't the message on the brick have been more pointedly political? Why would people who think I'm moral scum have called me babe in that first message?"

Davis leaned forward. "I think we should do some investigative work."

She frowned. "What?"

"Tail Elton."

She blinked at him for a moment before laughing out loud. "You mean have a stakeout at his house or something?"

"Exactly."

"I don't even know where he lives."

"How many guys in Portland can be named Elton Nedermeyer?"

She tilted her head. "Okay. What do we have to lose? When?"

"Friday night."

"Can't. I've got Natalie's wedding shower."

"Saturday night."

"It's a date," she said. Then, quickly, she corrected, "I mean, you're on."

Her correction was a depressing confirmation that he had made the right decision to follow everyone's advice and get far, far away. But he couldn't go to South America not knowing whether Celia was safe.

Which meant they needed to crack this nut very quickly.

Sixteen

Elton lived in a modern apartment complex in the suburbs, in a place called The Meadows. Despite the name, the two-story buildings were set back from the road in a grove of evergreens. Elton's place was on the second floor. On Saturday night, Celia and Davis were hunched down in the front seat of Davis's Ford, their eyes fastened on the apartment window that faced out on the parking lot.

After an hour of watching a blue glow emanating through his curtains, discouragement was beginning to set in, along with a crick in Celia's neck from sitting tensely in the Ford compact's bucket seat.

Davis groaned. "Nothing like watching a guy watch television to give you a feeling of accomplishment."

Celia attempted a few yoga stretches, modified for the cramped space. "I suppose we can deduce that Elton doesn't exactly have a wingding social life."

"If that really is Elton in there," Davis said. "What if there really is more than one Elton Nedermeyer in Portland, and we've been staring at the apartment of the wrong one?"

They had parked under the branches of a giant Sequoia in the parking lot, so the lights from the streetlamps wouldn't hit them. It made the car's interior seem very dark and cozy, though there was still a little twilight left. When she turned and looked into Davis's humor-filled eyes, Celia's heart responded with a peppy somersault. "Nope," she said. "I checked this out with Natalie at the shower."

"You told her we were going to spy on her wedding photographer?"

She shook her head in mock disgust. He certainly didn't give her much credit for private-eye finesse. "No, I told her I needed Elton's number because I wanted to get a portrait done of Gazpacho in a Santa hat to use on my Christmas card this year."

"And she believed you?"

"Absolutely! She told me I had reached new heights of pathetic oinkdom and that I seriously need to re-think the priority Gazpacho has in my life before I go completely round the bend."

"Sounds like she bought it, all right." His eyes narrowed on her. "So you managed to live through the shower?"

"It really wasn't that bad at all," Celia admitted. Of course, it helped that it had been at Natalie's condo, and that Natalie's mom had orchestrated most of the event. Celia had felt more like a maid of honor fig-urehead than anything else. "And by the way, Natalie really liked that cheese wedge dish you sent."

"No incidents with Babs?"

"Babs was on her best behavior," Celia said.

Davis looked amazed. "I should have crashed that wedding shower. I have a feeling you're covering up something."

She laughed. "I'm serious, it wasn't that bad. Any-way, it was better than sitting at home watching tele-vision. I don't have a wingding social life, either."

He gave her a once-over that sent heat shimmying through her. "You keep wearing outfits like the one you've got on and you will."

Yes! She suppressed the urge to pump her fist in triumph.

After she and Davis had made this spying date, she'd gone out and bought the sexiest top she could find on sale and teamed it with her skimpiest black miniskirt. She was glad to know her purchasing had not been in vain. Not to mention, Davis hadn't brought up the subject of Argentina in forever. Maybe that had just been a passing whim. "I didn't think you'd noticed."

His blue eyes turned smoky. "I'm not a blind man. After all . . . that tiger-stripe pattern . . ."

Despite the fact that her insides were revving like crazy, she lifted her shoulders in a nonchalant shrug. "I felt like something different. You like it?"

He didn't answer for a moment, but kept looking into her eyes, as if trying to see right into her soul. He swallowed, hard. "Sure, it's . . . sexy."

Deep inside, some part of her began to quake in anticipation, like a fisherman watching a fish circling his line. Deciding to try a little of that boldness Natalie had advised, she put her hand on his arm. "I bought it especially for tonight."

"I see—detective-story wear. Trying to play femme fatale?"

"Maybe."

His eyes strayed down her face, to her neck, and the cleavage her shirt bared. Then, swallowing again, he cleared his throat and faced forward. The change in his demeanor was jarring. It was as if he were snapping down a window shade. "Actually," he stated flatly, "I wish you'd worn something else."

Celia's hopes, and her hand, dropped. "Why?"

"A shirt like that? It's not good private-eye wear."

"Oh, and who are you? Elsa Clench for the Sam Spade set?"

"It makes you conspicuous."

"So? I have to stay out of sight anyway. There's no way we can let Elton see me without him getting suspicious."

He drummed his fingers on the steering wheel. His jaw clenched. "It's just not the kind of thing I'm used to seeing you wearing."

Now she faced forward, too, so he wouldn't see her face go red. Unconsciously, she hiked her shirt up at the shoulders. "I know I'm thrifty, but it's not as if I walk around in paper sacks. I wear things like this sometimes."

"Not around me you don't."

"Then, I'd think you'd find it a refreshing change to see me in something besides work clothes or sweatshirts."

He flicked another wary glance toward her shirt—as if it might bite him. "That shirt is just not how I think of you."

She crossed her arms, as if that could hide her growing irritation. "Well, how *do* you think of me?" Obviously not as romance material.

He lifted his shoulders again. "You know."

"How?"

He gritted his teeth as though he were admitting something unpleasant. "Like a friend."

"A friend." The word made her stew. "What kind of a friend?"

He turned to her, his face screwed up in puzzlement. "What do you mean? How many kinds of friends are there?"

"All sorts—like Elaine was a friend to Jerry on *Seinfeld*, for instance. Am I that kind of friend?"

He laughed. "No, not quite."

She wasn't sure how to interpret that laughter. "Well . . . Am I a friend like the *Friends* friends?"

He sighed. "Definitely not."

Now she had him. "You don't even watch *Friends.*"

"So?"

"Then, how do you know that's what I'm not?"

"I talk with Tom the TV critic, and I skim *People* magazine at the dentist. We're just not like that."

"Well, what am I to you then?" she asked hotly. "Ethel Mertz?"

"No . . ." He appeared to be turning the matter over in his mind. "Well, actually more like Fred Mertz."

The words echoed around the car's interior for a moment before Celia could actually absorb them.

Fred Mertz? Was this some kind of joke? She whacked Davis across the arm.

"Ouch!" He lifted his hands to ward off any more blows. "What's the matter with you?"

"I'm insulted! How dare you call me Fred Mertz?"

"Well, I can't say you're like Ethel," he explained logically, "because she was *Lucy's* buddy. I don't think of myself as Lucy."

She felt her brows beetling together. "What, are you saying you identify with Ricky Ricardo?"

"Well . . ." He gave it a moment's thought. "More or less."

Her mouth parted in astonishment. "The hot-blooded Cuban nightclub bandleader? *That's* who you identify with?"

"I only meant that . . ."

"Mr. 'Babalu'?"

". . . just in that context of . . ."

"The mambo king?"

"Okay, maybe it's not—"

His words cut off, and he raised his hand to shush her. His voice dropped to a whisper. "Someone's coming out."

They pivoted in unison to study Elton locking his apartment door and walking down to his car. He was in the same uniform she had seen him in last time: black T-shirt, black jeans, black sneakers.

"Is that him?"

"Yes." She'd forgotten this was Davis's first glimpse of him. "What do you think?" she asked.

"I think it's very appropriate that the guy's a photographer," Davis observed. "He looks like a negative."

Elton got into his car and pulled out of the parking lot. A few seconds later, Davis swung onto the street behind him. Celia hunkered down farther in the seat. "Where do you think he's headed?"

"I don't know."

"He didn't have a camera or any photography equipment with him."

"Maybe it was in his car already."

"I guess it would be too lucky if he headed into town. Say, to my apartment."

"If we caught him red-handed? That would be a stroke of luck."

"Or maybe proof that we're born detectives."

Davis's doubtful snort mirrored her own misgivings on that score.

Elton's car signaled.

"He's turning into this strip mall," Celia said.

They followed the car to the front of a Safeway. Davis parked his car between two minivans near the grocery store's entrance. The van to their left partially hid them, but they could still observe Elton as he passed through the automatic double doors into the store.

Davis laughed. "Yeah, we're such brilliant detectives we just might catch him buying a package of Vienna sausages."

"That would be a crime, of sorts," Celia said. "To Julia Child, at least."

"Look, Elton doesn't know me, so I'll go track him down. You stay out here."

He disappeared, leaving Celia to wait. And to stew. *Fred Mertz!*

She pulled her skirt down and her shirt up in frustration. What a dope she'd been. She'd tricked herself out in full tigress harness, only to have Davis reveal that he thought of her as William Frawley. Well, maybe she deserved it. She'd turned Davis down once, after all. What had she expected? How many times had she called *him* a pal?

Damn. Did he *really* see her that way? Had that one kiss just been momentary madness on his part?

Five minutes of those kinds of thoughts was all she could take. What had happened to Davis?

Unable to stand not knowing what was going on, she pulled her cell phone out of her purse and dialed. Davis picked up after one ring. "Where are you?" she asked.

"In the cereal aisle." He was whispering. "Elton's a Captain Crunch man."

"So we can deduce he has an upper palate like sandpaper. Anything else?"

"Besides the cereal, so far he's picked up a two-liter Pepsi, cool ranch–flavored Doritos, and two frozen macaroni and cheese dinners. Oh, wait."

Celia sat through a few moments of muffled footsteps and the faraway sound of a Muzak rendition of the love theme from *Titanic.* "Okay, he's through. He's in the express line."

"Did he buy anything else?"

"Dental floss."

"No yellow envelopes?"

"Nope, sorry."

"Where are you?"

"I'm hiding behind a Hostess rack. I'll wait till I see him finish at the checkout line, and then I'll follow him out."

"Okay," she said.

She'd almost beeped off when she heard Davis say, "There he goes."

She put down the phone and looked left. The van next to them had pulled out, leaving Celia exposed. She was staring right at Elton.

For a second, his face scrunched, perplexed. Then he broke into a grin and walked over. Self-consciously, Celia hopped out of the car.

"Holy guacamole!" Elton did a bizarre wild-and-crazy-guy shimmy. "Look at you! Sexy mama!"

His voice sounded much better. There was just a slight slurring now, so that *sexy* sounded a little like *shexy*. Time healed all wounds, she supposed—even self-inflicted ones. "Hi, Elton."

"I didn't expect to see you here."

"Oh, well, I . . ."

He shifted his bag of groceries over to the other hip, and the Captain Crunch box poked out the top. "This is a long way from Goose Hollow."

She went cold at the mention of her neighborhood. "How'd you know where I live?"

"Natalie told me."

A likely story. "Did she?"

"Yeah. So when am I going to meet this parrot of yours?"

She narrowed her eyes. "Why?"

"Natalie said you want to have some pictures of him."

"Oh . . ." It had never occurred to her that Natalie would relay her lie about Gazpacho's Santa portrait to Elton.

"I've never done pet photography, but I hear there's money in it." He chuckled nervously. "Not, you know, like I'd overcharge you or anything. I only meant that there were lots of people who . . ." He broke off and looked around the parking lot a little uncomfortably. "So what are you doing here?"

"Waiting for somebody." She shifted uncomfortably. *Please, please get out here, Davis.*

"A date, I guess, dressed like that." Elton not so subtly peered down her shirt. "Or should I say, *un*-dressed."

"Dressed is fine." The grocery store doors parted for Davis, and Celia could have wept with relief. "Oh, here he is now!"

Elton turned. As he watched Davis approach, his smile faded, and his chest seemed to deflate a little more.

"This is Davis Smith," she told Elton.

Davis was one cool customer, she had to admit. If he was surprised to see her gabbing with the object of their investigation, he didn't let on. He stuck out his hand for Elton to shake.

Elton had to move the bag again. "Nice to meet you," he mumbled, offering a pale, limp hand.

The conversation, awkward to begin with, sputtered to a dead stop. Davis looked at Celia. Celia looked back at Elton.

Elton seemed jealous—of Davis. She turned in wonder and could readily understand why. She kept seeing Davis through a filter of how he'd been before. But his appearance now was startlingly different than her old friend. His clothes were sharp and draped his thinned-down frame in a way that drew notice to how tall he was. His jaw was more prominent, and his blond hair was stylishly mussed. It made her want to run her hands through it and muss it some more.

Davis caught her staring at him, and she felt her face heat up.

"Davis will be at Natalie's wedding and rehearsal dinner," she told Elton.

"Yeah?" the photographer said without enthusiasm.

They stood in silence for at least another half minute. Davis was smiling and staring off into the parking lot, while Celia was watching Elton closely for signs of guilt. Unfortunately, the guy's whole appearance screamed guilt. He was all tics. His eyes cut shiftily from one thing to the next; his legs jangled nervously beneath him. His fingers drummed anxiously against his paper bag. It was hard to tell whether this was normal behavior for him or not. Nothing about the guy seemed normal, including his clothes, which were a carbon copy of what he'd been wearing the first time she'd met him. Did the guy just have one favorite T-shirt, or did his entire wardrobe consist of nothing but Marilyn Manson shirts?

After what seemed like an eternity, Elton cleared his throat. "Well . . . guess I'll see you around."

Both Celia and Davis broke into relieved smiles. "Right!"

"Bye!"

They got into the car quickly and sat in stunned silence for a moment before looking at each other.

"Yeah, we make great detectives," Davis said.

Celia leaned against the passenger door and shuddered with laughter. "I thought I was going to lose it before you showed up. Didn't I tell you he was creepy?"

Davis sobered. "You were right. And he didn't like me."

She had to agree. "He definitely seemed to change demeanor after you came on the scene. He almost seemed jealous. And get this—he knows where I live.

He named my neighborhood. Don't you think that's suspicious?"

"Maybe. But if it makes you feel any better, I noticed something about Elton that would indicate he's not our brick thrower."

"What?"

"His handshake. He's completely noodle-armed. The guy probably hasn't ever lifted anything heavier than a Minolta in his entire life. So how's he going to heave a brick through a third-story window?"

Celia bit her lip. "Oh."

"Especially if he had to throw it across a street."

"It's a narrow street," she reminded him. "And it was only half a brick."

"It would still take good aim. Frankly, Elton didn't seem up to the task."

Celia had a hard time letting go of the notion of Elton as her persecutor. "But he definitely could have taken the picture . . . and he seems so odd."

"He's definitely a nut, but he just might not be our nut."

They spent the fifteen-minute drive back into Portland in disappointed silence. The atmosphere in the car was downright gloomy. To eliminate Elton as a suspect left them with only Lyle . . . and the rest of the world.

When Davis parked on her street, he nodded up toward her apartment building. "I'll come up with you."

As they climbed the second flight of stairs, Mr. Zhirbotken's apartment door slammed closed. Davis stopped and tilted his head toward the door. "That always happens."

"He just likes to check who's in the building," Celia replied. "It's a little nerve-wracking, but in a way it's like having a live security system. He sees everybody who goes in and out of this place."

Davis frowned. "Too bad he couldn't have seen who was tossing bricks through your window."

Inside her apartment, all was quiet. Corky and Ellen weren't there. No surprise there. The soul mates spent most weekend nights out together now. Corky was teaching Ellen the fine art of hanging out in bars.

Davis still appeared to be in a Sherlock state of mind. He peered around her apartment with an intense expression.

"Do you want to check under the bed?" Celia asked him. "Maybe you won't find any intruders, but there's bound to be a few sinister dust bunnies under there."

Gazpacho squawked at them, and Davis strolled over to look at him . . . from a safe distance. "I hope you don't think I'm being pushy. I just worry."

She followed him to the bird perch and petted Gazpacho on his soft feathered head. "No. To tell you the truth, it's been great having someone looking after me this week. A new sensation in the life of Celia Snowden."

He smiled that sexy smile of his, and it felt as though something were squeezing the air out of her lungs. How could a man aim such a sexy smile at a woman he'd compared to Fred Mertz?

He ramped up the wattage on his grin, and her insides liquified.

Feeling heat glow in her cheeks, she lowered her gaze, which unfortunately fell on her tiger-striped shirt. She'd really thought it was seductive looking in the store . . . but apparently it hadn't done the trick.

Of course, maybe the problem was that *she* hadn't done her part. She hadn't really gone for broke.

Deciding to go for it now, she put her hand on his shoulder. "You look like you could use a massage."

She rubbed the stiff muscle under her hand, but instead of relaxing, he seemed only to tense all the more.

His blue eyes stared into hers questioningly. Her face was flaming, but she didn't care. Her insides were purring with desire.

"Can I get you something, Davis? Coffee, tea?" She added, not really joking, "Me?"

His expression changed. His smile faded, and he shot out a hand to hold her arm, as if she needed bracing. And maybe she did. Her legs were beginning to go rubbery on her. She was afraid that Davis would hold her at arm's length, which would be really humiliating.

Instead, he started pulling her toward him. "Heaven help me," he muttered as he bent down to kiss her.

She lifted up on her toes and met him halfway. As their lips touched, it felt as if the world tipped crazily. The man didn't seem to need heaven's help in this particular endeavor. He was an expert kisser. She closed her eyes as a wonderful light-headed sensation seemed to lift her to the clouds. This definitely hadn't happened when he'd kissed her on the stoop.

What was so different now? So right?

Before when he'd kissed her she'd been so shocked, she hadn't been able to take anything in. Now, after dreaming about this for so long, she greedily tried to absorb everything. The way his lips slanted against hers with just the right pressure. He held her firmly, but not so tight that they couldn't move and explore. A year of carefully platonic friendship evaporated in an instant, the kiss transforming their world into something vastly more complicated, more delicious. She ran her palms over his shoulders and looped them around his neck. She fluttered her fingers along the crisp hairline at his nape, loving the bristly softness of it. His hands lowered to her waist, investigating a few curves along the way, then pulling her to him more roughly. She tilted her head and gently nipped his lower lip.

God, she loved the feel of him, the smell of him. He was so incredible . . . so sexy. What had she been waiting for? She should have done this months ago, as soon as Ian had bailed. Or before. She should have dumped Ian. Davis was far superior. He was perfect. He was . . .

Groaning.

It was as though the sound was ripping out from somewhere deep inside him. Celia pulled back, startled. "What's wrong?"

He gulped in a deep, shuddering breath, but couldn't seem to speak.

"I know." She draped herself against him again. "I feel the same way. This is crazy, isn't it?"

"Yes," he said. "It is."

The tone in his voice gave her pause. He didn't mean crazy the way she meant it—a wonderful, irresistible madness. He meant *insane*. Demented.

Her body, boneless with disappointed lust, began to slide toward the floor. She grabbed on to the lapels of his linen jacket.

"So much for being a tigress," she muttered.

His brows knitted together, and he stared down at her. "What?"

"Nothing." She hated the prickliness in her tone. Hated it, but couldn't get rid of it. "Sorry—I didn't mean to ruin a perfectly lovely evening of spying by attacking you."

"Celia . . ." He cleared his throat and began working his jaw in that way she was so familiar with. It was the way he looked when he was getting ready to say something unpleasant.

Maybe this was the downside of falling for someone you know too well, she thought. You could read them too easily. And unless she was mistaken, Davis was about to remind her of how much he valued their friendship and how he wouldn't want to lose it. . . .

In other words, pretty much the same speech she'd been practicing a few weeks ago to use on him.

She pushed her hands against his chest, ready to cut him off at the pass, rejection-wise. There was a hard little lump underneath his jacket. "What did you do, bulletproof your blazer before we went to spy on Elton?"

He shut his eyes. "Paper's not bulletproof."

She frowned and investigated the shape of the bulge. It was envelope-sized. Whatever he was carrying around with him had to be pretty important, or he wouldn't be closing his eyes at the reminder of it.

"The envelope came today. I was trying to find the right time to tell you."

Half expecting to find an envelope containing another awful picture of herself, she reached into his inside breast pocket and pulled out an envelope of a completely different sort. Travel bug that she was, she gasped instinctively when she saw an airline logo.

And then that split second of elation evaporated. Airline tickets?

It felt as though something had knocked her backward. She found herself reeling away from him, toward a chair. She needed to sit down. "So you're really going?"

He nodded.

How could she have forgotten?

"When?" But she didn't wait for his response. She peeked into the envelope and saw the date. June third. Saturday.

As in, a week from right then.

She gaped at him, speechless.

"I was going to tell you," he said, "but there didn't seem to be a right moment."

How about the hour that we were sitting bored in the front seat of your car, waiting for Elton to come out? How about any time tonight? "Davis, this ticket says it's for next Saturday."

"I know . . . It's a cheapo ticket I bought off the Internet. I didn't have a lot of choice. It leaves on a Saturday night, and it's got a million stops—"

"I'm not concerned about your itinerary," she said, interrupting. "You're *leaving.* Did you quit the paper?"

"Leave of absence."

A million words were spinning around her head, but she didn't seem capable of putting them into any kind of order. He was leaving her. He had it all planned.

"I know this looks sort of bad . . ." Davis said.

All she managed to sputter out was, "N-next Saturday is Natalie's wedding."

"It's okay. I don't leave till late in the afternoon. I can still go to the wedding with you."

"I don't care about that," she said, nearly exploding. "I just can't believe you're leaving so suddenly. And that I . . ."

Oh, Lord. She'd thrown herself at him, expecting him to be so grateful that she was at last stamping him with the Celia Snowden seal of approval.

"Celia, don't look like that. It's no big deal."

"No big deal? I attacked you!"

"I liked it," he said.

Liked it so much he'd groaned and pushed away from her. She crossed her arms. She couldn't help it—she felt wounded. *The wounded tigress.*

"I told you that I was thinking about leaving," he said.

"Precisely—*thinking* about. You didn't tell me you were going next weekend. That's a pretty big omission."

He nodded. "I should have told you, but you've had so much to deal with, I just didn't feel good about it."

"And how long will you be gone?" she asked, flipping through the itinerary that she'd just said she had no interest in. She had to go through the pages a few times before she finally understood. "There's no return ticket here." Pure depression struck her system. "You're not coming back?"

He chuckled uncomfortably. "Of course I'm coming back."

"When?"

"Oh . . ." He shrugged. "In a couple of months."

"A couple?"

"Well . . . three. Maybe."

She collapsed onto the sofa. "I've got the wedding this week. Natalie's going to be in high gear. I probably won't have a moment to see you before you go!"

"It's no big deal. I'll understand if you don't have time."

For some reason, that was the most crushing statement of all. No big deal? He didn't even want to spend any time with her before he left?

"Look, we should obviously talk this over. Would you like to go out for a drink or something?"

And be given a love-you-like-a-sister speech? "No thanks."

"But you just said you were upset that we wouldn't have any time to be together . . ."

"I meant after tonight. Tonight I'm still absorbing the shock."

He laughed. "C'mon. You're acting like a woman

in one of those movies of yours. This isn't that big a deal."

She darted a quelling look his way, and his smile faded. "In those movies of mine, when someone says something's no big deal, it usually means disaster is right around the corner."

"Why don't we go out for a drink?" he asked again.

"No thanks. I'm going to stay in and drink." Already she was ticking off a mental checklist. Emergency vodka? Check. Orange juice? Check.

"Well, maybe I'd better go." Davis edged toward the door.

Best friend/potential lover abandoning her?

He sent her one last doubtful glance as he backed toward the door. "I'll call you, okay?"

"Check."

Clearly, he had given her one chance, and she'd blown it. Then he'd gone looking for love and had come up with Kyra. When that didn't work out, he'd decided to try Argentina.

Argentina!

She'd thought he was just *talking*. The way she planned things there was always considerable lag time between getting an idea and acting on it. She hadn't thought Davis was actually going to toddle off to Argentina immediately.

She snorted derisively as she slurped up the last of a screwdriver. He thought he was going to write his book down there? That was a laugh. He'd probably . . .

Write a book. This was Davis. He usually did what he said he was going to do.

Including, apparently, going to South America.

After draining her emergency vodka, Celia crawled into bed and went over the whole night again. Their

Holmes and Watson gig seemed like ancient history now. What had gone wrong?

The next thing she knew, she was revived by a splitting headache and the sounds of voices in the next room. Whispers and laughter and the occasional bump. Carefully, she sat up in bed and cocked her head. Then, last of all, she carefully squinted open one eye.

Sunlight trumpeted at her optic nerve, making her cringe. She squeezed her eyes shut again and felt her way out to the living room.

"Hey, you're alive!" Corky bellowed in greeting.

Celia swallowed. Did people have to be so loud? "Am I?"

"We were a little worried last night when we saw the empty vodka bottle, but you look okay. A little green, maybe. Something the matter with your eyes?"

"No, they're just seeing the world today in atomic flash-o-vision."

"If you want some coffee, it's in the thermos on the kitchen counter," Ellen said.

Celia bestowed her thanks upon them and crept toward the kitchen. Last night's conversation with Davis started to flood back to her consciousness, but she tried to shut it out and just concentrate on rehydrating. She drank some water—she'd sucked down all the orange juice last night—then hit the coffee. She'd swigged down a cup before she finally felt human again.

In the living room Corky and Ellen were being very industrious, pointing at the different boxes stacked around the living room and tossing things into a few empty boxes. Gazpacho, playing foreman to all this activity, was perched on Corky's shoulder. Every once in a while, he leaned over and tried to nip his ear playfully.

She leaned over the kitchen counter. "What are you guys doing?"

"Moving boxes," Ellen said.

"Did you get a storage space?"

Ellen looked at Corky. Corky looked at Ellen.

"Didn't you tell her?" he asked.

"Golly, no. I never really thought . . ." She looked up at Celia. "Well, I knew you'd be relieved to have us out of your hair anyway."

A knot of apprehension formed in Celia's stomach. They had gotten an apartment. Okay. She would deal with this. Heck, at least she'd have her place back to herself. She'd be alone again.

Really alone. Just an oink and her parrot.

Thank heavens she had her bird.

She struggled mightily to fight off self-pity. She even managed a smile. "Where are you going?"

Corky wiped his beefy forearm across his brow. "Well, since Davis is headed to South America, he offered to let us house-sit for him. He said it would be helping him out."

The smile froze on her face. All she needed now was a reminder of Davis. "When did you guys work this out?"

Ellen looked at Corky. "Was it Thursday?"

Thursday. As far back as Thursday Davis had been busily making plans. And since Celia had been sitting next to him or eating with him or talking to him on the phone for a large portion of that day, she could only imagine that he had to work pretty hard not to let her know what he was up to. Namely, stealing her roommates.

She cleared her throat. "That'll be a good deal for you guys."

"We really appreciate your letting us stay here for so long," Ellen said.

"Yeah, you've been great," Corky added. "But this place *is* small, and Davis said we'd be helping him out."

"I'll bet," she said.

"I just know you'll be glad to be all by yourself again!" Ellen said. "Personal space is so important to good *ch'i.*"

Corky grinned. "Sure, just think—no more Bruce Springsteen . . ."

"No more messy Italian dinners," Ellen added.

"No hopping over boxes all the time."

Celia sniffed in nostalgia. She hadn't minded any of that.

Okay, she'd minded the Bruce Springsteen. But mostly just from a parrot-corrupting point of view.

"By the way . . ." Corky tilted his head and looked at her. "There's been something I've wanted to discuss with you, Celia."

"What?"

"Well . . ." He tilted his head to the disgustingly contented bird on his shoulder. "Would you mind if we took Gazpacho?"

Seventeen

Monday morning it was the silent treatment all over again. When Celia came into work, she plopped her deli coffee cup down on her desk and greeted Davis with a pert nod. Then she punched her computer terminal on, dropped down into her chair, and studiously avoided looking his way for two hours.

Davis ached to say something to her. However, he didn't know what that something should be. He just didn't trust what was happening. Celia was acting almost like a jealous lover. But how could that be?

Hadn't she made it abundantly clear that she wanted to be just friends?

Hadn't Olga told him, in no uncertain terms, that a woman didn't want to be hit on by a buddy?

Hadn't he suffered through their stakeout trying like hell not to stare at the way her breasts filled out that sexy little shirt? He'd been dying to kiss her then, to leap on her like some hormone-charged teenager in a lover's lane. But no, he'd refrained.

For as long as he could, at least.

In her apartment, it had seemed that she was coming on to him. In fact, Celia hadn't seemed very happy when he'd cut the kiss short. Could he believe that Celia was falling for him? Maybe it was just the danger she was in. Having bricks thrown through her window and poison-pen letters delivered to work was bound to shake a woman up. Maybe make her do things she didn't really mean to do, like deck herself out in sexy little tiger-striped shirts and vamp her friend.

He didn't want to set himself up for disappointment again. His only consolation was that he would be out of here soon. A week wasn't too long to endure an awkward silence.

He was working on his last column, but it felt as if he was simply typing. The paragraphs were coming out lifeless. In frustration, he punched over to his E-mail. Buried among the usual catalog of work-related memos and annoying spam was a message that surprised him.

C. Snowden   re: our "friendship"   5/29 10:17 AM

He cut his gaze over to her desk, but Celia remained turned away from him, stiff backed.

He clicked on the message, which was short and to the point.

Ricky Ricardo never *kissed Fred Mertz.*

Smiling, Davis hit the reply button. He drummed his fingers for a moment, trying to think what the best reply should be. Should he pour his heart out on the screen? He was tempted to, but he wasn't sure Celia would be in a receptive mood. She seemed to be back in wiseacre mode. He decided to answer her in kind.

Now that *would have been groundbreaking television.*

He moused over to the send button, but at the last minute added another sentence to his message.

I'm coming back.

He hit send.

He turned his attention back to work and checked his E-mail periodically for a reply. But not a peep did he hear from Celia until she let out a short shriek.

He swiveled. Her eyes were riveted on a letter that was written in eerily familiar bold capital letters. Looking ill, she wordlessly passed the paper to him.

WATCH THE BIRDIE!!!

"When did you get this?" Davis asked her.

"The damn thing's been on my desk all morning. It was just in a plain white business envelope—not yellow—so I didn't think anything of it when I was sorting my mail." She turned and started fidgeting with her purse. "He's threatening Gazpacho! I've got to get home!"

"Isn't your place locked?"

"Of course, but what if he's figured out a way to get into my place?"

Seeing that she was hell-bent on checking on her parrot, Davis could only follow her. He grabbed his jacket off the back of his chair.

"Oh, Davis, you don't have to—"

"Forget it. Of course I'm going with you."

They slipped out and barreled over to Celia's apartment. As they charged up the staircase, Davis stopped on the second landing with the odd feeling that something was different from usual. He nodded toward Mr. Zhirbotken's door. It was firmly closed. No head poked out to glare at him. "Your neighbor's not spying today."

"He's an engineer for Intel," Celia explained. "He's at work. He only polices the landing on nights and weekends."

There was no sign of forced entry of Celia's apartment door. Inside, Gazpacho was safely in his cage, looking put out to be roused from a midmorning nap. He shouted a petulant bar of "Born to Run" and proceeded to preen himself, pointedly ignoring them.

"Seems okay to me," Davis observed.

Celia was checking the lock on the living-room window. She raised the shade and peered out toward the street and the building opposite. "The fire escape worries me."

"I doubt someone's going to climb a fire escape

that lets out on the street to break into your place in broad daylight," Davis told her. "That wouldn't be very stealthy."

"Right—they wouldn't do it during the day." Celia closed her eyes. "They'll wait till nighttime, when I'm here by myself."

"Corky and Ellen are here, too."

"Not for long." She sent him an accusing stare.

"Oh, right."

The awkwardness that passed between them reminded him of Saturday night, when they had been standing in this very room, locked in each other's arms. He braced himself against a strong flare of desire kindled by the memory. He couldn't forget that the kiss had been followed by the present coolness between them.

Celia flopped into an armchair and hugged her arms around herself protectively as she stared at the parrot. "Poor Gazpacho. He's a potential kidnap victim now."

"Like Pattie Hearst." Davis shook his head. "I bet the Symbionese Liberation Army could have used that bird."

Celia ignored the wisecrack. "I should have agreed to let Corky take Gazpacho when he offered."

"Corky wanted to take him?"

She nodded.

"What did you say?"

Her eyes widened. "What kind of mother do you think I am? I said no, of course."

"Oh."

She sighed. "And then this morning Corky looked so depressed I had to tell him I *might* consider joint custody. But I can't leave Gazpacho here now."

Davis gritted his teeth as he took in Celia's pride and joy. Of course, he had to offer to take the creature—finger lopping beak and all. If Corky was going to get joint custody, the wretched pile of feathers would end up at his place anyway.

He cleared his throat and tried to strike a bright, generous tone. "I'd be happy to look after him for a while."

"Liar." Her lips turned into a wry smile.

So much for his stab at appearing heroic. "Well, I'll take him, at any rate."

"That's beyond the call of duty. I'll board him at my vet's for a few days until we can see how things shake down."

They had brought Davis's car, so they loaded Gazpacho and his paraphernalia into the Ford and drove him over to her veterinarian. The parrot was definitely peeved as Celia said goodbye to him. "Think of this as a safe house, 'Spacho. Be a good birdie."

Gazpacho sent her a disdainful look that said that being a good birdie was for wimpy parakeets. Nevertheless, Celia fell on him in a flood of emotion. The vet tech pursed her lips as mistress and bird performed a parting ritual of chirping on her part and wing flapping and screeching angrily on his.

When they were finally pried apart and Gazpacho disappeared through the door leading to the boarding area, he blurted out an ear-splitting bar of "Born in the USA."

Celia dashed a tear from her eye.

"Good grief, Celia," Davis said.

She pierced him with a sharp gaze. "You obviously know nothing of abandonment issues."

"You're not abandoning him," he reminded her.

"No, but I feel like I am." She sniffed and added pointedly, "Unlike some people, I find that discomforting."

Davis battled the urge to grab her by the shoulders

and shake her. Didn't she understand that he was exiling himself to Argentina for the good of them both? He'd tried being a good platonic buddy. It was a no go. And she'd made it clear that his amorous attentions were mostly unwelcome.

Or mostly welcome. Davis was about ninety-eight percent certain that Celia didn't know *what* she wanted.

They were halfway back to the office before he broke their steely silence. "Didn't you get my E-mail?"

She snorted with laughter. "Oh, yes."

"Well?"

She pivoted in her seat. "You keep saying that you're going to come back. I guess you think that's very reassuring. 'I shall return.' It just sounds like MacArthur before he pulled out of Manila. With me playing the role of the beleaguered Phillipines."

"That's a little melodramatic," he said.

"Ha!" she cried, melodramatically.

"Celia . . ."

"Don't 'Celia' me. I'm the one being left—by you, by Corky, and even Ellen. All I'll have left is Natalie. Oh—and the crazy guy taking weird pictures of me and threatening my bird. Can't forget him!"

Davis frowned. "I hadn't considered that."

"Obviously not!"

He shook his head. "I meant I hadn't considered that angle of the note," he clarified. " 'Watch the birdie' is what someone says before he takes a picture."

Celia's mouth formed an *O* of understanding. "Elton!"

He hated to incriminate a guy on such thin evidence. "Maybe I'm wrong."

"No—you're right. Elton knows I have a bird. Remember? He asked me when he was going to meet

Gazpacho because Natalie told him I wanted to have pictures done." Her breath caught. "Plus he looked annoyed that I was with you—maybe he felt jealous. And that was just a day and a half before I get this weird note. A day and a half would be about what it would take to get a message through the city postal system, wouldn't it? Isn't that sort of an odd coincidence?"

"Well, yeah. But it isn't proof. And you have to remember that before we became suspicious of Elton, we'd been thinking that the thrown brick was a response to the Stan and Mike article."

She shook her head. "I haven't received one E-mail from angry readers that even hints toward one of them being the brick lobber. I don't think our guy is trying to make a political statement."

"We're still not sure that it's not a woman," Davis pointed out.

"Right. Taking pictures of me in a Nurse Diesel bra?"

"A woman would know how humiliating that would be."

"I don't have any female enemies that I know of, except maybe Olga. And even I don't think she would do something like this—she seems to like her sabotage to be in liquid form."

"I think you ought to come stay at my place this week."

She drew up proudly. "That won't be necessary."

"If Gazpacho needs a safe house, why shouldn't you?"

"I've still got Corky and Ellen with me." She lifted her head proudly. "Temporarily."

"What about after that?"

"What do you care? You'll be gone."

Frustration nagged at him. How could he explain

that what he really wanted more than anything else in the world was to gather her into his arms and keep her safe from this wacko? Celia was all wounded pride and prickly defensiveness. "I'm sorry, okay?" he said. "Can we please bury the hatchet?"

She lifted her chin. "As long as you don't intend to bury it in my back."

He groaned. "I apologize for not telling you sooner about my leaving. I'm sorry about stealing your roommates. I thought you'd be glad!"

"I might have been if it hadn't all seemed so sudden, so sneaky."

"I apologize for that, too. Now, can we please call a truce?"

Arms crossed, Celia pursed her lips and scooted down in her seat. Then she sent him a sidewise smile. "This really isn't fair. You have me over a barrel."

Davis couldn't think of one bit of leverage he had in this situation. "I do?"

"Of course—you're my escort to the Glass wedding festivities, remember?"

He smiled down at her. "Don't you know I'd be your escort even if you weren't speaking to me?"

"That would be a blast."

"But it won't come to that, will it?"

She shook her head. "I can't hold a grudge. Not against a man who's sat with me through as many Jacklyn Smith movies with me as you have."

He stopped for a red light. "Then, it's a date?"

She tilted her head. "A real date? As in pick me up at the door . . ."

Taking a chance, he said, "And kiss you good night."

She blinked up at him, and for a moment he was about to say to hell with waiting for Friday night. He was ready to kiss her right there.

Celia sat up and cleared her throat. "You're on."

Davis felt his pulse accelerate. He hadn't been so happy to have a girl agree to go on a date with him since he was sixteen. Judging from his and Celia's reactions to each other, no one would have guessed that they had spent a score of Friday nights together before this one.

The light changed, and he crossed through the intersection, feeling equal parts joy and trepidation. Five days before he was scheduled to fly off to Argentina probably was a hell of a time to try to jump-start a love affair.

Once they were afloat, Celia had to admit that Natalie's idea for the barge ride on the Willamette for her rehearsal dinner wasn't bad at all. In fact, easing down the river on their candlelit raft, surrounded on both sides by the lights of the city, felt almost like a fairy tale. Natalie had hired a four-piece combo to play old jazz standards, and part of the deck was designated for dancing. Not far away stood the beautifully set banquet table. All the guests marveled at the fact that Natalie had dared schedule a boat ride in Portland in early June, and it wasn't raining.

"Of course it's not raining," Celia heard Babs say to a distant relative, "it wouldn't *dare.*"

But what Celia marveled at was the fact that everything was *working.* Natalie, in an ice blue silk gown, was absolutely stunning. Angus was, as Natalie had predicted months ago, an incredible babe in a tux. More amazing still, he was sober.

It was the first time she'd seen him upright since the airport. But the memory of that encounter was still so strong she had to resist the urge to wipe her mouth when she spoke to him.

"I see you're over your jet lag," she said.

Angus gazed at her in confusion. He probably wasn't certain who she was. Natalie hadn't thought to introduce them, knowing they had already met before. "D'I know ye?"

"Yes, ye do. I'm Celia, Natalie's maid of honor."

He frowned in confusion.

"Airport," she reminded him.

He shook his head and slurped down a glass of champagne.

She patted him on the arm. "Don't bust a gray cell."

He looked at her as if she were crazy. "I canne understand a thing yer sayin'."

All the party details Natalie had worked out were clicking right along. The waiters handed out trays and trays of hors d'oevres to smiling guests. Natalie's relatives and old friends and coworkers, very few of whom Celia actually knew, mingled with manic friendliness, as if they were at a high school reunion. Elton, almost unrecognizable in a conservative blue suit, looked almost like something from the land of the living. He unobtrusively shot candid photos and was followed by John, his assistant, whose face Celia couldn't get a really good glimpse of, since he'd spent the entire evening obscured by a video camera.

"Worried?" Davis asked Celia as she watched Elton.

She swung her gaze over to her date. That was the other fairy tale that seemed to be shaping up. Davis, wearing his best suit, had come to pick her up. They had joked with each other in the car on the way over as if nothing strange at all were happening. As if he weren't breezing out of her life the very next day. But as the barge floated along, and the champagne lulled her senses, and Davis stared at her with those incredible blue eyes of his, she had to remind herself that this was no more real than a dream. Tomorrow, the wedding would be over, Natalie would be off beginning real life again with Angus, and Davis would be getting on a plane and flying far, far away for God only knew how long.

No, this dreamy feeling wasn't real. But it was oh so tempting to believe that it was. To believe that she and Davis had a chance to start fresh in this romantic setting.

If his question about Elton didn't drag her entirely back to reality, it gave her a little tug in that general direction. She shook her head and took another sip of champagne. "I've given up worrying about all that. That note came Monday, and nothing else has happened all week. Whoever was bugging me probably has gotten bored and given up."

"I hope so."

"I even picked up Gazpacho today," she said. "I didn't want to leave him at the vet anymore—he hated it."

"*He* hated it?"

"Okay, I wanted him home. But I could tell he was ready to be the bane of my existence again."

Davis nodded. "Well, maybe the brick lobber really has decided to call it quits. Let's keep our fingers crossed."

Channel Seven's six o'clock anchorwoman, Jane Russo, danced by in the arms of one of Natalie's uncles. Celia smiled. Natalie was really being generous to offer a forty-dollar partridge dinner to her bitter rival.

Davis offered her his arm. "Would you care to dance?"

Celia tilted her head, listening to the band's rendition of "Dream a Little Dream of Me."

"Can't. It's not a waltz or a cha-cha." Not that she ever wanted to do *that* dance again.

He took her hand anyway, and she felt a bolt shoot through her at the touch of skin to skin. Suddenly she became very aware that she was dressed to the nines in the slinky, sleeveless black dress Natalie had insisted she buy during one of their shopping expeditions. It was fitted and high-necked, and in it she could almost imagine that she was Audrey Hepburn.

He pulled her gently toward the dance floor. "Never mind. Just two-step."

She could hardly play tug-of-war with her date in the middle of Natalie's party. She smiled, relenting. "I don't two-step very well, either."

"I promise not to squeal if you step on my toes."

They glided across the dance floor a few times, listening to the music, looking at the lights. *Just a dream, just a dream,* Celia kept repeating to herself as she pressed against the very real chest beneath Davis's lapels. And felt his very real hand at her waist. His hand in hers. The heady smell of cologne was real, too. But the feelings swirling inside her were not something she could bank on. She repeated that to herself, too, as her heart drummed crazily.

He looked down at her, and she could almost see her own dopey expression reflected in his eyes. "Celia."

Just her name. Whispered in a husky voice that she'd never heard from him before.

She blinked up at him, unable to speak.

Just a dream, just a dream.

"I really messed everything up, didn't I?" he asked.

"No, it was me," she said, remembering the kiss on her stoop. "All those weeks ago . . ."

"That's what I did wrong. I should have—"

"No, *I* should have."

Davis laughed. "Do you have any idea of what I'm trying to say?"

"I don't even know what *I'm* trying to say."

He pulled her closer. "What I'm trying to say is what I should have said last Saturday, but I didn't know how because I'd pissed you off with the ticket thing."

She tilted her head. "What?"

"I'm crazy about you."

Maybe not a dream. A silly grin stretched her lips from ear to ear. "You've done a fantastic job hiding it!"

"Of course. That's what I was trying to do."

"But why?"

"Because after my last attempt at sweeping you off your feet backfired, I asked Olga why a woman friend would be turned off by a male friend making advances, and she gave me this long speech about how women get so much harassment from men that they want their men friends to stay strictly platonic."

Celia rolled her eyes. "Why on earth did you ask Olga?"

"It seemed logical. She writes a column."

"But her perspective is skewed. Of course, *she* might be plagued by men hitting on her all the time. That's not exactly my problem, though."

Davis nodded toward Elton, who was shadowing Natalie as she made her rounds of the guests. "You certainly had a strong reaction to him."

She lifted her brows. "Well, yeah. So would anyone, except maybe Elvira."

"Well, okay. Maybe I made a mistake." He sighed. "And I certainly began to wonder what kind of expertise Olga can have about relationships when out of all the men in the world she chose to go out with Kevin Muldoon."

"I've developed my own theory about that," Celia

explained. "I think she's just seeing how the other half lives. You know, slumming with the jerks the rest of us have tried and discarded. When in reality she'll probably discard him, too, and end up with a perfect George Clooney clone who will worship at her feet."

Davis laughed. "Probably so. Poor Kevin. Doomed to be a discard, like Elton."

"No, Elton is a never-picked-up."

Suddenly, Elton was coming toward them, as was John with the videotape rolling, but only because Natalie was bearing down on Celia like an ice blue streak. She had a ferocious look on her face. "Celia! What am I going to do?"

Celia and Davis stopped dancing and turned toward her. "What's the matter?"

"It's that bitch, Jane! Do you know what she just told me?"

"What?" Celia and Davis asked in unison.

"She's been offered a job in Los Angeles! A major market!"

Celia frowned. "You knew she was probably leaving."

"But I thought she was going to be fired. I didn't expect her to take off in a blaze of glory!"

"Nat, I'm sorry."

"And get this—Boise Barbie is getting her job!"

Poor Nat. "She told you this *tonight*?"

"Oh, yes." Natalie was practically snarling now, even as the videotape was rolling. "Gleefully, she told me. When I was surrounded by as many guests as possible, I might add. Including the station manager."

Natalie snatched a glass of champagne off a passing waiter's tray and downed it like a person crawling out of Death Valley might suck down a canteen of water. She practically tipped the champagne flute upside down to catch the last drops of liquid.

"Don't let it spoil your evening," Celia told her. "This is your night."

Natalie grabbed another glass of bubbly.

"Careful," Celia warned.

"Oh, I've never had any problem holding my liquor." Natalie shot a look at Angus, who was pushing her mother around on the dance floor. "Unlike *some* I could mention."

Uh-oh. "You know what I would do?" Celia suggested quickly. "Just act like it doesn't bother you in the least. Water off your back. For tonight be Portland's answer to Katie Couric—so perky and bubbly that no one will see you sweat."

"You're right!" Natalie said, sipping thoughtfully at her glass now. She gave Celia a quick hug that was like being engulfed in an ice blue cloud of Chanel Number Five. "I knew I could count on you!"

She floated away, bubbling with forced laughter and greeting people with slightly mad gaiety.

"I hope she's okay," Celia said.

Davis pulled her close and started their feet moving in rhythm as the band played "Stardust."

"Natalie? She's indestructible. You don't have to worry about her."

Good thing, too. Because in Davis's arms, listening to a languid saxophone playing "Stardust," Celia didn't feel like worrying about anything.

An hour later, however, as they sat at the long banquet table, Davis began to doubt his words concerning Natalie. After dinner, it was impossible not to notice that a pall had fallen over the evening that had begun with such promise.

The band was still playing romantic standards, there still wasn't a cloud in the sky, and the dinner had been absolutely delicious. But their hostess was looped. And the guests seemed to be dragging. Full of food, they lolled back from the table, barely able to converse with their neighbors on the seating chart. Maybe the pre-dinner dancing and drinks had gone on too long (obviously they had for Natalie), because everyone seemed sated not only foodwise and drinkwise, but also conversation-wise. Davis caught several people sending furtive glances toward the shore.

He'd been looking pretty longingly in that direction himself. Not that he was in any hurry to end the evening. In fact, he would have loved to prolong the night that had seemed to bring him everything he'd ever wanted. He'd felt he could dance with Celia forever on this floating paradise. The only thing that he found more amazing than having been finally able to talk to Celia about his feelings was the fact that this glorious moment had taken place in a setting orchestrated completely by Natalie's mad fantasy.

After dessert, Natalie stood up, her fists planted on the table in front of her to keep her from weaving, and announced that she wanted to make a toast. She picked up her seemingly bottomless champagne glass and lifted it, sloshing champagne all over the plate that had held her two helpings of tiramisu. "F-folks, I would like to toast the person who made this all possible," she slurred. "Who, most of you might guess, is also the person I love more than anyone else in the world."

"Uh-oh," muttered Celia out the side of her mouth. "I think we're about to be treated to an ode to Angus. Let's hope she can keep it G rated."

Davis leaned toward her. "It might wake a few guests up if she can't."

Natalie gulped some champagne and continued, grinning. "Somebody once said, 'War is hell.' Well, I got something to say to that someone. The real hell is planning a wedding."

She hiccuped, and then tears started flowing down her face. "Unless you've got a friend like Celia." She gestured toward Celia, who seemed to shrink in her chair as all eyes turned to her. "Celia Snowden, folks. That's who I love more than anyone else in the world. It isn't my mommy, or my hubby, or even my jobbie. It's my buddy." Her lips curled into a toothless, child-like smile. "Come on up here, Celia."

Celia was frozen in distress. Davis had to give her a nudge. She let out a groan only he could hear and then scuttled forward to get this over with. At the head of the table, Natalie sloppily draped herself over her. "My pal Celia! Let's everybody give her a big round of applause!"

Tepid clapping ensued. Most people just looked uncomfortable, but no one had anything on Celia, who looked so embarrassed she would have been a good candidate for spontaneous combustion. "This is great, Natalie," she muttered. "But now maybe people might want to get back to dancing, or at least eating."

Natalie grinned a goofy grin. "Course! Me, too. Just as soon as I get my picture taken with Celia." She put two fingers to her mouth and blew a piercing whistle. "Hey, Elton! Get over here and take my picture with my friend Celia!"

Elton was only five feet away from her. "Maybe you two should stand next to the guardrail so I can get a good shot of the skyline behind you," he suggested.

Natalie nodded and grabbed Celia's hand, leading her over to the rail. To everyone's dismay, Natalie hopped up and sat on the rail itself. "I want this for pos-pos-prosperity. Me and Celia. C'mon, maid of honor, haul your carcass up here."

"Um, I don't know if that's a good idea." In fact,

Natalie seemed to be weaving precariously on her perch.

"Sure, it'll be sort of rustic," Natalie said. "Like two old friends sittin' on a fence. You probably did a lot of that in Nowhere, Oregon, where you grew up."

"But this is a barge in Portland, not—"

"Celia!" Natalie barked. "Would you *get your ass up here?* You're just the maid of honor. I'm the bride. I outrank you!"

"Oh, all right," Celia grumbled, crawling up next to Natalie and hanging on to the rail beneath her for dear life. She grinned tensely. "Take the picture, Elton."

Elton stood about ten feet away from them, fidgeting with his camera. Finally, after much changing of speeds and checking the lens, he lifted his camera. "All right," he instructed them, "watch the birdie!"

Natalie was all open mouthed enthusiasm, but at Elton's command, Celia's face drained to a ghostly pale. Her eyes widened, and her gaze swerved toward Davis. Hers was a look of sheer horror. And shock. She was frozen with it.

Davis was on his feet in a second. He'd dismissed Celia's suspicions about Elton out of hand, and now look!

Watch the birdie? What did Elton have in that Minolta, a bomb?

That would be just his luck. The woman of his dreams was finally within his grasp, and some nut blows them all to kingdom come.

Well, not if he could help it. Davis ran forward, uncertain whether to attack Elton or try to save Celia. In the end, instinct decided for him. He swerved toward Celia.

"Watch out!" he cried.

Her eyes got even larger as he charged her like a

bull. She leaned back right before he got to her. Her own movement combined with his trajectory was a disaster. She flipped backward, falling overboard. Davis heard the dull splash and hung over the rail, gaping at the dark, brackish water below.

"Celia!"

The answer was splashing and a spluttering cough.

"Hang on, Celia!" He jumped on the railing, peeled off his dinner jacket, and dove into the water.

When he bobbed to the surface again, gasping from the cold, he sputtered up water and yelled Celia's name. "Where are you?"

She swam toward him, teeth chattering. "H-h-here!"

Soon, they were clutching each other, which did neither of them any good. But they couldn't seem to let go. They were shivering and laughing and burbling up drecky river water. In their waterlogged evening clothes, it was a struggle not to sink.

A spotlight flashed from above. They squinted through the glare up at the barge, where the silhouettes of all the guests were now gathered along the rail. He could make out John videotaping and caught a flash as Elton snapped pictures of them. The camera obviously wasn't rigged with explosives.

"Celia? Davis?" It was the suddenly sober voice of their hostess. "Have you two gone insane? Get back on this barge *this instant!*"

"Disgraceful!" Babs seconded.

Some of the passengers snickered, which brought renewed gales of laughter from Davis and Celia.

Elton, apparently, was not their man.

Eighteen

They were still dripping as they drove back to Celia's. Still laughing, too. Celia's sides ached.

"Natalie will never forgive you for this," Davis said.

Their dip in the Willamette might have made them feel deliriously giddy, but it had rendered Natalie as sober as a judge. While attendants hauled Celia and Davis back onto the barge and threw blankets over them, the bride-to-be chewed them out in no uncertain terms. With good reason. Which only made them giggle more. Celia had tried to explain that Davis had only been concerned about their welfare, but Natalie hadn't been in the mood for explanations. They were banished from the barge and sent back to shore in a dinghy.

"She'll have her wedding tomorrow and after that her honeymoon, and when she gets back she'll probably have forgotten tonight," Celia said. "Besides, it's like the time Gazpacho messed up her car. It will provide good guilt to twist my arm with in the future. Natalie loves that."

Davis circled the block looking for a parking place. "Street's crowded," he observed.

Celia frowned. She'd been hoping Davis would come up and . . . Well she wasn't sure what she expected him to do. She knew what she *wanted* him to do, namely ravish her. But she doubted, in her present state, she looked particularly appetizing. "You don't have to park. You can just drop me off."

He slammed on the brakes, jolting them both forward. His eyes turned dark with intensity. Even with a dripping blanket draped over his shoulders he was sexy as hell. Why hadn't she ever noticed? Why on earth had they wasted so much time?

"You don't really mean that, do you?"

Her mouth went so bone dry, the only way she could communicate was by shaking her head.

"Good," he said.

They had to park two blocks away, but Celia didn't mind. Once they were on the sidewalk, Davis put an arm around her. They must have looked a sight, two people draped in Barge Bonanza blankets, but Celia was too deliriously happy to give a damn. The important thing about this moment was that she was walking arm in arm with Davis—not for the first time, though it felt like it. They had strolled like this before, but it had never actually felt like this. There had been no possessiveness in their touch before, no anticipation crackling in the air around them.

"Do you think Elton figured out what happened?" Davis asked.

"Oh, God, I hope not," Celia moaned. "When I was explaining to Natalie, I tried to keep out of Elton's earshot. He must have thought you were nuts."

"*Everybody* thought I was," he said. "And you, too, I'm afraid."

She flashed him a grin. "Guilt by association. For once I don't mind."

Suddenly, Davis stopped. She went a foot beyond him before realizing he wasn't with her anymore. She swung around. "What's wrong?"

"I just realized something," he said.

She tilted her head.

"I've never kissed you on the street before."

She laughed as he tugged her toward him. "You kissed me on my stoop. Doesn't that count?"

He ran his fingers through her wet hair. "Stoops and streets are completely different."

"I never knew," she said, cuddling against him.

"Here, I'll show you."

His lips touched hers, and something magical happened. For once, they were on the same page, relating to each other with the same need. No confusion. No holding back. It was delicious.

And it was made all the better because of the setting. Davis might have had a point about stoops and streets. She'd never thought of her street as romantic before, but now, with the stars and the tall lamps illuminating the old houses crunched so close together, she felt she was on a movie set. Neither of them was ready for their close-ups. Her Audrey Hepburn dress was still soggy, and water from her wet hair dripped down her back. Under his blanket, Davis's shirt was stained with brown. His uncombed hair stuck out in odd places as it dried. And frankly, both of them smelled a little fishy.

But she was beyond caring. They mashed as if there was no such thing as dry.

By some unspoken agreement, they broke off when it became clear that they were about to cross the line from exuberance to exhibitionism. She leaned against him and felt giddily nervous as they neared her apartment. Her newly empty apartment. Corky and Ellen had moved over to Davis's that morning. Their timing couldn't have been better.

"This is going to be the first night I've been in my apartment alone in forever."

"No, it won't."

She frowned. "It won't?"

His gaze smoldered down at her. "You won't be alone."

She gulped.

"Wait a minute," Davis said, stopping again.

This time she fell against him, primed for another kiss. She tilted her head up expectantly; it took her a few moments to realize that he wasn't even looking at her.

He was squinting toward her apartment house. "Who's that coming out of your building?"

Celia turned. They were still half a block away, so she couldn't see that well, but then, when her eyes adjusted, she sucked in a breath of surprise. The man at her front door was a regular string bean—tall and lean, with little round glasses and a long, thin ponytail.

"That's Lyle!" What was *he* doing there?

And then, as he hurried down the steps and turned onto the sidewalk, she saw something that nearly took her breath completely. He was carrying a birdcage.

It felt as though someone had punched her in the gut. "He's got Gazpacho!"

She took off running.

Hearing her exclamation and the tattoo of her stiletto heels, Lyle turned, then dashed off down the street.

"Stop!" Celia yelled. Though, of course, Lyle didn't. He skimmed the corner and sped away down a darker side street. The man might have disappeared, but Gazpacho's pissed-off screeches were like a radar signal.

Celia's heel dug into a crack in the sidewalk, and she flew forward, landing on her hands. "I'll get him!" Davis assured her as he raced past.

Hands stinging, Celia pushed herself up and limped forward again, but she was way behind. Davis, however, had thrown off his blanket and was closing the distance. She saw him tackle Lyle from behind. Both men and the birdcage went down. She let out a yelp of alarm. Lyle and Davis were actually fighting. She and Davis wouldn't have any relationship—platonic or otherwise—if he got beaten to a lifeless pulp. She had to do something.

And then, in a flash, something was coming toward her. At first she saw only a figure out of the corner of her eye swipe up Davis's discarded blanket. Then it leapt into the fray.

Celia let out a yell. "Davis, watch out!"

Lyle looked up, disoriented, and Celia tossed her own blanket over his head. Davis and the mystery man seized the moment and tackled Lyle to the ground. They secured their charge by sitting on him.

The two men stared at each other in surprise. But no one was more stunned than Celia to see her downstairs neighbor sitting on Lyle.

"Mr. Z!" she exclaimed. "What are you doing?"

"I heared the noise," he said. "Then saw the man with parrot sneaking out."

"Three cheers for nosy neighbors!" Celia said.

Davis laughed, but as he wiped a filthy wet sleeve over his brow, he winced.

He had a red bruise just to the side of his left eye. Celia knelt in front of him. "Are you all right?"

He grunted. "How about you?"

"Fine." She looked over at Gazpacho, whom she was worried about more than herself. He was pacing angrily in his overturned travel cage, which required him to crouch like Groucho Marx. Celia had to stifle the urge to give Lyle a quick boot in the ribs. "I guess we all came through okay. I suppose I should call the police."

"That I did already," Mr. Zhirbotken said.

She was *really* going to make an effort to keep the volume on her stereo down from now on.

Flashing red lights illuminated the street, and a police car screeched to a stop right in front of them. Two uniformed men hopped out of the cruiser.

At that moment, Celia sort of expected this to be the end of the matter. She supposed the ranking officer would take one look at Lyle wrapped in the wet blanket and tell his partner the equivalent of "Book him, Dan-O," but this was not the case. In fact, the two cops looked at the three of them, not Lyle, with suspicion.

"Sirs, we'll have to ask you to get off of that man."

Not in the habit of arguing with men carrying guns and clubs, they did as told. Lyle came up sputtering and rubbing his eyes.

"Are you crazy? Are you trying to smother me?"

"Are *we* crazy?" Celia marveled at the nerve of the jerk. *"We're* not parrot thieves!"

"At least I'm not a wife thief!" Lyle shot back bitterly.

"What?"

"You stole Ellen!"

A cop stepped between them so that Celia had to shout over his shoulder. "I didn't steal your wife. She left you because you're a controlling ass."

"You coerced her, and you seduced her!"

Celia's jaw dropped. "Are you insane?"

"I should have known when Ellen started sneaking out in the middle of the night that there was some kind of hanky-panky going on."

Celia could hardly believe her ears. And then, as she remembered *why* Ellen had said she was sneaking out in the middle of the night, she nearly lost it. "She wasn't meeting me, you dope. She was sneaking out to eat hamburgers."

"If that's so, it's only because of your corrupting influence! You two have been shacked up together for a month," Lyle said bitterly. "A month in that tiny apartment."

Davis shook his head. "Man, you've made a big mistake."

Celia put her hands on her hips. "Can't you tell whether your wife is a lesbian or not?"

"She never was, until you got your hands on her."

She groaned in frustration. "Lyle, your wife is at this minute out at the movies with a red-blooded, Bruce Springsteen–worshiping American male, who has also been living in my apartment."

"The three of you?" the cop asked.

"It was only a temporary arrangement," Celia explained.

They were dealing with two new officers, of course, so it took a while to explain just what was going on. The fact that both she and Davis were sopping wet— not to mention Lyle's confusion concerning his wife's sexual identity—made things even more difficult to sort out. Also slowing down the process was the choking rage Celia felt as she related the story of the brick thrown through her window, the menacing letters she'd received at work, and, most of all, the picture. When Lyle smirked at her description of the snap he'd taken from the rooftop across the street from her building, she wanted to clobber him. Only enormous self-control, and the sight of the guns hanging on the officers' belts, kept her from following her impulse.

The upshot of the evening was, the man had broken into her apartment and kidnapped her parrot, and Celia wasn't going to let him off scot-free. She didn't care what his motive had been.

"I only wish I could sue him for damages to Gazpacho's psyche," she declared as she and Davis were finally climbing the steps to her apartment. They had escorted Mr. Zhirbotken back to his place. The man had earned her eternal thanks.

She lifted Gazpacho up to eye level, and the parrot blinked at her wearily. "Poor baby!"

Davis sent her a dubious look. "I hate to tell you this, but that bird of yours had a pretty damaged psyche already."

The criticism made her bristle, but only for a moment. Looking into Davis's laughing blue eyes, she found it impossible to be irate, even on her bird's behalf. "I'll let that comment pass. This time."

"Why?" He beamed an impossibly sexy grin at her that made her insides feel as if they were turning to Jell-O. Which, she discovered, was not a bad feeling.

Not bad at all.

"Because I was hoping to seduce you," she said as they pushed the door open. She would have to repair her lock tomorrow. "For the moment I refuse to say anything that might jeopardize my success."

"You couldn't fail," he replied in a husky voice, "because I had the exact same idea."

"Good. Then, stop dissing my bird."

When she closed the door behind them, she felt unaccountably edgy. God knew, this wasn't the first time she and Davis had been alone in this apartment, but this time the air in the two little rooms felt charged. She busied herself putting Gazpacho back onto his perch, where he looked happy to be.

So how was this mutual seduction supposed to come about? Should she just throw herself at Davis?

She glanced down at herself. Audrey Hepburn had never looked this bedraggled. She was an absolute mess. Her dress was stained with dried dirt from the river. Her arms were dirty, her hands had bloody streaks where she'd landed on the sidewalk, and when she reached up to feel her hair, she discovered that it was matted rather like a dog's might have been after a dip in the Willamette.

She wrinkled her nose. Right now she was *not* the kind of creature a man would want flying at him on a Friday night. "I'd better get in the shower and wash the river off of me."

He nodded. "Me, too."

She blinked at him. Did he mean . . . ?

She swallowed. Of course that was what he meant.

He smiled as he took her in his arms. "No sense wasting water." He pulled her to him for a kiss. Their lips met, and it felt as though all the static in the air became an electric current connecting them. "We don't want to be hydro-hogs." He rained little kisses down from her lips to her chin.

She shivered and gripped his arms for support. "N-no." A gasp escaped her as he nipped at her ear.

Her hands seemed to move of their own accord up to the buttons of his shirt. One by one, she started undoing them. Her task was made slightly more difficult because of the damp material, but she discovered a zeal could overcome that little obstacle.

Luckily, it wasn't far to the bathroom from where they were standing. The one advantage, she supposed, in having a tiny apartment. There was no in-house destination that couldn't be reached in ten or fewer steps.

But she couldn't have said how many steps it took them. It seemed as if they simply floated in that general direction, and the next minute they were staring at the claw-foot tub. Now there was a decision to be made.

"Bath or shower?" she asked.

"Your pick," he said.

She started running the bath. When she stood up

from turning the water on, Davis reached for her hand and pulled her to him. She tugged off the shirt that she'd unbuttoned. When that task was accomplished, he turned her around. She frowned in confusion until she heard and felt the zipper that went down her back unfasten. The dress fell in a puddle around her ankles. He undid the strapless bra she'd worn, and it fell away. Next she squeezed out of her pantyhose. When she turned to him, she was wearing only a skimpy pair of panties, and Davis's eyes were alight with appreciation that sent a bolt of desire through her.

To hell with waiting for a bath, she thought. She flipped the lever, and hot water sprayed from the shower head. She stepped in and tugged Davis after her. He stripped faster than she would have thought humanly possible and joined her in the steamy confines of the shower curtains.

She'd never done this. She'd thought it would be awkward, a little embarrassing, but she was actually too frenzied to feel embarrassment. Davis grabbed a bar of soap and set about lathering up her entire body. She sucked in her breath as he took his time with her breasts, circling them lovingly. He bent down and kissed her lips. "You're beautiful, Celia," he said. "More beautiful than I ever imagined."

She closed her eyes and let his words wash over her. Let his hands and that innocent little bar of soap work their magic. She felt enveloped by steam and caresses; when he reached the V between her legs and began to gently lather her there, she had to grab hold of his shoulders just to make sure she could remain standing. He caressed her until she thought she was going to faint, and then he moved lower, down her thighs, working all the way down to her feet.

He washed her feet.

She was practically weeping with desire and the need to reciprocate.

She got her chance when he stood. She took the bar from him and began her own routine—though she had a hard time concentrating. Davis kept bending down to kiss her. Her hair. Her lips. Her neck. She melted against him. She could feel his erection pressing against her. She reached down and explored the velvety hardness of him. Moaning, he quickly pulled her toward him, so that they were both kissing directly under the pulsing jet of hot water. It rinsed over them in a steamy cascade.

And then he flipped the water off.

She blinked, surprised.

Davis stepped out of the shower, grabbed a towel off the rack, and began drying her with the same thoroughness that he had used when washing her. Inch by inch, she was rubbed down, kissed, and thoroughly cherished.

When her turn came, she was not so patient. She snatched up a towel and made quick work of reciprocating. She was revved up and ready to streak across to her bed.

She kissed him and thought she could sense him holding back. *Please don't let him have changed his mind.* "Is something wrong?"

He closed his eyes and released a heavy, mournful sigh. "Yes."

A lump formed in the pit of her stomach. This was a fine time to be having second thoughts! "What is it?"

His voice came out husky, raw. "Protection."

She tilted her head. "Protection?"

"Condoms," he bit out. "No condoms."

Relief flooded through her. Wouldn't you know he'd be Mr. Careful, Mr. Considerate? She performed a Barishnykov-like jeté to the sink. She reached up and flipped open the medicine cabinet, where there was an unopened box of Trojans. She tossed it to him.

"A gift."

He caught the box and looked at her dubiously. "You just keep them around?"

"Are you complaining?"

He shook his head and reached out to her. A quick tug was all it took to bring her to him. They kissed as they performed an entangled pas de deux across the hall to her bedroom. There, they fell on the mattress in a snaggle of arms and legs.

"Your skin feels so good, it's like silk."

She was in an agony of desire. She'd expected that things would move quickly once they hit the bed. If she'd had to guess, she would have bet that Davis was a meat-and-potatoes kind of lover. A few kisses and then bang. Right now, after their hijinx in the shower, that sounded okay to her. Great, in fact.

But the thing was, she was wrong about Davis. He had an inventiveness that was as surprisingly wonderful as it was impossibly frustrating. Celia was ready for a little consummation. As in *ready*. She'd never been so *ready*.

But he seemed to have the endurance and creativity of a practiced Don Juan.

Patience, however, had its rewards. Celia had never experienced such dizzying heights. Need seemed to radiate through every pore of her body, and he fulfilled her every wish, spoken and unspoken. Their desire spiraled until she feared they would both go spinning off into some frenzied stratosphere, but they found completion and after the fireworks came skimming back safely to earth.

They lay together for a long time, breathing heavily, shocked by what they had experienced. When Davis lifted up on his elbows and looked down into her eyes, she couldn't help it. She smiled. He smiled, too, and then averted his face so that she couldn't see him chuckling. She felt him shake. She let out a snort of laughter. Suddenly, they were in a heap, practically weeping.

"I'm sorry," she said. "It's just . . ."

"I know."

"And to think, all the time we've known each other we could have been doing this instead of eating grilled cheese sandwiches and watching movies."

"But that was nice, too," he said, bending down to kiss a little bead of perspiration that was escaping down her neck.

"You mean you think what we just did was *nice?*" she asked, stunned. To her it had been an earth shattering experience.

"No, what we just did was magnificent," he said. "It was dynamite."

She pulled the covers over her head and groaned. "Oh, no! Are you *sure* you didn't write that letter?"

He gave her a quizzical look. She explained about the Olga-Inga letter Kevin Muldoon had written.

He laughed. "I thought something strange was happening. You kept saying odd things to me. I couldn't figure it out."

She snuggled up to him. "No more speaking in code," she promised.

"No." He kissed her forehead, then worked his way down her nose to her lips. She moaned and felt herself slipping away into that happy oblivion once again.

He awakened to an alarmed cry and a bump. When he opened his eyes, Celia, wearing nothing but an oversized T-shirt she had acquired at some point during the night, was holding her head and wincing.

Davis sat up. "Are you all right?"

"Oh, sure. This happens practically every morning."

"You wake up screaming?" That could be a problem.

"No, I hit my head on the ceiling. It's one of the hazards of attic dwelling."

"Is that why you were yelping?"

She threw out her hands toward the sunlight pouring through the windows. "No! It's almost ten. Natalie's wedding is at eleven."

A bolt of alarm shot through him.

"I've got to get going!" they both cried in unison. "I've got to—"

Here, their words diverged.

"Get dressed!"

"Pack!"

Celia, who had been scurrying toward the bathroom, stopped dead in her tracks. "What?"

He jumped out of bed. "Well, I've also got to get home and get dressed."

"What?" Her needle was stuck in a groove.

"I can't wear my suit from last night," he explained. "It's filthy."

"You said *pack,*" she pointed out. "You said you were going to go home to *pack.*"

Despite their promises of last night, it sounded as though she was speaking to him in that code again. Did the word *pack* have some alternate meaning he wasn't aware of? "That's right," he said carefully.

"You mean you're going?"

He shook his head in confusion. "Going home, or going to South America?"

"To South America!" she said with growing hysteria.

"Of course I'm going," he said. "You knew that."

She looked as if she was about to explode. "I knew it before last night."

Ah. His muzzy brain latched on to the crux of the problem now. "I've paid for the ticket, Celia. I've made the arrangements. I've quit my job, for heaven's sake."

"You took a leave of absence," she pointed out. "They'd take you back immediately, no problem. You know that."

"I was going to write that book, remember?"

"But you could write that here just as easily." She rolled her eyes. "Listen to me! I'm begging!"

He reached out for her arm and pulled her toward him. Even after their draining night, given their state of undress, it was hard to resist the impulse to drag her back to the bed and make love to her again. But he sensed right now that she needed words, not sex. "If you're worried about my coming back, you don't have to beg."

"I'm not concerned about your coming back," she retorted. "I'm concerned about your desire to leave in the first place. I thought last night meant something."

"It did. It meant everything to me."

"Everything except giving up a nonrefundable ticket," she said. "Which, if you'll recall, is one way. You could decide to stay for two years."

"Then, this *is* about whether I'll come back." He didn't have to be reminded that Celia tended to think that the world was abandoning her. "I wouldn't have made love to you last night, Celia, if I didn't have every intention of getting back to you. And now I couldn't possibly stay away for long."

She lifted her chin. "Three months *is* a long time.

Anything could happen. You could fall in love with someone down there. Some *senorita.*"

"You could do the same."

She sniffed. "Despite what Lyle said, I *don't* go for *senoritas.*"

"You know what I meant." He shook his head. "Celia, *you're* the one who is always itching to go do something different, to go to exotic new places. Now you're acting as if I'm committing a crime for wanting the exact same thing."

"But I wouldn't leave now! We just . . ." Her face turned a shade redder. "Well, I thought we were starting something."

"We are." He pulled her closer and tried to look into her eyes so that she could read how sincerely he meant his words. "What do you want me to promise? That I'll write? I will, every day. E-mail *and* snail mail. I'll call you all the time—pester you with phone calls if that's what you want. Heck, we spend half our time on the phone anyway."

"But that's when we were friends," she pointed out. "Things are different now."

He put his hands on her shoulders. He had to stifle the urge to throttle her, and maybe shake loose the impression she had that he was going to walk out on her today and abandon her forever. "I'm not Ian," he told her.

"You're acting like him."

He sighed heavily. "Listen, you need to get dressed, and I need to run home. We can talk at the wedding reception."

She stepped back. "If you're so pressed for time, you don't have to come to the wedding."

He didn't know how to answer that. He was beyond frustrated now; he was getting mad. And anger was something that he'd never felt toward Celia before.

He turned back and started throwing on the clothes that he'd dropped on the way to the shower last night. "You're the one who sounds like you're trying to push me away," he pointed out. "But I'll be at that wedding whether you want me to be or not."

She lifted her chin. "All right."

He left, wondering why the hell he felt so frustrated. Why for the first time in his life he wanted to strangle someone. And then, as he was walking back to his car, it struck him. She had no idea—not even a clue—about how deep his feelings for her ran. To her, this was all a new fling, another love affair she was embarking on. While ever since last night he'd been working on the presumption that this was *it*.

But now he wondered if *it* was all he'd hoped it would be.

Nineteen

Celia sped to the waterfront hotel as fast as she could, but she still just squeaked in at the last minute.

She parked her car and ran inside the hotel as quickly as her lavender-dyed heels would allow. All things considered, she'd pulled herself together pretty well. Never mind that she'd just had the most incredible night of her life. Never mind that she had finally found her dream man right under her nose, only to have him declare his intention to fly about as far away from her as he could get without opting for an icy tundra. Never mind that emotionally she felt as though she was skittering across thin ice. She had managed to shower and mousse her hair and put on makeup and do justice to the dreaded pale lavender strapless.

Might as well look good when Davis said goodbye to her.

So good, perhaps, that he might just decide not to get on that plane at all?

She shook her head. That was the most desperate kind of wishful thinking—especially coming from someone encased in pale purple taffeta.

She followed signs that read GLASS WEDDING. It seemed entirely appropriate that the name McDougall was nowhere in sight. She could see the door leading out to the green space that was set up with folding chairs and fantastic sprays of roses everywhere. The band from last night had been replaced by a soothing classical quartet playing "Jesu, Joy of Man's Desiring." Many of the chairs were already occupied by well-heeled guests, most of whom she recognized from last night. And from the withering or humorous looks she received from the people milling about in the hall and just by the doors, they remembered her, too.

Just get through this, she told herself. If she was lucky, she would never have to be a bridesmaid again. In fact, it was almost guaranteed, since she was out of single, marriageable-aged friends. When the time came, she intended to convince Ellen and Corky to elope.

She ducked into the room that had been set aside for last minute bride preparations and encountered a sight that was the last thing she'd expected. Chaos. Babs, holding the wedding dress, was chasing Natalie around a screen. Though her hair was done, Natalie was dressed in a pair of jeans. Plain old blue jeans. Celia had never seen *that* before. Both women were screeching at each other.

"Get it away from me!"

"Don't be a *fool!* Put on the damn dress!"

Natalie shrilled like a child refusing to eat broccoli. "You can't make me!"

Unfortunately, the bridesmaid cousins were nowhere to be seen. They had probably scattered the moment Natalie and Babs started going head-to-head.

Celia cleared her throat. Both women turned, gasped to see her there, and rushed at her.

"Celia!" Natalie cried.

"Celia! Thank God you're here!"

Celia sucked in her breath. If Babs Glass was glad to see her, something earth shattering was going on.

"Will you please tell Natalie to stop playing prima donna and put this thing on?"

Natalie ducked behind Celia, cowering. Celia's brows pulled together in puzzlement as she took in the dress, which was a full-skirted taffeta—a Windsor princess special, as Natalie would have sneeringly called it. No wonder Natalie didn't want to put it on.

"That's the wrong dress," Celia informed Babs.

"Natalie *doesn't fit* in her dress. The store sent this one as a replacement."

Natalie whirled Celia around for support. "It's a *size twelve!*"

"Because *you're* a size twelve," her mother pointed out.

"I am not!" Natalie declared stubbornly.

"Natalie . . ." Celia, though amazed how quickly those Cheetos had piled onto Natalie's once-slender frame, couldn't see how any of this mattered right now. "There are guests outside."

"Is that my fault? Mother will just have to tell them the wedding is off."

"You want to call off your wedding because your dress doesn't fit?"

Natalie put her hands on her hips. "Can you think of a better reason?"

Babs gesticulated angrily with the dress. "What am I supposed to say? That the wedding is canceled due to flab?"

The word hit Natalie like a slap. "Yes! Go tell them that, Mother. And while you're at it, tell them that the wedding is also canceled because the bride doesn't love the groom."

"Don't be childish."

"It's the truth."

"Then, you should have thought of that two months ago."

"But I didn't. I'm thinking of it *now!*"

Celia felt as if she had stepped into a rabbit cage inhabited by two pumas. She had the strongest urge to see if she could sneak back out the door and find the hotel's bar. She tiptoed a few steps toward the exit before Natalie stopped her by grabbing her arm in a viselike clutch.

"*You* don't have to tell them," Natalie assured her, as if Celia ever had any intention of facing down that crowd. Her friend stared at Babs icily. "Mother will do it."

"Natalie, you're being childish," her mother said, which Celia thought might just be the understatement of the year. "You've just got bridal jitters."

"It doesn't matter what I've got. I can't get married."

"You can."

"No, I can't." She looked at her mother pleadingly. "And would you please explain it to Angus for me?"

Her mother practically cried with relief. "*That's* what I'll do—I'll get Angus!"

Celia let out a bark of surprise. "Doesn't Angus know what's happening?"

Neither of them was listening to her. "*He'll* be able to convince you that this is all a lot of foolishness," Babs muttered to herself as she sailed toward the door with outstretched arms.

Natalie nodded. "That sounds like a good idea. You do that."

Her mother fled the room, dress still in hand. The silence she left behind felt like a roar.

After the door had slammed behind Babs, Natalie let out a long sigh, shook her head, and marched over to the door and flipped the lock. "That poor deluded woman. She seems to think this wedding is the most important thing in the world."

Celia felt faint. This was *Natalie* talking? "My God, Nat. What's happened?"

Natalie seemed surprised she would ask. "It's simple. I've changed my mind." She went back to where her things were gathered in a little pile. Willy-nilly, she started dumping clothes and shoes and cosmetics in a duffel bag.

"But you've made so many plans—you're just going to toss them away?"

"You know, I've decided planning isn't always the best thing. Look at all that planning that we did for our trip to Thailand. All the maps and guidebooks in the world couldn't keep us from getting stuck in that typhoon."

Celia wondered whether now was the moment to admit that she had skimmed her travel guide's little section on the rainy season. "But you said you were so happy, so in love—"

Natalie snorted. "Spoken on a sugar buzz."

"Look, just because a dress is a little tight . . ."

"The dress was simply the last straw. I was popping out of it, Celia. And I looked in the full-length mirror, and I just decided that this *just isn't me.* It's just not. I was just so desperate to be what I wasn't, what Mother thought I should be, that I've become someone I just don't recognize as me at all."

"But what about the windows slamming on your youth? My God, you're going to be an oink."

Natalie raised a brow at her. "Could I possibly be more of an oink than I am now?" She snatched a facial wipe from her bag. "My real trouble is work, and I'm about to remedy that." She hurried to the mirror. "I'm leaving Channel Seven."

Celia's jaw went slack.

"You remember that job in Eugene?" Natalie asked, wiping her expensive bride makeover from her skin.

Celia nodded, numbly.

"Well, screw it, I'm driving down there this afternoon. I'm going to beg them for the stupid job if I have to!"

"But what about all the hippies? You said you'd hate it down there."

"I will, but I'm going nowhere here. My station doesn't see me as Jane Russo replacement material. Fine. I'll go down and be a big fish in a little pond like Barbie from Boise, and I'll show them. I'll come back as queen bee—or better yet, I'll go to San Francisco or Los Angeles or Seattle. Or New York! There's a whole world to conquer out there. Why am I beating my brains out for people who don't appreciate me? I should be on C goddamn NN."

"But Angus . . ."

Natalie sighed as she wiped off makeup at a furious pace. "Poor Angus. They'll just have to pickle him in Guinness and send him back to Glasgow."

She gathered up her duffel and headed for the sliding door that led out to a pool area. She was sneaking out the back way, apparently. "That's it, then—wish me luck!"

"You're going *now?*" What was this, cut-and-run day? Celia followed her. "But, Nat . . ."

Natalie grinned. "Don't you start, too. She nodded toward the wedding dress she'd left in a puddle on the floor. "Take it if you think you can use it. Say, if Fozzie ever proposes."

Celia huffed. "Not likely! Not after what happened this morning."

Natalie's brows shot up. "This morning? You mean you and Davis spent the whole night together?"

"For the first and probably the last time."

Natalie's eyes widened. "Oh, I wish I had time to hear you spill! When I get back from Eugene, we'll need to have coffee." She gave her a quick hug. "And you know, Celia, you look *dynamite!*" She laughed merrily and then hoofed it out the back door. Celia watched her friend run across the pool area in a crouch, then disappear behind a hedge.

At the same time, someone started pounding on the door. *"Hey, Nat-lie!"* Angus cried, giving Celia the impression that he would be a good Stanley McKowalski if a theater company in Scotland wanted to do *A Streetcar Named Desire.*

Giving Natalie just a few more moments' leeway, Celia bided her time strolling to the door, then counted to ten and flipped the lock. Angus fell into the room. "Where's Nat'lie?"

Celia looked at him and sighed. He *did* look great. Even the combination of tux and kilt couldn't disguise the fact that the guy was a major hottie. In fact, those hairy soccer-toned calves of his were an additional enticement. Too bad her affections were otherwise occupied, or she might have been available for lending succor to the jilted groom.

Come to think of it, she might be available soon anyway.

The reminder of Davis made her stomach clinch painfully. She turned with impatience to Angus. "Natalie is gone, Angus. But if you need help, I can loan you any number of books that deal with abandonment issues."

But none of them can stop people from abandoning you, she almost added. Angus would probably figure that one out for himself.

She left the room and started walking slowly back out toward her car. As she reached the hotel lobby, she heard Davis calling her name. At the sound of his voice, her heart was a tight, painful knot in her chest. She turned and got a load of him, and she felt almost faint. He was all spiffed up in a different suit. He looked incredible, sexy. As he came toward her, thoughts of last night raced through her head. How could he leave after something that earth shattering?

Unless, of course, the earth hadn't shattered for him.

"What's going on with the guests?" she asked him.

"Natalie's mother was beginning to make some kind of announcement. What happened?"

"Natalie bugged out big time. She's running away to Eugene."

Davis sent her a look of confusion. "Eugene? Are you serious? That's anarchist central."

"It's also where she's been offered a job."

Davis considered this for a moment. "Well, she'll never run out of things to complain about there."

"Who knows? Maybe she'll give up shaving and take to folk singing." Celia shrugged. "She was right to punt the wedding. It never would have worked."

"Well, I suppose even Natalie is entitled to her one moment of sanity."

Having used up the safest topic of conversation, they lapsed into silence.

"You look incredible," he said after a moment.

"Lavender isn't really my color."

They stood awkwardly, unable to think what they should do next. The first of the guests were trickling out with bemused looks on their faces. Soon, she realized, all of the guests would be gone, and she and Davis would have to part ways, too. And after their argument that morning, she couldn't just let him go. She'd sounded like a harpy.

"Look," Celia said hurriedly. "I'm sorry about this morning. I didn't express myself very well."

He reached out and took her hand in his. Their fingers threaded together. "I'm listening now."

She swallowed. "Well . . . First off, I know you're not like Ian. It's just that I felt so giddy and happy—and then your saying you were going home to pack was like having the rug pulled out from under me."

"I guess that wasn't very tactful," he agreed.

"I just don't want you to go," she said in a rush before she could lose her courage. "Last night was incredible. I want to spend the summer with you."

A series of emotions paraded across those blue eyes that were pinned on her face so intently. "I guess that cinches it." A smile broke across her face. "Then, you're staying?"

He dropped her hand. "No, I'm still going."

She watched him cautiously, fearing that rug was about to be yanked out from under her again. "I'm not following."

"Let me see if I can put it more clearly for you." He paused and then said, "I love you, Celia."

Her legs went wobbly. Her heart skipped a beat. But something was wrong. He was saying that he loved her, but his tone indicated that this wasn't necessarily a good thing.

"As a matter of fact, I've been in love with you for about a year now," he admitted.

"What?"

"I don't know if it was love at first sight, but it was pretty near it."

She stepped back. "I never knew. You never told me!"

"Because you always made it clear you didn't want to hear it. You kept me in a little compartment reserved for a male friend who would be a good fallback when you needed an emergency date, or a hard-to-reach lightbulb changed . . . or when you needed a shoulder to cry on about Ian. For a long time I didn't mind being in that little compartment, because I loved you and I just wanted to be around you under any terms. But those little compartments can get pretty stuffy. When I realized that, I decided to take a leave of absence and visit Antonio."

She listened to what he was telling her with a sense of unreality. Davis didn't bandy words about. If he said he was in love with her, she doubted he was speaking on a whim. She wanted to say something, to put into words all the jumbled thoughts reeling around inside her head, but it felt as if the breath had been knocked out of her body.

"You probably think I'm pretty loopy for confessing all this now," he said. "But I wanted you to know why I'm still going to Argentina."

She shook her head. "If you love me . . ."

"Don't you get it? I don't just want to spend a summer with you—I don't want to be the flavor of the month before you decide what you really want is, say, a strapping Swede. I couldn't deal with that. This way, I'll be gone for a while, and if what we feel now is something lasting, we'll know it."

"B-but—"

He pulled her to him, and suddenly his arms were around her and they were kissing. As his lips touched hers, she felt dizzy with confusion and desire. She grabbed the lapels of his suit, wanting to hang on to him physically in some way. How could he do this? Was he punishing her for not realizing he was in love with her before? Was that it?

He pulled back from her. She felt almost as if she were panting. "I guess that'll have to hold us till I get back."

"Davis, wait! You can't just leave."

He smiled. "Don't stress out, Celia. I'll be in touch."

He turned and walked away. As if it weren't costing

him a thing. In fact, he seemed as proud and straight as she'd ever seen him.

While *she* was noodle limp with shock. Her first instinct was to run after him, but what more could she say? She told him she didn't want him to go as bluntly as she could, and he'd come out with the fact that he loved her as the reason that he wanted to take off. What had happened to the old persistent, predictable Davis? Why was he disappearing just when she needed him most?

She felt about as low as a person could get, but the day was apparently not over yet. From the direction of the defunct wedding party, she heard someone calling her name. She turned and saw Elton bearing down on her, his face red.

"Oh, hi, Elton." He looked upset. But, of course, he'd just lost his big client. "Sorry about the wedding."

He snorted derisively. "I'll bet you are. You're all heart. So shensitive!"

The words were like slaps. She recoiled slightly. "Are you all right?"

"Sure. Fine," he bit out. "But this morning Natalie told me the reason you went overboard last night. You thought *I* was stalking you? That I was going to perpetrate some violence?"

Celia took a deep breath. All that seemed so far in the past now, it was hard to even remember. "I'm sorry."

"Were you so repulsed by my asking you for a date that you had to make up some weird stalker fantasy about me?"

"Somebody *was* stalking me," she said in her defense. "I just didn't know who."

"S-so you just jumped to the conclusion that it was me," he sputtered. "I paid you a compliment and wanted to get to know you better, and you treated me like I was some sort of nut. Thanks. Thanks a lot!"

As she digested his anger, she began to see the situation his way. From his point of view, she had behaved pretty despicably. "I'm sorry, Elton."

His lips twitched down into an unforgiving scowl. "Yeah, well, you can just find somebody else to take your parrot's Santa pictures!"

He turned and stomped out of the lobby toward the parking lot.

He, too, seemed to have gained a little stature and swagger from having chewed her out. She seemed to be a great ego booster in that regard.

She glanced anxiously around the hotel lobby, just in case there was someone else who wanted to come flying at her. If she stayed where she was, it would only be a matter of time before Babs or Angus found her again. She crept out of the lobby and then made a quick dash to her car.

But where could she go now?

The last place she wanted to retreat to was her apartment. She didn't want to look at her rumpled sheets and remember just what she had been up to during the rumpling. She couldn't go to Natalie's.

Which left only one pathetic alternative.

She headed for the office. Along the way, she tried to console herself that she was in just the right mood to edit obituaries. She would be channeling her negative energy in the right place for once. Unfortunately, she would have to explain to Marie that this week's "Unions" column had dissolved before her eyes.

But as it turned out, her boss was impressed to see her there on yet another Saturday. She cackled with glee at the outfit, too. "Don't tell me the Salvation Army is trafficking in pastel taffeta!"

Celia grumbled a response and shuffled toward her

cubicle. Once there, she looked across at Davis's cleared desk and felt a knifing pain in her chest. She must have been insane to come here. She collapsed in her chair and clicked on her computer. As it booted up, she fidgeted through her drawers for paper clips, pens . . . anything to keep her gaze from cutting to the left and that empty desk. She hoped that Marie would leave her in peace, but no such luck. The Warden came strolling over and sat down on the edge of her desk.

"I've got news about 'Unions,' " Marie told her.

"Me, too," Celia said.

"Better let me go first." Marie smiled. "Snowden, your dream has come true. Starting tomorrow, that dumb column is going to have a new name."

Celia let out a harried sigh. *Great!* Being harassed by Marie was just what she needed right now. "Let me guess . . . You want to call it 'Here Comes the Chump.' "

Marie's face contorted into a confused mask. "What?"

"Or how about this for short and sweet—'Dead End.' "

Marie looked offended. "Are you crazy? *I* thought we could call it 'Ever After.' "

Celia straightened. "Oh. This is for real?"

"Of course!"

It was a victory, of sorts. But Celia was hardly in the mood for jumping up and down and squealing. "It's great. I like it. But it will have to be next week," she informed her boss. "Natalie Glass called off her wedding."

Marie frowned. "Damn! I guess we could put in a notice saying we're revamping the column. Make it sound like we've got the Keebler elves over here hand carving new typeface or something."

Celia nodded. "That would probably work."

"Glad you think so. But the downside of that is, next week you won't be writing the column."

Celia glanced up at her, alarmed. Hadn't this morning been traumatic enough? Was she going to be fired, too? "I swear, I had no idea Natalie's wedding was going to fall through. I would have had a backup . . ."

Marie laughed.

For a moment, Celia felt uneasy. Something was terribly wrong, but she couldn't put her finger on it.

And then it hit her. She'd never seen Marie genuinely smile at her before. Ever. The woman didn't smile at her workers. She scowled, smirked, or screamed, but never smiled. Celia rolled her chair back, trying to get distance from her boss, who she feared was about to snap. Maybe she'd been breathing newspaper ink for too long.

"Don't be a dope," Marie said, still grinning. "You're not being yanked off your column because of that harebrained anchor woman. You're being promoted!"

"Promoted?"

Marie clapped her on the arm. "It just came through last night. You, Celia Snowden, are going to be the assistant editor of the soon-to-be expanded *Portland Today!*"

Celia sat in mute surprise, letting the words sink in.

Obviously, Marie was pleased by her speechless reaction. "I like the way you handle things, Snowden. The way you stood up to Caselli over the gay marriage thing. The way you handled the harassment from those loony readers. Shrugging off tossed bricks and abject humiliation. You've got guts."

Guts? Celia felt hysterical laughter bubbling up inside her. And a little pride, of course. After all, coming from Marie, having guts was the highest compliment. It was like having John Wayne tell her she had true grit.

Should she confess to Marie that the bricks and humiliation had been meted out by Lyle, not angry readers? That *she* hadn't even wanted to do the gay wedding in the first place?

Nah. "I don't know what to say . . ."

"Of course not!" Marie said, slapping her on the shoulder. She looked critically around her little cubicle. "We'll have to do something about this little box you work in. You'll need a setup that looks a little more authoritative." She glanced over at Davis's emptied cubicle. "Okay, we can just adjust Dashiell Hammett's space into yours. Give you a little breathing room." She pushed herself up and stuck out her hand. Celia shook it limply.

"You're moving on up, Snowden."

"Like the Jeffersons," Celia muttered.

"Huh?" Marie squinted at her. "Oh, right! Ha! Keep that sense of humor. You'll need it if you're going to start managing." She started to walk away, but then turned. "Oh, by the way, you'll still be editing the weddings and obits. Also a lot of other stuff we'll divvy up later. We'll have a meeting soon." She was about to go back to her desk again, but then turned back once more, giving Celia's wedding outfit a pointed up-and-down gaze. "And now that you're getting a promotion, you might want to lay off the shiny pastels."

Celia leaned back and tried to take it in. So. Without meaning to, she'd scored a professional success. This job wasn't the dead end she'd feared. She was now going to be . . .

The Wardenette.

Her heart sank.

Oh, Lord! In a few months, she would be well on

her way to becoming like poor workaholic Marie. In twenty years, she would be telling young coworkers about how tough things had been at the turn of the century. By that time, the whole paper would probably be nothing *but* wedding announcements, sex advice, and horoscopes. But she wouldn't notice, because she wouldn't have left the building in at least a decade.

Meanwhile, Natalie would be reading the evening news for NBC. Ellen and Corky would have the most successful Italian pub-yoga center in America. And Davis . . .

Davis would probably be just a memory. The one that got away that she would think of wistfully while she ate her sandwich at her desk at lunchtime. He'd be writing mysteries. And, maybe, he'd still be her friend.

For some reason, that seemed the most depressing prospect of all. In fact, she didn't think she could stand it.

A glutton for punishment, she spun her chair around to face that empty desk of his. The reminder of the fact that she'd probably just lost him was painful. As painful as . . .

Slowly, the muscles in her body started to go limp.

Davis said he'd loved her for almost a year. And all these months, he'd been sitting there. Five feet away from her.

All these months . . .

She mentally reviewed what had happened during that time. All the greasy sandwiches they had shared, the dumb conversations. He'd been in love with her the whole time, but he'd never said anything. She'd been so self-absorbed, she'd never even suspected.

And so he'd watched her be over the moon about Ian, and then listened to her whine when Ian had dumped her. Afterward, he hadn't uttered a peep when she had complained about how there just weren't any interesting men around to date.

She'd been looking right through him, taking him for granted. Treating him like her fallback date. It must have made him feel like hell.

When she'd found out Davis was a dance whiz, she'd been surprised. She'd thought she'd known everything about him. But come to find out, she hadn't known the first thing about him. Not even what she could have found out if she'd only paid attention to what was going on right in front of her.

No wonder Davis didn't trust her now. No wonder he thought her feelings were fly-by-night. He had poured his heart out to her. He was about to take off for South America for heaven only knew how long, and she hadn't even told him that she loved him.

She jumped out of her chair, snatched her purse off her desk, and sped toward the elevator as fast as her four-inch heels would allow.

"Hey!" Marie shouted. "Where are you going in such a hurry?"

"Airport!"

Davis hunched over a drink at the bar at the Portland airport, cursing himself for being one of those early arriving travelers. Most of the time it gave him a feeling of security to know that he wasn't rushed. Today, however, it just seemed to give him extra time to brood.

Maybe he was making a big mistake. Maybe he should go back. . . .

He took a swig on his beer.

No. He couldn't go back now. He didn't want to

go back to being a lovesick puppy. This would be better. Better for both of them.

He let out a ragged breath. Who was he kidding? This would be torture.

He was just beginning to wonder if he changed his mind whether he'd ever see his luggage again, when Celia, still wearing that damn lavender dress that looked both sexy and slightly girlish, was suddenly standing next to him. At first he thought she was a mirage. Then the mirage spoke.

"You can't go," she announced.

He jumped off his barstool and grabbed her shoulders, more to steady himself than anything else. "What are you doing here?"

"Keeping you from making a terrible mistake," she said.

He tilted his head. "What do you mean?"

"You're being reckless, Davis. Do you realize all the terrible things that could happen to you in three months in Argentina? You could get caught in a flood."

"It's not the rainy season," he said.

"But what about diseases? They've had outbreaks of cholera down there . . ."

"I got vaccinated."

"Earthquakes?"

"There's higher tectonic volatility in Portland," he replied. "*I* check these things."

She crossed her arms. "Okay . . . But there's one mistake you obviously haven't thought through clearly."

"What's that?"

"Leaving me."

He sighed in exasperation. "We've been all through this."

"Not with all the facts, you haven't. Because the fact is, you might think that you're the only one in love here, but you're not. I love you, too."

He gaped at her. He'd dreamed of hearing these words, but he'd never imagined he'd hear them in an airport bar with CNN Headline News blaring in the background.

He wasn't sure he could trust them.

"I know what you're going to say," she said. "You're going to say why didn't I realize this days or weeks ago? It's the same thing Natalie's mother asked her when Natalie went nuts and called off her wedding. But you know what? Natalie was right."

"But—"

"I know," Celia interrupted, "you're going to tell me that I'm just saying I love you because you're leaving."

Bingo.

She frowned up at him. "But don't you realize how foolish that is? I didn't know you loved me. If I had, I might have thought of this earlier—maybe months earlier. And if I had, you would have believed me, right?"

"Well, yes . . ."

"So why can't you just be glad that I'm realizing it now? Sometimes it just takes a little pressure to understand what's really important." She let out a tired breath. "Does that answer your question?"

He couldn't even remember asking a question. All he knew was that his head was beginning to ache, and he had the strongest urge to kiss her. "Celia, you know what I think?"

She blinked at him stubbornly. "What?"

"I think we're both suffering from overexposure to Corky. What you're saying is making sense to me."

Her face broke into a smile, and she wrapped her arms around his waist. "Maybe you're just desperate to believe I love you."

That was one thing he couldn't deny. "True."

"Good, because I'm desperate for you to believe me, too."

He looked around. They were drawing stares from the other patrons in the bar. He didn't particularly care about that. But he was about to hop a plane to South America. "This is such bad timing. I'm about to leave . . ."

She shook her head. "No, you're not. You're staying here."

"But I've already promised my place to Corky."

"So come live with me for a while. It'll be cozy."

She did make it sound like a no-brainer. "But what about my book? I've already told the paper I'm leaving . . ."

She laughed. "You don't have to worry about that. You'll have an in with your boss."

He frowned. "How do you figure that?"

"Because I'm now your boss's assistant."

He fixed a disbelieving stare on her. "Marie promoted you?" When she nodded, he laughed.

"So you see, there's another reason you have to stay."

"What's that?"

"I'll need someone to make certain I leave the office sometimes. I don't want to turn into the Warden."

He waggled his brows at her. "Are you sure it's not too late? You sounded awfully comfortable giving me orders."

She tightened her grip around him. "Here's another one. Kiss me."

He complied happily. Suddenly, the ticket in his

breast pocket weighed nothing. The airport around them faded away. It was just him and Celia, and this kiss. He could have gone on kissing her for hours, in fact, except the flight he was supposed to take to Los Angeles was called, and he instinctively stiffened.

She pulled back and watched his face anxiously. "Is that your plane?"

After a moment, he shook his head. "Not anymore. The only place I'm going to is your apartment, remember?"

She broke into a triumphant smile. "We're going to have a great time, Davis," she said, taking his carry-on bag from him and tugging him back toward the terminal's exit. "We can put your writing table in the corner next to the stereo. My apartment is just perfect for two people and a parrot."

Hold the phone.

Gazpacho.

Reality sank in fast. His steps slowed as if he had rubber cement on his heels. He'd just gotten used to living in a Bruce Springsteen–free zone again. Not to mention, he enjoyed having all ten fingers.

He began to gaze with longing back at the terminal where his flight would be taking off. To a land without Gazpacho.

Celia turned to him. "What's the matter?"

"Couldn't Gazpacho go live with his uncle Corky?"

"No!" Celia said. "Besides, you'll want to get to know him if he's going to be your stepbird. He's really an amazing parrot."

"I know him already. That's the problem."

She bit her lip. *"Davis."* She gave him that look. That dewy-eyed, kissable look that was going to be his undoing, his doom.

Davis sighed. "What the hell." He let Celia tug him along toward the parking lot.

After all, when two people really loved each other, it would be foolish to let an ornery bird come between them.

ABOUT THE AUTHOR

Liz Ireland lives with her family in Oregon and is currently working on her next contemporary romance.

From Best-selling Author
Fern Michaels

__Wish List	0-8217-7363-1	$7.50US/$9.50CAN
__Yesterday	0-8217-6785-2	$7.50US/$9.50CAN
__The Guest List	0-8217-6657-0	$7.50US/$9.50CAN
__Finders Keepers	0-8217-7364-X	$7.50US/$9.50CAN
__Annie's Rainbow	0-8217-7366-6	$7.50US/$9.50CAN
__Dear Emily	0-8217-7365-8	$7.50US/$9.50CAN
__Sara's Song	0-8217-5856-X	$6.99US/$8.50CAN
__Celebration	0-8217-6452-7	$6.99US/$8.99CAN
__Vegas Heat	0-8217-7207-4	$7.50US/$9.50CAN
__Vegas Rich	0-8217-7206-6	$7.50US/$9.50CAN
__Vegas Sunrise	0-8217-7208-2	$7.50US/$9.50CAN
__What You Wish For	0-8217-6828-X	$7.99US/$9.99CAN
__Charming Lily	0-8217-7019-5	$7.99US/$9.99CAN

Call tool free **1-888-345-BOOK** to order by phone or use this coupon to order by mail.

Name_____

Address_____

City_____ State _____ Zip _____

Please send me the books I have checked above.

I am enclosing $_____

Plus postage and handling* $_____

Sales tax (in New York and Tennessee) $_____

Total amount enclosed $_____

*Add $2.50 for the first book and $.50 for each additional book.
Send check or money order (no cash or CODs) to: **Kensington Publishing Corp., 850 Third Avenue, New York, NY 10022**
Prices and numbers subject to change without notice.
All orders subject to availability.
Come visit our website at **www.kensingtonbooks.com**.

Thrilling Romance from
Lisa Jackson

__Twice Kissed	0-8217-6038-6	$5.99US/$7.99CAN
__Wishes	0-8217-6309-1	$5.99US/$7.99CAN
__Whispers	0-8217-6377-6	$5.99US/$7.99CAN
__Unspoken	0-8217-6402-0	$6.50US/$8.50CAN
__If She Only Knew	0-8217-6708-9	$6.50US/$8.50CAN
__Intimacies	0-8217-7054-3	$5.99US/$7.99CAN
__Hot Blooded	0-8217-6841-7	$6.99US/$8.99CAN

Call toll free **1-888-345-BOOK** to order by phone or use this coupon to order by mail.

Name_____

Address_____

City_____ State _____ Zip _____

Please send me the books I have checked above.

I am enclosing $_____

Plus postage and handling* $_____

Sales tax (in New York and Tennessee) $_____

Total amount enclosed $_____

*Add $2.50 for the first book and $.50 for each additional book.

Send check or money order (no cash or CODs) to:

Kensington Publishing Corp., 850 Third Avenue, New York, NY 10022

Prices and Numbers subject to change without notice. All orders subject to availability.

Check out our website at **www.kensingtonbooks.com**.

Discover the Magic of
Romance With

Kat Martin

__The Secret
0-8217-6798-4   **$6.99US/$8.99**CAN

Kat Rollins moved to Montana looking to change her life, not find
another man like Chance McLain, with a sexy smile and empty
heart. Chance can't ignore the desire he feels for her—or the suspicion that somebody wants her to leave Lost Peak . . .

__Dream
0-8217-6568-X   **$6.99US/$8.99**CAN

Genny Austin is convinced that her nightmares are visions of another
life she lived long ago. Jack Brennan is having nightmares, too, but
his are real. In the shadows of dreams lurks a terrible truth, and only
by unlocking the past will Genny be free to love at last . . .

__Silent Rose
0-8217-6281-8   **$6.99US/$8.50**CAN

When best-selling author Devon James checks into a bed-and-breakfast
in Connecticut, she only hopes to put the spark back into her relationship with her fiancé. But what she experiences at the Stafford Inn
changes her life forever . . .

Call toll free **1-888-345-BOOK** to order by phone or use this
coupon to order by mail.

Name_____
Address_____
City _____ State_____ Zip_____
Please send me the books I have checked above.
I am enclosing $_____
Plus postage and handling* $_____
Sales tax (in New York and Tennessee only) $_____
Total amount enclosed $_____
*Add $2.50 for the first book and $.50 for each additional book.
Send check or money order (no cash or CODs) to: **Kensington Publishing
Corp., Dept. C.O., 850 Third Avenue, New York, NY 10022**
Prices and numbers subject to change without notice. All orders subject
to availability. Visit our website at **www.kensingtonbooks.com.**

DO YOU HAVE THE
HOHL COLLECTION?